Praise for
THE KIMONO TATTOO

"*The Kimono Tattoo* is an intelligent escape—into the past, into the mind, into a fascinating culture. Finely crafted and perfectly paced, this literary thriller remains engrossing long after the last sentence, opening a world that lingers in the imagination."

–Jeannette Cooperman, St. Louis Media Hall of Fame journalist, essayist, and author of *A Circumstance of Blood*

"Debut novelist, Rebecca Copeland offers a smart, entertaining read in *The Kimono Tattoo*. Readers who relish mystery, suspense, literary fiction, and romance will find it all in this multi-genre gem!"

–Johnnie Bernhard, author of *A Good Girl,
How We Came to Be*, and *Sisters of the Undertow*

"In a tale as intricately patterned as a Jacquard-weave obi, Rebecca Copeland's American heroine finds herself entangled in the delicate threads of Kyoto's kimono industry as well as the darker skeins of yakuza, tattoo parlors, and rebellious youth. The reader is quickly drawn in to the dangerous twists and turns while Copeland's detailed knowledge of Kyoto comes through on every page—a treat for all who love this city, and a great read."

–Liza Dalby, anthropologist, artist, and author of the best seller, *Geisha; Kimono: Fashioning Culture*; and the novels *The Tale of Murasaki* and *Hidden Buddhas: A Novel of Karma and Chaos*

"An intriguing mystery wrapped inside the beautifully rendered world of Kyoto. Rebecca Copeland's intimate knowledge of Japanese culture and custom shine throughout this novel. "
–Susan Perabo, author of *The Broken Places* and
T*he Fall of Lisa Bellow*

"It is not simply an exciting page-turner you cannot put down, but also an intricate thriller uniquely informed with the "kimono and tattoo philosophy," and immensely enriched by the protagonist's double perspective as both an insider and outsider—an American scholar living and working in Japan. The novel brings you so vividly into the kaleidoscope of the modern-day Japan, you want to make a trip there the next day, holding a copy of *The Kimono Tattoo.*"
–Xiaolong Qiu, author of the award-winning
Inspector Chen Series

日本文学と着物文化に対する深い造詣と理解に脱帽し、
モザイクのように組み合わされた緻密な謎に圧倒された。
桐野夏生

English translation:
"A delicate and intricate novel, pieced together like a mosaic, that just blew me away. The author shows a strikingly deep knowledge of Japanese literature and kimono culture."
–Natsuo Kirino, Edgar-Award nominated author of
OUT, Grotesque, and other novels

THE KIMONO TATTOO

Rebecca Copeland

BROTHER MOCKINGBIRD

Library of Congress Control Number: 2021930307

Cover Design by: Alexios Saskalidis
www.facebook.com/187designz

For information please contact:
Brother Mockingbird, LLC
www.brothermockingbird.org
ISBN: 978-1-7344950-5-8 Paperback
ISBN: 978-1-7344950-6-5 eBook
First Edition

In memory of my father and mother,
who first brought me to Japan.

CHAPTER ONE
PIGEONS

The white parasol caught my eye. I watched the tip gliding along the green hedge, running parallel to the parking lot outside my window. Fair complexions were prized in Japan and particularly in Kyoto, where many claimed the traditional values and tastes were stronger. Most women carried parasols when the sun was bright, shielding themselves from the skin-darkening rays. Many carried them even when the sun was dim, and long into the autumn months. I recalled the way neighborhood women approached me when I was a little girl out on errands with my mother. They would stroke my porcelain skin, murmuring *kime ga komakai*. "Her pores are so fine." I thought I was close to royalty until the summer I was thirteen, and my parents returned to North Carolina on furlough. All the girls in that lazy town slathered up with baby oil and baked under the sun. They admired their tawny brown tans and the white lines left by their skimpy bathing suits. Next to them, my skin was practically luminescent. "Here comes Casper," they smirked whenever they saw me. Tired of the taunts, I spent an afternoon on a lawn chair under the sun until I turned crimson. My mother rushed me to the emergency room for third-degree burns. Far less painful to be a fine-pored princess in Japan.

I watched the white tip until it reached the corner and turned down my street. A woman in a grey kimono stepped into view. Even from a distance, I could tell the fabric was a *kinsha* silk. At the hem ran an asymmetrical design in gradated shades of blue and pale pink resembling a mountain ridge, a flowing stream, a spring haze. The woman seemed very chic, her face carefully shaded by her parasol.

I gauged from the color of her kimono she was in her sixties. She walked with assurance, her black sandals clipping silently over the pavement. With each step, her kimono snapped open at the hem, revealing the white under kimono. She held her parasol aloft with her right hand, and in her left she carried a shopping bag from the Takashimaya Department Store. I wanted to catch a glimpse of her face, but a flock of pigeons took flight from outside my window, blocking my view. When the fluttering of wings subsided, the woman stepped beyond my field of vision.

I often watched the tourists streaming beneath my second-floor window. The narrow lane outside my house provided a convenient shortcut between the austere Nanzen-ji Temple and the zoo. Kyoto was never at a loss for tourists. It did not matter the season. The pretty lanes and winding paths buzzed with foot traffic as honeymooners, giggly school groups, and elderly couples trekked dutifully from one famous site to the next, buying souvenirs, snapping photos, and sampling the celebrated cuisine. I enjoyed their excitement as I sat at my desk stacked high with dictionaries and square-lined manuscript papers.

I was working a deadline for Logos International Translation Agency run by Mrs. Tomoko Shibasaki on Teramachi. The agency was small but had ongoing contracts with Lysis computers and the comically named Tomato Bank. It occasionally got requests from subsidiaries of Sumitomo. For the most part, the requests were ad hoc, last minute, and ran the gamut from marketing brochures to press releases for small manufacturers with international aspirations. I had little choice about what I translated. I worked on commission and was contracted to complete three translations per week, more if I could manage it. Mrs. Shibasaki also employed her son Hiro, who was more work than help. It wasn't that he lacked the language aptitude the job required; he just didn't care. As the only native speaker, I was responsible for all the final copy, constantly correcting Hiro's mistakes, but in such a way he didn't realize he was being corrected. The linguistic gymnastics I performed were exhausting.

Still, a job was a job. I knew what to expect and hardly taxed myself. Besides, I could do most of my work at home, occasionally making an office appearance.

This was not the career I expected. When I finished my Ph.D. in Japanese literature, I landed a coveted tenure-track position at a private college in Iowa. I secured myself a husband, too. All seemed to be on track. Five years later, when I returned to our tidy bungalow after a six-month research trip to Japan, I found he had moved the Asian Studies Department secretary into our bedroom.

"Well, you know, dear," my mother scolded, "it's hard for a man to feel important when his wife devotes so much time to her career."

She had no room to talk. True, she packed our home and followed my father halfway around the world to Japan, supporting his calling as a missionary doctor. But even so, she rarely was home. She was too busy with her work supervising nurses to be proficient at the Betty Crocker routine.

To dig the knife in a little deeper, the department I supposedly sacrificed my marriage for denied my tenure. So here I was: forty, divorced, and back in Kyoto, back to the only home I'd ever really known, even though it wasn't really mine.

Rusu. That's what they called being away from home in Japanese. My friends got a good laugh out of my situation. The word "rusu" sounded much like my name when pronounced Japanese-style. Ruth. It fit. I was perpetually "away." Never home. In other peoples' houses, but never in my own.

I reached the last fold of the marketing brochure when the doorbell cut through my thoughts. I avoided answering the door if I could. The telephone, too. The answering machine could take a message just as easily. I hated having to explain why the Nakatas were not home and who I was. When I got to my name, Ruth Bennett, it inevitably gave the caller a start. They assumed I was Japanese. The door was another matter. There was no getting past my flame red hair and statuesque frame. Some people would be so terrified when they caught sight of me, they'd turn on their heels and leave. Even when I greeted them in Japanese, they couldn't accept the redheaded barbarian before them was speaking their language. They'd wave their hands wildly in front of their faces like the blades of a windshield wiper turned on high and say in Japanese, "I'm sorry, I don't speak English."

"But I'm speaking Japanese," I would say. It would be to no avail. They were convinced we could not communicate and would hurriedly withdraw.

The bell sounded again. Insistent. My caller was not going

to leave. I thumped down the steep wooden stairway trying not to lose my house slippers. The *genkan*, or entryway, of the house was large, befitting the home's luxury. To reach the front door I remove my house slippers and stepped down into a pair of genkan sandals. I didn't use the peephole or try the intercom as a proper housewife would. I just opened the door cold and found the lady in the grey kimono standing on the narrow front porch. Now it was my turn to stare.

"My name is Tokuda," she said with a respectful bow. "Miyo Tokuda. I have come at the bequest of Shōtarō Tani Sensei. I am terribly sorry to arrive unannounced like this. But there is a matter of some urgency." Her Japanese was slightly accented, not the soft lilt typical of Kyoto but something more rustic.

Curious, I invited her in. Miyo Tokuda skirted past the blue Italian leather sofa and chose to kneel on the floor by the low table. She bowed formally, nearly touching her head to the Persian carpet. I was relieved I vacuumed recently, but her actions forced me also to sit on the floor. I returned her bow with a less enthusiastic one. At that point, she pulled a box of Kyoto sweets out of her shopping bag along with a large bundle wrapped in a purple *furoshiki* cloth. When she had emptied the paper bag of its contents, she folded it into a neat parcel the size of an envelope and placed it in her lap.

"It's not much, but I hope you will accept this small token of my appreciation," she said as she pushed the box of sweets across the table.

Wagashi rice confection was a favorite of mine. I wanted to unwrap them right there and dig in, but I knew better. Proper protocol was to wait until she left. I thanked her for the gift and

excused myself momentarily while I dashed to the kitchen for
refreshments. I had just made a pitcher of chilled barley tea. I
grabbed it along with the crisp, cinnamon-flavored cookies Kyoto
is known for. I set these on a tray and rushed back to my visitor,
who moved the mysterious purple parcel on the table in front of
her.

Kneeling, I set the tray of tea and sweets down and slowly
positioned a damp hand towel on a bamboo holder for my
guest. She watched silently as I set the glass of tea on the wicker
coaster and placed it in front of her. I acquitted myself rather
well in demonstrating ladylike manners. Ms. Tokuda gave a slight
bow. She quietly moved the glass to the side and began deftly
unknotting the cloth. I watched as she pulled the wrap away,
revealing a plain wooden box, the kind precious ceramics are
packed in. She turned the box towards me and slid it across the
table.

"Sensei would like you to translate his novel," she said,
indicating the box.

"His novel?" Shōtarō Tani was a highly regarded writer
but disappeared years ago following some disagreement with
his father. He was one of the favorite writers in my graduate
seminars because he was surrounded by such mystery. It was not
unusual for a writer to commit suicide, or even to run afoul of
the law, but just to vanish? Some rumored he moved to Europe.
Some presumed he was dead. And for a writer, not writing or
publishing was a kind of death. The literary world had all but
forgotten Shōtarō Tani.

"When did he write this novel?" I asked. Only one of
Shōtarō's works was translated, his early novella, *The Prodigal Son*

Does Not Return. Largely credited with spearheading a revival of the Naturalist School of writing popular in the 1910s, Shōtarō's work was darkly confessional and emotionally claustrophobic. *The Prodigal Son* revolved around the reasons he refused the family kimono business and the abuse his father heaped on him. Although the translation of the work was excellent, it was hardly noticed among English-speaking readers.

Given the lack of positive reception the work received, I wasn't exactly thrilled by the prospect of translating a Shōtarō Tani story. But I was intrigued, even flattered.

"Bennett-san, the novel is not yet complete. Sensei is still writing it. He finished the first chapter and is now at work on the second. When that is done, I will bring it to you for your translation."

"I see."

Actually, I didn't see at all. This method of production was highly unusual. Granted, Japanese writers occasionally published stories serially in journals before presenting them as a complete book, but to see chapters translated before the book appeared in its entirety was strange.

"I have strict instructions on procedures, what we expect of this translation, and how you return it to us when it is complete. You'll find it all explained in this contract."

Ms. Tokuda pushed a formal white envelope across the table towards me. It was thick. My name was written vertically down the length of the envelope in black ink, clearly in brush. I wondered if it was her hand or Shōtarō's.

"You will find a small gratuity enclosed as well. When you submit the translation of the first chapter, we will provide additional compensation. Once the entire novel is translated, you will be paid in full. It is all explained in the instructions. But, please, feel free to ask me whatever you wish, and I will do my best to answer."

"Well, I am wondering why Shōtarō Sensei prefers to have his manuscript appear first in English."

"Sensei has very good reasons. After his disinheritance, his family, particularly his older brother Akira, made it difficult for Sensei to submit his work to appropriate publishers. They may exert influence over the Japanese press, but they have no power with American publishers. We plan to publish first in English."

"I understand."

Ms. Tokuda confused me momentarily when she referred to Akira as Shōtarō's older brother. Shōtarō had been the only son. But then I remembered. When he refused to succeed to the family headship, his father forced his older sister Satoko to marry Akira Hamada, who then assumed the Tani name, ownership of the kimono business, and all the rights and privileges of the first son. It didn't seem fair to me. Before her marriage, Satoko had been a very savvy businesswoman. When I was in high school, I saw many advertisements for Tani Kimono in the ladies' magazines.

"Look at this photograph," my dance teacher once told me.

I whined that Japanese women were not as liberated as Americans. All of fifteen years old, I thought I knew what it meant to be an independent woman, and I arrogantly complained Japanese women were too submissive. Insulted, my teacher, who ran her own dance studio for nearly thirty years, punched indignantly at the photograph.

"Here's a woman who has made it in the business world."

I looked down to see a fashion tableau of Japanese models in kimonos designed like Paul Klee paintings parading along Fifth Avenue. I didn't get it. I asked her what made them independent.

"No, Ruth, not the models, the designer. Satoko Tani. She is revolutionizing the kimono industry, and she's only twenty-seven years old."

That was 1978. Years later I read in one of the tabloids the Tani family took advantage of the old-fashioned marriage system and adopted Akira Hamada as their male heir and Satoko's husband. By then my dance teacher had died, but I could still remember how her eyes shone when she brandished the magazine under my nose.

"Bennett-san? Please look inside the envelope and let me know if you have any questions."

I picked it up and slowly slid my finger under the flap to break the seal. I pulled out a large stack of bills, wrapped neatly in a stiff white paper band. Since it would be rude to thumb through them, I set the stack aside, but if they were all ¥10,000 notes, like the top bill, then the stack amounted to a hefty sum. A piece of white paper was folded beneath the bills. I pulled it out and unfolded it to find a set of instructions typed in English.

The contract continued for a page and a half with the kind of boilerplate language I'd encountered before. But two items struck me as odd: the secrecy I was expected to maintain regarding the translation and the amount of the compensation. I would receive over $2,000 just to accept the job and another $2,000 each time I completed a new chapter. I'd have to work twice as much for Logos to make a similar commission.

Mrs. Shibasaki made it very clear when she employed me

I was not to moonlight. The translation requests she received were always time sensitive, and she'd lose her reputation in the business if she couldn't deliver on demand. Any translation I did had to be approved by her first. An infringement of that rule could result in dismissal.

"Tokuda-san, the terms outlined here are very generous. But as you may know, I am employed by Logos International. I would need to clear this request with my employer first."

"Under no circumstances may you mention this translation to anyone else. I refer you to the first clause in the agreement."

She pointed to the document I had read.

"But I could lose my job if I accept this assignment."

"Do you like your job so much?"

"It pays the rent."

In fact, I didn't have any rent. The Nakatas were close friends of my parents and refused to take any payment. Apparently, my parents helped them in the decades following WWII when so many Japanese were impoverished. As missionaries, my parents were sent over with enough provisions to last their four-year term. But seeing the poverty around them, they soon gave away whatever they could, and their four-year rations were spent in less than a year. What they lost in supplies, they made up in good will, acquiring friends and supporters, seeing their four-year term extended ten times.

But the translation work was my only source of income. Taking on a job like the one Ms. Tokuda proposed, as attractive as the money was in the short run, was risky. Once a translation was done, there was little guarantee another would be waiting. I had already lost one job. It was more than a job. It was my career.

I didn't think I could afford to lose another, even a crappy one.

"Bennett-san, if you accept this translation assignment, Sensei will make it worth your while."

"That's very generous, Tokuda-san. But please understand you are putting me in a difficult position. I'm just not sure I can ..."

I glanced nervously at the clock behind my guest and realized I'd need to leave for work soon.

"Do you want to know why I have come to you?"

I was dying to know.

"Sensei was pleased with your translation of Yuriko Daté's *Kimono Killer.*"

"I am surprised he noticed such a clumsy translation."

I replied as modesty demanded. In fact, I labored for two years over that translation and was ecstatic when it won a distinguished award, one of the few designated for Japanese-to-English translations. I believed it would secure my tenure. But, the chair of my department was not impressed. Translations, she argued, were not original work. I did not write the work, but as I translated it, I lived it. I entered into the weft and warp of the words, unraveling the threads and reweaving them into a new work. I even met the author during the process. Yuriko Daté was delightfully candid, full of insights and anecdotes about her writing process.

So, when I returned to my campus later that summer, I wrote an article about her and published it in a small women's studies journal. Not enough "academic rigor," the powers-that-be judged.

Life was far better with Logos International where every day was just like the day before. There's something to be said for predictability. I was tired of surprises.

Yet, I was beguiled by the possibility of another literary translation.

"Sensei thought your translations of kimono dyeing and weaving were particularly skillful. It is clear you understand the spirit of the kimono. You looked past the words, Bennett-san; you felt the power of the art."

I blushed and lowered my head as if to deflect the compliment. I labored over getting the kimono terms just right. It was a challenge since I was translating words that didn't have an equivalent in English, because they do not exist in the English-speaking world. I had to find a way to bring my Japanese world into my English world. The effort was exhausting. Some nights, after a day of translating, I felt depleted, rather like a medium at the end of a séance. It was the kind of exhaustion that ended with fulfillment.

"I love kimonos," I said.

Ms. Tokuda smiled and then broke into a laugh, raising her hand gracefully to cover her mouth, but not before I caught a glimpse of her teeth. They were deeply discolored, perhaps from smoking. That might explain the husky rasp of her voice. The contrast between the decayed interior of her mouth and the genteel nature of her gesture was a bit disconcerting.

"Oh, Bennett-san! You are more Japanese than a Japanese."

I heard that a lot. Because of my profession before I became a translator, my time was devoted to studying Japanese traditions and literature. Naturally, I seemed to know more than the average Japanese about their own history. On the other hand, I knew embarrassingly little about America or American history.

My Japanese friends were far more familiar with Henry David Thoreau or Mark Twain than I was.

"No one else can handle this translation, Bennett-san. You know Sensei comes from a very long line of kimono designers. He is counting on you to help him. His story needs to be told. It's a matter of life and death."

Ms. Tokuda bowed deeply, the tips of her fingers sliding slowly off her knees to touch the Persian carpet.

Despite myself, I said yes.

CHAPTER TWO
HERONS

I went back to the living room after I saw Ms. Tokuda to the door and started clearing the table. She had ignored the tea and cookies. When I picked up the pillow on the floor, I noticed her folding fan beside it. I opened it, just to be sure it wasn't mine, and saw a lovely design of thin-legged herons stepping primly through water swirls and falling leaves. I rushed to the front door to see if I could catch her.

I looked up and down the street, hurrying to the corner. I'd been too slow. When I turned back to my house, I nearly ran into a black sedan driving much too quickly on the narrow lane. It almost filled the small road completely. I had to flatten myself against the wall of the zoo to avoid being run down. Because the windows were tinted, I couldn't see the driver.

When I got back to my house, I placed the fan on the shoe cabinet near the front door. Then, I carried the manuscript upstairs to my study. I was eager to get started on the translation, but a glance at the clock on the bedside table reminded me I had to hurry if I was going to finish my work for Logos International on time. Tokuda's visit set me back at least an hour. I put the manuscript box down on my bed and returned to the promotional marketing brochure. "Our patented new interface system will reduce . . . blah, blah, blah."

Once done, I hurriedly changed into a light linen suit, raked a comb through my hair, and scooped my papers into my tattered briefcase. I had one minute to catch the 2:03 Number Five bus. Fortunately, the bus stop was just a block from my house.

Mid-afternoon buses are not normally crowded in Kyoto, and today was no exception. A clutch of schoolgirls from the Notre Dame academy, housewives returning from some market or another, and tourists all merged on the busy sidewalks. The Number Five edged past the Kyoto Zoo, possibly the worst zoo in existence with its cramped, dismal cages. Next up was the Heian Shrine, its vermillion *torii* gate resplendent in the afternoon sun. The stop did double duty with the Kyoto Municipal Museum.

At Sanjō Kawaramachi, I fished exact change out of my purse and dropped it in the fare box as I rushed off the bus. I had five minutes to get to Logos International before I was officially late. I was already regretting my decision to accept the Shōtarō Tani translation.

Speed walking through the Teramachi shopping arcade is no easy task. I dodged mothers with strollers, old women with canes, and men on bicycles, none had predictable routes and when least expected veered into my path. Logos International was located on the second floor above Omni God, a trendy clothes shop, and a stone's throw from the Kyoto City Hall. The staircase leading to the office was narrow and dark, but the office space itself was large and airy. Mrs. Shibasaki had her own room overlooking Oike-dōri and the Kyoto City Hall. I had a cubicle in the main area, as did her son, Hiro. I didn't have a door I could close or a window, but I did have some privacy and could spread my papers and reference books around without annoying Mrs. Shibasaki.

Next to Mrs. Shibasaki's office was a long table used by our freelancers or *freeters*. They stopped by and did odd jobs for Mrs. Shibasaki whenever they had need for some extra cash, and whenever she had more assignments than Hiro and I could handle. I was delighted to see the freeter Maho at one of the desks. She gave me a big smile when I walked in.

"Cutting it close as usual, I see," she chided in a breezy English.

"Is the boss in?"

Maho tossed her head in the direction of Mrs. Shibasaki's office. To my surprise, the door was closed.

"Is she with a client?" I asked. Normally, she left the door open, ever vigilant about the comings and goings in the office.

"I don't think so. It's been closed since I got here."

"When was that?"

"Between you and me, a few minutes ago."

Maho gave a wink. She was as impulsive and irreverent as she was impish. Maho had a Mohawk for one thing. Today, the upper fringes were dyed pink. You never knew what color to expect. She dyed it orange for Halloween last year. For Christmas, she colored it green and red. If her hair weren't startling enough, she sported a pierced nose, a slew of piercings on her ears, and a tattoo on her upper arm.

I liked her.

She grew up in California and seemed more at home with surfboards than she did with rickshaws. Maho's father was on the faculty at UC Santa Barbara, in psychology, until returning to a position at Kyoto University. After twelve years in the States,

Maho couldn't adjust to the different customs she encountered here in her "home" country. As soon as she graduated high school, she began running with a group of rappers, DJs, and manga creators. I'd run into her with them a few times along Kawaramachi. They looked rough, but they weren't bad kids, just kids in search of something different. Mrs. Shibasaki couldn't stand Maho's appearance, but she couldn't deny her talents as a translator.

"Ruth, is that you?" Mrs. Shibasaki stuck her head out of her office door. "Thank god! I need your help."

She was wearing a formal "visiting" kimono. But her heavy obi was so loose it looked ready to slip off.

"Oh, Maho, so you're here, too?"

Maho and I both exchanged surprised glances. We had never seen Mrs. Shibasaki wearing a kimono. She always dressed in designer suits, wearing her mane of thick, dark hair with ribbons of grey at the temples.

"Ruth, my sash came undone on the way over. I don't know how to knot this thing, and I'm about to exhaust myself trying. Can you help me? I know you wear a kimono for your dance lessons."

"I can try, Mrs. Shibasaki. I've never tried to tie an obi on someone else. Let me see what I can do."

Maho and I both pushed our way into her office, which had been turned into a dressing room with a rich assortment of undersashes and ties, hairpins, and hair spray. Next to the bookshelf was a full-length mirror I'd never seen.

"I haven't worn a kimono in such a long time," Mrs.

Shibasaki said. "It must have been at some New Year's Party in Dallas way back when. And really, in the States, no one would know if I did it right or not. But here . . . oh, Ruth, can you help?"

"It's probably better if we start all over again. Let's take your obi off."

"Why are you wearing a kimono if you hate it so much?" Maho asked.

"I don't hate it, Maho. I just don't feel comfortable in a kimono. I feel like I'm a foreigner or something. Oh, no offense, Ruth."

I smiled and scrutinized the way she wrapped the kimono. She hadn't allowed enough length at the bottom and too much of her white tabi-clad heels were showing. I untied the cords and wraps and fluttered the kimono open and away from Mrs. Shibasaki's slender body, noticing the beautiful under kimono she was wearing of pale pink embossed silk. Checking that the hem touched low on her heels, I wrapped the fabric around her body, left side over right, lifting each edge up slightly at the ends.

"Maho, give me one of those kimono *himo*. No, no the long narrow tie."

I spoke a little harshly, afraid the slippery silk would slide out of place before I could cinch it down. First, I wrapped a tie around Mrs. Shibasaki's hips and pulled it as tightly as I could, then bloused the kimono over the tight tie, smoothing it out in a neat fold and quickly tied another one above it. We covered this with a tight band to smooth the folds and cords. Now it was time for the obi.

A *fukuro* obi is long and difficult to manage, though not as tricky as the much heavier, double-sided *maru* obi. Fortunately, both her kimono and obi were made of thinly lined silk, light and easy to knot. I pulled each end tight and listened as the silk sighed in resistance.

"What's the occasion, anyway?" Maho asked.

"Hiro has an *omiai*," Mrs. Shibasaki blushed as she spoke.

"But please don't tell him I told you!"

"Well, of course it's not a real omiai," Mrs. Shibasaki continued, seeing our stunned expressions. "I wouldn't insist on anything so ridiculously old-fashioned as an arranged marriage. I just like to call it that to rattle Hiro. It's really just a blind date. A client of mine has a daughter he thinks would be perfect for Hiro. Hiro's not getting any younger! And the girls he's been seeing . . . well, let's just say I don't think of them as marriage material!"

She had a point there. Hiro had just turned thirty-six, and I think most of his "girl friends" were women he met at the hostess bars he frequented with our clients. It would be fine if he fell for one of the women and offered to marry her, but that didn't seem likely. Hiro was not particularly interested in marriage.

"We're supposed to attend a tea ceremony. That's why I'm wearing a kimono. It'll be an evening event by torchlight. Sounds romantic, doesn't it?"

"Hiro's going to sit through a tea ceremony?" Maho clearly was still trying to reconcile the notion of Hiro and a marriage meeting.

"Well, no. Hiro won't be there. Only the women will attend the tea ceremony. It'll be me, the mother, and her daughter, Erika. You know what they say, far better for the women in the two families to get along than for the intended . . ."

Maho scrunched her face in disgust. "Guess I'm never getting married."

"Hiro will join us later with Erika's father. They'll be taking us to dinner at the Miyako Hotel. Are you sure you've got everything tight enough?"

"Don't worry," I said, as I gave the sash a final tug. "You'll be fine."

"Great. I can hardly breathe now as it is!"

"Once you relax it will feel more comfortable. Really. You look beautiful! Is this *yūzen*?" I asked. The kimono was dyed exquisitely, a pale blue background with a frothy splash of waves ran along the hemline, while a smaller splash draped one of the shoulders and sleeve. Lithe little fish frolicked in the waves. Here and there silver embroidery highlighted the fish, making it seem that their scales were glistening. Her obi was a silvery grey and so soft a silk it was nearly iridescent. The design on the obi was a subdued brown in a pattern resembling bamboo baskets, the type once used to catch and carry fish. How clever, I thought. She means to reel in a little fish tonight!

"It is yūzen. My goodness, Ruth! Are you sure you're not Japanese?"

"Not a Tani Kimono by any chance?" I asked, brushing aside her Japanese quip.

"Not a chance! Do you know what those run for? If I had that kind of money, do you think I'd be working?"

She turned to admire herself in the mirror, gave her upswept hair a careful pat, tucked a tube of lipstick into her silk handbag, and headed for the door.

"Oh, I almost forgot. Did you finish the software marketing brochure, Ruth?"

"Yes, let me run and get it." I felt a small frisson of fear shoot through me, remembering my meeting with Tokuda and my rush to finish Mrs. Shibasaki's translation. I'd been hasty. Hasty in agreeing to Tokuda's request. Hasty in wrapping up my job for Mrs. Shibasaki.

"No, I don't have time to check it now. I'm sure it's fine. Just put it in an envelope and take it to the post office, okay? Tomorrow's fine. But send it express."

"Thank you, Mrs. Shibasaki."

"No, thank you! You saved me. I'd forgotten that you'd translated the kimono novel for that horrible Daté woman. You really know a lot about it."

With that Mrs. Shibasaki swished out of the office.

"Wait, who is the 'horrible Daté woman'?" Maho asked.

"She's the author of *Kimono Killer*. Want to wrap things up here and get a bite to eat?"

I went to my cubicle to collect an express mail envelope. I noticed Mrs. Shibasaki left my next assignment on my desk. I stuffed them both in my briefcase. Maho busily pulled at the spikes in her hair as we exited the office, locking the door behind us.

The Seiryū was a hole in the wall, but often the best noodle shops are. The owner was a Chinese immigrant who had probably been in the country for years but still carried the patina of "outsider." Not as obviously as me, of course, but visible, nonetheless. We could hear him and the kitchen staff shouting to one another in Chinese. It was still a little early for the evening rush. Once we got his attention, we ordered plates of fried *gyōza* dumplings and yakisoba noodles.

"So? Tell me about the horrible Daté woman." Sensing a

good story, Maho leaned forward, slipping back into English.

"Ok, for starters, she's not horrible. Mrs. S. just doesn't like her because she's almost her age, and she runs around with younger men."

"How much younger? You mean like Hiro's age?" Maho snickered.

"No, I mean like your age."

"Seriously?"

"Absolutely. And she goes through them like candy. Though in truth, I'm not sure who tires of whom first."

"I love it!"

"Well, she can get away with it because she's famous. But let a normal woman try something like that and all hell breaks loose!"

"So how do you know her?"

"I wouldn't say I know her. But I met her a few times while I was translating her novel."

"Did she have one of her boy toys hanging around?"

"No. I really think a lot of that is for show. She was very elegant when I met her. Had me in for tea and sweets at her old house on the hillside, just above the Philosopher's Path. She was very patient with all my questions about the novel."

"What kind of questions?"

"You know, little details. The novel is set in the past and features a young kimono maker, so I had to work my way through all those technical terms."

Our beer arrived, and Maho and I took turns pouring each other a glass, careful to bring the foam to the top without spilling over.

"*Kampai!*" I clinked my glass with hers.

"Cheers!" She responded with a smirk. "Nothing like a cold beer to end a long day."

"What was long for you, Maho? You barely sat in the office for more than ten minutes today!"

"I know. But sometimes just being in 'polite society' is exhausting. I mean, I get so tired of constantly listening to the snickering behind my back. And the glares. Like today, on the bus, two high school scumbags kept throwing paperclips at me. They thought they were really cute."

"I'm sorry."

"Look, I don't dress like this for attention, contrary to what everyone thinks. My parents are always trying to psychoanalyze me, telling me I need to find another way to display my rage—or whatever. I guess it's true in a way. I want to show on the outside how different I am on the inside. I'm not like people here. I'm not like anyone. But I wish people would just leave me the fuck alone sometimes."

"Was it better in the States?"

"In a way. But not really. I only felt comfortable at the beach around Ventura. There were just a lot of cool, creative people down there, and no one cared what you looked like or where you went to school. I'm going back one of these days."

The waiter dropped our gyōza and noodles off, checking to make sure we knew which bottle contained soy sauce and the thicker spicy sauce. We took our smaller saucers and mixed the soy sauce and vinegar to suit our tastes. The gyōza were still hot, but we couldn't wait. We each pulled a dumpling off the stack and dunked it in our sauces before taking a tentative bite. Hot water and oil gushed from the opening I made in the gyōza skin and dribbled down my chin as I reached for a tissue.

"What about you, Ruth? Do you like it here? I mean you must, to live here like you do."

"Sure. It feels like home to me."

"How can this possibly feel like home?"

"Well, for starters, it's the only home I've ever known."

"Ruth, I don't mean to pry," Maho shifted in her seat staring into her beer.

"No, that's okay. I mean, I went through a phase where I guess I hated it here. I hated the way people starred at me all the time. No matter what I did, I always felt like I was doing something wrong. You know how you have those dreams where you're walking around and suddenly you realize you're naked? It felt like that."

"More like nightmares!"

"And my parents made it worse. Especially my mother. She was always scolding us for any little infraction. 'What will people think?' she'd ask. 'You're a representative of Christ—do you want people to think all Christians misbehave like this? Ruth! We've got to be good models for Christ.' It got to the point where I was afraid to do anything wrong, afraid I'd send a whole nation to hell if I 'set a bad example'!"

"Whoa! And I thought I had pressure!"

"Sorry, I didn't mean to be so melodramatic! It was just hard feeling like I was always on display."

"You don't have to stay here now, though. You've got choices.

Why not can go back to the States?"

"I feel even more out of place in America."

Maho frowned slightly.

"I guess I feel about Kyoto the way you feel about Ventura, California. It's hard to explain. But the minute I leave Japan, as soon as the airplane wheels lose contact with the runway, I start to feel ungrounded, too. And even after we touchdown in the States, or wherever I'm traveling, I constantly feel as if I'm still up in the air. It doesn't feel real. I feel I'm floating over unfamiliar landscapes. On the other hand, the minute the jet touches down in Japan, regardless of whether it's Narita or Tokyo or Osaka or wherever, I feel home. It's a very physical feeling, you know? I can feel the tension in my chest subside. I can breathe again."

"Wow! That's exactly how I feel, only going the other way! That's weird. I wonder why our feelings are so polar opposites."

"Probably it's just because of where we grew up. Those early memories lock onto us. From as far back as I can remember, I was in Japan, speaking Japanese, seeing Japanese faces, well, other than my parents and my brother. For the longest time, I thought eventually my face would change, too, and I would grow to look more like my playmates."

"Guess you're still waiting for that to happen!" Maho snorted and then continued, "What about your brother, did he also await the day he'd be 'turning Japanese'?

"I don't know."

"You should ask him sometime."

"I can't."

"The silent type, huh?"

"No, he disappeared."

Maho's playful smirk dissolved into shock. It didn't make sense, did it? It still doesn't. And I don't know how to explain it any better than to say, he disappeared. Because that is what happened. He was there with me one minute, waiting to cross the train tracks at Yase Hieizan-guchi, and then he was gone. It happened so long ago, and so much has been lost to the blur of time. I was only twelve. Mother gave us train fare and told us to head up to the mountains, take the cable car to the top of Mt. Hiei. The breezes there were delightful, and the cable car ride thrilling. It wasn't unusual for parents to send children off on their own in those days. And Mother rarely had time for the two of us, anyway.

When we came to the train crossing, I grabbed Matthew's hand. It was sticky and soft and before I could stop him, he slipped out of my grip. I can still see his sturdy legs in his short pants and the luminescent arc of his slender neck. He was almost seven. He had seen a puppy on the other side standing alone beside the tracks. Afraid the puppy would get hurt, he darted across just as the train was nearing the crossing. The gates had already gone down. But he was small enough to glide easily beneath them. I saw him reach the other side. And then the passing train obstructed my view. When the last train car finally rumbled past, my brother was gone. No puppy, no brother, no sign of either. I will never forget my mother's panicked expression when she reached the police station where I awaited her and asked, "How could you have let him cross without you?" How could I?

"Ruth?"

I looked up at Maho, realizing I was staring into space. I wanted to explain, but I couldn't make myself speak. And Maho didn't press for more details. I liked her all the more for it.

"Split another beer?" I asked to break the silence.

"I ought to head home."

"Yeah, me, too. I have work to do."

After paying our tab, we walked in silence for a block or more, trying to avoid other pedestrians. Maho was not one to find silences awkward, but even so, she asked in a way that seemed deliberate. "Besides dyeing techniques, what's *Kimono Killer* about? It sounds kind of cheesy."

"Oh, I wouldn't say it's cheesy. It's historical fiction. The history part of it involves the famous kimono shop, the Kariganeya, and the invention of the yūzen dyeing technique. But Daté spiced it up with a fateful encounter between an impoverished apprentice and the boss's daughter."

"Ah, a love story!"

"Yeah, and like all the best love stories, it's a tragedy."

"What? Did they all get killed by a kimono?"

"Kind of. The young apprentice poured his life into the kimono he was making for the empress, but he was sabotaged by a jealous co-worker and disgraced. The disappointment ruined him, and he threw himself in the river. Then his girlfriend went crazy, wrapped herself in the fabric he had made, and ran barefoot alongside the river, cutting her feet on the sharp rocks. When she couldn't run any further, she collapsed and died. Eventually, the kimono went and got revenge on the scoundrel co-worker."

"Sounds like a kabuki play. They all die in the end!"

"All but the kimono. Kimonos take on a life of their own. That's what they say. You don't own a kimono, a kimono owns you."

"That's what they say about tattoos, too!" Maho glanced down at the one on her right arm, a fanciful rendering of Nausicaä on her jet glider. "Like this one here. Sometimes Nausicaä takes over my life and sends me off on all kinds of wild adventures!"

"I'd like to hear about some of those adventures!"

When we reached Sanjō-Ōhashi, we said goodbye. The air was cooler now that the sun was down, and I decided to walk home from Sanjō. It was a long walk, but one I enjoyed. I knew shortcuts that snaked in and out of alleys and narrow paths. I could smell the dinner preparations in the houses I passed along the way. Many had their windows open. Here and there I caught a whiff of mosquito smudge or heard the splash of water being readied for the evening bath. At some houses, the sound of the television. At others, murmured conversations. I wondered about the people who lived in those houses. Families sharing stories, discussing the events of the day. Ordinary people leading ordinary lives. Were they happy? Certainly, every family nurses wounds and tends to hidden pains. Aren't they all flawed? Maho's certainly was. Her Ph.D. father and perfectly polished mother were hardly model parents judging from the way they pressured Maho. And mine? I brushed the thoughts from my mind and hurried home. That is to my borrowed home. I had a translation waiting.

CHAPTER THREE
BUTTERFLIES

Shōtarō Tani had been a good-looking man. Perhaps he still was. I have a distinct memory of a photograph of him in a small convertible, top down, hair tousled by the wind, rounding a corner on a steep seaside drive. I saw the photo in one of those infamous weekly tabloids like *Friday* or *Josei Seven*, though why I was even looking at such a rag is no longer lodged in my memory. I just remember the photo. The car was a foreign make, maybe a Lamborghini or a Porsche. It wasn't the car; it was the aura. He looked free and happy gliding along the slender belt of highway, a jagged seacoast to his right, the mountain wall to his left. The sun was bright above him. I could almost taste the salt in the air and feel the breeze tangling his hair. I can't remember where he was at the time. California? Amalfi? The place was no more important than the car. What mattered was he wasn't here. Not in Japan. He was out, enjoying his own private adventure, as private as one can be with a paparazzi capturing you in a telephoto lens from some unknown perch.

There were other photos, too, all from the early 1980s, shortly before Shōtarō's disappearance. He would have been nearly thirty by then. I remember one of him leaning casually

against a large column, dressed in summer-weight trousers, his
white linen shirt unbuttoned at the neck and the tail flapping out
beside him. His arms were crossed over his chest and his head
cocked with his chin jutting up towards the camera. In other
photos, he is with women, none of them Japanese, all of them
laughing. Shōtarō Tani was a party boy. He liked expensive
wines, Cuban cigars, and European women. And he had the
money to get what he wanted. Most of his riches were his by
birth, but he hadn't done too poorly in promoting his writing
and establishing a following, even in the brief time he was active.

Apparently, Shōtarō was still writing. Did that mean he
was back in Japan? Had he reconciled with his father? That
seemed unlikely given the circuitous approach to publishing.
I suspected we had yet another chapter in the family angst he
had exploited so well before. There was only one way to find
out. I lifted the lid and pulled the pages from the box. It was
too late to begin translating in earnest, but I wanted to at least
have a look. The manuscript pages were covered in an outer
wrapping of thick white washi paper, delicately embossed
with the Tani family seal. Certainly, a formal way to present
an unpublished, unfinished novel! I pulled the wrapping apart
and fanned the pages out on the desk. They were type printed,
not done by hand, which was unusual for a writer of Tani's
generation, but a relief to me. The characters would be easier to
read. I flipped to the last page to check the number. Fifty-three.

Setting the packet back on the desk, I slipped downstairs
to pour myself a glass of wine. Sauvignon Blanc was my drink
of choice, and I had half a bottle in the refrigerator. I grabbed
a glass and carried the bottle back upstairs to my room. It

was ten p.m. A leisurely drink and a quick perusal of the manuscript would be just what I needed for a good night's sleep.

As soon as I pulled off the title page, I discovered what looked like a diary. Writing in diary form was hardly unusual in Japan; some of the earliest prose texts were journals, or more accurately, art diaries. This diary was in a female voice; and that was surprising. All of Shōtarō Tani's earlier works hewed closely to his own experience. Perhaps he was assuming a female persona, maybe as a way to distance himself or disguise himself? The more I thumbed through the pages, the more I noted the diarist appeared to be Shōtarō's sister, Satoko. Or at least that was the way it was being presented.

August 29, 1982
Shugakuin Hazamacho, Kyoto

Hot and muggy with the likelihood of rain.

I love kimonos. I love the story each one tells, implicit in the weave, imbued in the dye. A little old-fashioned perhaps, maybe even a little superstitious, but I believe each kimono contains the spirit of its creator. The materials used to make kimonos are obtained from living beings, the silk spun from the body of the worm or from the sinewy fibers of the flax and hemp. The dyes used on the fabrics are all derived from living plants, flowers, grasses, and more. And it is the craftsman then who breathes new life into the lives pulled from the earth. It is the magic of the human hands and the wonder in the human heart that turns these natural elements into beautiful fabrics animated by the bodies of their wearers. Kimonos communicate the stories of their past to their wearers. It is important, then, for the kimono and the kimono owner to be well matched. And it is important for the kimono owner, and I use this word sparingly, to appreciate the spirit of the kimono. When you do, the combination of your spirit with the kimono's, creates a beautiful presence.

This is my kimono philosophy.

Is it odd to have a kimono philosophy? My father chides me for it. But the art of the kimono is in my blood. It is my lineage. Samurai may follow the way of the sword; tea masters, the way of tea. I follow the way of the kimono.

There was a time when my father indulged my love of kimonos. He himself had no interest in the garment, at least not beyond whatever profits they accrued to the family business. He paid for my classes in textiles, even sericulture. With every chance I got, I attended exhibits and explored as much of the dyeing and weaving techniques as I could. But it seems it was all just a joke to him. He would never allow me to devote myself to the family business. That was to belong to Shōtarō, and Shōtarō wasn't interested.

"The only thing women are good for is wearing our product, Satoko!" I'll never forget the way Father sneered when he said that. "Don't imagine you're ever going to be anything more than a shopkeeper's wife."

To the outside world, Father clinged to old-fashioned values, I knew he had other intentions.

The voice that came through in the diary installment was confident, excited, but bitter as well. I say "installment" because with the next page, the form changed to that of the epistolary. And this time the voice was tied to Shōtarō's persona.

> April 15, 2004
> Castelmola, Sicily

> My Dearest Satoko,
> Your letter calling me back to Japan took me quite by surprise. I swore when I left, I would never return. I have grown accustomed to my life in exile here, far preferring my sunny villa in Southern Italy to our pretentious Kyoto house. But I have missed you. I was sorry I was not able to return for Mother's funeral. I appreciate the letter I received with notice of her death. Did you send that, too? There was no note, but it was postmarked Kyoto, so I assumed it was you. I thank you for honoring our agreement not to correspond. Until now, that is. Maybe we took our fears too far, but I worried if Father learned of my whereabouts, or of your communication with me, he would make things difficult for the both of us. I have to say, things have not been difficult for me. To the contrary, I have flourished here on foreign soil, growing fond of my hermit's life. No more flashy cars. No more leggy women. The quiet anonymity suits me. During the day I stroll the flagstone lanes, enjoying

the luxurious play of light along the white walls, the
red flowers cascading from flower boxes, the patches
of blue sky darting over the rooftops.

I still write, of course. And I think of home when
I do. I think of you. How many letters I have written
to you, long ones, explaining everything. I'd even walk
the winding lane to town determined this time to post
one to you. But each time I'd change my mind and
tear the letter up, scattering the tiny pieces over the
ledge where the road bent, watching them sail like
tiny butterflies into the sea below.

The letter went on for several more pages. Although I only
intended to thumb through the manuscript, I was finding myself
being drawn in, puzzled by the haphazard, patchwork nature
of the piece. The writing seemed similar to Shōtarō's style, as
far as I could remember from my graduate school days long
ago—lyrical, expressive, somewhat overly emotional. But it was
different, too, lacking the polish of his earlier works. I wondered
if this chapter was really finished. Could Tokuda have given me a
draft by mistake?

And then there was the long lacuna in Shōtarō's writing. His
last published work came out in 1987. I remember the date because
that was the year I took the course on Japanese contemporary
fiction in graduate school. I elected to write my end-of-term paper
on one of Shōtarō's novels, hoping to leverage my knowledge of
kimonos into a better grade. My plan was a bust. My grade was
fine, if I recall, but Shōtarō's novel had little to do with kimonos.
The focus was on a young man's friction with his father, the same

focus in his earlier works. I remember some surprisingly violent scenes—of coming to blows with the father when he forced the man's sister to marry and forgo her own professional aspirations. By the end of the novel, the father disowned the son and silenced the daughter, which is what happened to Shōtarō, as well.

Shōtarō Tani didn't exit the limelight immediately. He became a media sensation: scion of an old-Kyoto family gone bad made for good television. It was after his sister's wedding ceremony that rumors of Shōtarō's disappearance began to spread. He was conspicuously absent from the ceremony, though to have attended would have meant crashing the occasion, since his father had forbidden him access to the family. But thwarting his father was one of Shōtarō's pastimes. When he failed to appear at previously scheduled television interviews, people noticed. It was as if he had just vanished. Brief reports in the major newspapers on his curious absence led to speculation. Most assumed Satoko's new husband forced Shōtarō into hiding. This same husband, teaming with the father, compelled Satoko to relinquish any involvement she once had in the company. She, too, all but disappeared from the public eye. Her absence, however, was less noticeable.

I took another sip of wine and returned to the manuscript. The narrative style of the piece shifted yet a third time. We moved from a diary to a letter and what appeared to be a straightforward, first-person narrative, more representative of Shōtarō Tani's earlier writing.

Her letter was simple. "Come home now," she wrote. "It's urgent. Meet me at the Benibana Inn,

Shiobara Hot Springs in Nasu. I'll be there by 5 p.m. on May 7."

We agreed not to contact one another until Father had died. Satoko would then be able to free herself of Akira. I was pretty sure Father was still alive. But the urgency in Satoko's letter compelled me to act. I hurriedly packed and caught a flight to Narita, then took the train to Shiobara. My connections were bad, and by the time I got to the Benibana, I'd been on the road for two days.

It was an odd place to meet. I appreciated that it was far from Kyoto, and that's probably why Satoko chose the site. But there were inns closer to Kyoto that would have been equally discreet.

By the time I reached the inn, Satoko had already checked in. But she was not to be found in her room, the gardens, or the baths. When she still had not returned by 6 p.m., I decided to go look for her. It was unusually chilly for May. There'd been a snowfall a few days earlier and patches still lingered here and there. I had only a cotton jacket, so I walked briskly along the stone path until I came to the suspension bridge spanning the Hōkigawa River. Uncertain where to go, I stepped out onto the bridge and looked down on the rushing waters below. I shivered against the damp mist rising up from the spray. The sun had set, and the river was etched in shadows. Even so, from the bridge, I saw what looked like a woman resting along the rocky shore just out of reach of the water. She was lying on her stomach with her head cradled in her arms, her hair spread haphazardly around her. Difficult to discern in the waning light, she seemed to be wearing a richly patterned kimono. The way she was lying, with her hair spread out in all directions, I was surprised her kimono was not in disarray. I hurried down from the ridge unable to imagine how she had come to be there. Had she slipped? As I drew closer, I realized she was not wearing a kimono. She was naked. Had her body been painted? Stumbling over the rocky ground I crept up beside her, calling to her. She didn't move. I jostled her shoulder, noticing when I did her skin was cold to the touch. I also noticed the design coloring her back, legs, and arms was not paint. It was a tattoo. Or tattoos. Across her left shoulder ranged a design of red maple leaves, each leaf so finely wrought you could feel them shimmer in the light of the newly risen moon. Along the other shoulder was a cluster of cherry blossoms, tissue pale, almost translucent. From the branches of both the maple and the cherry dangled *tanzaku* poetry slips. Each slip was so intricately painted the woman's skin became the washi paper of the slips, lightly flecked with different squares of pigment, resembling crushed dried flowers and grasses. If it were lighter, I'm sure I could have read the poems on each of the slips. That's how fine the tattoos were. Hesitating, afraid of what

I'd see, I rolled the woman over. Her eyes were open, staring but unseeing. And her mouth was covered in a thick dark blood.

"Satoko!"

That familiar face was so grotesquely displayed. I wanted to hug her to me, but I was afraid. There was something ghastly about her lying there naked under the moonlight. When I glanced down, I saw her entire torso was covered in tattoos from her collarbone to the midline of her thighs. All the tattoos were of kimono motifs, fans, incense burners, peonies, and scrolls. I could not stand to look. I struggled to my feet and stepped away from her. Her head rocked slightly with the violence of my action and when it settled, her eyes stared up at me, empty.

I should have at least closed her eyes or left my jacket to cover her. But I couldn't think of anything except leaving. Why had she sent for me? Or had she? Anyone could have written that letter with its cryptic demand. But if Satoko didn't write it, who did? And what might that person have in store for me?

I rushed back to the Benibana, uncertain of my next step. I should raise the alarm, inform the police; recover my sister's body. But what then? What would happen when my own whereabouts were discovered? How would I explain what had happened? What if my presence here implicated me in Satoko's death? I could well imagine my father trying to pin the blame on me. What a convenient way to get rid of me and simultaneously get his revenge. But would he really have his own daughter killed? Was Satoko murdered? Stripped of her clothes, covered in tattoos . . . something evil had taken place.

The innkeeper eventually trundled up to the front counter, after the third time I pounded the bell. He looked troubled when I told him I wanted to leave.

"At this hour? The trains have stopped running now, sir. And besides your sister has already paid in full for two nights lodging. I strongly recommend you spend the night. Enjoy a good dinner. Wild boar is on the menu this evening. Have a flask of saké, a nice long soak, and then start fresh in the morning. Who knows, your sister will probably return later tonight. She may have just gotten caught up in her stroll with her friend."

"Her friend?"

"A woman in her early sixties, I'd say."

"Did she say who she was?"

"The woman? No sir, she was not one of our guests. But they seemed like old acquaintances."

"What did she look like, this other woman?"

"Can't say for certain. I didn't really get a good look. Didn't try to either. It's not any of my business, you know. But I'd say she looked like she might be someone in the arts."

"Why do you say that?"

Well, on account of the way she was dressed. She was wearing a very elegant kimono. Your sister, too, for that matter."

"My sister was wearing a kimono?"

"Oh yes. A light brown, I believe. Or maybe it was yellow. Not fancy or anything but tasteful, like the older lady."

"Was she wearing a coat?"

"Come to think of it, no. And she must be feeling a little chilly now if she's out without it. The temperatures drop suddenly here in the mountains. Once the sun goes down, it gets pretty cold. Especially for folks not used to it."

I was struck sharply with sorrow at the old man's words, seeing Satoko lying naked on the cold rocks.

"Oh no, sir. I'm sorry to upset you. I'm sure she's just fine. Probably stopped off at a café with her friend and forgot the time. She'll be back soon, just you see. Wouldn't it be better for you to wait here?"

I thought about it. The old man had a point. It would be difficult for me to get anywhere now without a car. And the prospect of running around an unfamiliar town in the dark seemed foolish if there was a killer about. Besides, I hadn't slept in days. I was worn to the bone. I asked for paper and pen. I wanted to record exactly what I saw. I needed a good record of events, should the police discover me.

When he heard my decision, the old man's face

brightened. He hustled me back to my room, urged me to change into the night robe the inn prepared, and then he set off to have his young assistant start my dinner service.

"Wait a minute!" I yelled at the manuscript on my desk. "Your sister is lying dead on a rocky shore, and you're just going to sit in the room she paid for and drink saké without doing anything about it?" I understood Shōtarō's wish to remain undetected. But how horrible could it be to confront his father?

I checked the clock by the bed. A few minutes past eleven p.m. I wanted to keep reading, but my head was swimming. Perhaps I'd had too much wine. I could hardly make sense of what I'd just read. This work was nothing like Shōtarō's earlier writing. For starters, it was stylistically inconsistent, and it was, for lack of a better word, fantastic. A woman's tattooed body? And a kimono tattoo at that. Were there really such tattoos?

I stepped into the bathroom to wash my face. Looking at the pale red eyebrows above my eyes reminded me some women tattoo eyebrows on their faces, eyeliner, too. But the kimono tattoo was different. Besides, it would have normally been hidden from view. Those eye tattoos are visible for all to see, though I suppose they look more or less "natural." At least that's what they tell you. I'd have to look tattoos up online tomorrow and see if I could learn more about patterns and designs. But, right now I had to sleep.

I slipped out of my jeans, collapsed on the bed and closed my eyes, but I couldn't get the image of the woman's naked body and the kimono tattoos out of my mind. I sat up in bed and switched on the light. I hadn't seen it before . . . not exactly. But I had read it. Actually, I had translated it.

I got out of bed and crossed the floor to my bookcase, skimming the titles until I came across the dark violet binding with "Kimono Killer" scrawled in red down the spine. It was the description of the famed kimono fabric, wasn't it? I flipped through the pages. There.

The bolt of fabric, stretching the length of the workroom, was drenched with color. Sumptuous, luxurious color. Shunsuke stood back and took it in, his masterpiece, a fabulous tableau of crimson maple leaves and delicately pink cherry blossoms. But it was the detail he mastered that set his work apart from the others stretched across the drying boards in the workroom. The maple leaves on his fabric were so finely wrought, you could see the delicate ribbon of veins running through each shimmering leaf. The malachite green along the bark of the trees produced a soft spongy lichen. On the other side, for the designs were planned in asymmetrical blocks along the shoulders and the hem of the kimono when assembled, the cherry blossoms were tissue-pale, almost translucent. Beneath the petals sprigs of new leaves burst forth a gentle red. From the branches of the trees, he had painted dangling poetry slips, each slip richly textured in different colors and pigments to capture the wispy softness of paper. Some resembled the ink wash technique called "sunset," where lighter hues blended to darker at the paper's edge, while others mimicked "moonrise" or "latticework" patterns. The paper slips dangled gently from the branches fluttering in the invisible breeze. Some blowing upwards, others twisting to show the darker backside. And on each he had meticulously painted verses in thin India ink. It had taken him days of practice to imitate all the different calligraphic styles. And now, with this single bolt of silk, he had created an imaginary three-dimensional montage of poetic elegance, ornamented surface upon ornamented surface, layer upon layer, paper, blossoms, and silk. Soon this gorgeous cloth would rest upon the empress's own soft skin.

Shunsuke was exhausted. He had been working nearly non-stop on his fabric for most of a fortnight. He had to win the competition. He had been an apprentice far too long and under far too ignoble conditions. He knew he was better than the other young men the master had brought into his service, men from better families but with far less skill. Shunsuke had to prove his worth; but mostly, he had to win his release from his master, so he could set himself up in his own studio.

Shunsuke heard stealthy footsteps in the corridor. They paused outside the closed door to his workroom. Then he saw a small white note glide softly beneath the door. Ochiyo!

CHAPTER FOUR
CROWS

Crows were everywhere, cawing and swooping past in a swish of blue-black wings. Why they were here, I didn't understand. The English garden outlined a rangy privet hedge in need of trimming. Cosmos and poppies bloomed in a wild tangle. I followed the gravel path that wended through the flowers, past statues of cupids and timid maidens into an open field lush with daisies and day lilies. On a hillock just ahead, I saw a lilac bush in full bloom, thin white sheets of paper fluttered amidst the hanging lavender globes. Tanzaku poetry slips. At the time, I didn't think it the least bit odd to find tanzaku in an English garden in North Carolina. I was certain I was in North Carolina, where my father grew up. When I was a child, our family returned there every five years when my parents took their furlough. In the distance, I saw the faint purple outline of the Blue Ridge. But the crows were wrong. North Carolina crows were never this big, or boisterous. These were closer to ravens. The lilac bush was gone now, but one poem slip still fluttered in the breeze, gliding softly in my direction like a wayward feather. I reached out to catch it when, in a swoop of black wings, it was gone, clenched tightly in a crow's crooked black beak.

I had been dreaming, lying flat on my back in my upstairs

bedroom behind the Kyoto zoo. The crows were particularly noisy this morning. Probably enjoying the treasure trove of trash left behind by yesterday's zoo goers. And then I felt the flash again. Only it wasn't light. It was a ringing bell. The front door bell. Who on earth was at the door this early in the morning? I stumbled out of bed and grabbed for my jeans, struggling to find a sweatshirt to pull over my head. It wasn't cold, but I didn't have time to put on a bra and my T-shirt was thin. The clock next to the bed clicked as the numbers rotated—nine o'clock. I'd slept late!

Mrs. Miwa, the neighborhood busybody, was at the door. I sensed it would be her before I even opened it. Her salt and pepper hair was cut in what at one point might have been a saucy pageboy but now looked like a slightly deranged version of the bob worn by the diminutive actress Linda Hunt. Her glasses were perpetually smeared and had the unfortunate effect of magnifying her eyes, fitting since she was always trying to peer into my business. I couldn't imagine what neighborhood law I had broken this time! Sleeping past sunrise? The last time she was at my door it was to inform me it was the responsibility of the house owner to sweep the area in front of the house. I did sweep, whenever I saw an accumulation of grime, but apparently that was not enough for Mrs. Miwa. I promised to sweep every morning, and I had tried. So, if sweeping was not the reason for her visit, what then?

"Ruth-san, are you not aware of our policy regarding late night parking? Section Seven Article iii of our *Neighborhood Association Handbook* clearly states any car pulling into or exiting a parking space after nine p.m. should not use the headlamps. It is quite distressful to those who live in front of the parking pad. There have been complaints, Ruth-san." Her Japanese was formal but clipped while the speed with which she fired off the neighborhood association rules was impressive.

"*Ohayoo gozaimasu*, Miwa-san. It looks like another fine day."

"Yes, yes, good morning. Now about the car." She switched to English in a display of authority.

"Mrs. Miwa, I quite understand the parking regulations. I am familiar with Section Seven Article iii of our *Neighborhood Association Handbook*. You may not be aware of this, but I have no car."

"I *am* aware that you have no car. I am referring to your visitor who was parked here last night. When whoever it was left at approximately 11:37 p.m., he failed to dim the lights. There've been complaints, Ruth-san."

I was just about to tell Mrs. Miwa I had no visitors last night when she turned abruptly on her heels, but not before reminding me to please be sure to follow the association guidelines.

I guess someone took advantage of the empty parking pad beside my house. I hadn't noticed anyone when I'd come home last night. It occasionally happens. But usually it's during the day, when a tourist, desperate for a parking space, takes a chance and parks in the space belonging to this house. If they leave late at night, they're not supposed to turn on their headlights until they've cleared the parking pad. The bright lights shining into the windows beyond the pad were annoying. I could understand that. I just couldn't understand who would park here so late at night, after all the tourist sites had closed. There are no restaurants around here to speak of. Probably it was some group of kids. But how typical of Mrs. Miwa to put the blame on me, the resident foreigner!

I took advantage of my proximity to the broom just inside the doorway to give my street a perfunctory sweep. The way a candy wrapper leapt up off the asphalt when the broom passed over it and drifted lightly in the air before landing on the mound of debris reminded me of the dream I was having before Mrs. Miwa's visit. I had been dreaming of a poem slip, hadn't I?

That's when I remembered the manuscript stacked on my desk, waiting like a dark door. The body in the story had been tattooed shoulder to thigh with kimono designs. The way the author described her; she was practically a human pattern book. That's what I couldn't understand. Shōtarō Tani's "fiction" had always been much closer to autobiography. Had he decided to turn over a new leaf with his re-entry into the literary world and create something fantastically farfetched? But if so, why kill off his sister? She had always been a source of support for him. Why not kill off Satoko's detested husband or even her father?

I'd have to reserve my judgment until I'd read a bit more. And not being an expert on tattoos, there were some vocabulary items in the chapter I didn't understand. But mostly I was curious about the way the body was decorated. As Shōtarō Tani had described the tattoos, they seemed to represent the kind of lush design so typical of kimonos, pretty blossoms, butterflies, and birds floating among wave-like clouds and cloud-like pine branches. On other areas, the design was more narrative, representing scenes from classical literature or classical works of art. It was not unusual for kimono designers to draw from famous screen paintings or woodblock prints. I recalled the magazine my dance teacher showed me years ago, with the fashion spread of kimonos designed by Satoko. Some were wonderfully modern, with bold geometrical styles, while others seemed influenced by the Genroku prints of the seventeeth century. They cost a fortune. But they looked "familiar," and tapped into a modern desire for a past Japan. They worked well for women who were sent abroad in diplomatic service. The woodblock print designs were usually familiar overseas making the kimono even more elegant in the eyes of the foreign admirer.

But the description of the tattoo with the poem slips resembled the kimono Daté portrayed in her novel. Was this just a strange coincidence? Tokuda said Shōtarō admired my translation. Had he also admired Daté's work enough to appropriate it? Of course, if we're going to play the appropriation game, it seemed both of them had "borrowed" their ideas from the famous diptych screen painting by Tosa Mitsuoki. And that stood to reason. Mitsuoki was a great favorite of the Empress Tofukumon'in, who also patronized the Kariganeya, the famous kimono shop that featured strongly in Daté's historical novel. Tattoo, kimono, screen painting...they were all intricately entwined in a way that was as baffling as it was beguiling. I needed to take another look at Daté's novel. It had been years since I translated it. I had a vague recollection of Tosa Mitsuoki's screen painting, but I needed to refresh my memory of it. Undoubtedly, I could find what I needed on the Internet. Before that, though, I needed a cup of coffee.

I ground the coffee beans and started the drip pot, enjoying the aroma of the special roast an old college friend had sent me from Hawai'i. I toasted a giant wedge of bread, Japan's answer to Texas toast, then slapped a wafer-thin slice of processed cheese on top to melt while the coffee finished. I was too lazy to slice fruit, but I managed to locate a carton of yogurt in the back of the refrigerator.

I carried my coffee, toast, and yogurt back into the living room and sat down next to the low table where Tokuda and I conversed earlier. Was it really just yesterday? I turned on the TV and flipped through the channels. It was too late in the morning for the BBC, but NHK usually had reliable news segments throughout the morning. The female announcer was looking very grave as she gave the latest report on the Japanese Nikkei index. I was not particularly interested in what NHK had to offer me this morning and was reaching for the remote when the reporter switched to a breaking story. The nude body of an unidentified woman was found in Tochigi Prefecture, near the Nasu Shiobara Hot Springs area. The reporter added, there was no evidence of foul play.

I looked up from my toast to see crime scene investigators in orange vests scrambling over rocks beside a swift moving river. Two men were carrying a stretcher towards a blue vinyl tent erected over the crime scene. There was no footage of the body, but the place looked bleak and cold with grey wet rocks surrounded by tall conifers. The river roared ominously nearby.

What a chilling coincidence, but I doubted the body was tattooed like a kimono! I switched channels to see if I could catch other stations airing the same news. Finding dead bodies on riversides was not common in Japan, and usually news like this was quickly sensationalized. But no matter how many channels I clicked through, I couldn't find any other reports.

Quickly depositing my dishes in the sink and pouring myself another cup of coffee, I clomped upstairs to turn on my computer. Maybe the news outlets had picked up the story by now. I scanned the usual sites: *Yomiuri, Asahi, Mainichi, Japan Times*, but none had anything to report. On a whim I typed in the name "Satoko Tani." There were old pages about her kimono innovations, exhibits, and travels. In photographs she looked vivacious and active, always in motion, getting into an airplane, stepping onto a sidewalk, her face aglow with intelligence and confidence. But there was a marked paucity of reports about her after her marriage.

Satellite pages led me to earlier reports about her brother: his debut, his award, the rift with his father. But nothing beyond that. I did come across a fairly recent report on Tani Kimono. Their business was seeing a downturn in profits. According to the report, this was not unexpected as many other kimono manufacturers were seeing similar declines. The reporter blamed the situation on the fact that women were no longer wearing kimonos. Given the convenience of wearing Western garments, women lacked confidence in how to wear a kimono properly and so avoided the attire altogether.

Another article echoed the same opinion but offered a bit more hope that the kimono would not go the way of the dinosaur. The author recognized that plenty of women (and men as well) still wear kimonos to pursue traditional arts, which were far more abundant in a place like Kyoto, where the Tani Kimono business was located. An English-language article decried that nowadays the kimono is only worn by the rich or by professional geisha, which I knew to be patently false. And a fourth observed the energy and excitement younger kimono wearers were putting into salvaging vintage garments or wearing kimonos in nontraditional ways. I frequently saw these kids about town, young men dressed in Doc Martins and kimonos or college-aged girls shortening kimonos and layering them over leggings and high heels. Some purists looked askance at their unconventional ensembles. But most welcomed their creativity. Besides, I thought the purists' view was anachronistic. Even at its earliest, the kimono was frequently worn in eclectic combinations. I was reminded of the schoolteachers in the nineteenth century who combined items of a man's costume with those more traditionally worn by women. They completed their ensemble with leather boots newly imported from Europe.

I glanced at the bedside clock and was startled to see it was 11:30 a.m. I needed to get moving if I wanted to be at my dance lessons on time. Nihon buyō teachers were particularly strict, and mine was no exception. She did not brook tardiness. Once I saw her tell a woman who was two minutes late, she would not teach her that day. She'd have to come back next week. Classes started on time, or not at all. She took the woman's pay and then sent her on her way. I had heard it wasn't the first time she had enforced her tardiness policy so stringently.

Normally, I changed into my kimono at home and went to my lessons ready to go. I disliked changing at my teacher's studio. There wasn't a lot of space or a mirror in the dressing room. I was going to have to rush, so I would have to change there. I banged around the room frantically searching for my cotton practice kimono, sash, and other paraphernalia. One time, in my haste, I left my cassette tape with the dance music at home. Another time I forgot my fan, which was tantamount to a violinist forgetting her bow. You just didn't forget that kind of thing. But there I was, fanless. The sensei looked at me with utter bemusement, shook her head, and handed me her own to use during the lesson. I wondered if she would have been as lenient with a Japanese student.

I walked the few blocks to catch the subway that went by the dance studio. The foot traffic by the zoo had picked up, and it took effort to dodge around parents with small children and those out for a casual stroll. When I made it to the corner by the Heian Shrine and the Kyoto Municipal Museum, I nearly collided with a man in a stained grey jacket and dirty baseball cap. He looked homeless, which was surprising. The homeless in Kyoto were usually invisible. Mostly they congregated down by the river where they could live more or less rent-free under the bridges. The river was a number of blocks west of where we were. I gave the man a wide berth as I continued my rush to the subway.

Japanese transit was always on time and always immaculate. As soon as I stepped aboard the subway car, the doors swooshed to a smooth close and off we went. I reached my stop in no time. The dance studio was a few blocks south of the station, down a tiny lane accessible only to bike and foot traffic. I slid open the front door to the studio, stepped out of my shoes and made sure to arrange them neatly off to the side of the entryway. I hurried up the stairs.

"Right arm, right arm," I heard Sensei calling out instructions to the two women in the class ahead of mine. "Look left...shoulder down...gaze up at the mountain...up, up. It's a mountain, you know!"

Our dances were frequently narrative, telling a story based

on a poem or play from the past. Sometimes they were just celebratory. And other times they were meant to capture the bittersweet mood of a woman waiting for her lover. Always they were elegant and very carefully choreographed. Each tilt of the head, each twist of the wrist was strictly regulated and done exactly as it had been done forever.

I kneeled at the entryway to the practice room, placed my fan parallel to my knees, and bowed to my sensei. She nodded her head in acknowledgement and went back to observing her students. I went into the dressing room to change.

I had been taking dance lessons since high school. Well, not continuously. There was the long hiatus when I was in the States for college and then for my unfortunately brief career as a college professor. In fact, I had only just resumed my lessons. There was so much I had to relearn. People talked about muscle memory, about being able to return to something physical after many years and picking it up again. But if it were true, I was an exception. I felt like I had to start over from the very beginning. And I had a new sensei. The woman who had taught me years ago passed away. My new sensei was generally pretty patient. She rewarded effort. She wanted her students to be obedient. I tried to please her on both scores.

The lesson was over now. The two women knelt and bowed in gratitude to the teacher, their dancing fans folded. Their greeting done, they walked quickly into the dressing room. I sat silently on the floor beside the door waiting for the teacher to summon me for my lesson.

"Are you going to the kimono exhibit at the Nomura Museum tomorrow?" one woman asked the other. They were both middle aged. But it didn't seem they'd been taking dance lessons very long.

"I have tennis lessons tomorrow. I could go Sunday. But, speaking of kimonos, did you hear about Satoko Tani?"

"Do you mean the daughter in the Tani Kimono family?"

I was supposed to be letting my mind empty in preparation for my lessons. But my ears pricked up at the mention of Satoko. I turned to stare at the women. Noticing my gaze, they lowered their voices. They had changed back into their street clothes and were sitting on the floor folding their practice gear. I had to strain to catch what they were saying.

"Did you hear about the body they found in Nasu Shiobara?"

"It was just on the news this morning, right?"

"Well, my husband texted me the police think it is Satoko. He works for a subsidiary of Fuji Network."

"How bizarre. I wonder what she was doing in Shiobara? Was it a love affair?"

"Ruth! Ruth-san! Are you sleeping? It's time for your lesson."

I'd been so intent on trying to catch the conversation in the dressing room, I missed my teacher's first call to class. I wanted to stop and ask the women for more information, but we weren't supposed to talk before class. We really weren't supposed to talk after class. Now that I was summoned, I had no choice but to enter the practice room and begin my lesson.

I knelt in the middle of the room facing my teacher, my dance fan folded in front of my knees. I bowed and asked for her guidance.

"From the beginning, Ruth."

I stood, turned away from my teacher, who was seated

primly on a cushion. Opening my fan and holding it above my face, I leaned back and twisted ever so slightly. I was a woman, abandoned by her man, gazing up into a mist-enshrouded moon, and thinking of times past. The music started and slowly I twisted my body, lowering the left shoulder first and then turning my head slightly, until I was gazing at the floor. My fan followed in a slow arc. Now the fan was a mirror reflecting the moon behind me. Gazing into it, I saw the misty orb of the moon in the reflection and my face. Time passed. I aged. My man was gone.

Could the body by the river really be Satoko's?

"Ruth!"

Sensei cut through my thoughts, and I saw I had reached my favorite part of the dance. I knelt on one knee and closed my fan slowly one fold at a time until only two folds were left open. Now my fan was a letter. With the finger of my right hand, I pantomimed rubbing an inkstone. I turned my hand over, and my finger became a brush. I dipped it once in the ink, dabbed the ink, and then brought my brush to the paper to write. I was writing a letter to my lover, but the only letter I could think of was the one Shōtarō Tani supposedly wrote to his sister, the sister he left lying dead and exposed on the riverbank. Did I then have proof of a murder sitting on the desk back at my house? I mean, it had to be murder, right?

"No, no, no!" Sensei clicked off the cassette tape. "Don't turn your hand all the way up. We don't want to see the underside of your palm. Now try it again."

I rubbed the imaginary ink again, dabbed the imaginary brush, which is my finger, and brought it to my imaginary letter paper.

"There! You did it again!"

Sensei got up off her pillow and knelt beside me.

"Like this."

She moved her hands lithely through the air, delicate but strong. I could smell the ink. I could sense the weight of the brush in her gesture. I could feel the woman thinking, longing, remembering, as she pulled the brush off the inkstone and prepared to write.

"Don't act it out, Ruth. This isn't a mime show. You need to feel it. Now, again.

She started the cassette again, but I was not ready, and I missed the cue.

"No! Again."

We repeated these four or five times until she let me move to the next steps. Holding my fan behind my back, I staggered slightly with the emotion, one step back, two, and . . . my mind returned to the riverside, imagining the tattooed body spread ghoulishly over the rocks.

"That's enough now Ruth. Go home and practice that much. Listen to the music. Feel the mood. Do you understand? You think too much."

I knelt before her, placed my fan before my knees, and bowed.

I nodded affirmatively.

"Ruth, of course I want you to get the steps right. I want perfection. But that comes later. Right now, I just want you to feel it. Do you understand?"

Sensei had some free time before her next lesson, so she called me into the practice room to chat after I had changed into my street clothes. She often did so when she had a spare moment. And it was a treat for me. Sensei was famous. Local television stations frequently sought her out whenever they needed an expert on traditional culture. Thin, graceful, inevitably dressed in a kimono with her hair swept high atop her head, she was the image of a *bijin* beauty from the past. Even so, her tastes were quintessentially modern. She preferred to dine on French cuisine and when she wasn't preparing a performance, she enjoyed taking her Alfa Romeo roadster out for drives in the mountains. She was a fan of Yuriko Daté, and she would frequently talk to me about her latest novels.

We exchanged some pleasantries when I decided to ask her if she was familiar with Tani Kimono.

"Of course. They make excellent kimonos. Or at least they used to. A Tani Kimono is always supple, and the colors are deep, they show up well on stage. Years ago, the family was a great patron of the school and would donate kimonos for our performances. I even collaborated once with Satoko Tani, back when she was more involved in the business. But it's been years."

"You worked with Satoko Tani?"

"Once, yes. I choreograph my own dances, you know. And I worked with Satoko on creating the kimonos for one of my pieces." I may have a video tape of the performance downstairs if you would like to see it."

"I would like that very much."

"I'll have my assistant locate it. You can pick it up the next time you come."

I could tell my teacher was ready to wrap up our conversation, but I needed to know more about Satoko. I played my "foreigner card" and pretended not to pick up on her cues.

"Why do you think Tani Kimono didn't retain Satoko or promote her to president? From everything I've read, the business has been declining ever since her husband took over."

"Ruth, did you ever stop to think they don't want the business to continue?"

The thought stunned me.

"Everyone says the kimono business is no longer profitable," Sensei continued. "They say the business is dying, but I don't agree. The kimono business, all the traditional arts, are communal operations. It's important to establish good relationships with other professional businesses that depend on kimonos, like the dance schools, the tea schools, and such. We are their best source of advertising. And even though women are buying fewer kimonos these days, they are willing to pay more for the few they do buy. Much more. A business with the history and customer base Tani Kimono has can work to stay afloat. If they are losing profits, perhaps it's because they don't want to stay in business."

With that, my teacher squared the seams of her kimono, smoothed the fabric over her knees, and pulled herself up tall and straight on her floor cushion. It was time to end our conversation. I bowed, offered the appropriate parting words, and headed down the stairs.

CHAPTER FIVE
CRANES

Back out in the small lane in front of the dance studio, I heard the drum teacher two houses over instructing her students on the proper way to hoist the shoulder drum. A few houses down a shamisen lesson was in progress. The neighborhood was a haven for the traditional arts. After my class, I liked to saunter slowly back to the main road and soak in the atmosphere. When the windows were open, such as today, the sounds tumbled pleasingly into the street. The arts were very much alive. Different, I suppose, from the way they had once been taught and appreciated, but alive, nonetheless.

Today, I didn't feel like lingering. I was eager to get home, so I could make sense of what Shōtarō Tani had written. Was Satoko really the woman by the river's edge? If so, where was Shōtarō? Had he asked Tokuda to hire me to *translate* his discovery of her death? Or was he expecting me to go to the police with this information? What evidence could I offer, a work of fiction by a writer who many presume to be dead? I could imagine the welcome I would receive. Once they uncovered my own past, wouldn't they treat my information as further proof of my instability?

I took the subway to Higashiyama-Sanjō to connect to the No. Five bus and jumped on. The bus rumbled past trendy tourist shops as it headed towards the bright vermillion gates of the Heian Shrine. When the driver stopped at the museums, I suddenly remembered the Kyoto Prefectural Library was there. They would have today's newspapers, as well as issues dating back decades, perhaps even white paper reports on businesses in the prefecture.

Once inside the library, I asked at reception for the periodicals and was sent to the multi-media reference room on the second floor. The most recent newspaper they had came off the press late last night. There was nothing on the Shiobara body. So, I spent time scanning through the CD-ROM directory trying to locate information on Tani Kimono. I perused a few old newspapers on microfiche. But I quickly came to understand I would have to have a more efficient way of searching. The only thing I found was a general report on the kimono industry in Kyoto, listing the three leading kimono manufacturers. There was no mention of Tani Kimono, which was counted among the three, seeing an inordinate loss in business. What I did discover, though, was the interconnectivity of the kimono industry. My dance teacher had called it a community. But it wasn't just the consumers of kimonos who contributed to this community. The kimono manufacturers hosted a whole array of smaller manufacturers and businesses.

There were those businesses that specialized exclusively in the obi sash, which was often more expensive than the kimono itself. And then there were the manufacturers of the ties and tassels that accompany the obi. Separate businesses designed and made footwear to be worn exclusively with kimonos, not to mention the handbags and other accoutrements.

Beyond manufacturing, there were shops that specialized in cleaning kimonos, which was more complicated than it may sound because to really clean a kimono you had to take it apart at the seams and re-stitch it all back afterwards. There were businesses that refurbished kimonos: dying them modern colors, changing the length of the sleeves, or trading out the lining, for example. Scads of businesses specialized in teaching the proper way to wear kimonos. I was surprised to find that some wedding businesses did double duty as funeral parlors, which also allowed for the sale or rental of appropriate kimonos for mourning. But it didn't seem Tani Kimono had branched out into the lucrative wedding/funeral business.

Fewer were the number of companies that actually made the kimono. Among those I surveyed, most had histories dating back to the early twentieth or mid-nineteenth century. Tani Kimono boasted a four-hundred-year history. It would be devastating if they left the business. And there were so many satellite industries that depended on Tani Kimono. I was surprised the government hadn't designated them an intangible cultural property. If they did, Tani Kimono wouldn't have the freedom to close their doors or alter their business without government permission.

I hadn't gotten very far in my research when the library staff began making preparations to close. I still had about thirty minutes, but I was hungry and suddenly aware I'd skipped lunch. I packed up my stuff and headed out the door. By the time I rounded the corner to the zoo, the crowds had thinned. This was one of my favorite times of day. It was approaching twilight, *"tasogare"* in Japanese, a magical time caught between day and night. With the sun slipping beneath the horizon, the light is uncertain, making it difficult to distinguish what is seen. The word in Japanese alludes to this vagueness. Unable to see exactly who is walking towards you in the twilight, you call out, "Who is that?" Or, *tasogare* as it would have been in years past. In classic plays and ghost tales, tasogare is the time of day when strange things happen, when peculiar creatures step out of the shadows, when dream worlds become real.

The zoo was now long closed and looking a little bereft. Just an hour ago it would have been teeming with people, the air sparking with shrieks and peals of laughter. Now, it was silent. I'm sure the animals were ready for a break, tired of being ogled and teased all day long. The man in the stained grey jacket was sitting alone on a bench in front of the zoo. The soft twilight glow painted over the stains and wrinkles in his jacket, making him look almost presentable. Here he was, an elderly suitor on a park bench awaiting a lover.

It was only a block to my house from the zoo. I began running through my mind what I had left in the refrigerator to eat. Nothing except a few take-out bags, their contents a mystery. I turned back and headed for the Fresco, where I picked up some prepared food and rushed back out for the walk home. It was dark now, not even a hint of the earlier twilight, and a wind had come up. It would probably rain tonight.

As I turned into my street, I noticed a black sedan parked in the pad by my house. Was it the same car that had been there last night? I'd have to let whomever it was know they couldn't park there. Mrs. Miwa would be proud of my diligence.

The side windows were tinted, and I couldn't tell if anyone was in the car. Most people here backed into a parking space, but this car pulled in front first, making it awkward for me to peer in through the windshield. No wonder its headlights annoyed my neighbors. I walked behind the car and came along the driver's side. I was ready to tap lightly on the side window when the car's engine roared to life. The headlights flashed on the high beams, and the car screeched into reverse, backing out so quickly, the rear bumper nearly hit the zoo wall on the other side of my narrow street. I instinctively jumped backwards, lost my balance, and dropped my grocery bag, spilling my dinner across the asphalt.

"What the hell?" I shouted at the retreating red taillights. As I collected my groceries, I noticed a fresh pile of cigarette butts. "Pigs!" I muttered to myself, stomping up the stairs to my front door. Even inside I could smell the stale, acrid odor of cigarette smoke.

I scooped the rice into a bowl, found some sauce for the tempura, and ate in front of the TV. I missed the evening news and couldn't find any more coverage of the Shiobara mystery body. I checked out the usual gossip show. The host was shouting at one of his panelists in typical over-the-top fashion. They weren't discussing the Shiobara case, so it must not have been hyped into sensational news yet. I scarfed down my meal and headed upstairs to see what I could find online.

I was excited to see a few more reports on the body in Shiobara. But the more I read, the more my excitement faded. Investigators were not giving much away. The *Yomiuri* site announced a female was found nude, but if authorities had identified the body, they weren't saying. The *Asahi* site was much the same. They offered, however, that the body had been dead for some time. How long, they did not disclose. But they noted that, even though the riverside was generally well traveled by tourists, passersby had failed to see the body because it was tucked deep within the underbrush and covered by leaves.

Speculation of foul play was now even greater, but the medical examiner had not determined the death was a homicide. On none of the online sites was the death the leading story.

Maybe the body in Shiobara wasn't Satoko's after all. In Shōtarō Tani's account, the body was visible from the bridge. Could I really be sure about what I'd heard at the dance studio? The woman who had made the claim, the one whose husband worked for the news network, had put on a gauze facemask as she prepared to venture back outside. Perhaps she was sensitive to the dust or pollen that was so rampant over the last few weeks? But it meant her words were muffled.

And what about the chapter I was now translating? Was the similarity between the story and the Shiobara body just a wild coincidence? Could Shōtarō himself be the one who put the body there? But why murder Satoko? Maybe she wanted to sell the kimono business and was planning to cut her brother out of the considerable proceeds. Nothing made sense. More puzzling still was why Shōtarō had drawn me into his family drama. I really *should* consult the police. But subjecting myself to all those questions again, the smirks, the pompous patronizing . . . I had too many bad memories of trying to convince police of a crime they didn't believe existed. That was a long time ago. So long ago I thought I'd sealed the door to those memories. It disturbed me to discover the door was still ajar, so I decided not to speak to the police.

I knew the contract also forbade me from trying to contact Shōtarō Tani, but this extraordinary coincidence seemed to warrant discussion. Maybe I should start with Tokuda.

I pulled the contract out of my desk drawer and read it again. Even though it noted Miyo Tokuda would be my contact person, there was no contact number. There was no information anywhere about how to reach anyone related to the project, only the post office box number on the self-addressed envelope. I suppose I could write to whoever checks the box. But that would take who knows how long. I'd rather just try to meet Tokuda, but, how? I wasn't even sure where the Tani Kimono store was. Perhaps there was a website. I went back to the Internet again and searched but came up empty. Many of the traditional businesses had not yet bothered to enter the Internet age.

Who else knew Tokuda or how to reach her? Yuriko Daté! She knew about the kimono industry in Kyoto. I started thumbing through my desk for my address book. It was almost too late to call at nine o'clock, but Daté was a night owl.

"Ruusu-san! What gu-do tai-min-gu!" she said in tortured English when I introduced myself. She was funny like that. Breaking into English in the middle of a phrase and then switching immediately back to Japanese. "I haven't heard from you since you got back to Japan! But I'm so glad you called. I'm just finishing another novel and will be looking for a translator."

"Wonderful! I hope this one includes lots of kimonos, too."

"Of course! Lots of kimonos and lots of murders, too! And this time, the killer's a person! But that's not why you called me. How can I help you?"

I explained in brief I was trying to reach someone who worked for the Tani family, and I needed to find the address or a phone number.

"I see. Well, I know I have that information somewhere. It's going to take me a while to locate it. I can never remember where I put things, you know. I suppose I need a secretary.

The one I had the last time you were here left me. But you probably knew that. It was in all the scandal pages."

I did remember the incident. It seemed her young male secretary, and of course much more than a secretary, grew jealous over Daté's flirtations with other men. He made a scene after one of her award ceremonies. Packed his bags the next day. I was surprised she hadn't replaced him. Maybe she had really cared for him.

"Ruth-san, why don't you stop by tomorrow afternoon? You still remember where I live, don't you? I'll have your information for you then. But we can also spend some time catching up. I'll see that we have a light lunch. Say, 1:00?"

As I hung up, I remembered why I so enjoyed working with Daté on *Kimono Killer*. She was always so approachable. If I had a question about a passage I was translating, I'd call her and ask. She never appeared to be bothered by my intrusions nor did she belittle me for needing to ask, though in truth she was sometimes amused by what had stumped me. "No, no, Ruth-san. You are over-thinking this! When I write about the character being on the edge in the dark, I'm not referring to some deep psychological moment. I mean, the character was standing at the edge of the verandah and it was nighttime. Nothing more." I looked forward to seeing Daté again.

Feeling energized after the phone call, I decided to read more of Shōtarō's work. I was hoping I could read through to the end tonight, though that seemed overly optimistic. I pulled the manuscript off the desk, turned the light on by the bed, fluffed the pillows against the wall, and curled up against them. I paged through the manuscript until I found where I had left off.

Dear Satoko,

I could not sleep. How could I? Every time I closed my eyes, I saw you lying there alongside the river. You were so cold, so unlike the sister I remembered. I could see you now in my mind's eye as you had been in high school, your silky black hair in braids. You kept it that way all through school, even though it was out of fashion. You always seemed so self-assured. That's why I remember the time you came home, flushed and agitated. You wouldn't tell me why. When I asked, you shut yourself in your room and refused to come downstairs for dinner even when Mother called. Do you remember?

I never told you, but the next morning I followed you when you left for school. You turned off of Ichijō and headed in the exact opposite direction of school. It was early still, and not many people were out on the street, so I had to be careful you didn't see me. It was hard to keep up. You were on your bike and I was on foot. But the hills slowed you down. I watched as you leaned your bike against the wall by the Shisendō gate and turned to walk the long, bamboo-lined path to the garden entrance. It was not yet opened. But you stood outside the entranceway talking to a boy I didn't recognize. Not that I would. I didn't know any of your friends. You never brought them home.

The bamboo grove was thick. I suppose you figured no one would see you there. I was small still, and able to crouch down without being too obvious.

You were crying. The boy bit his lip. It was cold, and you had wrapped a long black muffler around your neck. Your breath came out in wispy clouds. Suddenly you stood up on tiptoe and threw your arms around the boy's neck. He buried his face in your muffler. And then, just as suddenly, you pulled away, hurried down the bamboo pathway, got back on your bike, and pedaled briskly back the way you had come. I had to dart behind a light pole to avoid being seen. I watched as you sailed down the hill, and when you were out of view, I stepped out from my hiding space, and looked up the pathway where the boy had been. He was gone.

Later I learned his name was Ryohei Miyazaki. You and he frequently slipped away from your various lessons and practices to meet at the Shisendō. That was back when you still had hopes of becoming a kimono designer. Ryohei's father was a well-known yūzen dyer, and I imagine you and Ryohei dreamed of future collaborations, both in romance and career. Holding hands in the cool bamboo bower next to one of the Shisendō tea cottages, did you talk through the different designs you envisioned? The greens of your dyes would be greener than any before, the delicate edge of your flowers, finer than the finest.

I don't know what made you cry that morning. I was only eleven and can't be sure of the sequence of events now. But when Ryohei finished his first year of high school, his father pulled him out of school and had him work full time in the family business.

Ryohei had a natural talent for the art and an intuitive understanding of how to encourage the truest colors from his dyes.

I recall another time years later. It was well after you had graduated high school. I had already started publishing my stories in odd journals here and there and was just beginning to savor the taste of literary fame. I was selected for a prestigious prize and featured in an article: "Exciting Young Writer Channels Literary Spirit of an Earlier Age." It was when I showed our father the article, triumphantly expecting him to understand finally my true calling. He became more aggressive in his insistence that I return to Kyoto and stop "wasting his money with my silly scribbling."

I well remember the argument we had. I had come home for Mother's birthday party, we were celebrating her sixtieth year and Father and I were alone in the family sitting room, doing what we did best, quarreling. Our exchange that afternoon was more heated than usual. Both of us had come to a temporary end to our tirade of words and were sitting silently in our easy chairs glaring at one another when you came to retrieve your portfolio of sketches. Father's eyes sparked spitefully as they shifted from me to you.

"Where are you going?" he shouted. Do you remember? He yanked the portfolio out of your hands, knocking several of the design sheets loose and sending them sailing to the floor. When you tried to gather them up, he snatched the sheets from your hands.

"I've been lenient with you long enough, Satoko. And here you are at twenty-nine, sneaking around as if you were still a girl in high school with that, that apprentice."

He spit out the word "apprentice" like it was a curse, when in fact, Ryohei had long since finished his apprenticeship to his father and was now head dyer. His fabrics were more and more in demand. And a number of kimono connoisseurs claimed it was his love for you that inspired him. I don't know whether or not Father was aware of the gossip.

"Look, leave Satoko out of this. Your fight is with me," I glared at him.

"My fight is with both of you, dragging the Tani name through the mud."

"Who do you think you are, Satoko, carrying on like you're some kind of kimono-maker? What you are is a baby-maker, and you better get to it or you'll miss your chance. And I don't mean with the Miyazaki apprentice either."

Father grabbed the large fabric shears lying on the table and sliced through your design sheet, the white strips fluttering delicately to the floor while the blades of the scissors winked with a brutal glitter. I can still hear the icy sound of the metal slicing the soft washi paper and the whispery sigh of the paper hitting the floor.

"From this day forward, you will not see him again.

If you care about our family traditions, our kimono traditions," he said as he took another slice with the large fabric shears, "you will do as I say."

His words were ominous. It wasn't just the menacing way he held the shears. There was something else, something behind his words. I didn't understand at the time. But you did. I saw you blanch. You collapsed to your knees and sat back hard on your heels.

Snip, sigh . . . more strips fluttered through the air, landing all around you like feathers torn from a white crane. When they all settled on the floor, you bowed low, your forehead nearly touching the floor, stood slowly, and left. You didn't say anything further. Father glowered after you, veins bulging in his forehead.

"Father, don't do this," I protested.

"You may not speak to me. This is a family matter and does not concern you. You are no longer part of this family."

"Father, please. I'll do what you want me to do. I'll take over the business. Just please, leave Satoko alone."

"You are dead to me. I want you out of this house now."

He marched out of the room leaving me with the paper carnage.

Where was our mother in all this? She, after all, was the legitimate Tani, the one who was born to the business. Father was an adopted son-in-law, like Mother's father. In both cases it was because the families failed to produce male children, but our mother hadn't failed. She had given birth to me. And how she must have celebrated to have finally been able to offer up a male child. I suppose my refusal to take over the family business had been a bitter disappointment.

Instead of helping you, Satoko, I ran. Nothing has changed. I'm still running, leaving you vulnerable and alone. Forgive me.

The chapter ended here at page fifty-three. I hoped there would be more about Satoko's death and what happened to Shōtarō after he left the Benibana Inn. Hopefully, the next chapter will tie up some of the loose ends. And I hope the ends tied will not as closely resemble today's news reports. I wish I had the complete manuscript. It's hard to translate without knowing the whole of the parts.

Even so, as the story continued, it began to more closely resemble vintage Shōtarō Tani. Of course, the second-person address was somewhat odd. But the themes were much the same. There was the acrimony between the father and the son, though this time it was more clearly directed toward Satoko. Perhaps she was the stand-in here for the Shōtarō hero. Instead of the writer son defying the father, it was the artist daughter. Except, she wasn't being all that defiant. It appeared Satoko was not willing to fight her father. Or perhaps more accurately, she had no means with which to defy him. Her brother did not seem particularly dependable. Sure, he protested, but he did little else.

I couldn't get past the resemblance to *Kimono Killer*, either. On the surface, there wasn't that much to justify a comparison. But at a deeper level you had the same kind of hopeless situation, an aspiring artist struggling against all odds to maintain balance in a world askew. In Shōtarō's story, the actual kimono apprentice, Ryohei, didn't need to fight for his art. But Satoko did. She seemed to fill the role of the kimono apprentice in *Kimono Killer* who had only his talent to rescue him from ignominy. And when his rival sabotages his design, he has nowhere left to turn.

"Shunsuke!" The master's voice boomed down the corridor. Shunsuke dropped the rag he had been using to mop down the workshop floors and hurried to his master's quarters. He paused outside the door and coughed softly to acknowledge his presence.

"What is the meaning of this, Shunsuke?"

Shunsuke entered the room and knelt before his master. The older man was clutching the silk fabric Shunsuke had labored over month after month. He glowered down at the apprentice, veins bulging in his forehead, and his hand trembled as he gripped the material.

"Master?"

"You dared to enter a flawed piece in the contest for the Empress?"

Shunsuke looked in dismay as the master unfurled the fabric, now wrinkled and soiled from handling. He pointed angrily at the section with an embroidered crane, its white feathers embossed with gold thread. Here and there the threads were frayed, and the mother of pearl flecks Shunsuke painstakingly applied to the bird's wings were scraped away.

Shunsuke blanched. He reached for the fabric, but the master took the long knife he had on the table at his side and sliced into it just far enough to rend the cloth. Then he took both hands and slit the fabric in two. The scream of the silk echoed through the room.

"You will never work for this shop again. Get out."

Shunsuke stumbled from the house barely conscious. Passersby mistook him for a drunk and paid him no mind until he leapt from the bridge, crashing into the swollen river below. His body bobbed and drifted like a broken doll before coming to rest on the rocky shoals. At just that moment, dyers upstream, unaware of the tragedy below, began to rinse their fabrics in the currents. The frothy river, now a deep red, washed over the emaciated body of the hapless apprentice.

And so, the kimono took its first victim. The master's daughter, Ochiyo, would be the second. Deeply in love with Shunsuke, she wrapped herself in the torn fabric that ruined her lover and went insane, running up and down the rocky shoreline until her bare feet bled, staining the shoals red yet again. The master was so distraught, he closed his shop and released all his apprentices. My favorite part of the novel came next.

In the Edo period, they recycled cloth. Some of the scraps

from this kimono were sewn into altarpieces and others into banners and dedicated to the local temple. The villain Takitarō, who had secretly sliced through the embroidery threads in order to sabotage Shunsuke, began to suffer from nightmares. He kept dreaming he was being choked, and he'd wake up in a sweat. So, one evening he went to the local temple to pray for relief. Because the temple was near the fateful river, it was built high up off the ground to prevent flooding. Takitarō lit a stick of incense and was praying before the altar when a strong wind began to blow. The altar banners swayed back and forth when he realized they were made out of the kimono he ruined. He began to back away from the altar when one of the banners broke free of its tether and flailed out at him. With a shriek he turned to run, tripped, and fell headfirst off the temple parapet and onto the river rocks below, breaking his neck.

The temple decided to decommission the banners, since they seemed to be haunted. Other worshippers at the temple would report seeing a young woman sumptuously arrayed when they first approached the altar room. But when they came closer, they realized it was just the altar banners waving in the wind, only there was no wind. The priest responsible for discarding the banners had been brought up in a family of artists and knew how exquisite the fabric was. He couldn't bear to destroy them. Instead, he took the remnants to his older brother, who made his living painting fans for elegant women. He was always being asked to transfer his beautiful drawings to fabric, so his customers could wear them. But whatever he painted on fabric was short lived. The paints would fade, or if a lady got caught in a sudden downpour, her kimono ended up irreparably streaked.

The fabric the priest brought the fan painter was just as durable as it was sumptuous. No matter how many times he dipped it in water, the colors did not fade. Uncertain how to achieve the same effect, the fan painter set to work experimenting and challenged his apprentices to create a fabric with a similar design. They plied their paste, dyes, and needles, thinking they could never make anything as exquisite as what the unfortunate apprentice had made. The fan painter eventually succeeded in perfecting a dye-resist technique. The "yūzen" dye process, the fan painter's name was Miyazaki Yūzen, grew so prominent, he ran the Kariganeya out of business.

I checked the clock on the bedside table and was surprised to see it nearing midnight. My eyes were burning from all the reading, but I wanted to go over the passage about the tattooed body one more time. Could I have possibly misread the section? As I recall, Shōtarō's narrator used the word *shisei* to describe the tattoos on the woman's body. There were other options. He might have referred to the tattoos as *irezumi*, literally "inserted ink" or *horimono*, "a carving." But he used shisei, which combines the character for stab or pierce with that for blue. To me, shisei was a more literary choice and took the edge off the initial shock of a woman with a full body tattoo.

As I paged back through the manuscript, I noticed only the first and last pages of the chapter were numbered. The pages in the middle were not. I thumbed over the pages, starting at the beginning and working towards the end, looking for words that would place me in the scene: bridge, river, body, tattoo . . . I couldn't find the page with the scene. I started again, widening my key words to hot spring, inn, Shiobara. I found those without much effort. There was the reference to the letter Satoko sent to Shōtarō in Italy, begging him to return to Japan and instructing him to meet her at Shiobara Hot Springs. And there was the scene where he was waiting for her in the inn. Satoko's things were in the room and the innkeeper assured him she had checked in. Shōtarō waited, grew impatient, headed out to search for her. And then? The page was gone.

CHAPTER SIX
CUCKOOS

Summer mornings in Japan arrived early. Skies brightened just before four o'clock, though the sun didn't officially rise for another hour. Early sunrise was to be expected for a land called "The Rising Sun." The owners of my house installed room-darkening shades in all the bedrooms. But I preferred waking to the natural light, even though the day started earlier and earlier as the summer wore on.

I stretched, enjoying the soft grey light filtering into the bedroom. It was a good day to run. Not too hot, yet. Having taken the day off yesterday, I needed to run today. I lay in bed charting the course I'd take. I decided against the usual run along the Philosopher's Path. I'd be there later this afternoon when I visited Yuriko Daté. Today was a good day to run to the Kamo River, but I had to get moving. If I waited too late, I'd be battling traffic all the way there. I got up, shed the T-shirt I'd slept in and got dressed. That's when I saw Shōtarō Tani's manuscript scattered across my desk and remembered my late-night search for the missing page. It had to be here somewhere. I'd start the search again after my run.

It was 5:30 a.m. when I got to Nijō Avenue. The traffic was so light I ran most of it in the street. When I reached the Kamo River, I headed north in the direction of the mountains. The cool air, the near isolation, and the rhythmic pounding of my footsteps coaxed me into a meditative state. I began to reflect on the missing page and my earlier search.

I checked under the desk, behind it, too, thinking the page might have sailed off on its own. I had even checked in the covers on the bed. No luck. The page was gone. Working myself up, I checked to see if other things were missing: my passport, my credit cards, and the cash Tokuda gave me. Those were the only valuables I had. They were all where I had left them. Only the page was missing. I went downstairs to check the back door and the patio. I locked the sliding door, realizing I had left it unlatched the other day after I'd brought in the laundry. There was a wall around the yard and a side gate that stayed locked, so I usually didn't worry excessively about the door. And, why would someone "break in" to the house to steal ONE page? It didn't make sense. "It'll turn up when I least expect it to!" I told myself. But now, there was even more reason to contact Tokuda. I had to get to the bottom of this story and the bizarre coincidence with the Shiobara body.

I caught the tip of a stone buried in the path and lurched forward, regaining my balance just before I landed on my face. It was time to pay attention to where I was. The Kamo River run was beautiful, especially this time of year. The river was full from the runoff of mountain snow and early spring rains. Everywhere the green grew lush and thick, from the canopy of leaves overhead to the tangled river grasses swaying along the banks, and here and there on the sandbar islands dotting the center of the river. Long-legged herons perched gracefully at the river's edge waiting for fish. The inevitable crows, mourning doves, and an occasional black kite competed for attention. The clouds, rising above Mt. Hiei, home of the famous Enryaku-ji Temple, changed from grey to pink to puffs of white. Kyoto was placed where it was because of Mt. Hiei and the Enryaku-ji monastery. The mountain was to the north, the direction of the "demon gate"and was believed to offer a protective barricade against malicious spirits. Perhaps the mountain's protection was only offered to native inhabitants, though. My little brother and I had not been as lucky, had we? If anything, the mountain had acted like a gateway to sorrow. It was time to turn back.

It was nearing 6:30 a.m. when I reached Nijō Bridge. I crossed the river and snaked along neighborhood streets to avoid the increasing traffic. I was home by 7:00. After cooling off for a few minutes on the patio, I went inside to shower. I thought more about the missing page and the tattoos described, and it suddenly occurred to me I should ask Maho for advice. She might be able to tell me if it would be possible to get a tattoo so richly layered it looked like a kimono. If the tattoo was too far-fetched, then I'd know Shōtarō's description was embellished. Maybe his time in Italy really had influenced him to be more imaginative. It was too early to call Maho now. I decided to send her an email with a request to call. Within minutes, my phone was ringing.

"Ruth! You're finally going to do it?"

"Do what?"

"Get a tattoo? I knew you had a wild streak!"

"No, sorry. I don't need the information for me. I mean, I'm not planning to get a tattoo. It's for a project that I'm working on.

"The boss has you translating about tattoos?"

"No, it's not for her. I mean, it's not a translation exactly."

"Not exactly?"

"I was just wondering if it were possible to get a tattoo that looks like kimono fabric."

"Sure, anything's possible, but it would be pretty unusual. Seriously, you're not planning a tattoo for yourself? That sounds like the kind you'd get. Ha, think how easy it would be if you didn't have to actually wear the kimono. You could just take off your clothes and there you'd be!"

I shuddered thinking of Satoko lying on the rocks. Hadn't Shōtarō mistaken her tattoos initially for fabric?

"If I wanted a kimono tattoo, what'd I do?"

"How big a tattoo are we talking? Western or Japanese?"

"Japanese, I guess. What's the difference?"

"Japanese tattoos are usually all connected. Western tattoos can be completely separate."

"In that case, Japanese. I'm talking about a full body, from shoulder to thigh."

"Wait. Is this one of those, 'It's not for me, it's for my friend' kind of discussions?"

"No, I swear. But what if it was?"

"Well, if it WAS I'd take you to my *horishi* and you could ask him!"

"Would you do that even if it wasn't? It'd be really helpful."

"I'll see what I can do. He doesn't like being interviewed. Too many foreigners have been turning his art into some kind of deep, dark oriental mystery. But I'll explain you're different. So, what's the tattoo you want to know about? Is it like a picture of a geisha or something?"

"No, it's not like that. And I haven't actually seen it myself.

It was described as if the skin were the palette for a variety of kimono patterns and dye motifs. Some of the designs were very intricate. I'd just like to know how much time it would take to get a tattoo like that."

"Got it. I'll make a call and get back to you later."

"Thanks, Maho. I really appreciate it."

After we hung up, I realized I hadn't asked her how she was or what she was doing up so early. But maybe it wasn't early for Maho. To tell the truth, I didn't know that much about her. Perhaps I was just jumping to conclusions when I assumed she was a late riser.

I still had a few hours before my meeting with Yuriko Daté. I'd need to stop on the way and pick up a gift. Fruit was usually a good bet. But I couldn't recall seeing a fruit stand between my place and hers. The shops along the Philosopher's Path were mostly for handcrafts and tourist trinkets. I decided to go to the Fresco now instead of hoping to find something appropriate on the way.

Orange kumquats had recently come into season and were lined up prettily in the fruit case. I opted instead for two large mangoes packaged together in a gift box for ¥4,000, nearly $40. Not cheap by any means. But Daté seemed more of a mango person to me. To make the present even more festive, I carried it over to the florist to see if I could have it gift-wrapped.

The florist was happy to oblige, wrapping the box in bright blue tissue paper with yellow ribbons. She pulled a green sprig out of a box on the counter and affixed it to the present. "*Sabisu*," she said as she handed the box to me, meaning that she was giving me the sprig for free. When she saw my quizzical look, she explained. "It's for the Aoi Festival." That's right. Today was May 15th, the day of the annual Hollyhock Festival. I had completely forgotten. Normally, I'd go stake out a spot along the parade route. I wouldn't have time today. I asked the florist if I could have a few more sprigs. I was sure it seemed greedy, but I thought it would be fun to wear one in my hair and give another to Daté.

I rushed home to change clothes. I'd decided to wear a kimono and it took longer to dress than if I were just slipping into a skirt and top. I opened my kimono chest and pulled out one drawer after another before settling on a light hempen yellow kimono. Finding the right obi was an even greater challenge, but one I enjoyed. I pulled a few out of the protective white paper wrappings and set them alongside the kimono, finally deciding on a woven black sash with a green hollyhock design. I offset the sash with a cord that was close in color to the kimono. I tended to be conservative in my color combinations, unlike Daté. She teased me about it whenever I gave her the chance. "Why so dour, Ruth? Use a little imagination."

I was just pulling my gear together when Maho called.

"Ruth, I talked to my horishi."

"That was fast."

"He wants to see you. Can you come over now?"

"I'm really sorry, I've already made plans."

"Can't you cancel them? He said it's important."

"I really can't. I'm scheduled to spend the afternoon with Yuriko Daté."

"Ah, that horrible Daté woman!"

"She's not horrible."

"She is to me. She's sucking up your time. Okay. I'll try to explain it to Sensei. But let's plan on tomorrow morning. Nine?"

"What's so urgent?"

"I don't know. When I told Sensei you wanted to ask questions about a kimono tattoo, he got really quiet. I thought maybe we'd lost connection. And then he said so softly I could hardly hear, 'Bring her here.'"

"Wow, not what I was expecting. Okay, I'll be there tomorrow at nine. Where should I go?"

"The studio is pretty hard to find. Let me meet you at Fushimi Station on the Keihan line. Be there by 8:30. Okay?"

"Okay. And thanks, Maho."

I hadn't expected my inquiry about the tattoo to invite such an urgent response, and now I was intrigued. Did Maho's tattoo artist have information about Satoko? I mean, was she really tattooed? And by the same token, was she really dead? I was tempted to call Maho back and cancel my visit with Daté, but I just couldn't.

It took close to twenty minutes to get from my house to the start of the Philosopher's Path. The path followed a canal built in the late nineteenth century. Today, it was full of people in search of a quiet place to stroll. Most were tourists, Europeans with big bellies and bigger cameras; older women with sun parasols spread one alongside the other like a mobile canopy; and inevitably middle-aged men walking alongside mini-skirted young women who were clearly there for monetary gain. The men looked deliriously happy, walking with vigor and pride while the women, towering over their escorts in their high heels, just looked bored as they texted messages on their cell phones with dexterous thumbs.

Daté lived in a modest estate wedged between Hōnen Temple, one of the most peaceful temples in Kyoto, and Ginkaku-ji, one of the most popular with tourists. Built atop a high stone retaining wall, her house always made me think of a castle. The steps to the front door were steep, and I wondered how Daté navigated them late at night when she returned inebriated from one of her parties. Before I could ring the bell, Daté was there, holding the door wide and smiling just as widely. She was wearing a beautiful, indigo *tsumugi* kimono with a light green obi woven with scenes from the Aoi Matsuri, a procession of ox-carts, horses, and beautiful women in twelve-layered robes.

"Ruth-san! Don't you look lovely. How nice of you to go to the trouble to wear a kimono! Let me see, now turn around . . . well done, Ruth. You're getting better."

"All thanks to you. I always appreciate your guidance."

"Please come inside."

"Thank you. I am sorry to bother you."

"Ruth, Ruth enough of this formality. Come. Have a cup of tea. Let's relax a bit."

Daté led me through her formal sitting room, decorated in a very tasteful, minimalist style, a *hinoki* slab table in the center, and a single cushion. I paused to appreciate the fresh arrangement of flowers in the alcove, white peonies in a black *Bizen* vase. Then I noticed the hanging scroll. It looked quite old. The brown satin brocade mounting was fraying slightly, and the silk background was discolored in spots. But the painting was captivating. A person was resting alongside a stream holding a round fan. Blue water spilled into frothy waves at the bottom right of the scroll. In the upper left corner were the outlines of rocks and a waterfall along with a tumble of orange chrysanthemums. It wasn't easy to tell whether the person was male or female. The paint on the face had worn away, leaving only the faintest suggestion of an expression, from the languid position of the body, with black-clad feet poking out from under billowing robes, I guessed male. The outer robe was a somber brown damask festooned with maroon colored fans etched in black. The inner robes, like the face, had faded and were now but a whisper of white.

"Do you like it?"

"Very much."

"That's the work of Miyazaki Yūzen-sai. It's a seventeenth century scroll. But I picked it up for a song at a little shop off of Kita-oji."

"He was founder of the yūzen dyeing technique, right?"

"So, they say. But he started as a fan painter. See the fan the person is holding? The design is unfortunately faded now. But that would have been an example of the way Yūzen-sai decorated fans. That one is round. But most of his work was on folding fans, as you can see in the pattern on the robe."

"I love all the different dimensions of fabric. You have the brocade mounting and the ribbon of trim around the silk painting that plays on the chrysanthemums. And then the silk offers painting upon painting. It's just resplendent!"

"I wonder if this wasn't a sort of advertisement for Yūzen-sai. He presents several examples of his fan painting within the larger painting."

I would have stood there longer admiring the scroll if Daté

hadn't urged me on. She led me into her study, which offered a stark contrast to the sedate silence of her sitting room. Her study was a maze of bookshelves and file cabinets. There was a desk in the center laden with papers, books, and boxes. I noticed a blue light flashing intermittently beneath a sheaf of papers and realized her laptop was underneath. On the wall not covered by bookcases she had a large framed picture which I could tell was by Takabatake Kashō, the famous magazine illustrator. This print, like many of his illustrations, was of a woman in a kimono. She was seated in a train and gazing wistfully out the window as a summer scene glided past. The print was awash in gentle greens and muted blues—so fresh I could almost feel the breeze from the open train window.

"So, you like Kashō?"

"I do," I replied. "The women in his prints may look melancholy at times, but they seem so bold. I mean look at this woman. She's going somewhere. And you just wonder where, and why. I guess that's why I like him so much."

"Well, let's get the two of us moving, too. Please, join me on the verandah."

Daté prepared low-slung chairs and two narrow tables on the verandah overlooking the garden. She must have recently had the tree limbs and hedges trimmed as everything looked manicured and clipped. A few azaleas were still in bloom. A river of white pebbles snaked through the garden, edged by moss and patches of grasses, mostly miscanthus but also sweet flag and golden forest. A stand of irises sheltered against the garden wall offered a splash of deep blue color. The blooms nodded lazily in the soft breeze.

No sooner had I settled in my chair than a handsome man stepped out onto the verandah with a tray of iced barley tea and two damp towels. He knelt by our chairs and placed the tea and towels on our tables.

"Let me introduce my chef, Masahiro. He has prepared a light lunch for us this afternoon. I hope you will enjoy it.

Masahiro bowed slightly and then withdrew without uttering a word.

Daté still had a taste for young men. I strongly doubted all he did was cook for her. When I turned from Masahiro to look at her, she was smiling suggestively.

I pulled the box of mangos out of the bag I had been carrying and handed it to her. "Please add this to our light lunch if it suits you." I also produced the extra sprig of hollyhock which she pinned to her hair with great enthusiasm.

"Are you enjoying being back in Kyoto, Ruth-san?"

"Yes. Very much."

"Are your parents still here?"

"No, they retired some time ago. They live in the U.S."

"They were missionaries here, weren't they?"

"Yes."

"And you never thought of following in their footsteps?"

"Never."

"I couldn't really see you riding a bicycle in black trousers and white shirt and going door to door with pamphlets!"

"I'm sure I couldn't see me doing that, either! But that's not the kind of missionaries they were. They worked at the Iwakura Christian Hospital. My father was a surgeon and my mother a nurse."

"Well, if I had to have surgery, I'm sure I'd want a doctor with God on his side! Hard to fail when you work for the Almighty!" Daté laughed at her own joke. "Did he? Did he ever lose a patient?"

"He was an obstetrician. So, he was more accustomed to welcoming life into the world!"

"Sorry, I hope I didn't offend you. Anyway, small chance I would have ever met your father!"

I was used to people making jokes about my parents' profession. Mostly, they were made in fun, but my father did have a number of difficult cases and a few setbacks. When I mentioned this to Daté, she was eager for details.

"Once a young woman who was mentally challenged was brought to the hospital by her parents. She was pregnant. Her family did not know how, but they wanted her to have an abortion. My father understood, but he felt disconsolate performing the procedure or any surgery on a young woman who could not give consent. Then there was another time when a woman with a history of heart disease died in childbirth. She had been warned against carrying a pregnancy to term for this very reason, but she had persisted. My father performed a C-section to try to relieve the stress, but even so her heart gave out. He once showed me a photograph the woman's family had sent him of the baby's first visit to the shrine. It was poignant to see the baby's grandmother there, but no mother."

"That's sad. But I guess some women will go to any lengths to give their parents grandchildren!"

"There was one other case like that. But this time, the baby died. He would have been the parents' first son. I remember my father telling my mother about the shock he had, though, when the woman's husband stormed into the recovery room, mad with grief, and berated my father for saving the mother but not the son. 'You should have put the life of the baby first,' he shouted. 'You stole my son from me.' The mother of course heard the exchange and also began to accuse my father of making the wrong decision."

"That's crazy!"

"I was in grade school when it happened. The family pressed charges. They had no legal grounds and could get no more than a token condolence payment from the hospital. Even so, my parents suffered during the year leading up to the trial. My father was full of guilt, but he was also dismayed by the bereaved father's behavior. In the end, the husband divorced the wife. My father discontinued his surgery practice once the lawsuit was over and went into administration full time after that."

Masahiro returned and set a tray laden with dishes down between us. He slowly placed each dish on our individual table trays, carefully arranging them in front of us.

"I'm sorry to dominate the conversation with stories about my parents. Just look at this feast! I thought you said it would be light lunch."

Masahiro prepared boiled tofu, vinegared octopus, tempura okra and lotus root, and grilled sweet fish. Each lightly seasoned and served exquisitely in an assortment of small dishes of varying sizes and glazes. Midway through the meal, Masahiro brought out a small flask of chilled saké and poured each of us a glass.

"Daté-san, what do you know of the Tani Family?"

"I suppose I know as much about them as they know about themselves . . . or will admit!"

Really? Are you writing a book about them?"

"Writing? I already did. You should know—you translated it."

"*Kimono Killer*? But I thought the family in that story disappeared after their disastrous run-in with the killer kimono."

"Yes, *that* family did. The apprentices died, the daughter lost her mind, and the business collapsed. But that wasn't the Tani family, Ruth-san. The Tanis are descended from the other family. I didn't feature them particularly in the story. They really don't come in until the end. But you remember the priest who couldn't bear to destroy the kimono remnants that were used as temple banners?"

"Right, right. He couldn't destroy something so beautiful, so he gave them to his older brother."

"Well, that's where the Tani Kimono got its start."

"You mean the story's true?"

"Of course it's true. I write *historical* fiction. I don't have enough imagination to make this stuff up! I didn't set out to write about the founding of the Tani family or even to write about kimono dyeing. I had planned to write about Empress Tofukumon'in. She is such a perfect subject, the daughter of a Tokugawa shogun *and* the consort of an emperor. But the more research I did for the project, the more I became interested in the way she patronized the arts. A lot of the businesses and arts at the time, kimonos but also pottery and painting, competed for her patronage. So, I decided to recast the story and focus on a particular competition. Now that part I invented."

"The part about Shunsuke's kimono being ruined and then seeking revenge?"

"For the most part. But there was a kimono, intended for Tofukumon'in, that ended up in a Buddhist temple, eventually making its way into the hands of the artist who would be credited as the founder of yūzen. You saw his painting hanging in the alcove. Miyazaki Yūzen-sai. He was the Tani predecessor. That much is true. The rest is mostly my invention."

"Wait. You mean there really *is* a killer kimono?"

"Absolutely! You know temples keep meticulous records about who donates what and when. Unless the temple falls victim to fire or war, the records survive. I was able to dig up the ledgers on this particular donation, but it was almost impossible to read. The paper was compromised by insects and age. If Satoko Tani hadn't helped me out, I don't think I could have managed."

"So, you worked with Satoko on the project?"

"To be perfectly honest, she's the one who gave me the idea for the kimono story in the first place. Somehow, she learned I was interested in Tofukumon'in. She read an interview in which I mentioned my future plans. She contacted me to tell me about the kimono. As she described it, the remnant is the Tani talisman of sorts."

"I had no idea!"

"I'm surprised, you're such a scholar."

"I *was* a scholar of modern literature, but that hardly gives me expertise in textile history!"

"You're still a scholar, and you know more about kimonos than most Japanese women of your generation, so I wouldn't be so quick to downgrade your knowledge."

"That's very kind."

"You know you should never refer to the Tani talisman as the "killer kimono," right? I mean, not to any Tani."

"So then, that much is made-up?"

"You have to give your readers something to enjoy. I have no idea how the young apprentice Shunsuke died. Only that he drowned. For all I know he got drunk and fell in the river. And the same thing might have happened to Takitarō, the apprentice who I assumed compromised the fabric. The records only note that he died a short time later. There is no indication that he was attacked by an angry altar piece!"

"And the daughter?"

"All we really know is that an apprentice to a subsidiary of the Kariganeya worked long and hard on kimono fabric for Tofukumon'in. Although the finished product was exquisite in every way, the kimono was rejected. Shortly thereafter the apprentice died, followed by a second apprentice from the same shop. The daughter of the shop owner was reported to have gone insane. And in the years that followed, the Kariganeya went bankrupt. That's all."

I remembered the way Maho reacted to my synopsis of the story, exclaiming it reminded her of a kabuki play, where everyone dies in the end.

"The Tani family was not amused," Daté continued.

"How do you know?"

"I know because they tried to sue me for defamation of character."

"Why?"

"Well, they were aggrieved on two counts. First, they

claimed that my story suggested the Tani predecessors acquired the kimono remnant through an inappropriate act. In my story, the young priest is supposed to destroy the fabric. But he gives it to his older brother, who is none other than Miyazaki Yūzen-sai, to whom the Tanis trace their origins."

"But that's just fiction, right?"

"Apparently not. The Tanis claimed Yūzen-sai studied the fabric his brother brought to him and from doing so invented what would become the yūzen technique. Then, when he was preparing his own sons to carry on the family tradition, he bequeathed the precious remnant to his youngest who became such a successful kimono marketer he ran the Kariganeya out of business. Understandably, they were outraged by my depiction of this family heirloom as being some kind of killer. But they only stood to make things worse if they publicized the suit and drew attention to what would otherwise have been overlooked."

"Then, did you win the lawsuit?"

"Oh, we didn't let it get that far. My lawyers negotiated with their lawyers, I paid them a tidy sum, and we let it go at that. I haven't heard from them since."

"So, I guess that put an end to your relationship with Satoko."

"That's something I could never understand. She was the one who told me about the remnant in the first place. She even showed me pictures."

"You saw the remnant?"

"Not the actual fabric. I saw photographs of it.

"What did it look like?"

"Well, I tried to describe it in the novel, but even my best efforts could not capture the beauty, especially the tanzaku slips."

I felt myself shiver at the mention of the tanzaku slips. They kept reappearing. I was getting ready to ask about them when Daté's handsome "chef" returned with a fresh flask of saké. He refilled our glasses and quietly withdrew.

"During the entire encounter with the Tani family, I never saw any trace of Satoko. And I never felt comfortable revealing she and I had discussed the kimono remnants, nor that she had shown me photographs. She never said anything about the family, and I never really had a face-to-face discussion with her husband, Akira. But there was just something about the entire situation that seemed odd."

"How do you mean?"

"I mean, it was as if Satoko was going behind her family's back to make sure I knew about the kimono fabric. And frankly, if she hadn't alerted me to the existence of the remnant or told me where to look for the temple records, I never would have been the wiser. Since the family seemed upset about my disclosures, and not just my depiction of the kimono as somehow lethal, I got the impression they were at cross purposes."

"Were you ever able to talk to Satoko about it?"

"No, during the proceedings, she was nowhere to be found. And when it was all done, it was made clear I was not to contact anyone in the family directly. All future communication was to go through our attorneys now."

Daté lifted the flask and filled our glasses.

"So, tell me why do you want to contact the Tani family?"

Given Daté's unfortunate history with the Tanis, I could

imagine she would be concerned to learn of my involvement with them. I was beginning to find it strange as well. Hadn't Tokuda said Shōtarō Tani liked my translation of *Kimono Killer*? And why was that? Because I had done a good job translating the descriptions of kimonos? I felt as if Tokuda's seamless story was beginning to unravel. I couldn't make sense of what had happened. Tokuda appeared out of the blue with a chapter to translate saying she or rather her boss was drawn to me because of *Kimono Killer*. When I read the chapter, I discovered what appeared to be a death that may or may not have really happened, described in language that seemed to have been culled from Daté's work. Truly, what *did* I want with the Tani Family? I prepared a response to what I assumed Daté would eventually ask.

"I read something by Shōtarō Tani recently and have been wondering what happened to him. I was hoping to interview him and heard a certain Ms. Tokuda was the one to contact to set this up. But I don't know who she is or how to reach her. I thought if anyone would know, you would. But I'm sorry to have brought this up. I didn't know about your unhappy history with the Tanis."

"I wish I could help you with this, Ruth-san, but I've never heard anyone in the Tani household mention a Ms. Tokuda. And are you certain Shōtarō Tani is still alive? It's been close to twenty years since I've even heard his name."

"Yes, I believe he's still alive. Who do you think I should contact?"

"It's a delicate situation, isn't it? He was disowned by the Tanis, after all. I don't recommend you contact them. If you really think Shōtarō is still alive and still writing, you should contact his publisher. Didn't he write for Bungei Press? I'll see if I can find a contact there to help you."

She picked up a small bell from the table and rang it a few times. Her chef reappeared. Apparently, he was also her secretary.

"Please bring me my address book."

Masahiro nodded and then withdrew.

"I'll be happy to give you the address for the Tani house, too, if you really want to follow up there, but you should use caution. They aren't a very happy family, especially with the family head they have now. Unhappy families can be very unpleasant."

"Thank you for all of your help. I'll promise to be discreet."

"I always wished I had done more to befriend Satoko. When we met years ago, she seemed somewhat desperate. But I had no idea I would lose all access to her. At any rate, what that family did to her was really tragic."

"You mean, forcing her to marry Akira."

"It was more than that. Their treatment of her was brutal. I honestly thought she was a brilliant kimono designer. I mean, I saw a few of the designs she and her lover collaborated on. They were masterful. Satoko was the true heir to the Tani legacy. After she married, there were rumors she had gone insane and was spending a lot of time at a "resort" near the sea. In meetings with me she was hardly insane. And there were just as many rumors she was still deeply involved with her lover and was the secret "inspiration" behind his best designs. He has won a lot of design competitions, you know. His kimonos are now in such demand he doesn't need to rely on other shops to market his products."

"Is that Ryohei Miyazaki?"

"Yes, how'd you know?"

Daté shot me a puzzled glance.

"Oh, like you said, I'm a scholar," I said with a wink, completely disarming her. "Wouldn't he be the true heir to yūzen, with the name Miyazaki?"

"Oh, it's a common enough name. Just think, Hayao Miyazaki, Aoi Miyazaki, they can't all be related! And names, as you know, are in flux, Ruth-san. Tani was a branch family, from what I understand."

Not to mention Tsutomu Miyazaki, I thought to myself. He was the horrible serial killer and cannibal who preyed on little girls in the 1980s. Maybe murder runs in the family along with yūzen dyeing. With all this talk of the family's cruelty to Satoko, I couldn't get the image of the tattooed corpse out of my mind.

Masahiro returned just at that moment with Daté's address book. She flipped through the pages, realized she didn't have anything to write with, and sent Masahiro back to her office for pen and paper.

"I heard Satoko continued to see Ryohei even after her marriage," Daté said, a smile curling impishly at the edges of her mouth.

"How was that possible?" I asked. "I thought her husband was very controlling."

"I think he didn't care. As long as she kept her behavior out of the public eye. He had more than his share of other women. I guess he figured as long as she was conducting her own extramarital affairs, she couldn't complain about his, not that he would have listened to her complaints anyway. I think it was a way he leveraged his power. She completely withdrew from the family business. If she really wanted to interfere in the way Akira ran the business, she could have. Most of the employees would have been loyal to her."

"That's interesting."

"Here's the address you wanted. Now, why don't we walk a bit in the garden?"

We had been sitting on the verandah for quite some time. Daté offered me a pair of garden sandals, and we stepped down onto the white gravel. She pointed out rocks she had shipped in from other locales, river rocks from Kamikōchi, the foundation stone from a Heike hideaway in Shikoku. There was a gate along the back wall that led into the Hōnen Temple grounds.

"That section of the temple isn't open to the public, but occasionally I let myself in and take a secret stroll."

I must have been staring at her with a look of shock because she quickly added, "It's not that clandestine! I know the head priest. And let me say, he's very handsome. Look," she said as she twisted the handle, "the gate was installed by the temple and it opens *in* to my garden. I'm still waiting for the priest to pay a visit!"

Masahiro came out after us and was lighting the lamps in the stone lanterns. It was too early in the year for fireflies. Still the soft glow of the lanterns filtering between the pine needles and maple leaves seemed magically romantic. I suppose the late afternoon saké helped make the scene more intoxicating. The cry of the cuckoo rose out of the bamboo thickets behind Daté's gate.

It was time to leave. I had taken up too much of Daté's time.

"Let me call a cab for you."

"Please don't bother. I really don't mind walking."

"But it's late, Ruth-san. You must be tired."

"I rarely get the chance to stroll along the Philosopher's Path under the moonlight. It will be a treat, a lovely way to end a perfect day."

"In that case, I won't insist. But at least let me send Masahiro with you. I really don't like the idea of you walking alone."

"I'll be fine."

Japan was such a safe country. I'd never felt nervous about walking alone. We exchanged protests and pleasantries, bowing with each utterance. I turned and walked down the steep stairs, careful not to lose my balance. I looked back up at Daté when I reached the street, bowed once more, and then stepped into the shadows.

The road was narrow, barely wide enough for one car. The streetlight was out at the bend by Hōnen Temple, and the road was flanked on either side by high walls and higher trees. The interlocking branches made a tunnel that blocked the soft glow from the moon. Once I made the next turn, the road opened up, with restaurants and residences.

I listened to my own breathing and the soft clip of my zori sandals snapping against my heels. I thought I heard another set of footsteps behind me. Daté must have decided to send Masahiro, after all. I turned to look but couldn't see anything but a tunnel of darkness. The footsteps stopped. Feeling frightened, I picked up my pace. I thought I could hear the other footsteps just under my own. I slowed. They slowed. I sped up, they sped up.

I glanced quickly over my shoulder but saw only shadows.

Had I drunk too much saké? No, I was more alert than ever in my life as every nerve in my body pulsed. I was now on the long straight street in front of Hōnen Temple. The temple gates would be closed. A tall stand of bamboo loomed over the surrounding hedge. There was an empty lot across the street—the for-sale sign in the middle of it nearly hidden by thickets of weeds.

I needed to head toward the Philosopher's Path where there might be more people.

I could see a streetlamp ahead, marking the road down. It seemed very far away, but I was there sooner than I thought. I took a quick right and began heading down the hill, pulling over to stand behind a utility pole, so I could look back up the street into the light. If someone was following me, I'd be able to see them when they entered the circle of light. I waited. A cat trotted soundlessly across the street, but I saw no other movement. It was completely still.

Once I reached the Philosopher's Path, I slowed to a stroll. I could feel my heart rate return to a normal beat. And then I heard someone stumble behind me. I turned quickly and caught a glimpse of a dark form darting into the shade of a tree. My heart pounded.

"Who is it?" I tried to shout. But my voice sounded more like a rasp. "Who is it? Who's there?" I tried again and managed to produce a louder sound. There was no answer. I turned and ran.

I remembered there was a phone booth just up ahead. If I could get to it, I'd call. Who would I call? I didn't want to call the police. It would do no good to call Daté now. I'd call a taxi. I was pretty sure I could remember the number of the MK cabs.

I could see the phone booth in the distance now, the interior light glowing like a beacon in the dark. The green phone inside seemed to almost pulsate with hope. I ran as fast as I could towards the light and slammed on the door to open it. It didn't budge. Pull! It reads "pull." So, pull, goddamn it! The door sprang open. I jumped inside and slammed the door shut, then fished through my purse for some change. I found a ¥100 coin.

I explained I needed a cab on Shishi-ga-tani just down the street from the Philosopher's Path. The dispatcher promised to have a car to me in five minutes. She hung up, but I pretended to stay on the line. Let whoever was following me think I was talking to the police.

Deciding I gave the taxi enough time, I opened the door and stepped back out onto the path. I started running. The canal was on my left, like a gaping abyss. I heard what sounded like a rock skittering along concrete, and then a splash. When I reached the street, I looked hopefully to my right. A few blocks away, I saw a taxi driving toward me, its red "call" light illuminated. I waved my arms and ran towards it, relieved when the taxi pulled to the side of the street and opened the automatic door.

I practically dove in the back seat.

"Close the door! Close the door!"

The taxi driver turned around to look at me, simultaneously pushing the button to close the door. I starred through the glass into the darkness searching for the sign of my pursuer. Nothing moved.

CHAPTER SEVEN
PEACOCKS

Sunshine was pouring thick and golden like honey through the window when I awoke. I nestled deeper in the pillows and squinted as my consciousness gently pulled itself forward into wakefulness. I thought of my brother, and the time our grandfather gave us honey from his beehives on the farm. My brother squealed with delight when the honey oozed out over his hand. Sticky little hands. I could feel the press of his hand against my palm. So small. I should have held on to it. I should not have let him cross the track by himself. I squeezed my eyes tight to block out the sun, the luminescent white of his slender neck disappearing into the darkness behind my eyelids. I squeezed my eyes tighter to erase the memory. I counted my breaths, rolled to my side, my back to the window, and opened my eyes.

The kimono I wore last night was hanging on an airing pole alongside the wall by the closet. I remembered now my near hysterical run from Daté's house. The balls of my feet felt tender from where they had pressed against the edges of the zori sandals. Once I had gotten into the taxi, I had stared out the window as it sped along Shishi-ga-tani. But I hadn't seen any sign of a pursuer. Had I just imagined being followed?

Well, if I was going to be such a scaredy cat, I had no business walking around alone at night. I needed to either work on improving my nerves or get in the habit of calling taxis before I had another meltdown.

I rolled out of bed and examined the skirt of my kimono, just to be sure I hadn't kicked any dirt up on it in my mad dash. I didn't notice any damage, just the usual wrinkles where the obi and cords had been tightened around the waist. I didn't have time to deal with that now, I needed to get dressed to meet Maho. The trek to Fushimi would take time.

What did one wear to meet a horishi? Whatever the outfit, I'm sure it wasn't part of my sartorial repertoire. It was funny, I always knew just how to dress when wearing a kimono. The season, the occasion, the mood all helped to determine what was appropriate. But with "my native dress," I was never certain. And what was my native dress anyway? Blue jeans and a T-shirt? That was almost always my default selection, and today was hardly any different, though I did decide to dress up a bit with a pair of black jeans topped off with a long-sleeved purple blouse.

I took a short cut to the Keage subway stop that skirted behind the mansions by the Nanzen Temple and ran alongside a small canal. The dew last night was heavy and as the ground warmed in the sun, a gentle mist rose alongside the canal and covered the narrow pathway. I felt like I was walking into a milky white tunnel.

The Nanzen Temple grounds were nearly empty as I cut across them. There was a man feeding pigeons by Sanmon gate. People love Kyoto because of its rich history. Almost any point in the city will yield a story about an event that happened there in the eighth century and a later event in the eleventh century and so on. History wraps the city in layers. The waves of history undulate and overlap, it seemed, allowing us to go backwards in time even as we went forward. And my history was there, too, my stories also settling into the sediment. Whenever I saw the great Sanmon at Nanzen Temple, I remembered the way my little brother and I used to play there on occasion. We would wrap our arms around the pillars of the gate and try to touch each others' hands. Our arms were too short, but each year we seemed to get closer and closer.

The pillars were lighter in color near the base, from all the hands that patted and rubbed the wood in passing. My brother's handprints were there. And mine, too, pressed into the history of the temple, becoming part of the story.

The man feeding pigeons was wearing black gloves. He moved his hands awkwardly, as if he had a palsy of sorts. He glanced over at me and caught my eye just as I turned to look in his direction. Neither one of us had wanted to establish eye contact. We both hurriedly looked away but not before I realized it was the homeless man I had seen earlier by the zoo. I wondered if the temple priests had started to provide shelter for the homeless.

I left the temple grounds and headed along a pretty lane surrounded by elegant restaurants and private homes leading to the station. The train at Keage was there when I arrived and my connection to the Keihan line at Sanjō was simple. I made it to Fushimi with fifteen minutes to spare. I stood outside in front of the station and looked up the road leading to the famous shrine. All the tourist shops were still shuttered, but delivery men on motor scooters were already busy rumbling up the narrow stone-paved street. I watched one swerve as a woman threw a pail of water from the doorway of her shop. She bowed in apology. Further up, a man with a hose was dousing the street in front of his shop. When the first tourists arrived, the stone pavers would glisten with a fresh application of water.

"Sorry to keep you waiting!"

I turned to see Maho rushing up behind me.

"Not at all, I just got here! Don't you live nearby?"

"Not exactly! Anyway, I've been spending time in Saiin."

"Oh, I'm sorry, I didn't realize you would have to make a special trip all the way out here."

"It's not a big deal. I'm glad to do it. Besides, I'm curious to hear what my horishi has to say!"

"So am I! And a little nervous. You said he sounded upset."

"Not really upset. I don't know how to describe it. Anxious, I guess."

Maho had dyed her Mohawk peacock blue. She was wearing a black tunic over a red miniskirt with purple leggings and green sneakers. Maho attracted a lot of attention as we darted around pedestrians rushing to the station. She guided me down an alley dotted with bars and cafés. Most were closed and shuttered. The few that were open smelled of stale cigarettes and spilt beer. I could imagine the vibrant evenings, the noise, the drunken jostling. It was a rough neighborhood.

Tattoos were still not warmly received in Japan and were associated with gangsters and the underworld. Many establishments: restaurants, hotels, public baths, and the like wouldn't serve someone if they had a visible tattoo. I glanced over at Maho, colorful, unconventional, confident in her own peculiarity. I could only imagine the opposition she had encountered.

Maho turned into a smaller alley and we snaked around trashcans and empty liquor crates. At the end of the passageway, she entered a non-descript building. The foyer was dark but spacious and smelled slightly of incense. Given the chaotic jumble outside, it felt oddly calm. About midway down the corridor, she stopped and knocked on a door. I noticed there were no names or numbers on any of the apartments. We waited in the semidarkness. I could hear someone moving on the other side of the door. A lock turned, and the door opened. A petite woman wearing blue jeans and a Hello Kitty T-shirt held the door for us and smiled when she saw Maho.

"It'll be just a few minutes. Please take a seat. I'll bring some tea."

We were ushered into a small room that wouldn't have looked out of place in anyone's house. Two couches faced a large television. Cushions were tossed about on the floor and sports magazines competed for space on the coffee table. The woman returned with a tray and two cups of hot tea, which she set before us after first sweeping the magazines off to one side.

We sipped our tea but otherwise were silent.

Maho's horishi entered the room. We stood to greet him, a short man, muscular and completely bald. He was wearing the loose cotton garments often favored by the Buddhist clergy. They looked like karate-gi but were dyed a light brown with an orange undertone. I recognized the dye as *kakishibu*, derived from the juice of unripe persimmons. The horishi indicated we were to follow him into another room. We headed down a hallway until we reached what must have been his studio. It was Japanese style, with tatami mats, a low table upon which was a neat stack of books and a black lacquer calligraphy box. Curtains covered one of the walls, and it looked like there was shelving behind the curtains. The horishi gave us each a cushion, and we sat.

Maho introduced me, telling me the master's name was Hori-ichi. I bowed, thanking him for taking the time to meet with me. He nodded, folded his arms across his chest and stared at me. No one spoke for some time. I was uncertain if I was supposed to speak. Instinct told me to keep quiet and ride it out.

"I understand you have questions about a tattoo?" Hori-ichi asked, finally.

"Yes. I'm curious if it would be possible to get a tattoo with kimono designs?"

"Why?"

"Well, it seems unusual. I thought most tattoos are of heroic characters or images from myths and legends . . . dragons, samurai, peacocks, peonies, that sort of thing."

"No. Why are you curious about a kimono tattoo?"

"Well, I mean, I wonder if it would be possible."

"A horishi is an artist. We make art. Anything is possible. But you are right, kimono tattoos are rare. In fact, I only know of one. And what I want to know now is how you came to ask about it."

The term horishi comes from the word to carve, *horu*. He uses his needles to carve under the skin and deposit ink. This particular horishi was staring at me so intently, I felt as if my skin were being pricked and gouged. It was clear he was not accepting my nonchalance.

"I read about the tattoo."

"You read about it? But you've not seen it?"

"No, I have not seen it."

"Where did you read about the tattoo?"

"I am sorry, I can't give you any more information."

The horishi turned his head to one side and squinted. "And what did you read?"

"I read about a woman whose body was covered in a tattoo that looked like a kimono. And I just wanted to learn more about tattooing."

"How was the tattoo described?"

"It had several different elements, from an assortment of dye patterns to poetic scenes. What fascinated me was the suggestion that the tattoo was so elaborate, it represented several layers of fabric. It must be very difficult to achieve that with tattoo ink."

"Not for a talented horishi. About the poetic scene, did it look like this one?" The horishi pulled a book off the table beside him and opened it to a page that had been marked. When he handed the book to me, I saw it was a museum catalog, and the illustration he marked was of Tosa Mitsuoki's tanzaku screen. I felt a shudder run up the back of my spine.

"Yes," I could only manage a whisper. When I looked up from the book, the horishi locked onto me with his gaze. He shut the book with a snap and returned it to the table. Then he shifted on his cushion, so his knees were nearly brushing mine.

"I don't know you, and I don't know what you are involved in. But you must stop. It's dangerous. You may already be in danger. You may have invited danger on the person who wears this tattoo. You must stop."

"What do you mean? Who has this tattoo?"

"That's enough. You've been warned."

"Please. Please just tell me why it is dangerous."

"Maho," the horishi turned to Maho who looked stricken. "You will leave now. Do not bring your friend here again."

The horishi stood up and walked out of the room. Maho and I exchanged glances, both of us uncertain of what had just happened.

"What did you do?" Maho asked with an accusatory note.

"I don't know what just happened."

But I had an inkling.

Maho and I walked down the hallway to the front door of the apartment. The woman was already there, waiting. She watched us scramble into our shoes. When we stepped out into the dark corridor, I heard the door lock behind us. Maho and I did not speak to one another until we were out of the building, out of the twisting maze of alleys, and back on the main thoroughfare. The sun was bright. I could feel my excitement rising, and along with it a sense of dread. Satoko did have a kimono tattoo. Why else would the horishi respond the way he did? That also meant she was likely dead.

"Ruth, what's going on? I've never seen the horishi like that. What are you into?"

I needed to tell Maho something, she deserved as much. But we couldn't very well stand there on the street and chat, so I asked her to stop for a coffee and a bite to eat.

We found a restaurant that had just opened and placed an order. Our waitress brought a large round tray brimming with the sweet-sour sushi the area was known for. We picked up our wooden chopsticks, pulled them apart, and dug in.

"What are you hiding from me, Ruth? I need to know. I feel like I've done something wrong."

I evaded her questions at first, telling her it was just my interest in kimonos that led to my questions. But she knew better. She persisted, and I finally broke down and told her the whole story, starting with Tokuda's sudden visit, the translation request, the missing page, the body that may or may not be Satoko, all of it. I knew I was breaking my contract with Tokuda, but I couldn't stop myself. It was all getting out of hand, and I needed to tell someone.

"The tattoo sounds fantastic, Ruth. I wish I could see it."

"So, do you think your horishi was the one who did it?"

"That I don't know. But my horishi is the best there is. If Satoko could afford a tattoo as elaborate as the one you described, she would have gone to the best. But let me ask my boyfriend. He's got more tattoos than I do and has a pretty good rapport with this horishi, because he works for his brother. He's the one who introduced me to him."

"Thanks, Maho, I'd really appreciate it if you could find out more. But be careful, okay? I'm not really sure what I've gotten myself into, and I don't want to drag you in with me."

"Based on the way the horishi looked at me, Ruth, I'd say you already have."

"I'm sorry. I really didn't think the tattoo was real."

"I'm not worried," Maho shrugged. "Besides, I'm curious now."

After the first few pieces of sushi, we slowed down.

"How long do you think it would take to get a tattoo like that? And wouldn't it cost a fortune?"

"It would take years, Ruth. If it was as extensive as you say it was, I'd say at least ten years, and she probably couldn't go more often than once a month. The body just couldn't take it. I can't even imagine the cost."

"I suppose money would not have been a great concern. But I just don't understand why. I mean, why would someone like Satoko spend all that time and money on a tattoo, especially one no one would likely see, except, I guess, her husband."

"People do all kinds of things you wouldn't expect them to do. Just because she was tattooed didn't mean she was some kind of deviant. You're just buying into an age-old stereotype."

"I didn't mean that. I just don't think it's common for women like her to have a tattoo. Do you?"

"No, you're right. She was making a very bold statement, that's for sure."

"But why? Who was the statement for?"

"Not everyone gets tattooed for the shock value, you know. That's what I keep trying to explain to my parents. Tattoos are a way for me to release my inner self. I don't have the words to express myself half the time. Tattoos do it for me."

She lowered her collar and exposed her right shoulder, revealing a pink, frothy wave somewhat similar to the famous Hiroshige woodblock wave devouring a fishing skiff with Mount Fuji in the background. But instead of a skiff, Maho's tattoo had a round-eyed cartoon-like girl on a surfboard. Rather than terrified at the oncoming wave, she flashed a peace sign.

"This was my first tattoo. I designed it myself and had it done in Venice Beach. It speaks for me."

"I guess that's you on the surfboard?"

"Well, sure. But that's me in the wave, too. My life has been about crossing oceans, catching waves, and turning waves pink.

I'm not afraid. This is me, Ruth."

I could see something very beguiling and poignant in the image. It was girly and cute but at the same time bold and defiant. I liked the idea of Maho turning typhoon waves pink.

"Probably it's the same for Satoko. The tattoos speak *for* her. The tattoo becomes her, so she doesn't need to show it off. She enjoys it for herself."

I could see her point. For Satoko, her tattoos could very well have been an expression of her own self-love. Perhaps it was her love of kimonos that inspired her to become the very living embodiment of a kimono.

"I just can't imagine the pain."

"It hurts like hell; I won't lie to you."

"And to endure that for ten years?"

"But that's part of it, too. Pain is also a language. Kind of like you were saying about kimonos. It's expressive. We've been taught to be afraid of pain, to avoid it at all costs with our pills and hospitals. But it wasn't always like that. Pain has been used as a gateway to ecstasy. Ecstasy in the sense of transcendence. Pain pushes you. It takes you places you didn't expect to go. And when you're done, you feel like a soldier returning from battle, or a mystic back from a vision quest. After a tattoo session, I feel cleansed and calm."

"I hadn't thought of it that way."

"In a way, the pain of the tattooing is mine. It's mine to control. I own it. And it takes away the pain I can't control, the pain of my parents' disappointment in me; the pain of the men who've used me; the pain of wanting to be somewhere and someone else."

Maho's eyes grew shiny as she spoke. I knew she struggled with self-doubt and had had a difficult childhood. But I had never heard her speak with such self-assurance or, for lack of a better word, wisdom.

"Sorry," Maho smiled self-consciously. "I didn't mean to get all philosophical on you. It looks like you're not convinced."

"No, no. Don't be sorry. You've given me a lot to think about. There's something so specific about these particular tattoos. Why a kimono?"

"Well, maybe they represent what her husband and father took away from her. So, in a sense, maybe the tattoo *is* defiant."

Maho signaled to the waitress for more tea.

"You would know better than me," Maho continued, "but in the old days didn't commoners in Japan line their kimonos with elegantly painted silks?"

"Yes. Only the upper classes were allowed to wear kimonos made of silk. But if a member of the lower class had the money for it, he would line his plain kimono with silk and smugly stroll about knowing that inside he was luxuriating in its smooth elegance."

"Maybe that's what it was like for Satoko. She couldn't wear her passion on the outside, underneath her kimono she revealed herself."

"I guess. Kimonos are themselves so expressive. A woman's choices, her style, speak for her, like a second language, a language of fabric."

"But fabric is fragile," Maho countered. "It can tear and fade. A precious kimono can be stolen. Heck, your whole wardrobe can go up in smoke. But if you are alive, your tattoo is forever."

"If she's dead, do you think it's because of her tattoo?"

The waitress came and cleared away the empty tray.

"You ought to try to visit Satoko, Ruth. Go see for yourself if she's still alive. Pretend you're a journalist or a scholar doing research on women in the kimono industry."

"I suppose I could stop by the Tani store. Maybe she's there. Who knows?"

"Or why don't you try to interview her lover? You could pretend you want to talk to him about his designs and then strategically shift the conversation to kimono businesses, Tani Kimono, the lovely daughter of Tani Kimono."

"Hmm, I'm not sure I could be that subtle."

"I'd be happy to go with you and wait for you at a coffee shop nearby or something."

"I appreciate it!"

It was nearly noon when we left the restaurant. Maho and I rode back to Sanjō and parted company. I headed home to regroup. Maho had given me a lot of suggestions, but I decided my next step should be to contact Tokuda. I would use the missing page as an excuse to ask her about Satoko. And then where would that lead me?

I was beginning to feel uneasy about contacting Tokuda. If she was Shōtarō's secretary, she probably didn't have anything to do with the family. And I couldn't get the horishi's warning out of my head, the way his eyes bored their way into mine as he told me I had to stop. But I just wanted to ask Tokuda about the manuscript she'd given me. I really felt I had no choice but to do what I could to find her.

As soon as I got home, I fished out the numbers and

addresses Daté gave me. I called the Tani Kimono office first. A man answered. For whatever reason, I expected it to be a woman. In my most proper business Japanese, I asked if a woman named Tokuda was in the Tani employ. The man assured me there was no one there by that name. I apologized for my mistaken assumption, and then asked if by chance Satoko Tani was there. Again, the voice replied in the negative. "Mrs. Tani does not come to the shop." I noted a slight change in the tone of his voice. He had lowered it, as if wishing not to be heard.

"In that case, would it be possible to reach her at home?" I was hoping to solicit more information.

"I'm sorry. We don't provide information about the Tani family or household."

My questions were beginning to seem impertinent. Taking a chance, I asked for Shōtarō Tani.

"Shōtarō Tani? I'm sorry, may I ask who is calling?"

I suspected the shop phone might have caller ID. I probably should have gone to a pay phone to place the call, but I hadn't been thinking.

"Oh, I'm sorry not to identify myself sooner. My name is Nakata," I said as politely as I could muster, using the name that would have popped up on caller ID.

"I am writing an article about distinguished kimono families in Kyoto. I was hoping to set up an appointment to speak with members of the Tani family about their experiences, family history, interesting anecdotes from the past, that sort of thing. Would you know how I might reach Shōtarō Tani?"

"I cannot help you with that."

"Would it be possible to speak with Mr. Akira Tani, the

company president?'"

"Just a minute please."

I was surprised to have gotten this far. I hoped the Nakatas wouldn't mind my borrowing their name. If I could conduct my interview over the phone, I might be able to get away with disguising my identity.

"Ms. Nakata, is it?"

It was the same person who had answered earlier.

"Mr. Tani is extremely busy and frankly, he's not sure what information he can offer beyond what has already been stated in our company brochure. Do you have that? I'll be happy to mail it to you if you provide an address."

"Certainly, I have the brochure," I lied. "I was just hoping for some more personal insights, and I am positive Mr. Tani has more to share than he realizes. Of course, I understand he is very busy running such a successful business. But if it might be possible to make an appointment to speak with him by telephone, I would be most grateful. I would only require five minutes or so of his time—ten at the most."

"I will have to consult his personal assistant and get back to you. May I have your telephone number?"

Assuming he already had it, I offered the number, thanked him for his understanding and noted, as I hung up, that I was counting on his help.

Once that call was done, I looked up the number for the Tani estate and dialed it. A woman answered, one of the household helpers. I went through the same set of questions. The woman assured me there was no one in the household employ named Tokuda. When I asked to speak to Mrs. Satoko Tani, I heard her draw in a breath and demand to know who I was.

"My name is Nakata and I am writing an article on distinguished kimono families in Kyoto. I was very much hoping I might be able to speak with members of the Tani family. I assumed Mrs. Tani could help me with this. I have heard so many wonderful things about her and her contributions to the kimono industry."

"Mrs. Tani is not available. I'm afraid we can't help you."

"Certainly, I understand. I hope Mrs. Tani is not unwell . . ."

"She's not available, as I said."

"Yes, yes, I see. I would be just as grateful to speak with her younger brother, Mr. Shōtarō Tani. Might that be possible?"

This time the breath the woman drew in was noticeably louder.

"Mr. Shōtarō Tani is no longer part of this household, perhaps you . . ."

"Oh, I beg your pardon, I didn't realize. Could you tell me how I might reach him?"

"I'm afraid that is quite impossible."

"Then might Mr. Akira Tani be willing to speak with me briefly." I was wondering if I should ask next for the father.

"What exactly is your business with the Tani family?"

The woman was beginning to grow cross.

"For an article, as I explained. I am contacting the most distinguished kimono families in the area. Yours is the first I've called. But I'll also be consulting Watanabe Kimono, Azuma Kimono, and . . ." I picked up the scratch pad beside the telephone and made the sound of flipping through paper. "And, Miyako Gofuku Erizen." I recalled from my earlier research at the Kyoto

Prefectural Library those were the largest kimono businesses in the area.

"I see. Well, I'm not at liberty to help you with your project. Please call the others first and call back next week. I will have discussed your proposal with my employer by then and will have a better sense of his interest in your request."

"Yes, I'll do that. And for whom should I ask when I call back?"

"I will answer. There is no need for you to ask for anyone."

I don't think I could have continued my pretense much longer. Lying was a lot of work. So was translating. Mrs. Shibasaki was good enough to give me some time away from the office, but that didn't mean I had time away from my assignments. I needed to get a start on them if I was going to have anything to show her next week. I went upstairs and dug my briefcase out from under the pile of dirty running clothes I had dumped on the floor yesterday. My assignment was yet another cell phone company trying to market to short-term travelers. I set the document on my desk alongside the Tani manuscript.

The doorbell startled me just as I was pulling up the cover sheet. I pushed back from my desk and hurried down the stairs, hoping it might be Tokuda again. But before I could get even halfway down the stairs, the ringing turned to pounding. And then I heard shouts.

"Police! Open up."

CHAPTER EIGHT
HAWKS

"Coming!" I stepped down into my clogs at the entryway and unlatched the door. I had barely turned the handle when two men pushed roughly from the other side and burst in, knocking me into the shoe cabinet beside the door.

"What are you doing?" I shouted. My back throbbed from the hit it had taken. I instinctively reached behind to rub what was surely going to become a bruise when the man closest to me grabbed my arm and pushed me up the step and into the hallway. He and his partner followed me inside, roughly kicking their shoes off. I was startled by their boldness. Usually people do not step up into a house without being invited, but nothing about this encounter was ordinary. I had never seen these two officers before. In fact, I wasn't even sure they were officers. They were not in uniform.

"Who are you?" I demanded, suddenly afraid. Both men pulled identification holders out of their pants pockets and flashed them at me. I caught sight of an emblem of some sort but did not have time to read their identification.

"Please, show me again. I can't read so quickly."

The man who did not have hold of me pulled his identification holder out again and held it out while I read aloud, "Detective Takuya Kimura, Kyoto Metropolitan Police."

"What is this about, Detective Kimura?"

"We have some questions for you. May we come in?"

It appears you already are! But I knew to be careful. It is never a good idea to mouth off to a policeman, and this caution is especially true of Japanese policemen, who have a largely unchecked authority and a propensity to abuse it.

"Shall I bring some tea?" I ushered the two men into the living room. The second had released his grip on my arm, and I rubbed it as I started for the kitchen.

"No! Sit."

I sat on one side of the room and they on the other. Detective Kimura began, "How do you know Satoko Tani?"

"I'm sorry, but you must be mistaken. I've never met Mrs. Tani."

Detective Kimura's partner slammed his hand down on the coffee table with a loud smack.

"Don't lie."

"I'm not lying."

"Then why were you calling around looking for her?"

So, that was it. My phone calls this afternoon were traced. I suppose I could have denied the calls, but I didn't think I'd done anything wrong.

"I have questions about traditional kimono makers."

"Who is Hideo Nakata?"

"He owns this house."

"And who are you?"

I was sure they already knew who I was. If they were clever enough to trace the phone calls, they would have been smart enough to pull my personal information.

"Ruth Bennett."

"What is your business here?"

"I work for Logos International Translation Agency. Would you like to see my Alien Registration Card?" I started to rise, but Kimura motioned for me to sit back down.

"Why are you interested in Satoko Tani?"

I reiterated my interest in kimonos.

"You told the Tani's housekeeper you were writing an article. Who are you writing for?"

"Well, I guess that wasn't exactly true. I'm not really writing an article for anyone in particular, but I'm interested in kimonos. I just had some questions, that's all."

"What kinds of questions?"

"I'm curious about the history of the Tani family."

"Out of the blue you want to know about the Tanis?"

"No, it's not exactly out of the blue. Earlier I translated Yuriko Daté's *Kimono Killer* and in doing background on it, I learned about the Tanis."

"Who's upstairs?" Kimura asked.

"No one. I'm here alone."

"I heard someone upstairs. Just now."

"That's not possible. No one's up there."

"I guess there's only one way to find out."

Kimura signaled to his partner who rose and headed to the stairs. I could hear him climbing noisily and then walk into my bedroom. The thought of him pawing through my things made my stomach knot.

Kimura kept his eyes riveted on my face, a slight sneer curling the corner of his lip. It wasn't long before the other man stomped back down the stairs. He tossed the Tani manuscript on the coffee table and shoved the contract in my face.

"What's this?" he demanded.

"It's a translation. I mean, it's a contract to translate this manuscript here."

"I know that. I can see that, can't I? What I want to know is where did you get this?"

I explained my encounter with Tokuda.

"Shōtarō Tani is dead. So, who really wrote this?"

"No. He's not dead. He's in Italy. Or he was."

"His family declared him dead several years ago."

I knew that, of course. It had been in the papers. Once he'd been missing for seven years, they got a court order to list him as legally dead. But there was really no proof; a body was never uncovered.

"But how do you know he's not just overseas somewhere?" I asked. "He describes his life in Italy here. It's all here."

I pointed at the manuscript on the coffee table. Kimura turned it around and thumbed through the pages brusquely. I wondered if he would notice the missing page, and if he did, how I'd explain that. Now I was pretty relieved the pages weren't numbered.

"And what does it say about his sister?" Kimura asked, continuing to scan the pages.

"I don't know, I haven't gotten very far." I lied again.

"Well, that's too bad, Bennett-san, because we're going to

have to take this manuscript as evidence."

"Wait, evidence of what?"

"Evidence of a murder."

"Murder?" "Whose murder? Was Shōtarō Tani murdered?"

"Shōtarō's dead, long dead."

"Then who?"

The two men looked at each other knowingly but said nothing.

"But you can't take this manuscript. It's my only copy, and I'm under contract to finish it in a few days!"

"Your translation of this novel is over. And if Miyo Tokuda, or whatever her name is, contacts you again, let us know. Here, I'll leave you my card."

Kimura scooped up my papers and rose to his feet. His partner followed suit. They marched over to the entryway, stepped into their shoes, and left as abruptly as they had arrived. I stood on the stair staring at the closed door for several seconds. How did the police know to come to my house?

If Shōtarō Tani was really dead, then who wrote the manuscript? Who was Miyo Tokuda? I wished I'd paid more attention to the story when I'd had a chance. The mixture of epistolary entries and descriptive narrative gave the work a patchwork quality, but I assumed it meant to echo the image of the tattoo etched like kimono patterns across the woman's body.

I just didn't know what to believe. Earlier when I had talked to Daté about Shōtarō, she suggested I contact his former editor at Bungei Press. They might know how to contact Miyo Tokuda, too, assuming she was really Shōtarō's secretary. I would have to figure out a way to return her money to her.

Daté gave me the mailing address for the press, but I hadn't noted any editor's name. I opened up my laptop and started a search for the webpage. They were located in Tokyo. As I was scanning for a phone number, Maho called.

"Ruth, what're you doing?"

"It's a long story."

"Well, I've got some information for you about the tattoo. If you've got time, meet me and Hawk at Sanjō Ōhashi."

"Hawk?"

"My boyfriend, Taka. But he goes by Hawk, since that's how it translates into English. He thinks it has some funny association with me, since I have a Mo*hawk*."

"When do you want to meet?"

"When can you get here? We're about ten minutes away."

"It'll take me longer than that. I'll leave here as soon as I can."

"Good. Let's meet at the Starbucks then."

I straightened a few things up and headed out the door. I didn't really feel like following up on Satoko Tani or the tattoo anymore. The translation was pretty much a bust now. But I wanted to talk with Maho about what happened.

It was dark by the time I reached the Starbucks. Maho and her companion were halfway through a *matcha* frappe.

"I'm sorry to keep you waiting. Let me get a coffee and join you."

"I don't want to talk here, Ruth. Let's buy some beers and go sit down by the river. We can stay there as long as we want, and no one will bother us."

I hadn't drunk beer down by the river since I was in high

school. It sounded like a great idea to me! We picked out a six-pack of Yebisu Premium and snacks at the Lawson's across the street and headed down towards the river. No one else was there, though occasionally a couple strolled by, appearing oblivious to anything around them.

Hawk opened a can of beer and handed it to me. I had to bite back my laughter. He really did look like a hawk with his prominent nose and his bright eyes darting from side to side.

"Hawk works for Hori-ichi's brother, Daisuke Muroya, a woodblock artist. He and the horishi collaborate on projects. Hawk is there all the time, cleaning up the studio and stuff. When the brothers get together, he hangs out until they're finished because Muroya likes to have him around in case they run out of booze or food. When that happens, he sends Hawk down the street to one of the *izakaya* bars. Hori-ichi doesn't usually discuss a client's tattoo, but since his brother sometimes helps him, the conversation can come up. Hawk overheard some stuff."

"I don't like talking about what goes on between Hori-ichi and Muroya-Sensei, but Maho trusts you. And after what she told me about your meeting with Hori-ichi, it sounds like Mrs. Tani might be in trouble, or worse."

Hawk finished his first can of beer, then crushed it down flat and opened another.

"Hori-ichi's been working on Mrs. Tani's tattoo for more than twelve years. He told his brother when she first started coming in, she often had welts covering her back and legs, like she'd been beaten or whipped. She told him if her body was going to be marked, she wanted to be the one to mark it. He thought it must have been her husband. You probably already know this, but a lot of Hori-ichi's clients are with the underworld. You know, *yakuza*."

Hawk ran the nail of his index finger down his cheek to indicate a slash or a scar, the universal symbol of yakuza in Japan.

"Hori-ichi sometimes hears things from his other clients." Hawk took a swig of beer and then continued. "He asked around about Mrs. Tani's husband and learned he had some unsavory business habits. Seems he and Mrs. Tani's father are into horseracing and gaming. Hori-ichi wasn't exactly certain, but he thought the marriage with Mrs. Tani was arranged to clear a debt the father racked up with the younger. Now, they're just siphoning money out of the kimono business to prop up some shady investments."

"Like what?" I asked.

"I'm not really sure. Mrs. Tani's husband acted like he owned her. Hori-ichi said the bastard beat her. Looks like he bragged about it to his yakuza associates. Said he liked to take her into the family storehouse, tie her to the center post, strip her, and whip her. Usually about once a month, but sometimes more. No one could hear once he shut the door. And she never told."

"What a prick!" Maho looked thoroughly disgusted.

"When he bragged about it, he said she was into it. He said she understood he had to discipline her, to make her submit."

"I find that hard to believe," I offered.

"She probably couldn't stand the thought of losing the kimono business," Maho said. If she tried to divorce him, wouldn't she lose it? I mean, it's not like her father was going to help her get rid of the bastard."

"I guess you're right." I needed another beer. I put my

empty into the plastic bag and pulled out a full beer. A couple who looked like they had already had too much to drink stumbled past.

"On the other hand, it's not our place to judge," Maho crushed her empty and threw it, missing the plastic bag. I put it in the bag and scooped out a full one for her. The last one. "You don't know. Maybe she *did* enjoy it. Maybe she really was into it."

"Maybe," Hawk said, looking remorsefully at the bag of empty cans. "But that's not what Hori-ichi thought. He was sure Mrs. Tani was in a fucked-up situation. He thought the tattoo was her way of leveling the field a bit. It must have really angered her husband."

"I wonder how he allowed it. I mean, wouldn't he have tried to stop her?"

"Maybe he did . . ." I murmured.

"I'll go get us another six pack," Maho said as she stood up and brushed the dirt off the back of her jeans. "You guys keep talking. I'll be right back." She turned and followed the path up to Sanjō.

"This is the part I will never forget. Hori-ichi told his brother when Mrs. Tani first started coming to see him she said, 'My husband enjoys watching the welts form.' Seems her skin had hardly a single blemish, except for fading welts, not even so much as a freckle. He was excited about having such a perfect canvas for his art. And at the same time, he was a little reluctant to mark her, but she insisted. That's when she said, 'My husband enjoys watching the welts form. I want to take that joy away.' So, that's why I think she wasn't into it."

"Yeah, I agree."

Maho came back with a second six-pack of Yebisu Premium. She tossed down a pack of spiced peanuts, even though we still had rice balls and curry buns left.

"So'd you get to the part about the tattoo yet?"

"No, I was getting there. Give me another beer first."

Hawk pushed the tab down, taking a long drink.

"She had photographs of a kimono. Well, not a complete kimono, it was more like pieces of fabric. She called it the Tani talisman and said that's what she wanted. Hori-ichi said she was very precise and had already mapped out where she wanted different patterns and on what parts of her body. He advised her to avoid tattooing over her sides, along the ribcage, and over her breasts because he worried about the pain it would cause. But she insisted."

I winced visibly, unable to even imagine the pain myself.

"Hori-ichi went over the photographs with his brother, and they worked up some designs. I mean, they couldn't completely reproduce the whole fabric. She was too small. But Hori-ichi was able to condense it. He said it was the most intricate tattoo he had ever done. And the most beautiful."

"How did she handle the pain?" Maho asked.

"That's the thing, Hori-ichi couldn't believe how tough she was. Most of the time she was silent, biting on a towel until her breathing became so labored he had to stop. When he did, she'd tell him to keep going. When it really hurt, the tears would squeeze out of the corner of her eyes and saturate the mat where she lay. She almost never moaned or whimpered like a normal person would have."

"Women are better at tolerating pain, anyway," Maho

interjected.

"Hori-ichi says that, too. If they're really committed, they can handle the pain. It's the day trippers who come to him for a butterfly or some kind of one-point tattoo who yowl and moan. He usually doesn't work on them anyway but sends them to the Thunder God Parlor outside Pontocho."

"What did the tattoo look like? Did they ever talk about it?"

"I saw the sketches. I oversee straightening up Muroya's studio. He has a file on Mrs. Tani with the sketches he and his brother did. Occasionally, they'd have to re-do an area, I mean the sketch for the area. Tattoos are fluid. They grow out of the horishi's inspiration, so it's not always possible to follow a sketch exactly. That's why they were constantly amending what they'd done. The lady didn't seem to mind."

"So, she wasn't trying to reproduce the talisman."

"Well, that really wouldn't be possible, would it? I mean there's a difference between skin and cloth!"

"I can see there would be!" I laughed, but Hawk continued without so much as a smile.

"Even so, Hori-ichi said the design breathed on her. I guess that's true of any tattoo. The wearer gives it breath. Hori-ichi was especially pleased with his work on Mrs. Tani. He said the tattoo looked like real silk, maybe because her skin was already as smooth as silk."

"Or maybe it's the magic of ink and blood," Maho interjected. "When a horishi's a real artist, like ours is, his tattoo will breathe on its own, dragons will soar, snakes will writhe, and flowers bloom. In this case, skin became fabric."

Hawk nodded in agreement. "Hori-ichi said he would watch

the tattoo billow and shimmer as he worked on her. He swore he could see the strips of cloth tremble like they were blown by a breeze."

"But why go to all that effort to get a kimono tattoo?" Maho asked. "You know, it cost a fortune. If I'd that kind of money for a tattoo, I'm sure I'd get something a little more active, like Tomoe the woman warrior or Benzaiten sitting on her dragon. Something that tells a story."

"Maybe her kimono tattoo tells a story," I suggested.

"Hori-ichi thought so. He thought it might be a story in code. She was very specific about certain patterns, and also about the poems he had to carve on the poem slips."

"What were the poems?"

"I don't know. They're probably in Muroya's notes."

"Do you think you could get a look at them? Or make a copy?

"I don't know, Ruth. It's not like I can just carry them off to a convenience store and make a copy. After your little visit to Hori-ichi, you can be sure he and his brother are keeping a sharp eye out. But I'll see what I can do the next time I'm asked to clean up the studio."

"Be careful, Hawk," Maho warned. "You don't want Muroya to find out."

"I don't want you to lose your job on account of this," I added.

"No, it's not like that. It's more of an apprenticeship than a job, but he does make my life hell whenever I step out of line."

A cell phone started to ring. Maho rifled through her bag, thinking it was hers. When we saw that it wasn't, I scrambled about in my purse trying to fish the phone out before it went to voice mail.

"Ruth-san! This is Daté. I'm sorry to call you so late."

"No, not at all. I'm down by the Kamo drinking beer."

"How fun! If I'd known you were there, I would have joined you."

"Please do!"

"I can't now, I have an early start tomorrow. I must go to Tokyo to judge a story competition. I wanted to let you know I have some more information about the Tanis and the talisman I thought you'd like to have. I'll try to send you a copy before I leave tomorrow, then we'll get together."

"That would be wonderful. When would you like to meet?"

"Let's see. I'm just going up for the day. Let's meet the day after tomorrow, shall we? Same time as before?"

"Excellent! I'll see you then!"

"And Ruth-san, don't expect another gourmet lunch. I'm afraid I've lost Masashi."

"Oh dear, I'm sorry to hear that."

"So it goes. I'll see you the day after tomorrow. Take care!"

"Yes, thank you."

I snapped my phone shut and tucked it back inside my bag. Maho looked at me, so I let her know it was Daté with more information about the Tanis.

"Ruth, did you actually invite that horrible Daté woman to come over and have beers with us?"

Maho repeated Mrs. Shibasaki's terminology about Daté just to rile me. I rolled my eyes and said, "Well, I thought it would be fun! But don't worry, she's not coming."

"Well, I wish she were. I'd love to meet her." Maho smiled and stuck her tongue out at me.

"Hey, Maho, we've got to get going." Hawk stood and started collecting some of the trash. Maho followed suit.

"Are you going to the office tomorrow?" she asked.

"Thanks for the reminder! I'll have to polish off the assignment Mrs. S. gave me tomorrow morning, and I'll be in after that. How about you?"

"Most likely."

"See you then, I guess."

We parted company. Hawk and Maho headed along the bank of the Kamo River towards Shijō. I walked up to Sanjō Ōhashi and set off for the bus stop.

I awoke to the sound of rain and dipped deeper into the covers, enjoying the rhythmic pattern on the roof. I allowed myself a vacation from running on days when it rained. I was just about to doze off when I remembered I had that translation to do for Logos. It was still there on my desk where I'd left it when the police barged in. The last time I saw Mrs. Shibasaki, she was rushing to get ready for her tea ceremony and marriage meeting. I wondered how they went.

I got up, stretched, and shuffled the papers around on the top of my desk, half regretting the cops hadn't confiscated my assignment along with my Shōtarō Tani manuscript. Marketing brochures are not the worst. I think that prize goes to non-disclosure license agreements. The brochure wasn't very long. I should have a document ready in a few hours. I slipped into a pair of sweatpants and went downstairs for a cup of coffee.

After three cups of strong coffee, I was ready to face the translation. The rain, the after buzz from the beers last night, and the incredibly dry material I was translating conspired to make it nearly impossible for me to keep my eyes open. As I fought my way through the manuscript, I found myself reflecting on Tokuda and my susceptibility to her request. The chance to translate something with an actual plot was such a treat compared to what I was doing now. I'd been at this job for nearly a year. And up until now, I hadn't really minded the grind. But the challenge of grappling with a real literary text had been tantalizing. And now the prospective future of more brain-numbing Logos assignments was daunting. My mood had turned as grey as the rain. Maybe Daté would ask me to translate her latest novel. She had said she was almost finished. Well, if it comes to that, I was going to be sure to ask for Mrs. Shibasaki's understanding. Trying to go around behind her back had not been a good idea.

I wrapped up the translation, just as my own self-recriminations reached an end. Did you know that for a mere ¥3900 a week and an additional ¥300 yen per day after that you can rent your very own cell phone in Japan? And all incoming calls are free. And for your convenience, you can pick your cell phone up at all major airports in Japan . . . I don't know. It didn't sound like a very good deal to me. I downloaded my translation onto a jump drive. I would print it at the office.

When I arrived, Mrs. Shibasaki was in a foul mood. Hiro was there as well, a toxic combination if ever there was one. First, one would criticize the other and then there'd be a sharp exchange of words followed by sulking on both sides. I learned that no matter how harshly Mrs. Shibasaki rebuked

Hiro, she would be just as vehement in leaping to his defense if I or anyone else in the office sought to join the criticism.

Hiro smoked, which was bad enough, but he was slovenly and careless. The office would be a much more efficient place if he just wasn't in it. But, I had to admit, Hiro had his charm. He was rakishly handsome with his grizzled chin and thick mop of hair. He often wore a pair of softly worn jeans that clung to his trim frame in just the right places. I was a bit of a sucker for the scruffy look.

I was curious about the omiai marriage meeting, but judging from the way the two of them were sniping at one another, I concluded it hadn't gone well. Mrs. Shibasaki was complaining about him being out late the night before. And in truth, he looked like he'd just crawled out of bed. I couldn't imagine he would be very efficient this afternoon. At least he wasn't smoking.

Mrs. Shibasaki retreated into her office. I ducked into my cubicle, booted up my computer, and was preparing to print out my translation when Mrs. Shibasaki poked her head around the corner.

"Did you see the morning paper?"

I hadn't. I didn't subscribe. I could never keep up with the reading, and I felt like I was just contributing to the deforestation of the planet.

"Satoko Tani is dead. You mentioned Tani Kimono the other day when you were helping me dress. Goodness, what a disaster that omiai was! Anyway, I thought you'd be interested."

She placed the paper on my desk, and I glanced at the headline.

"Satoko Tani: The Nasu Shiobara Nude."

"Oh, my God," I half shouted as I snatched up the paper. It was true. The work I'd been asked to translate was an actual account of her murder. I wondered if I should call Detective Kimura and give him a more thorough description of Miyo Tokuda. Obviously, she was involved.

I ran my eye quickly over the article to see if her name jumped out at me. The piece was annoyingly short on specifics. It seemed only concerned with naming the victim and noting the fact she was found nude.

"Do you know anything more? Have they found out who killed her?"

"They're calling it a suicide."

"A suicide? But what about her clothes? They don't mention her clothes being anywhere nearby."

"I caught a brief report on the radio on my drive over. They're saying she took off her clothes before she entered the river. She washed ashore but apparently her clothes have not been found yet. They're still searching."

"So, are they saying she drowned?"

"No. She swallowed some kind of poison and was likely dead before she went under."

"So, the medical examiner didn't find any water in her lungs? Is that how they reached that conclusion?"

"Such detailed questions! Much more so than the report! I don't think they performed an autopsy. They often don't in the case of suicide anyway. It's just one more intrusion the family doesn't want. They speculate she took off her clothes, drank poison, and then stepped into the river. Eventually, she washed ashore, and now they're saying they don't believe anyone covered her with leaves, as was reported earlier. The covering was the result of the river water washing leaves and refuse over her where she lay. It was happenstance."

"What about a suicide note?"

"There's no mention of a note."

"Well, how did they describe the tattoos?"

"What tattoos?"

I guess the news reports or the police or both withheld the information about the tattoos out of respect for the victim or the victim's family. Even so, something wasn't right. Usually reports like these tried to posit a reason for suicide. I searched the article and found not even the slightest supposition. There was no specific time of death listed and no real specifics. The report only offered Satoko's death being discovered on May 14. No indication of when she had actually died and no indication of where she had died, other than her body was found along the Hōkigawa River. There was no mention of who discovered her. And despite the sensational headline, the article wasn't even front-page news. I wondered if family pressure accounted for the vagueness of the article.

"Do you think they'll have a funeral service for her?"

"They probably already have, and I'm sure it was quite private."

I handed Mrs. Shibasaki the translation I had just finished. She gave it a perfunctory perusal and noted the clients would likely be by tomorrow morning to collect it. She wanted me to be on hand in the event they had questions. Then she gave me a stack of assignments to work on in the office. I was hoping I would be able to take them home, but she wanted me to spend more time at my desk. I think she wanted me there to buffer whatever friction she was having with her son. He was almost forty and still living with his mother. I'm not surprised the omiai was a bust.

It was six o'clock by the time Mrs. Shibasaki decided to close the office. Personally, I think she held us there so long to punish Hiro. Not that he did any work. I hadn't accomplished very much either. I found it hard to concentrate when others were around. Plus, I was still perplexed by the whole Satoko scene. I was sorry Maho hadn't stopped by the office. In a way, I was relieved, too. I would have had a hard time suppressing my desire to talk to her about Satoko.

I straightened my desk up and hurried down to Teramachi Avenue, stopping at a take-out window for sushi before rushing to catch my bus. Tonight, I wanted to drink a nice cold glass of saké, eat sushi, and watch a stupid crime drama on TV. I should probably take some time out to work on my dance lessons, too.

I got out of the bus across from the zoo and crossed the street to walk to the narrow lane in front of my house. Just before reaching the entrance to the lane, however, a dark sedan pulled out onto Nijō Avenue. The windows were tinted. I caught a glimpse of the driver through the windshield, but I couldn't tell if there was anyone else in the car. The driver was wearing dark glasses and either had his hair slicked down with pomade or pulled back into a ponytail. The car was gone before I could get a better look. Black sedans are a dime a dozen around here. And tinted glass is unusual but not particularly rare. Even so, the hairs on the back of my neck tingled, and I had the creepy feeling of being watched. When I reached the entrance to my house, I saw a package at the front door.

CHAPTER NINE
TENGU, THE MAN-BIRD

The package wasn't delivered by the post office or any other delivery service. There were no markings on the outside wrapper other than my name. Someone left it at the door. The black sedan flashed before my mind's eye, and I wondered if there was a connection. How many times had I seen the car now? I could only remember the time it had been parked on the pad outside my house, but I felt like I had seen it someplace else.

I carried the package inside and placed it on the living room coffee table while I went to hunt down a pair of scissors. I was too impatient to change clothes, but I did manage to pull my pantyhose off before heading back to the package. It was wrapped neatly in brown paper, sealed at the edges, not taped. I carefully slid one blade along the seam in the wrapper, slicing through the glue used to hold the ends of the paper in place. The wrapper fell away to reveal a plain cardboard box. This box contained one large plain brown envelope, not sealed, with the brass fastener at the opening folded over to keep the envelope closed. I opened it and pulled out a thin stack of papers. A white envelope of soft washi paper was clipped to the top page. My name was on the outside. The handwriting on the envelope did not look familiar. I slid a blade of the scissors along the edge of the envelope and slit it open, pulling out several soft sheets of folded washi paper. It was a letter.

Ruth,

Soon you will have finished your translation of the first chapter. Shōtarō Tani Sensei and I eagerly await to see what you have done. Perhaps it was the excitement generated by the anticipation of waiting, but Shōtarō Sensei has completed his second chapter ahead of schedule. I have enclosed it here. Although we do not wish to impede your progress on your translation of the first chapter, we encourage you to look ahead to the second, as we feel knowing the progress of the novel may be instructive to your translation. Sensei wishes you to know how grateful he is for your assistance. He believes his novel will go a long way in helping bring justice to those who have been mistreated and misrepresented. Once again, he reminds you that you are not to share the contents of these manuscripts with anyone until we are ready for publishing.

Thank you for your understanding.

We look forward to your initial installment soon.

Shōtarō Tani /mt

I could not seem to extricate myself from this translation project. I was translating a novel being written by a dead man!

Or, maybe not. I could see writing about his family's dysfunction and his sister's bizarre death would exact a certain kind of revenge. But I couldn't see how publishing in English would get him very far. If he had information for the police, why didn't he just go to them directly? Unless, of course, he was himself the culprit. If Satoko's death was not a suicide, then wouldn't he be a likely suspect?

The prospect of speaking to the police crossed my mind. But in a way, I suppose I already had. Aside from my discussions with the horishi, I doubted I had any information the police didn't already have. Besides, they reached their decision on Satoko's death based on their own evidence. What was it that Daté said last night on the phone? She had information about the Tanis and the talisman. She was supposed to be getting home from Tokyo tonight, so I'd see her soon enough.

I was hungry. I didn't bother setting the sushi I had bought on a plate. I just unwrapped it and left it in its plastic case. Not very aesthetically pleasing, but there would be fewer dishes to wash. I went to the kitchen to get chopsticks and most importantly, a glass of saké. Good Kyoto saké from Fushimi! I went back to the living room and turned on the TV, flipping through the channels in search of a suspense drama.

I loaded a small saucer with soy sauce, mixing in lots of wasabi and dipped my sushi in it. I know that's not how you're supposed to eat it, but I like the way an overload of wasabi stabs into my sinuses. I took a bite and slowly savored the burn. The next piece I ate was less intense. I let the sushi settle then took a slow sip of saké. *Momo no shizuku.* "Dewdrops from the Peach." A very poetic name for a relatively inexpensive bottle of saké.

Eating alone was not so bad when you had a glass of saké.

Growing bored with my culinary ruminations, I began to thumb through the chapter Tokuda, or whoever she sent on her behalf, had left at the door. She carefully wrapped the manuscript in the same soft white washi paper she'd used with the first chapter. I unwrapped the packet to find the same style of type-print. I checked to see if there were page numbers on each page, and once again there were not. But the chapter was much shorter, twenty-five pages in all. I really wasn't sure what I should do with this packet. Should I call Detective Kimura? Should I just ignore it altogether and wait for Tokuda to one day appear in the flesh? I flipped through the pages until my eye caught the name "Miyazaki Yūzen." Curious, I opened the packet to that page and started to read.

When I rang the bell she answered immediately, wearing several antique kimonos in a surprising mélange of layers. Did she think she was going to impress me with her wardrobe choice? She led me into her sitting room and invited me to sit. She placed a cushion in front of a faded hanging scroll.

"It's by Miyazaki Yūzen-sai," she said.

Ah yes, my long-lost relative. I assumed her choice of scrolls was accidental. I had not given her much warning of my visit. None, in fact. I just appeared. I was tired of her public speculation about my family. Her improbable *Kimono Killer* had invited unwanted curiosity, curiosity that encouraged reporters to come sniffing after the so-called Tani talisman, our family relic. Having exhausted any interest in those old scraps, they eventually turned to me, Shōtarō, the long-lost Tani son. Each was eager to be the one to break the story and reveal my whereabouts. I did not care to give them the opportunity. It was time for Daté to stop. She brought me a cup of tea and sat at the table opposite me, apologizing for the unwanted attention her novel had brought, and in practically the very same breath, informing me she had a new novel in the final stages of production. It was like salt in the wounds. I demanded to see a copy of what she had produced so far. She was reluctant at first, but I managed to persuade her. She stood up and opened the sliding doors behind her, revealing what could only have been her study. I stood to follow her and accidentally brushed the vase behind me with the edge of my jacket. The Bizen-ware vase toppled over but did not break. The flowers it contained had long since wilted.

She turned back when she heard the soft thud of the vase tumbling to the tatami. I apologized for the disturbance and righted the vessel. The flowers I left as they were, strewn about the alcove in a puddle of water. I followed after her into the study. Her desk was a jumble of papers. She rifled through them for a few minutes before claiming the manuscript was not there. She must have carried it back to her bedroom. She told me she was going to go get it. I told her to look on the desk one more time. These things have a strange way of hiding in plain sight. Clearly, she did not believe me, but she turned to look again, humoring me perhaps. I was not humored. I picked up the laptop lying atop a letter pad and brought it down hard on the back of her head. Not hard enough. She staggered forward over the desk, sending papers flying everywhere and reached up with her hand to touch the back of her head, turning as she did to look back at me over her shoulder. I grabbed the computer power cord and yanked it out of the wall, wrapping it around her throat, as I pushed my knee down hard into the small of her back. She fought. She fought harder than I had expected. I caught her hand in the cord when I threw it around her neck and she pulled desperately against the noose. She fell forward on the desk and kicked up at me, nearly catching me in the tender spot between my legs. I pressed down harder, practically climbing on top of her as I pulled tighter and tighter. I could feel her resistance weaken and then disappear. The tension seeped from her arm, her legs, and her back, arched in desperate defiance, flattened and went limp. I looked up from the scene of carnage and saw a print of a woman staring out the window of a train. She looked worried. She had good reason to be.

I found my way to Daté's dressing room and pulled two waist cords out of her chest of drawers, knotted them together, and wrapped one end in a noose. Then, I went back to the study and slipped the noose over Daté's head. Just couldn't take any more of life, could you? All those pretty boys and none would stay. I looked up at the ceiling, trying to find a rafter or something from which to hang the body. There was a pendant light, but I didn't think it would hold. I settled on the transom between the two rooms.

I couldn't bear to read anymore. It was much too realistic. Was I reading an actual description or a gruesome fantasy? I pushed away from the table, overturning my saucer of soy sauce as I did. It splashed over the white pages of the manuscript. I didn't care. I reached across the table for my bag and pulled my cell phone out. My hands were trembling. I didn't think I could find Daté's number fast enough. I punched in the numbers for her cell phone and listened to it ring until it went to voicemail. "This is Ruth, call me immediately." I disconnected the call and went back to my address book, searching for her home number. I called it. No answer.

Hadn't Daté said she'd be coming home from Tokyo tonight? Perhaps she was still on her way home. She wouldn't be able to answer the phone in the Shinkansen if she were out of range or in a tunnel, or if she had her phone turned off. But I couldn't just sit there and wonder. I had to go to her house to see for myself. I left everything as it was on the table and scrambled barelegged into my running shoes.

I locked the front door and took off at a jog, my suit skirt riding up as I went. I thought about running all the way to Daté's house. I could make it there in fifteen minutes. But when I saw a taxi pass on the cross street ahead, I changed my mind and flagged down the next one I saw. It had already grown dark, and I was still a little jittery after my last nighttime run along the Philosopher's Path. When the taxi reached Daté's house, I asked the driver to stay. He told me he could wait for fifteen minutes, but he'd have to pull up ahead so as not to block the road. He also demanded I pay the fare I had already used.

I ran up the steep stairway outside her house and rang the bell. I could hear it reverberate inside. It was dark on the porch, but through the glass sidelight I thought I saw movement inside. I took a step back and held my breath expecting the door to open any minute, expecting to see Daté's face light up in surprise to see me standing there. I'm sure it would give her a good laugh when I explained what had brought me.

When no one came, I pounded on the door. It opened on its own accord as if it had not been completely latched. I heard a car door close and the sound of tires taking the turn beneath Daté's house. I wondered if that were a neighbor leaving, or if someone else had commandeered my taxi. I stepped into the entryway and called out for Daté-san.

There was no answer.

I called for Masahiro. She said he had left, but perhaps he'd come back. I couldn't help feeling someone else was in the house. I felt along the side of the wall for a light switch and found one, sending a beam of white light cascading over the hallway. There were no shoes at the entry step. I slipped mine off and stepped inside, peeking tentatively into the sitting room from the hallway. I could see the Miyazaki Yūzen scroll was still hanging in the alcove. The Bizen pot was on its side, wilted flowers were strewn across the alcove shelf. My heart started to pound. A dim light filtered into the room from the other end, where Daté had her study. I let my eyes follow the light and then I saw her. She was hanging from the transom. The tips of her toes brushed the tatami floor. Was she dead? I rushed to her side and wrapped my arms around her, trying to lift her up and take the pressure off her neck. Her body was limp. Before I could figure out how to get her down, the ties snapped and she fell forward into my arms, sending us both sprawling over the sitting room floor.

"Daté-san! Daté-san!" I called to her over and over. She wasn't breathing. I couldn't tell if she had a pulse, but I didn't want to take a chance, I rolled her onto her back and tilted her head back in preparation for mouth-to-mouth resuscitation. Something was lodged in her mouth. I pulled her lower jaw down and slipped my fingers into her mouth, pulling out a balled up piece of paper. It was an envelope, empty and torn. On the front side I saw it was addressed to me. Daté had spelled my last name wrong. Only one n and an extra e after the two ts. As I stared at the envelope, I remembered she said she was hoping to mail me some information on Tani and the talisman. Was this an envelope she had thrown away?

I heard the front door open and softly close. Someone else was in the house. Panicking, I slipped out onto the verandah and stepped down into the garden. I remembered there were garden slippers by the stone step. I made my way to the step, found the rubber sandals, and stepped into them, keeping my eye on the sitting room and Daté's body. A man stepped into the circle of light and looked out into the darkness of the garden. I had never seen him before, and he didn't look friendly. I took a step backwards. The gravel crunched, loudly. It did not escape his notice. I am sure he already knew someone else was in the house. My shoes were at the front door, and they didn't look like the kind Daté would wear! I turned and ran. I remembered the back gate that led into the woods alongside the Hōnen Temple. I found the gate and struggled with the latch. What was it Daté had said when she pointed to it the other day? The gate was installed by the temple and it opened *into* her garden? I yanked at the gate, and it swung open. I ran as quickly as I could through the trees. The sandals were of little use and soon I had stepped out of them as I scrambled blindly through the thick undergrowth. Tree branches whipped through my hair and stung my eyes as rocks gouged my feet. But I was not about to stop. I practically tumbled down the hillside to the road below, jumping down from the stone wall in order to make it to the asphalt. The wall was higher than I thought, and I landed hard. The taxi was nowhere in sight. The road was nearly pitch black. I looked over my shoulder at Daté's house and saw two men leaving from the front door and tearing down the steep front stairs. It looked like they had my bag.

That's all I needed to see. I ran. I ran as fast as I could without looking back, darting down the first narrow lane I came to that I knew would take me to the Philosopher's Path, and from there it would only be a short distance to Shishi-ga-tani where hopefully, just hopefully I could find a taxi or could make enough noise to invite the police. But right now, all I could think to do was run. I heard motorcycles rumbling down the lane behind me. I didn't think I could make it. The sound of the motorcycles was growing nearer. I darted down the narrow footpath to my right that flanked the canal on the side opposite the Philosopher's Path. At least it would be harder for motorcycles to maintain any kind of speed on the path. With any luck, they'd lose their balance and fall in the canal. I slowed down to look over my shoulder, afraid I, too, might fall. When I turned, I felt someone grab me from behind and pull me into the damp bushes. I started to scream, but a gloved hand covered my mouth. I clawed angrily at the hand and began to flail as I could feel myself being pulled deeper into the bushes and down a set of stairs alongside the canal.

"Please don't make a sound. You'll have us both killed."

The voice was cultured. Maybe that was why. I don't know, but I stopped fighting. I gave into the power of whoever was pulling me. It was pitch black now. I reached out around me but came in contact with nothing. All I could feel was the hand over my mouth, pulling my head back sharply and an arm wrapped tightly around my neck. I couldn't feel my legs. I felt as if I were floating in space. Every neuron in my brain was screaming at me to stay alert, but I couldn't will myself to concentrate. Everything went dark.

When I came to my senses, I was lying flat on my back on a cold, damp surface in utter blackness. I could hear water running nearby, not in a tiny trickle but gushing with force. My feet felt wet. Was I in a well? I squeezed my eyes shut, hoping to cancel whatever crazy dream I was in. When I opened my eyes, it was still pitch black and I was still flat on my back on a damp floor. The more I grew cognizant of my surroundings, the more my body began to ache. My bare feet felt like they were on fire, cold from the wet but burning with pain. Between the pulsing of pain, I could sense another beat. Something or someone was breathing beside me. I was not alone in my well, or wherever I was. Slowly, I turned my eyes as far as they would go to the left and saw the dimly lit silhouette of a man. His back was to me, and he was peering out of the darkness into further darkness. In the distance, off beyond his head there was a stream of light coming from somewhere. I wasn't sure, but it looked like moonlight.

"Lie very still," I heard him say. It was the same voice I heard earlier. Cultured, soothing with its familiar Kyoto cadence. In the quiet, I could hear the distant roar of motorcycles. I focused on the sound. It grew farther and farther away, and then it was gone. The only sound left was the rushing water.

"They're gone. I'm going to light the lamp, but you shouldn't sit up too quickly. I think you fainted."

So that's what it's like to faint. I must have passed out from lack of oxygen and just plain fear. The man had me in a pretty impressive chokehold. I reached up and rubbed my throat. That only made the palms of my hands sting. I tried to sit up. I ached everywhere and the mere exertion of rolling onto my side to push myself up was painful.

"Who are you?" I asked the man.

"I believe you know who I am Ruth-san," he said as he turned on the lamp. The bright circle of light illuminated his face from beneath, distorting his features into a grotesque mask. Instinctively I gasped. He raised the lamp and placed it on a stone shelf, his face now softened by shadows. It was the homeless man with the soiled jacket and the baseball cap. Only now, seeing him up close, I detected a gentle elegance. His cheek bones were high, his nose thin and straight, and the long hair that slipped out from under his cap was threaded with grey.

"I remember seeing you earlier, but I'm afraid I don't know who you are. How do you know my name?"

"I've been following you, ever since Niida contacted you."

"Who?"

"Niida. Yasuko Niida."

"I don't know who that is."

"Middle-aged woman, master of disguise. She stopped by your place last week. Actually, I was following her."

"Do you mean Miyo Tokuda?" The man's description fit.

"She may have called herself that. And I don't know if Niida is her real name, either. But she is dangerous."

"Who are you?"

"You know me, I'm Shōtarō Tani. I believe Niida contacted you about a book I had written."

"Wait, you're Shōtarō Tani? Then you aren't dead. I knew it! But why did you have Niida or Tokuda or whoever she is contact me about your book?"

"It's not my book. I didn't write it. I haven't written anything for the last twenty years, at least not in Japanese. I've kept a diary, and I write to Satoko, or at least I did. I was beginning to write in Italian and to find a following there under another name. And then this . . ."

Shōtarō's face darkened.

"So, you *were* in Italy?"

"Yes."

"But you didn't write the chapters Niida gave me?"

"Of course not. I haven't written anything since I returned to Japan. I probably never will."

Shōtarō slowly brought his right hand to his face and holding the edge of his glove with his teeth, peeled it away. His hand was swathed in a white bandage. He had no fingers.

"What happened?"

"Yasuko Niida."

He grimaced as he pronounced her name.

"I received a letter from Satoko urging me to come back to Japan. She told me she desperately needed my help. She couldn't explain in the letter, but she told me to hurry. The letter was unusual. It was printed, for one thing, and Satoko always wrote by hand, proud of her penmanship. I assumed she used a computer to write this one because she was rushed. I made travel arrangements and returned to Japan as soon as I could."

"Did you plan to meet at Nasu Shiobara?"

"No. We were supposed to meet here in Kyoto at an inn close to Kurama."

"Was she there? What happened?"

"No, she wasn't there. I waited for some time at the inn. And then Niida came to call on me. She said Satoko sent for me, asking to meet her at Yuki Shrine. So, I followed Niida. She led me off the main road and along a wooded path, telling me it was a shortcut to the shrine. It was late in the day, and the light was fading from the skies. Along the path, it was even darker. I had to be careful not to trip over the large roots that rose out of the dirt like giant serpents. The next thing I knew, there were two men behind us on the path. They quickly overtook us, grabbed me by the arms and pulled me into a thicket alongside an outcropping of stones. Niida knew the men. She shouted out directions. They pushed me down on my stomach and spread me out over the stones. Niida glared down at me with a venom I had never seen.

'You!' she hissed. 'Reluctant heir. What a shameful excuse for a son. You and your sister will be sorry.' I tried to talk to her, but she'd already disappeared in the shadows. It was too dark to see the men now, but I could not mistake the glint of the cleaver. One of the men spread my right hand out flat on the stone. There was the flash and then the sharp sound of metal striking stone. My fingers were gone. I opened my mouth to scream, and though I felt as if my lungs were being rent, I didn't make a sound. The sick scrape of metal on stone echoed in my ears along with the sound my fingers made as they fell to the ground like grotesque raindrops. One of the men kicked me until I slid off the stone ridge and down a steep embankment. I remember rolling over and over. And then, that was all."

"They just cut your fingers off and left you there?

"I remember coming to. I was in a small room in a house or a cottage. I was lying on a futon, wrapped in clean linens. I could smell cedar logs burning and heard murmuring voices. But, I didn't see anyone. Before I could call out, I lost consciousness again. The pain was excruciating."

Shōtarō turned and peered out into the darkness. I was so riveted by his story, I forgot to wonder about where we were or what had happened. I suddenly remembered how Daté's body had fallen into my arms, and I was assailed with sorrow.

"Why Daté-san?" I murmured inadvertently.

"I don't know why. When they first came after me, I just assumed Satoko's husband had put them up to it. Maybe he had found the letters I'd sent Satoko, and it infuriated him. He's a controlling son of a bitch. But even so, it just didn't seem like something he would do. He's an ass, but I don't think he's a murderer. Whoever attacked me had left me to die."

"Who rescued you?"

"I don't know. The next time I woke up, I was in a room in the Kurama-dera Temple, being tended to by a priest. It wasn't the same room I had awoken in earlier. This room was bright and spacious. Instead of cedar logs, I smelled incense. When the priest saw I had opened my eyes, he said, 'Ah, it's good to have you back. I was worried you wouldn't awaken. But now that you have, let's get you to a hospital.' I protested. I don't know why, but I didn't want to go to a hospital. It didn't seem safe. My family would be informed of my return and for all I knew, they, or at least some of them, were responsible for what had happened. I felt protected in the temple, and I begged to stay. The priest relented."

"You mean, you haven't had any medical attention?"

"No. I haven't. I don't put a lot of store by magic, but they say there are special powers in the Kurama Mountains. Have you heard of *tengu*? The man-bird of legends?"

I nodded in the affirmative, but he went on with his description just the same.

"Some suggest they weren't always grotesque creatures. They started out as priests who took to the mountains to practice spiritual austerities and learn the art of magic. Most think of tengu as troublemakers out to trick humans. I like to think I was rescued by a tengu. The fact my wounds were able to heal so well in such a short time gives me reason to believe in magic. I only wish I could acquire some of the tengu's famous military might. I have some scores to settle, but first I need to find out who with!"

"How are you going to do that?"

"When I left the mountains, I came down to the city and started to keep an eye on my house, where I grew up. The police stopped by several times. At first, I thought they were there with information about me. Later I learned they were following up on Satoko. She'd gone missing. Now, I know she's dead. But I wasn't aware of that then. I tried to think of ways to get a message to her. One evening, I saw one of the men who attacked me enter the house through the back gate. He was let in by someone, I couldn't tell clearly. It was a woman I'd never seen before. I knew a place where the top rim of the cement wall had crumbled, and I was able to look from there into the back garden. The woman led the man to the verandah and had him wait there while she retreated into the southern wing of the house, that's the wing where Satoko spent most of her time. The woman wasn't gone long. She came back out and handed the man an envelope and then hurried him out the back gate. When he left the estate, I followed him. He caught a taxi on Shirakawa-dōri. I caught another and was able to follow him. He led me to Niida's house.

"She lived in one of those small wooden houses near Senbon-Imadegawa. I waited until the man left, and then I slipped in through one of the back windows. Try forcing a window open with just one hand! Once inside it didn't take me long to discover what her friend had taken from my house. I found the Tani family seal on her desk, along with the embossed stationery we used to use in the shop. I also found information about you, Ruth-san. She had your address, a blurb in English about *Kimono Killer*, and your place of employment. I also saw she had one of Satoko's old journals, and the packet of the letters I sent Satoko from Italy. The sight of those letters made the blood pound in my head. Satoko would not have easily let the letters fall into someone else's hands. When I picked up the packet, I saw the print-out of a contract between you and me and the manuscript with my name on it. I felt the hairs on the back of my neck stand on end. I spread the manuscript out on the desk and started to read. It was a near verbatim copy of the letters I had sent Satoko, except when it got to what happened at Nasu Shiobara. Satoko asked me to meet her at Kurama, not Nasu Shiobara. I've never even been there.

"But things were slowly starting to make sense. Someone, maybe this Niida woman, had lured me back to Kyoto by pretending to be Satoko. Undoubtedly, she had lured Satoko to Nasu Shiobara the same way, by pretending to be me. But why? I had no idea who she was or why she might harbor a grudge against us. I turned back to the manuscript to read more, when I heard voices at the front of the house. Niida had returned. She was talking to a man at the entranceway, possibly the same man. Hastily, I scooped the manuscript pages together and tried to stack them back up. No matter how I tried, though, I couldn't get the pages in a neat stack. Desperate, I opened the window in front of the desk, hoping it would seem the wind had ruffled the pages. Then I hurriedly slid out the other window and slipped into the darkness."

"Did you follow Tokuda, I mean Niida to my house?"

"I didn't follow her. Instead I set up camp near your house and waited for her to come. I saw her goons drive her past your front door and park down the street by the noodle shop. Then I saw her strutting confidently up the street in her light grey kimono, looking prim and carrying the manuscript like it was a ticking time bomb."

"That must have been the day I met her. I had no idea who she was or what she had done. She seemed so civilized."

"She's very good. She's tricked at least three people so far, and one of us has not lived to give her account."

"But why?"

I could understand in a sick demented way why Akira might want to get revenge on his wife, so he hired Tokuda/Niida to do his dirty work. Jealousy would have driven him to attack Shōtarō. Or maybe he wanted both Shōtarō and Satoko out of the way so he could sell off the business and pocket all the proceeds. But what did any of that have to do with me?

"I don't know. Maybe she meant the translation as a diversion of some kind while she set out to kill me and Satoko. I can only assume you're some kind of smoke screen. What I don't understand is why she has such a deadly grudge against Satoko and me. She's got to be in league with Akira."

"So, you're pretty sure Satoko didn't commit suicide?"

"I'm sure. She was bidding her time until our father died. She was determined to get the kimono business back."

"Then why did the police rule her death a suicide?"

"Bribery. I assume the family paid for that. A murder inquiry would have been too involved and time consuming."

Shōtarō folded his arms across his chest and stared off into the darkness before he resumed speaking.

"But, I suppose I am also guilty of trying to hide the truth."

"What do you mean?"

"I took the page describing the tattoo."

"You did that? You came in my house?"

"I'm sorry, Ruth-san. I needed to read the manuscript, and I wasn't ready to confront you about it. So, I broke into your house while you were away. You left the backdoor open!"

"I know. I've learned my lesson."

"I hadn't been able to read all of the manuscript while I was in Niida's house, and I was afraid if I'd taken it then, she would have suspected someone was on to her. I wanted to catch her in the act, and to do that I had to learn more about her plot."

"But why just that page? Why not the whole manuscript?"

"Like I said, taking all of it would have given me away. You would have known someone had stolen it. But that page . . . I just couldn't let that description of Satoko get out. For all I knew, you really were going to publish it."

"I guess it would have damaged her reputation, or that of the family's, to have had her tattoos discovered?"

"Tattoos? No. That's not it. I didn't care about her tattoos. I certainly didn't care about the Tani family. In fact, I enjoyed her tattoos, at least from a distance. She wrote to me about them, describing what she was doing and why, the designs, the pleasure it gave her to watch her body become more and more exotic. I was glad she had found a way to explore her sensuality."

"By exposing her body to the tattooist, you mean?"

"No, no that's not it. She and her lover conspired on the design of the tattoos, and they both worked with the horishi. Occasionally Ryohei was there in the studio with her while the horishi plied his needles. She would write about the way they would make love later, when the swelling subsided, as if they were both wrapped in the original kimono."

"Then why did you take the page?"

"I was afraid that knowledge of the tattoo would reveal the truth of the Tani talisman."

CHAPTER TEN
HENS

The lamp began to sputter. Shōtarō turned it off, sending us into a tunnel of darkness.

"It does that sometimes. Don't worry. If I turn it off for a few minutes and then turn it back on, it seems to fix the problem."

As my eyes adjusted to the dark, I could see within it different gradations of grey. A pale light glimmered beyond Shōtarō's shoulder.

"Is that the moon?"

Shōtarō turned and looked behind him.

"Do you know where you are, Ruth-san?"

"Are we in a culvert?"

"Close. We're under the Philosopher's Path. We're under the path that flanks it. Straight across is the path you like to take so often. That's a streetlamp you see."

"How'd you find this place?"

"We're actually in an elaborate system of culverts and tunnels. If we pushed in deeper, we could take this pipe all the way to Nanzen Temple and on to the zoo and never once surface. Most of the entrances are covered now with iron grills, but there are still a few access points."

Shōtarō turned the lamp back on and pointed it behind me. I saw a round opening leading into darkness.

"Would you like to have a look around?" Shōtarō asked with the edge of a laugh in his voice.

"Not tonight."

The gaping darkness behind me emitted a cold damp draft like a frosty breath. I was shivering.

"We need to go to the police, Shōtarō-Sensei."

I could still see Daté sprawled on the floor between her study and her sitting room, her face frozen in a tortured grimace. I couldn't bear the thought of her lying there. I couldn't go back. And I couldn't go home, not after I saw the men leave with my purse. The police seemed to be the only option.

"Will you go with me? I'm afraid."

Shōtarō nodded his assent. "Can you walk?"

I tried to stand. My knees ached and the bottoms of my feet stung from the cuts and bruises I had suffered in my run through the Hōnen Temple woods. I could walk. But if the men on motorcycles gave chase again, I'd be in trouble.

"There's a phone booth over to the south. We can call the police from there. Here, let me help you." Shōtarō offered me the crook of his arm.

Normally, I don't allow men to help me. I bristle when they open my door or pull out my chair, but tonight I was only too happy to rely on Shōtarō's arm. For all of his slender elegance, he was strong. I could feel the muscles tense in his arm as he helped steady me, guiding me alongside the canal wall. Once we were back on the path, I was able to hobble on my own to the phone booth, the same phone booth I fled to after my last visit to Daté's house.

"By any chance, did you follow me down this path a few nights earlier?"

"Yes. I'm afraid I frightened you. I just wanted to be sure you made it home safely."

"So, you've been watching over me?"

"Well, I haven't meant to stalk you. But for whatever reason, you're my link to Niida."

I pulled open the door to the phone booth and stepped inside while Shōtarō stood just outside the circle of light. I didn't have any money with me. But emergency calls were not charged. I explained the situation to the dispatcher. I was on the Philosopher's Path, but I wanted to report a murder in a house by Hōnen Temple. Strange men had chased me. I had no shoes. At one point the dispatcher called in a colleague who spoke English, which only slowed our communication further. I continued to use Japanese, growing impatient with the dispatcher's faulty English.

"No, I do not want an ambulance. I want a police car. I want to go back to the house. No, I don't know the address of the house, but it belongs to Yuriko Daté. Yes, that Yuriko Daté."

We went over these details several times until finally I convinced them to meet me on Shishi-ga-tani, and I would direct them to the house. When I turned and stepped out of the phone booth, Shōtarō was gone. I called after him several times.

I turned and limped down the path until I reached Shishi-ga-tani. I could hear the sirens in the distance, and I picked up my pace, my knees shooting pain with each step. I stepped onto Shishi-ga-tani just as the black and white patrol car reached the intersection. It screeched to a stop and a uniformed officer stepped out to greet me. The flashing red lights played across my face in quick intervals, forcing me to squint. Seeing I was in little condition to stand, the officer allowed me to sit in the back seat of the patrol car while he took my statement. He wanted to take me to a hospital, but I refused, insisting I needed to return to Daté's house. I explained I wanted to retrieve my shoes. I told him I saw two men leave the premises with my purse, and I was afraid to go home. The officer relented, turned the car around, and headed to Daté's house up on the ridge above Shishi-ga-tani. I looked back as we pulled away, hoping to catch a glimpse of Shōtarō.

When we reached Daté's house, the front door was closed but not locked. I followed the police officer in. He wanted me to stay in the car, but I refused. I wanted to see if the men had taken any of her things, not that I was sure I'd be able to tell.

My shoes were arranged neatly in the genkan and my purse was resting by the shelving, as though it had been there all along. The police officer duly noted this and asked me to check the contents. My cell phone was there, my wallet, and my house keys, plus an assortment of other odds and ends that find their way in somehow. The police officer watched me as I went through my wallet. Nothing was missing. I could tell he was beginning to lose confidence in the veracity of my story. We went together into the sitting room. The vase had been righted, and the dead flowers removed. I was afraid to look across the room, knowing what I would find. But the police officer had already walked to the study. Daté was once again hanging from the transom.

"You say she fell on you?"

"Yes! She knocked me down when she fell. The cords broke."

The officer pulled out his phone and called dispatch. He described the scene and asked if he had permission to move the body. He was told to wait. Because of my initial report, headquarters had already dispatched a crime scene crew. He had the volume on his phone turned up so loudly, I could hear the conversation.

As he talked, I looked around the study. All the loose papers had been stacked neatly on top of Daté's desk and appeared far more organized than it had when I was here last week. I looked on the floor for the brown envelope that had been balled up and stuffed in her mouth. It was gone. I walked around the desk and looked in the wastepaper can. It was empty. Then I noticed that the Kashō print of the woman in the train was gone. In its place was a calendar of cats. The month was wrong.

I must have gasped because the police officer looked over at me expectantly. He cautioned me abruptly about not touching anything. I pointed to the calendar and told him about the Kashō print I had seen in its place earlier. I could tell the cop did not believe me. At least whoever was behind this had left the body! Even so, I could already tell the police officer was thinking of this as a suicide. I didn't know what I could do to convince him otherwise. I could beg the crime scene technicians to fingerprint the scene. But, what would fingerprints prove, other than the men were here? Daté had men here all the time. I remember the manuscript I received said she'd been hit over the head with the computer. I looked toward her desk, and it was still there.

"Please check the computer," I blurted out. "Whoever did this to her, hit her over the head with it first and used the computer chord to strangle her. They only hung her up there to make it look like a suicide. Trust me, this is murder."

The police officer turned around and stared at me without saying anything or acknowledging my claim.

"Please, you have to believe me. I can prove it. If you take me to my house, I'll show you the manuscript. Everything that happened here is described there in detail."

"I will take you home as soon as the team gets here. Until then, please sit down and don't touch anything." His tone betrayed his exasperation.

I retreated into the sitting room and sat on the floor by the alcove. There wasn't much light there, but I tried to survey the damage to my feet.

"Excuse me, we're trying to find Daté-san's next of kin. Do you know how we might reach them?"

I looked up at the policeman and realized I didn't know much of anything about Daté. From reading the blurbs on the back of her books, I knew she was born in Mie Prefecture. But, that's about all. I never heard her mention any siblings. And I got the impression she had a difficult upbringing without access to many benefits or opportunities. She did tell me once she lost her parents while still young. I told the policeman as much. He nodded and then noticed the pitiful condition of my feet.

"Were you running barefoot?" he asked.

"Yes!" I had told him this earlier, when he picked me up. I told him about my flight from Daté's garden, and the men who chased me on motorcycles. I told him all of it again, explaining I saw them leave the house with my purse. I offered as much detail as I could, but I left out the part about Shōtarō. If he wasn't going to speak to the cops, I didn't want to speak for him. I could tell the police officer was only half listening to me, but he did go through the motions of taking a few notes.

I heard a van drive up and stop in front of Daté's house, within minutes the crime scene technicians had climbed the steep flight of stairs and were filing through the door wearing white jumpsuits. The police officer met them there and began to tell them in a low voice about his encounter with me and the scene he observed. The men turned and eyed me. One took out his camera and took my picture as I sat there on the floor holding one of my battered feet. I had not been sitting in a very ladylike pose for a woman wearing a skirt. Just my luck to have my underwear documented forever at police headquarters. The photographer then proceeded to take photographs of Daté's body, suspended from the transom. When he was finished, another technician spread a white canvas sheet beneath the body. Once this task was done, he stood and put his hands under her arms while a third technician cut her down. She collapsed on the sheet, and they rolled her onto her back. The photographer took more photos. I started feeling dizzy.

My actions must have attracted notice. I heard one of the technicians ask why I was there. The police officer murmured something in response.

"Did you take her statement?" the technician asked.

"Yes. Several times," the officer answered, wearily.

"Then get her out of here."

That brought me back around. "Please, please understand nothing was like this when I came earlier. Papers were all over the floor and the body fell on me when I tried to check for her pulse."

"You touched the body?"

"Yes, yes. I explained it all to the officer. The body fell on me. And then men came in the house, and I ran. They took my purse. I ran out the back door there and through the trees and the bamboo grove by Hōnen Temple, and they had motorcycles, and . . ."

The white clad men exchanged glances. The one with the camera must have given the police officer a secret signal because he came and placed his hand under my arm and pulled me to my feet.

"Come on Bennett-san. You'll need to come to headquarters for questioning. But it's late. You can stop by tomorrow. I'll take you home."

"No, you don't understand, I can't go home."

"Don't worry. It'll be okay. Let's go."

He pulled me to the entry hall. One of the technicians followed us out and stood there, blocking the door to the sitting room, as I tried to put on my shoes. My feet were too swollen to slip into the shoes without unlacing them. As I bent over to loosen the laces, I thought I was going to pass out. I could feel the two men mouthing words to one another over my head. Finally, the policeman asked, "Is there someone we can call for you?"

"No, there is no one."

I stood up and followed the police officer out the door. Once back in the patrol car, I gave him directions to my house. I looked on the dashboard console and saw it was 11:37 p.m. It felt much later. Or maybe it felt earlier. My mind was numb and everything was blurry and slow, as if I were walking underwater. Maybe I *had* fallen into a well, a well like in a Haruki Murakami novel, and stepped through a wormhole in time.

When we reached my house, I convinced the officer to come

in, so we could be sure nothing was amiss. Also, I wanted to show him the manuscript I received earlier that evening. I had to admit, for his distrust of me, he was still very kind. He checked the closets, the locks on the windows and doors, and he went upstairs. I was embarrassed to see the leftover sushi scattered across the living room coffee table. The saké bottle was there as well. And my empty glass alongside it. There were soy sauce stains over the table. Great, just when I wanted to appear credible, I end up looking like a sloppy drunk. That's when I noticed that the manuscript was nowhere in sight.

I limped up the stairs as quickly as I could, calling to the policeman. He met me at the top of the stairs and tried to get me to calm down, but I couldn't be consoled. And I couldn't stay here either. I explained to him again the sequence of events. I think I even begged him to stay the night. He told me that would be against policy and once again, he asked if there was someone he could call for me.

I wanted to call Maho. She knew some of what was going on, but I didn't know exactly where she lived or what her living situation was. I thought she lived at home with her parents. I doubt they would have appreciated me barging over in the middle of the night with bloody feet and hysterical stories. If Maho was living with Hawk, then that was another matter entirely.

With little options left, I decided to call Mrs. Shibasaki. I had been working for her for close to a year now. I thought I could trust her. Of course, I'd have to explain everything to her. I hoped when Mrs. Shibasaki saw me looking ragged and pitiful, she wouldn't be too harsh with me for considering the other translation job.

I picked up the purse I tossed by the living room table and dug my cell phone out. I only had Mrs. Shibasaki's cell phone.

"Mrs. Shibasaki? This is Ruth. I am so sorry to call you so late."

"Ruth! What's wrong?"

I gave her a quick synopsis of the situation, explaining I was afraid to stay overnight in my house, asking if she would mind if I spent the evening with her. She was wonderfully gracious and invited me to come immediately.

I handed the phone to the cop, so she could give him directions. Meanwhile, I went back upstairs to pack up a few things. I opened my desk drawer to check on the money Tokuda/Niida had given me for the translation. It was gone.

The cop was waiting in the genkan when I returned. As he handed me my cell phone, I noticed the Kashō print was hanging above my shoebox. It had been dark when we entered, and I hadn't noticed. I grabbed the cop's arm and pointed at the print, unable to form an articulate sentence. "That's it. That's the Kashō. It's here." The police officer did not appreciate the significance of what I was telling him.

"Bennett-san, let me take you to your friend's house now. You'll come to our headquarters tomorrow, and we'll take your statement again. You must be very tired."

He was right. I wasn't helping anybody standing here sputtering, and I didn't want to keep Mrs. Shibasaki waiting. And I didn't want to stay in my house a minute longer. I locked the door and crawled into the back seat of the patrol car for the ride to Mrs. Shibasaki's house.

I hadn't paid attention to Mrs. Shibasaki's directions, having left that to the police officer. She lived off Yamato-oji Dori, not far from the Kennin-ji Temple in a beautiful old wooden two-story *machiya*. A light was on in the downstairs front room, suffusing softly into the street. The police officer waited in the car, while I went to the door and knocked. Mrs. Shibasaki was there immediately. She pulled me into the entranceway while at the same time bowing deeply to the policeman. He nodded and drove off.

"Thank you so much for letting me stay with you tonight. I'm so sorry for the inconvenience. I really should have told you sooner, I'm just so sorry."

"Ruth, it's okay. We can talk about it in the morning. But now, you need to rest. Let's get you into the bath and then to bed."

When she set a pair of slippers out for me, she noticed the condition of my feet.

"Ruth, what on earth? Can you walk?"

"Oh, I'm sorry. My feet look awful." I stepped around the slippers, not wishing to soil them with my feet.

"Come with me. I'm going to clean your feet."

"No, no, really it's okay. I can do it myself."

But Mrs. Shibasaki would not be told otherwise. She had me follow her through the house to the bathroom. I wanted to linger and look at the different rooms, they were each beautifully appointed with painted *fusuma* doors, graceful latticework transoms, and fresh tatami. We twisted and turned around a softly lit inner courtyard and I caught a glimpse of a moss-covered stone lantern, but I had to struggle just to keep up with my hostess. At the end of the hall, she slid a wooden door aside and led me into the bathroom. The tub was soft hinoki wood and the walls and floor tiled with cool grey slate. She handed me a large fluffy towel and told me to take off my clothes and wrap myself in the towel. She discreetly stepped out of the room while I stripped. My clothes were filthy. Before I could figure out where to put them in her pristine bathroom, she was back with a bottle of alcohol, other towels, and a small wooden tub. She pulled the cover off the large tub and a warm cedar scent suffused the air. Then she filled the small tub with warm water, sat me on the stool, and rinsed my feet with the hand-held shower nozzle, testing first to be sure the water was not too hot or the pressure too hard. When she began, the soft stream of water stung, making me wince. But gradually, the water began to feel soothing. I watched as the runoff turned from brown to clear.

"Ruth, I'm so sorry."

Those were the first words she had spoken to me since we entered the bath. I was touched by her solicitousness. I felt my lower lip tremble, and before I knew it, the tears began to fall. Mrs. Shibasaki stroked my back.

"It's all right, Ruth. You have your cry. I'm going to look at your feet."

She knelt on the floor in front of me and placed a towel over her lap. Then she firmly pulled my left foot out of the water and set it on her lap. She took up a second cloth and rubbed it with soap, which she then transferred to my feet, dabbing softly but deliberately at the cuts and bruises. When she was finished with the left, she went for the right. After Mrs. Shibasaki had soaped up my feet, she stood and showered them off with the hand-held nozzle. Next, she took up the bottle of alcohol and another cloth, and poured the liquid directly on my feet, one at a time. I cringed with the pain.

"You have a few deep punctures. The light's not strong enough in here and I can't really tell if there's anything still left in the wounds. But I'm going to take you to the clinic tomorrow. For all I know you need stitches. Have you had a tetanus shot recently?"

I couldn't remember.

"Go ahead and slip into the bath if you feel like it. I think a short soak will do you good. I've set a night robe out for you in the basket by the door. Your bed is ready for you in the first room down the hall to the right. I have the light on. If you need anything, I'm in the room at the far end of the hall. Try to sleep."

She slid the wooden door closed. I took off the towel and hung it on a hook by the door and then lathered up and rinsed off before slipping into the deep wooden tub and sinking into the water up to my chin. I closed my eyes and tried to concentrate on the tension leaving my back, but all I could see was Daté-san. Like a slide show of horrors, I saw her tumbling down on top of me; I saw the wadded envelope and the dark cavern of her mouth after I had pulled it out, and I saw her hanging a second time from the transom and tumbling upon the white canvas sheet. Again, and again.

As beautiful as the hinoki bath was, it began to remind me of the culvert beneath the Philosopher's Path and my hideout with Shōtarō. Where had he gone? If he'd been there, I'm sure we could have convinced the police to investigate her death as a murder and not a suicide. Maybe he was afraid of being implicated. I didn't know whom to trust. Hadn't he come sneaking into my house? What was it that he had said? The tattoo would reveal the truth? What had he meant about the Tani talisman?

I tried to ask him to elaborate, but then the lamp started to flicker, and I guess the fear of being left in total darkness made me forget about the talisman. Talisman, tattoos, thugs on motorcycles, thugs with cleavers, suicides . . . I couldn't bear to think about it anymore. But then I realized, I had my own means of escape. I had dance.

I lay back in the warm water and closed my eyes, seeing on the screen of my mind the dance steps my teacher had most recently taught me. "Oborozuki," misty moon. I tried to play the music in my mind and managed to do so for the most part. Head back, face the moon. Dip the left shoulder, lower, lower. Now slowly, slowly glance down. Look first with your eyes. Lower your chin…

I stood up in the tub and the water fell off my shoulders and breasts and splashed back into the tub, sending ripples everywhere. The night robe was just where Mrs. Shibasaki had said it would be. I slipped into it, unrolled the sash of Hakata silk and wrapped it around my waist. I was ready to sleep.

Mrs. Shibasaki set out the futon bedding in the middle of the tatami-matted room. The freshly laundered sheets were crisp and cool, as I slid in under the blanket. I turned out the lamp at my pillow and fell into a deep sleep.

I awoke to the smell of bacon and the sound of rain. I pushed back the covers and sat up, surveying my room. Soft light seeped through the white shoji screens on the doors. I slid them back and gazed out onto the pretty inner courtyard I had seen the night before. Ornamental rain chains in the edges of the courtyard flickered silver with the streaming water. The rain blurred the outlines of the plantings, the moss, and stone, and made the garden into a collage of greens and grays. Feeling a chill, I crept back under the covers and lay for a few minutes watching the rain. But the smell of the bacon was persistent. I felt guilty lying about in bed. Reluctantly, I pushed the covers back again, stood up, and dressed in the slacks and light green sweater I had packed the night before. With some effort, I managed to pull my hair back into a neat ponytail.

I followed my nose to the kitchen which was a wonderful amalgamation of modern and traditional. The ceiling was open to the second floor as was the case in traditional houses like this. Mrs. Shibasaki had completely remodeled the room, adding a polished wooden floor and stainless-steel appliances.

There were dishes on the counter, covered with mesh tents to protect the freshly prepared food from insects, though I could hardly imagine any in this house. It was absolutely pristine. The pride of ownership showed in the gleaming woodwork and carefully selected art objects. I noticed a pot of coffee next to the stove. I picked up one of the cups on the counter and helped myself, then foraged through the refrigerator for some milk.

"Oh good, you're up!"

I was surprised to see Hiro striding into the kitchen. Clean shaven, barefoot, and smiling brightly, he wiped his hands on the apron he had tied around his waist. His form-fitting jeans were torn at the knees.

"Let's get you some breakfast."

Before I could say a word, he wheeled around and popped two slices of bread into the toaster next to the stove, pulled plates and silverware out of their respective cabinets, and set a place for two at the counter. Then, he lifted a casserole dish out of the oven where it had been warming and set it on the counter in front of me. He removed the mesh tents to reveal fresh cut papaya and strawberries on one dish and bacon on the other.

"I see you already have a coffee. Take a seat. Let's eat while it's hot."

I hadn't had bacon for breakfast in months, and when Hiro pulled the lid off the casserole dish, I was surprised to find a scrumptious looking egg casserole with spinach, mushrooms, and salsa.

"Did your mother make this?"

"No, I did."

"Hiro, I didn't know you cooked."

"Like a pro!"

He dished a generous portion of casserole onto my plate and placed another spoonful on his own. Then he handed me the plate of bacon and the fruit.

"Please, help yourself."

I had to admit, I was famished.

"Is your mother going to join us?"

"She ate earlier. She's gone over to the office for a bit just to finish up some loose ends and let her clients know she won't be available today. I think she's planning to spend the day with you."

"I am sorry to make her go to so much trouble."

"Ruth, she likes you a great deal."

I'm always surprised by people's capacity for kindness. I never thought Mrs. Shibasaki cared that much for me.

"She told me a little bit about what happened last night—at

least as much as she knew. I'm really sorry about your friend."

Hiro reached over and wrapped his hand around my arm. His kindness also caught me by surprise. At work, he's a bit of a jerk—lazy, grouchy, showing absolutely no consideration to his mother or his co-workers. But here he was fussing over me with the bright solicitude of a mother hen.

"Thank you," I managed to mumble, biting my lower lip to keep from crying.

"My pleasure. I much prefer cooking to translating."

"*Tadaima*! I'm back!"

"How are you doing, Ruth? Is Hiro taking good care of you?"

"Yes. He's been wonderful."

"Please eat as much as you'd like. I have to be careful not to overeat. Hiro's always feeding me one delectable dish or another. He's the reason I had the kitchen remodeled this way."

"Your house is beautiful, Mrs. Shibasaki. But I must say I'm surprised you live in such a traditional home. I always pictured you in a modern condominium."

"Well, it's a compromise between old and new. My husband's parents had been miso merchants, and this was theirs. They lived upstairs, and all of this on the first floor was used for their business. The shop was in front, and back here was the shipping, storage, and production. My husband was determined to restore their house when we inherited it. This kitchen is an example. There's also the family room and our bedrooms that are more Westernized. I'll show you after you eat."

I knew Mrs. Shibasaki lost her husband about ten years ago to cancer. I could see why Hiro would want to stay in the house.

Kitchens like this one are not easy to find in Kyoto.

Mrs. Shibasaki poured herself a cup of coffee and then asked me to follow her into the family room. Hiro stayed behind to clear away the dishes.

The family room was upstairs. I followed Mrs. Shibasaki gingerly up the steep staircase, my feet throbbing with each step. The climb was worth it. The top of the staircase opened out into an airy space with high ceilings and generous light filtering through the frets of the *mushiko* windows lining the front of the second floor. Mrs. Shibasaki invited me to take a seat on the couch. She sat beside me.

"Now, tell me what this is about, Ruth."

I did. I went through the whole story, much as I had told Maho earlier.

"I am so sorry, Mrs. Shibasaki. I should not have accepted that translation. You've been so good to me . . . and I just feel awful."

"Ruth, this isn't *all* your fault, you know. I should have been more understanding of your feelings. I'm sorry you didn't trust me enough to tell me about the translation. I would have worked something out."

"No. You've been wonderful. I'm very lucky to work with you."

"Well, let this be a new start for us, okay? I'll try to find more interesting work for you, and in return, you'll be more honest with me."

I nodded my assent.

"Now, what are we going to do about your house? I think you need to change the locks. Let me make a call for you."

"I would really appreciate that."

"And while we are getting the locks changed, I'm going to take you to the doctor."

"I usually go to the hospital in Iwakura. There are a few people there I still remember from my parents' days."

"Yes, of course."

"Mrs. Shibasaki, I don't want to make you wait on me, though. It might take all day! I can take a taxi."

"Absolutely not. I'll take you, but let's go to the clinic in my neighborhood. The wait won't be as long. Then, we can stop by the police station and see what they are doing about Daté's murder."

Mrs. Shibasaki made some calls, lining up a locksmith in no time and arranging for Hiro to meet him at the house with my keys. When she went to retrieve her car from the garage down the street, I brushed my teeth and picked up my things. I was relieved to see Mrs. Shibasaki's car glide up to the front door, a silver Mercedes.

The clinic was not very far from Mrs. Shibasaki's house. I could have walked there myself. I was beginning to feel embarrassed about all the pampering I was receiving. I checked in with reception, presenting my insurance card and alien registration, glad I had the presence of mind to pick up the former last night.

I paid the modest consultation fee, took a number, and picked a seat in the waiting room. As soon as Mrs. Shibasaki had settled herself next to me, my number was called, and I stood and walked into the examination room. The nurse took my vitals, instructed me to remove my socks, and wait for the doctor.

The doctor was dressed in a long white coat and wore a gauze facemask. It was difficult to hear what he had to say through the mask. He poked and picked at two of the deeper cuts, which hurt like hell. As if he had not tortured me enough, he pulled out a pair of thin-nosed tweezers and probed one of the puncture wounds eventually fishing out a bamboo splinter in addition to releasing a fresh stream of blood.

"I ought to put a stitch or two in here, Bennett-san. But I think we can get by with some butterfly tape. You have to be sure to let your foot rest, though. No sports, okay? And limit your walking and standing."

I nodded in agreement. Anything to stop more pricking.

"I am going to write you a prescription for an antibiotic ointment you'll need to apply twice a day, after first thoroughly washing the affected area. Are you up-to-date on your tetanus shot?"

Because I could not remember the last time I'd had a tetanus shot, the doctor arranged for the nurse to give me a booster. I hobbled back to the waiting room with the prescription. The pharmacy window was located conveniently next to reception. I took another number and waited until called. Finally, I was finished with the clinic after an hour and a half. Mrs. Shibasaki was ready to take me to the police station.

She made some calls and found out where we needed to follow up on the events of the night before. We were instructed to go to the Kawabata Police Station in Sakyo Ward, which was the one closest to the scene of the crime.

The station was on Higashi Oji and very close to the Fresco where I did almost all of my grocery shopping. Mrs. Shibasaki dropped me at the entrance and went to park. The building was newer than most, three-stories, and covered in a greenish-brick facade that now looked sadly dingy. There were posters of wanted criminals on the sliding glass doors. I studied them as I waited for Mrs. Shibasaki to join me. Most of the posters were old and the photographs blurry as if taken from a surveillance camera. I didn't recognize anyone. I don't know what I had been expecting, but this left me feeling oddly disappointed.

Mrs. Shibasaki came up behind me as I was pondering the face of crime. She nodded to me and stepped assuredly on the rubber mat, causing the glass doors to glide open with a whispered whoosh. She strode through the doors, took in the layout of the reception windows with a quick glance, and then marched up to the window to her right. She cut a smart figure in her impeccably tailored summer suit, her hair swept neatly away from her face. I hobbled after her. She was greeted by a woman behind a glass pane who spoke through a cut out circle. Within minutes, Mrs. Shibasaki was called back to the glass window. I tagged along.

"Officer Suzuki is out. His supervisor, Officer Murano will see you. Please, go through the door to your right and down the hall until you come to Reception Room 12 on your left."

Mrs. Shibasaki nodded and proceeded towards the door. She held it open for me, and we walked down the long corridor, flanked with closed doors and glass-windowed walls.

We came to Reception Room 12. The door was open, and the curtains were not drawn, but it was dark inside. Mrs. Shibasaki stepped into the darkness and felt along the edge of the doorway for a light. Just at that moment, a man in a police uniform walked briskly up behind her with a file folder and a clipboard.

"Sorry, sorry, the light is on the far side of the room. Here, let me get it. Whoever designed this building wasn't really paying attention."

The police officer crossed the room, switched on the light, and turned back to greet us.

"I am Officer Murano. Please, take a seat. May I offer you any tea?"

I was thirsty, but we both declined. After we sat, Officer Murano walked behind us and pulled the curtains across the glass. Then, he took a seat opposite us and opened his folder. Mrs. Shibasaki introduced us. She explained I was involved in an unfortunate event last night in which I discovered my friend dead, and that I wanted to be sure the police had all the information I could offer. Officer Murano nodded, stared at his file folder for what seemed an eternity, then looked up at me.

"Bennett-san, it looks like you gave your statement to Officer Suzuki last night. Do you have anything you wish to add at this time?"

Honestly, I had *no* idea what I told the officer last night. So, it was impossible to know what to add. I thought it best to start from the beginning, from my first encounter with Tokuda. Murano scribbled notes occasionally as I spoke. When I had finished, he closed his folder, thanked us both for our time, and told me he would contact me if he needed any more information.

"Officer Murano, I know my story sounds crazy, but Daté-san was murdered. All I ask is that you find whoever did this and bring them to justice."

"We care very much about justice and will do everything in our power to see the case is investigated carefully."

"Have you spoken with Detective Kimura? He was investigating the death of Satoko Tani, who was eventually declared a suicide. And I have to say, Officer Murano, I find that determination questionable." Having Mrs. Shibasaki next to me gave me the confidence to speak more forcefully.

"Detective Kimura?"

"Yes, he's a plainclothes detective with the Kyoto Metropolitan Police, the one who visited my house a few nights ago."

"Bennett-san, are you sure he was with the Kyoto Metropolitan Police?"

"I'm certain. He let me see his identification before he confiscated the manuscript Tokuda had given me. Kyoto Keishi-chō."

"I'm sorry to say but the only Metropolitan Police are in Tokyo. Are you certain he was not with the Tokyo police?"

"He said Kyoto. He was with the Kyoto police. Please, maybe I misremembered the organization he was associated with, but I did not mistake his name—Kimura. He is a detective."

Officer Murano opened his folder and made another note. "Just a minute please," he said, as he stood and left the room. Mrs. Shibasaki and I waited silently. We did not wait long. The officer was back within five minutes with the announcement that there were no detectives named Kimura. With that, he ushered us out of the room and down the hall.

To say I was dispirited would be an understatement. I was angry at myself for being so gullible. I was also wondering if my carelessness had gotten Daté killed. If so, I could not forgive myself.

Mrs. Shibasaki sensed my attitude and offered to take me to lunch. I wasn't hungry, but I knew she must have been. She found a coffee shop on the corner, and we went in for a quick bite: spaghetti Napolitan for her and a potato-salad sandwich for me. I tried to pay the bill, it was the least I could do, but Mrs. Shibasaki refused to allow it.

"Ruth, why don't you stay the night with us again? You seem so discouraged. Let Hiro fix you a nice dinner."

I just wanted to crawl up in a ball and disappear, but I couldn't face being alone in my house, knowing how permeable it had been to intrusions. I thanked Mrs. Shibasaki for her offer and asked if we couldn't stop by the house briefly, so I could pick up a change of clothes.

The locksmith was there, with Hiro, when we arrived. Mrs. Shibasaki backed her Mercedes into my parking pad, and I clambered out of the car and hobbled to the front door.

"Ruth, great timing. Come here and see what we've done."

Hiro led me through the house pointing to each window and assuring me he had checked the locks. Then we went to the glass door that opened onto the patio and the door to the kitchen, showing me the new locks.

"You're in a veritable fortress now, Ruth. No need to be afraid."

Reassured, I went upstairs for a change of clothes, congratulating myself for having done the laundry a few days ago, at least I had done something right. For good measure, I scooped up some light reading material. When I came down, Mrs. Miwa was at the front door conversing with Mrs. Shibasaki.

I could not imagine what rule I had violated this time.

"Ruth-san, this special express letter came for you yesterday while you were out," she said, holding out a thin packet in a large brown envelope. The red line across the top of the envelope and the stamp along the side marked it for special delivery. "The postman was going to leave a collection slip for you, but I offered to hold onto it and give it to you later. I'm glad I caught you."

The packet was from Yuriko Daté.

CHAPTER ELEVEN
PHOENIXES

"Why don't you take a bath," Hiro suggested when we got back to his house. He was eager to get to the kitchen where he had plans for a special dinner. They were both trying hard to help me take my mind off Daté's death. I followed the corridor to the room I slept in the night before, put my bag down, and pulled out a change of clothes. The tip of the package caught my eye, and I set it on top of the tatami next to my bag. After my bath, I would see if I was able to face it.

I headed to the bathroom, enjoying the wave of cedar scent that met me as soon as I slid open the door. I removed the cover from the tub. A cloud of steam rose up and wafted across the room. I undressed and returned to the bathing room, hoping that by lifting off the cover earlier the heat had dissipated somewhat. It hadn't. I stirred the water with the long wooden ladle and then dipped some out in a bucket. I added cool water to the bucket as well and began washing up with that. Gradually, I dipped out more and more buckets full of hotter and hotter water until by the time I had washed completely, my skin was conditioned to the heat, and I was ready to step into the cauldron. I eased myself in, displacing the water over the edge of the tub as I sank to the bottom. The water stung where it lapped at my shoulders and chest. The heat began to seep into my back and knees, and I could feel my tension ease. I was lucky to know so many kind people. I was lucky to be alive. I closed my eyes and drifted along a wave of happy sadness.

"Ruth, feel free to add cold water to the tub. I'm sure it's really hot! No need for you to boil yourself alive!"

Mrs. Shibasaki called from the doorway. I opened one eye and thought about turning on the cold tap, but I was too comfortable to move. I was also beginning to perspire. I pulled myself up and sat on the edge of the tub, enjoying the whoosh of cool air that greeted me when I did. My skin was salmon pink.

What had I been thinking about last night that kept me so long in the tub? That's right, my dance lessons. My next class was scheduled for tomorrow. I would need to attend, even though I wouldn't be able to participate. My teacher would expect me to come in person to explain my situation.

I pulled the lid back over the tub to keep the water hot, opened the sliding wooden door to the sink area, grabbed a towel off the shelf beside the sink and dabbed at my skin. Even so, my skin remained damp, making it difficult to pull my clean clothes on.

"How about a glass of wine, Ruth?" Hiro called from the kitchen. It would be foolish to turn down wine. I stood up, leaving the packet behind, once again, and entered the kitchen. Hiro was grilling salmon steaks. He had a bottle of chardonnay on the counter, chilling in an ice bucket. Gone were the ripped denims he wore to fix my locks, replaced by a pale blue linen shirt and neatly pressed slacks. In some ways, he was his mother's son after all.

"Help yourself. Pour another for me, too."

"Is your mother joining us soon?"

When he nodded, mid-sip, I took down another glass from the cabinet and filled it for her.

The fragrance in the kitchen was divine. Hiro had prepared a marinade of sesame oil, cilantro, and lime which he sprinkled over the salmon as it grilled. He also had skewers of mushrooms, asparagus, and tomato. I pulled plates down from the cabinets and set them out on the counter. When Mrs. Shibasaki entered the kitchen, fresh from her bath, the counter was ready with three place settings.

"It's good to have you here another night, Ruth," Mrs. Shibasaki said.

"Thank you both so much." I wanted to say more but felt suddenly overwhelmed with emotion. I blinked back my tears and took a sip of wine to avoid a full disclosure of my feelings. The Shibasakis either did not notice or knew better than to push.

We spent the rest of the meal enjoying polite conversation, careful to steer clear of any emotional landmines. Mostly, we limited our topics to current Kyoto politics and some of the more unusual personalities in the translation business. I could tell Mrs. Shibasaki wanted to talk about our visit to the police department and was curious about the packet from Daté, but I just didn't want to return to those topics.

It was eight p.m. when I finished in the kitchen. Still too early to sleep, but not too early to bid goodnight with the excuse I was going to read.

I slid the door closed to my room, sat on the futon, and

picked up the packet from Daté. I ran my fingers over the lettering on the outside of the envelope. The characters were distinctively hers, round and somewhat childish, betraying the fact she had only gotten through high school. She'd left Mie Prefecture as soon as she could and made her way to Kyoto where she worked for a few years as a waitress in a coffee shop, saving enough money to attend a night class on stenography. She never completed the class and enrolled in another on the craft of romantic fiction. Writing about star-crossed lovers was fine for a while, but Daté found her real interests were in historical fiction. The fact that she was able to prove herself as such a formidable researcher with only a high school education was really nothing short of amazing.

"Ruth Bennett."

Two n's, two t's. She got the spelling of my name correct this time around.

I slipped my finger under the loose corner of the envelope and carefully pulled up the seal. I winced with a feeling of dread as I slowly slid the letter out. It was almost like communing with the dead.

Ruth-san,

After we met last week, I wanted to explore the history of the Tani talisman further. I am grateful to you for sparking my curiosity. I feel like a very sloppy researcher. In my earlier digging for *Kimono Killer*, I failed to investigate one of the most obvious archives, that of Yūzen-sai Miyazaki, himself. I was so focused on the ill-fated apprentice it didn't occur to me to consider his contemporaries. Yūzen-sai was quite an artist, as you know, well regarded for his painted fans. His shop was by Chion-in Temple. His art was so highly prized lords from around the land commissioned work from him, some even sending unglazed pieces of pottery they wished him to inscribe. Women, too, wanted him to paint their kimonos. That's what led Yūzen-sai to cast about for some way to make his kimono paintings last longer. I don't know all the steps and tests Yūzen–sai went through before he came up with his dye-resist technique. All I know is that coming across the remnant of the Killer Kimono—or what would become known as the Tani talisman—helped speed the process. If that is, in fact, what happened.

Sorry to be sending you such random notes. We can discuss this in detail soon, but I wanted to keep a record of everything while it's fresh in my mind.

Here, I'm enclosing a brochure I picked up at the Yūzen-sai Museum, as I thought you might like to have a look. We can stop there together sometime if you're interested.

I was able to view a few of Yūzen-sai's design books at the Museum research room. In one, he discloses the technique for "keeping the lines from blurring." The sample design shows a tanzaku—and looks very similar to the kimono fabric that formed the basis for *Kimono Killer,* not that I ever saw that fabric, mind you, but it resembles the photographs Satoko showed me of the Tani talisman. It could be that incorporating tanzaku into kimono designs was common at the time, but I have never seen it done.

From there, I went to the Kyoto Institute for Technology, which houses the Yūzen-sai family records. I came across the record describing the establishment of the Tani Branch family. Yūzen-sai produced five sons. Along the way, he had several different wives. The first wife was sent home, divorced around 1670, after she developed an incurable disease. It seems the next two wives died young but not before delivering children. As Yūzen-sai's work became more and more popular, he had several relatives and friends of relatives coming to him with their own sons and asking him to take them in as apprentices. He could not accommodate everyone, and afraid of a heredity dispute upon his death, he tried to establish his younger sons in alternative situations. His first son, Yūichi, of course, inherited Yūzen-sai's name and shop upon his father's death in 1736, as well as his father's secret techniques. Yūzen-sai sent his second son into the priesthood some years before that as had been the case for Yūzen-sai's younger brother as well, the one who rescued the talisman. His third son, he sent as the adopted heir to the neighborhood fan maker, the one who for years supplied the fans Yūzen-sai painted. The fourth son, Yūzen-sai kept on in his studio as insurance, in case the eldest son failed to live up to expectations or else pre-deceased him. The fifth caused the greatest concern. He had demonstrated great aptitude for business but had absolutely no talent for making anything and was apparently a bit profligate as well. Yūzen-sai set him up in his own shop in 1719, providing him a small amount of capital, and having him assume the surname of the wife he married. Like the third son, this one was also forced to sever his association with the Miyazaki family and was removed from the family records. It was this son, Yūzen-sai's fifth son, who became the ancestor of the Tani family.

Yūzen-sai sent him off with a bolt of dyed fabric as a symbol of his connection to the family. It was a very tender tribute, suggesting that this son, his youngest, was most likely the offspring of Yūzen-sai's favorite wife, Ohatsu, whom he married in 1693. The bolt is described in the record in some detail as follows: the main design image was a large *noshi* bundle. I guess you translate noshi as "ribbon" in English. In Yūzen-sai's time, they decorated gifts with narrow obi sashes bound together in the middle with thin sinews of abalone and other cords. On either side of the knot, the obi ends dangled down in a splash of color. Each sash would be decorated differently with auspicious motifs, such as pines, cranes, turtles, plums, paulownia, phoenixes, and such. Dyeing this noshi design onto fabric allowed the artist to really show off his skill at detail, his mastery of different techniques, and his ability to make the surface of the fabric look three-dimensional.

The parting gift must have been very beautiful. But what I'm getting at here is the bolt Yūzen-sai bequeathed to the fifth son, the Tani ancestor, is <u>not</u> the "killer kimono" remnant the Tanis have claimed as their talisman. The photographs that Satoko showed me of the talisman look nothing like the description of the parting gift in the family record. If the fabric the Tani's have in their storehouse is truly the remnant of the "killer kimono," the one crafted by that ill-fated apprentice, the one Yūzen-sai studied in his effort to develop the yūzen dyeing technique, then it is quite rare, not to mention priceless. By rights, then, this talisman belongs to Yūzen-sai's heir, his first son Yūichi and his descendants, and not to the Tani family.

I look forward to discussing the implications of this little discovery with you soon. At least now I understand the Tani annoyance with me for my novel. I always thought their lawsuit stemmed from my depiction of their heirloom as being some kind of 'killer.' In reality, they were upset because I exposed the family's theft of what legitimately belong to the Miyazaki family.

And speaking of novels, I've just sent the final draft of my latest novel to my editor. Yes, this novel deals with a set of vengeful serial murders in the Nishijin weaving community at the end of the 1850s, right around the time when it looked like the industry was on its last legs. Desperate times lead to desperate crimes! You're going to love it, Ruth-san. I am hoping you will translate it for me.

I'll call after I get back.

Daté

I sat there for a while just staring at the letter. Then, I read it again. According to what Daté discovered in the archives, Yūzen-sai sent his youngest son off with a newly dyed bolt of cloth, and not the exquisite remnant of the "Killer Kimono." But then what of the photographs Satoko had shown Daté of a remnant designed with tanzaku? Could she have possibly mistaken the ribbons of the noshi for poem slips? And who else knew about the so-called Tani talisman? They had never mentioned the piece in their advertisements. Nor had they ever displayed it or allowed a museum to do so. Satoko's photographs notwithstanding, could it be it simply did not exist? And what was it Shōtarō Tani told me in the culvert? He didn't want Satoko's tattoo to reveal the truth of the talisman. What did that mean? Had the Tani predecessor stolen it from the legitimate Miyazaki heir? If that were the case, wouldn't the Tani talisman by rights belong to Ryohei Miyazaki's family, the direct descendents of the Yūzen-sai heir?

I heard a soft knock at the door. Mrs. Shibasaki slid the door open when I answered. She had changed into a night robe of peach-colored silk. She knelt just outside the entrance to the room.

"Are you okay? It must have been hard on you to read Daté-san's letter."

I thanked her for her concern. She told me she just received word that Daté's funeral was scheduled for the day after tomorrow, at ten a.m.

"So, the police have released the body?"

"Apparently so."

"And they are sticking with the suicide explanation?"

"I'm sorry, Ruth."

"That's two murders that will go unpunished."

"Perhaps. But we can't really know for certain, can we?"

I stared at the letter in my hand. "I think we can. I am certain Daté did not commit suicide."

Mrs. Shibasaki sat there quietly for a few minutes. She bowed, bid me good night, and softly slid the door shut. I heard her footsteps retreating down the hall.

The morning brought no end to the rain. "A little early for the rainy season, isn't it?" I murmured more to myself than anyone else, but Hiro looked up from the sink where he was washing a large grapefruit. Breakfast this morning was lighter than the one yesterday, and following the heavy meal the night before, I was relieved.

"An early *tsuyu* means a hot summer!"

Hiro sliced the grapefruit and set one half in front of me. He picked a fancy fruit spoon out of the drawer and handed it to me as he pulled a slice of toast out of the toaster.

"Would you like some rose hip jam? I bought it in Ohara, out in the mountains. A British woman who lives out there makes it."

He passed the jar to me.

"Hiro, you should open a bed and breakfast!"

"Maybe I will."

I could imagine Hiro puttering around in his apron entertaining guests, but he'd need a wife. I was half tempted to ask about the marriage meeting but thought the wiser of it.

When we finished breakfast, I helped him clear away the dishes, then I went back to the room to gather up my belongings. Hiro offered to drive me home. I needed to avoid walking for another day or two, but I couldn't just sit around their house. It seemed I was healing, but I could still feel a ping of pain every now and then when I put too much pressure on the balls of my feet.

Hiro pulled the Mercedes around to the front door and I piled in. He offered to run me past the grocery store on the way, but I declined. I was already feeling bad about imposing on him and his mother.

"Don't hesitate to ask for anything, Ruth."

Hiro gave me his cell number once we reached my house. He also made sure I had the new keys and waited until I had successfully opened the door and stepped inside before he drove off. I was confronted immediately with the Kashō print of the young woman in green. It was a breathtakingly beautiful piece. But I wasn't sure I would be able to face it on a daily basis. The ominous way it appeared in my genkan was a reminder of my vulnerability not to mention Daté's murder. I was getting ready to take it down when I changed my mind. I'd decide what to do with it later.

I walked slowly through the house, checking the windows and doors. No access point seemed to have been breached. I would need to get ready soon for my dance lesson. Clearly, I would not be dancing. That being the case, I decided on a kimono of dark blue tsumugi. It was slightly better quality than what I normally wear to practice. I dressed carefully, selecting an obi designed with phoenixes and paulownia on a muted background. In truth, the obi was a bit too elegant for my kimono, but I was attracted to the image of the phoenix and all of its mythical associations.

Once dressed, I was eager to get started. I made sure to lock the door behind me as I left the house. I even went back in one more time to be sure the doors to the patio were locked. When I had checked them once again, I headed for Nijō to hail a taxi. The driver offered to give me a "kimono discount," in keeping with a new policy in Kyoto to try to encourage more kimono wear.

I was early, and my dance teacher was surprised to see me. When she had a break between lessons, I explained to her I had hurt my feet and would not be able to dance for at least a week. She looked mildly irritated.

"What about the recital? Do you think you will be ready? It's just over a month away, and you've got a lot of ground to cover in learning your dance."

"Yes, I still plan to participate."

"Well. Be certain. I have to submit the list of participants next week. And I will also need your contribution."

I had forgotten about the contribution. Japanese dance was not an inexpensive pursuit. Each performer had to make a contribution to the cost of producing the recital, covering the space rental, publicity, and more. This time my portion was to be ¥30,000, over $300. On top of the weekly fees for the lessons, it really added up.

I pulled the white envelope with her weekly fee out of my bag and placed it on the floor in front of me, bowing as I thanked her for her instruction. She took the envelope, placed it beside her on the floor, and invited me to get a cushion and sit next to her while she taught the next student. I was glad to do so. You learned a great deal watching others. You learned more by watching the teacher.

My lesson was up next, or would have been if I were in shape to practice. Since I was not, my teacher had extra time, and she invited me to have a cup of tea with her. She called down to her assistant who came upstairs a few minutes later with two glasses of chilled green tea and two plates of sweet bean-jam cakes. My teacher and I nibbled and sipped, and she eventually got around to asking about my feet. With some hesitation I went back over the gruesome account. When she learned what had happened to Daté, she was horrified.

I appreciated her concern and then I told her how thinking about dance helped me divert attention away from my sorrow, so I could find calmness.

"That's good, Ruth-san. Now keep that focus. Work through the dance in your mind, even when you can't be on your feet.

I thanked her for her advice.

"Ruth-san, what made you start studying dance in the first place? Were you looking for calm?"

"I suppose I was, in a way. I didn't even know I was looking for Japanese dance. I guess you could say, dance found me."

"That's the way with a lot of artists. How did dance find you?"

"Well, it is a bit complicated. I was attending boarding

school in Kobe, and I was angry."

"I thought you told me your parents lived in Kyoto."

"That's right. And that's part of why I was angry. There were other students at the school who commuted from Kyoto. I didn't understand why I had to board. I felt like my parents were trying to get rid of me. And honestly, I think they were."

"Surely not."

I know it sounds childish. But I couldn't help the way I felt—still feel. They sent me away after my brother disappeared. They said they were putting me in boarding school to make sure I was watched over, since they worked all the time and couldn't keep an eye on me, but I think they were trying to get rid of me.

"Of course, they didn't want to get rid of you." Sensei peered into my face sympathetically.

"Well, it is what I thought. I just grew angrier and my anger found expression in all kinds of self-destructive behavior. I dyed my hair black and wore black lipstick, for example.

"You mean like those girls who cluster around Harajuku in Tokyo?"

"Sort of. But there wasn't anything fashionable about what I was doing. I didn't have a lot of friends, and I didn't go out of my way to try to make any, either. I was just a very unhappy little girl who wanted the world to know just how miserable and ugly she was. My schoolwork suffered, my grades were awful, which made my parents more upset and only served to make me angrier. I was in a pretty desperate downward spiral until my Japanese language teacher helped to pull me out."

"Your language teacher?"

"They offered language classes at the Kobe school, because

so many of the students were recent transplants or else had been in international schools throughout their childhood. Many didn't know Japanese. I'd been speaking Japanese since I was a baby, in some ways I considered it my first language. I thought if I took a Japanese class, I could ace it without even trying. But the teacher saw through me. She pulled me out of the class I was in and worked with me one-on-one. She really made me work, too. She could see beyond my thorny exterior and understood how to communicate with me. Maybe it was because I was more comfortable speaking in Japanese. But she had me read books on Japanese history. We studied poetry. We talked about art. She was the one who introduced me to Japanese dance. She brought me to see her teacher, and I started to take lessons. That's when I learned to wear a kimono."

"How old were you?"

"By then I would have been fifteen. I went once a week. I stopped dyeing my hair. I started talking to my classmates. I felt as if I had found something that belonged to me. When I graduated from high school, I went to the States for college and couldn't continue my lessons. For a while I was at loose ends, but eventually I started to study modern Japanese poetry and that seemed to fill the space that dance had left."

"That's a great story," my teacher beamed. "I'm glad dance helped you find your way through the difficult time in your childhood. Do you mind if I use the story in my monthly newsletter? I think it could be inspiring."

I doubted others would find my adolescent angst inspiring, but I gave my teacher permission to do so.

"After what you've told me, I have a better understanding

of why you were so attracted to Daté-san's work. As modern as she was, she really was the embodiment the Japanese cultural past. And you are, too, Ruth-san. You may be a foreigner, but the Japanese past lives on through your work and your interests."

I could feel my face flame with the praise. I didn't think it was deserved, but Sensei's use of the word embodiment made me think of Satoko. With Daté now gone, I wasn't sure what to make of the tattoo.

"Why don't you discuss the talisman with Ryohei Miyazaki?" My teacher suggested.

I think my mouth must have dropped open in stupefication. I never considered talking to Miyazaki. It seemed a little too intimate to ask him questions about his lover's family heirloom— and particularly about his lover's body.

"But I don't know how to make contact with him."

"I can help you. I've worked with Miyazaki-san on recitals and such. It really is a small world for those of us who still appreciate the traditional arts. We do our best to support one another."

She pulled her cell phone out from the inner fold of her obi, flipped it open, and began scanning for Miyazaki's number.

"Here it is. Let me just give him a call and see."

I waited tensely beside her while the phone rang. I could hear a voice pick up on the other end. My teacher briefly explained she had a student interested in the history of the Miyazaki family, as well as the Tani family legacy.

"Now? Yes, I suppose so. Just a minute."

My teacher covered the phone with her hand and leaned over towards me.

"Can you go over there now? Miyazaki-san said he is on his way back to his studio from a delivery and has the rest of the afternoon free. Why don't you go over?"

I nodded, wide-eyed.

My teacher said her good-byes and snapped the phone shut.

"Good timing, Ruth-san!"

I thanked her for her help, but I was a little nervous about meeting Miyazaki. I didn't know what the parameters were for the conversation.

"I'll write down the address. You'll need to take a taxi. He said his wife will be at the studio for the next hour, so she'll be there to let you in should you arrive ahead of him."

"His wife?"

I guess I looked surprised because Sensei quickly added. "Well, of course. You didn't think he'd wait for Satoko-san forever, did you? He had the future of his family line to consider. Once she married Akira, he took a wife, the daughter of a family that was in the sericulture business for generations. Seems it's a good match. They have three children."

"But, I heard he still saw Satoko . . . I mean, intimately."

"That may well have been the case. Don't look so surprised. It's not that unusual."

"It's not?"

"I guess you foreigners are more squeamish about such things. But really, if all the parties concerned understand, I don't think it needs to be tawdry. Satoko and Miyazaki had a bond that was not easily severed. And it doesn't seem Akira much cared one way or another. Miyazaki's wife may have been bothered at first, I don't know. But I'm sure she came to realize Miyazaki was never going to leave her for Satoko."

Sensei stood and motioned for me to follow her. We went down the long, steep staircase to her private office on the first floor. She fished a piece of paper out of the desk drawer and wrote Miyazaki's address down. She asked if I wanted her to call a taxi, but I said I would walk the short distance to Shijō and flag one down there. I needed to pick up a gift of sweets or fruit on the way, if I could find a good shop.

"*Mizu-yōkan!*" Sensei suggested. "Water sweets."

"What?"

"There is a great yōkan shop on the corner. They have lovely gift boxes of sweet-bean confections. But I recommend the mizu-yōkan. It tastes great lightly chilled."

The suggestion of *mizu* on this watery day seemed like I was only asking for more rain, but I appreciated my teacher's suggestion. I found the sweet shop on the corner where I had passed it weekly without ever seeing it. I picked up a box of mizu-yōkan in assorted flavors, green tea, red bean, and persimmon, then stepped out onto Shijō and flagged down a taxi.

It took less than fifteen minutes to reach Miyazaki's studio on the fringe of the Nishijin district. The taxi pulled up in front of an old machiya—not unlike Mrs. Shibasaki's but more "weathered." There was a crisp linen curtain hanging over the front entryway with the studio name dyed in calligraphic lettering.

I called out from where I stood by the entry step. I heard my voice echo weakly through the dark interior. There was no response. I called again, this time louder, with more conviction.

"Coming!"

A woman's voice rang out and then I heard footsteps along the wooden floor. In seconds, a woman stepped out into the entryway wearing a cotton striped kimono with cords around her shoulders to hold her sleeves back while she worked.

"Oh, you must be Ruth-san. Please come in. Miyazaki just got back; he'll be with you in a minute."

The woman ushered me into a spacious Japanese-style sitting room. She placed a cushion on the floor next to a long low table and invited me to have a seat. I bowed politely, handed her the mizu-yōkan, and took my seat. I looked around the room as I waited. The scroll in the alcove was of a mountain scene full of fresh green leaves and rushing waterfalls. There were fresh hydrangeas in the vase beside it. This must be where Miyazaki met his customers and helped them place their orders.

I heard a door open down the hall and then footsteps. A tall grey-haired man strode into the room and bowed slightly, followed by the woman who had met me earlier. She had a tray with tea and a cold towel. I bowed to the man from my seat and thanked him for taking the time to meet with me. He sat at the table opposite me as the woman knelt between us and placed the cold towel in front of me before putting a teacup on each side of the table. She bowed and left the room.

Miyazaki was tall and trim in loose-fitting, light blue shirt and dark trousers. His face was smooth, with hardly a wrinkle to betray the fact he was in his fifties. When he smiled, his teeth flashed white and straight.

"I see that you like kimonos," he said as he nodded in my direction.

"I love kimonos," I replied.

"Tell me, what do you like about kimonos?"

"I like the way they reveal and conceal. They tell a story."

"What kind of stories do your kimonos tell you?"

"Well, first, the design on the kimonos and the fabric tell me about the season or the occasion. The way the kimono is worn with an obi and other accessories tells me about the wearer's taste, mood, or sense of daring. If the kimono is handmade, it carries the story of its maker. And if the kimono is old, it retains the memories of the past."

"I see! You do love kimonos."

"Yuriko Daté-san helped deepen my appreciation of the way to wear a kimono. When I first met her, I was nervous about doing it wrong. There are so many ways to make mistakes, but she told me the kimono would reveal the spirit of the wearer."

"I'd say she was correct!"

"I miss her now."

"Yes, I heard about her death."

"Before she died, she sent me information about the kimono she featured in her novel, *Kimono Killer*. Are you familiar with that novel?"

"Oh yes. Satoko and I talked about it on several occasions."

His reference to Satoko was so casual. It surprised me at first. Was he supposed to lower his voice, worried that his wife might hear him mention his lover's name?

"Daté-san told me the Tani family was upset with her characterization of the kimono. But what did you think?" I asked, hoping to draw him out.

"I thought she told a lively story. I didn't think it threatened the Tanis in any way and found their protest unnecessary. But let me tell you a bit about the so-called 'Tani talisman.' That is why you're here, right? To hear the story?"

I nodded.

"It is true the Tanis have a remnant of a kimono that dates to the late seventeenth century. And the story of the kimono maker's tragic death is also well known. But how the remnant of the kimono fell into the Tanis's hands is a bit more of a mystery. My ancestor, Grandfather Yūzen-sai, acquired the remnant from his brother, a priest. The brother was supposed to destroy the remnant, but he was certain Yūzen-sai would want to have a look at it, so he brought it over to his shop next to Chion Temple. Perhaps he fully intended to destroy the fabric eventually, but one thing led to another and the fabric escaped destruction."

This is all in Daté's novel, and I was quite familiar with the details.

"Grandfather Yūzen-sai painted on silk all the time, so he was not particularly impressed with the painter's skill, but what fascinated him was the fact that even after the remnant had been lashed by raindrops and splattered with spray from the river, it did not smear or spot. The paintings held up.

"Grandfather Yūzen-sai was a highly regarded painter and orders came from around the country for his designs. He painted on fans, pottery, and sliding doors. He also painted on kimonos. But his kimono paintings were always vulnerable to the weather. Women mostly wore his painted fabrics indoors, terrified if caught outside in a sudden downpour their beautiful designs would disappear before their very eyes. Of course, the impermanence and fragility were aesthetically appealing. But he wanted his paintings to be less susceptible to the caprices of the weather. When he saw this remnant, he understood. He needed to use a fixative in his paint. He studied the remnant and experimented. He tested, researched, analyzed, then he tried. Within a year, he discovered a process that allowed him to paint permanently on fabric. Once he perfected his technique, his designs were in even greater demand.

"For years thereafter, Grandfather Yūzen-sai treated the remnant with great reverence. But he also remembered the young apprentice who had poured his heart into the production of the kimono. As an artist himself, he understood the effort it had taken, the toil, the trials, the love. He could only imagine how splendid the original kimono was and how devastated the young apprentice must have been to have had his kimono marred. He was also mindful of the rumors surrounding the remnant and the temple's earlier decision to destroy it. He personally witnessed strange occurrences when he was in the presence of the remnant."

"Strange occurrences?"

"Yes, that's right. He told his sons that on occasion, when he was alone in his studio studying the remnant, he would catch sight of a young man just out of the corner of his eye. When he'd turn to look, there would be no one there. Grandfather Yūzen-sai assumed it was a trick of the light. It was dark outside and the lamp he used was sputtering. As he got older, he began to suffer from cataracts. But there was one time, while he was testing a dye, that he felt a hand on his shoulder. He turned quickly but saw no one. When he turned back, the remnant was on the floor. Of course, he could have very well knocked it off when he turned. But Grandfather Yūzen-sai concluded from these incidents that the spirit of the young apprentice still clung to the remnant.

"Just before his death he called his second son, who was now the head priest of the Kyo-an Temple and asked him to perform a *kuyō* ceremony for the young apprentice, a ceremony that would release his spirit from its attachment to the remnant and free him of sinful clinging. He felt the apprentice had suffered long enough. He needed to find his way to the next world. So, Grandfather Yūzen-sai gave the remnant to his son, the head priest, and told him to burn it."

"Burn it?"

"Yes, to release the apprentice's spirit. If the remnant remained, the apprentice's spirit would be forever bound to it. Grandfather Yūzen-sai recorded his wishes in the Miyazaki House Records. I can't recall the date now, but there's a line in the diary stating his desire to burn the remnant. He describes how he delivered the Tofukumon'in kimono remnant into his son's, Priest Ryosai's, keeping, so he could perform a kuyō for the apprentice on the next *taian* good-luck day."

"But he didn't follow through?"

"As with the priest before him."

"He was too captivated by the beauty of the silk?"

"Not exactly. On his way to his temple from his father's house, the priest stopped by to see his younger half-brother, the fifth son who had been set up in his own business. As they conversed about this and that, he mentioned the remnant and showed it to his brother. Now, both had seen the fabric on different occasions in their father's studio. The fifth son, always eager to find a new business ploy, convinced the priest to let him hold onto the remnant. He planned to shred the fabric and boil shards down, so he could market it as a magical medicinal tonic. The priest wished to honor his father's instructions, but his temple was just beginning a new building project and needed new capital. He saw his younger brother's plan to help raise funds, so he agreed to leave the remnant with him."

"But he didn't shred it?"

"No, he had to wait for his father to die first, since he didn't want his father to know the remnant had not been burned as instructed. Grandfather Yūzen-sai did not die right away. He held on for a few more years. In the meantime, the fifth son, who'd been set up in a branch family named Tani, filed the remnant away in his *kura*. Shortly before Grandfather Yūzen-sai died, his second son, the priest, was killed in a temple fire. And so, it seems the remnant was forgotten."

"You mean, it just remained in the Tani storehouse?"

"Apparently. Eventually, the fifth son died. New family heads came and went. And no one thought of the remnant until much later when it was discovered in the kura during an annual cleaning. At that point, no one really knew much about it. But they assumed it was what was left of the bolt Grandfather Yūzen-sai gave his son when he set him up in a branch family. In conversations between the Tanis and the Miyazakis, they reconstructed the history of the remnant, but no one took the time to read the Miyazaki House Records. They were dusty old archives by then, filed away in the Miyazaki storehouse. So the stories were crossed, and the remnant was resurrected as the Tani talisman."

"But given the history, it seems a pretty morbid talisman."

"I agree. And if you look back over the Tani family history, you will see that since the time of the original patriarch in the seventeenth century up to the present century, there has not been a natural-born Tani son until Shōtarō."

"I had no idea. Why do they keep the talisman around? It sounds cursed!"

"I'm not sure the Tani family knows the real history. The Miyazaki House Records are not published. And I only know they are there because I searched them out intentionally."

"What prompted you to do that?"

"Satoko did."

"Satoko-san?"

"Yes. She stumbled upon the talisman when we were in high school. She liked to go into the Tani storehouse and root through old boxes and books. Like the Miyazaki Storehouse, hers was jam-packed with all kinds of antiques, scrolls from China, rugs from Persia, Korean celadon. The Tanis were shrewd collectors. The recent family head, Satoko's father, has sold off a lot of it to cover his gambling debts."

"What did Satoko-san do when she found the remnant?"

"She could tell the piece was exquisite. She asked her grandfather about it and heard the story of the talisman. I suppose this was really what lit the fuse for Satoko. She grew more and more fascinated by kimonos from this point on. She'd spend days in the storehouse poking through boxes and drawers. On special days, her grandfather would let her take the remnant out and place it under the lights in the house, so that she could study it better. But mostly she preferred to look at it in the storehouse. She said the dim light there was better suited to the subtle luster of the gold threads and the sheen of the silk. After her grandfather died, her father didn't allow Satoko to spend as much time in the kura. He argued it was unhealthy for her to be in there so long."

"Did she ever find out the true history of the remnant?"

"She did. And I helped her with it. She was the one who recommended I check the Miyazaki House Records for a reference to the talisman. The records are not easy to read. The ink is faded, the pages are worm-eaten in places, and the style of writing is difficult to decipher. Eventually, I found the entry marking the day Grandfather Yūzen-sai set his youngest son up in the Tani branch family. There was a description of the bolt he sent with him, even a sketch. When I told Satoko this, it only inflamed her curiosity more. She decided she was going to open the remnant to see if there was any sort of clue on the underside."

"Open?"

"When the remnant was sewn into temple banners, the kimono fabric was folded over and sewn together to make it long and narrow. Satoko wanted to open the seam where it had been sewn together to see what was on the underside. As is often the case with embroidered fabric, the underside has a brighter gloss than the outer and can give a better indication of the true colors. Here, let me show you."

Miyazaki pulled a bolt off the stack behind him. It was a deep red silk embossed with an interlocking diamond design. He unfurled a small section of the bolt and pulled it over, so that the underside was showing.

"If you look on the underside, you can see the embroidered parts look brighter in certain sections. Over time, this brightness increases."

"Did her father allow her to open the seam?"

"She didn't ask. Once Satoko had a mind to do something, she went ahead and did it."

Miyazaki's eyes glistened as he spoke of Satoko.

"She learned how to open the storehouse and slip in when her father was out. Even during the day, the storehouse was dark inside. At night it was as dark as the deepest well. There were three windows for light on the second floor, but they were kept shuttered except for the weeks of airing in the spring and the fall. What this meant was she had to have a flashlight when she entered. And once the door was shut, no one could see she had a light on inside. She could work with very little fear of being detected."

"So, she opened the seam?"

"She did indeed. I was with her. Satoko was always a little more self-assured when someone else was with her. She said she felt frightened when she was in the storeroom alone."

"I'm sure I'd be terrified of being locked in!"

"That wasn't it. She was terrified of what was in the storeroom."

"Snakes?"

"Spirits."

"You mean, like ghosts?"

"I mean, all those old objects having known the touch of those long dead. There was a sense some of the objects absorbed the spirits of their previous owners, especially those who had not lived a happy life."

"Like the talisman?"

"Like the talisman. I sat with Satoko as she lifted the remnant out of its paulownia box and pulled the softly worn paper wrapper away. She placed the remnant on a clean muslin sheet she'd spread out on a raised platform in the storehouse. Then, with a thin needle she very carefully pulled the stitches out of the seam. The thread was mostly rotten and broke off with each tug of the needle. She was soon able to open a nine-inch slit in the seam. Once she did, she slowly pulled the remnant inside out.

"As she began to pull the other side of the remnant through the seam, we could tell immediately she was right. The threads on the underside were much brighter than those on the outer. This was in part because they hadn't been exposed to the fading elements as had the outer side, but it was also because many of the threads had been cut on the underside. They waved and trembled when Satoko pulled them into the light like the slender tentacles of a sea anemone shivering in an underwater current. 'They've been cut!' Satoko gasped."

"Wait. I don't understand. How could they have been cut? Wouldn't the embroidery have come apart?"

"Some of it had. When we looked again at the outer side, we could see places where the embroidery had been worn bare. We thought it was the result of age, and it was. But had it not been cut, the threads wouldn't have been so susceptible to that kind of wear. Satoko was afraid to continue pulling the cloth through the seam, afraid the tension would further stress the fabric. But, feeling compelled to continue, she persevered. When she had half of the remnant turned out, we saw that some sort of design had been embroidered on the underside. When we brought the light closer, we could tell it was the character for "under" or "*ura*" "back."

"Like the back of the fabric?"

"That's what we took it to mean at first. But it was odd. Why would the kimono maker label the back of the fabric? It is obvious."

Miyazaki flipped the fabric on the table back and forth. It was clear which was the front and which was the back from the embroidery.

"We stared at the character for a long time. *Ura* 裏. The underside. The backside. There just seemed something potent about it, even a little sinister. Moreover, the character was sewn over the cut threads as if in an effort to mend the rent but also as a way to send a message about the rent. The cut threads were integrated into the newer overlay threads that sketched out the character, and the overlay threads were nearly the same color. So, it was almost impossible to see the character at first. We might not have noticed if we hadn't been shining the flashlight directly over the spot.

Ura 裏 is an interesting character. The lower portion of it consists of the graph for clothes or robe, *koromo* 衣. The top represents the symbol for cap or the lid of a pot 亠. The middle is the word for home place or village. *Sato* 里. That was also the character for Satoko's name. We stared at the character for a long time trying to figure out what it meant."

"I guess you were trying to get to the other side of underside."

Miyazaki smiled politely at my feeble wordplay.

"Only we weren't able to see the humor at the time. Satoko

began to pull more of fabric through. The colors were glossy, and the fabric felt soft and fresh. She pulled a few more inches when we saw the *hiragana* symbol 'ki' and a few more inches beneath that and slightly off to the side the hiragana 'ri'."

"Kiri? You mean, 'fog?' Or probably 'paulownia'. Was it an indication of a kimono design, maybe? The backside of the paulownia?"

"Good guesses, Ruth-san! We looked closer and saw that the symbol 'ki' was actually 'gi.' The small marks making it a voiced consonant were compromised over time."

"You mean, the word was *giri* as in duty?"

"Another good guess. As just floating sounds, they could mean many things, but with the *ura* several inches above, it was obvious what it meant. *Uragiri*. Betrayal. The young apprentice was signaling his betrayal. Whoever cut the threads had essentially stabbed the apprentice in the back."

Miyazaki paused and looked straight at me for a few seconds before continuing.

"That's when I felt cold fingers wrap around my wrist. It was pitch black in the kura except for the thin yellow beam from the flashlight. With my other hand, I reached over and felt the fingers on my wrist, following the slender hand up the arm and sighed when I realized the fingers belonged to Satoko. 'Ryo!' she said. 'I can't breathe.' I turned to take her in my arms, and I must have struck her other hand accidentally. The flashlight flew out of her grip and clattered to the kura floor. We were nearly in total darkness. Satoko whimpered and buried her face in my chest. And that's when I saw the glow."

"The glow?"

"Yes, a blue wavering glow. I shook Satoko and told her to look. She turned for a second before letting out a low painful scream. The glow disappeared. I dragged Satoko down with me on the floor and we crawled under the platform, scrambling for the light. When we came back up and shone the light on the remnant, it looked much as it had before Satoko dropped the light."

"The glow was gone?"

"Gone. It was gone so completely, we doubted it had even been there in the first place. I don't know. I was sure there was an explanation, and I told Satoko as much. She wasn't as easily convinced.

"I helped her turn the remnant right side out again. She did not want to take the time to re-stitch the seam, but she smoothed the ends under and wrapped the remnant back in the washi paper before tucking it safely in the paulownia box again.

"We couldn't get out of the kura fast enough. But as soon as Satoko had secured the door, I wanted to learn more about the remnant. I told Satoko about the Miyazaki Family Records and that I would check if anything was written there."

"And that's when you found the record Miyazaki Yūzen-sai had left, of his wish to perform a ceremony for the remnant?"

"I didn't find it right away. It took me nearly a year. But when I came across the passage, I told Satoko what I found. She was convinced the spirit of the young apprentice still clung to the remnant, and she wanted to follow through on Grandfather Yūzen-sai's wishes."

"Did she?"

"It wasn't her decision to make. She had to convince her

father."

"I'm sure that wasn't easy."

"It was impossible. Her father always thought of the Tani talisman as a potential money-making opportunity. In fact, he was in negotiations with a museum to try to sell the remnant for an exorbitant fee. The negotiations fell through. But he used the remnant to bind Satoko to him. Anytime she wanted to pursue her own interests, he threatened to sell the piece. She stayed with the family, hoping Daté-san's exposure of the talisman would assist her in her quest to free the remnant from her father's clutches. It had the opposite result. Her story about the apprentice only served to increase the potential value of the remnant."

"I doubt Daté-san had any idea what she was writing would have such influence."

"No, I'm sure she didn't. And Satoko needed to find a way to perform a kuyo for the remnant and release the spirit of the apprentice, which she believed was unhappily attached to it."

"But she didn't ever succeed?"

"I think she probably did."

"She had the remnant burnt?"

"No. I think she relied on transference."

"Transference?"

"Yes. She devoted herself to trying to transfer the spirit from the remnant to its simulacrum."

"You mean, like another kind of art work? A painting or maybe a tattoo?"

Miyazaki stared at me sharply.

"So, you know about the tattoo?"

"Yes," my voice trembled.

Miyazaki silently picked the bolt of fabric off the table and began to roll it up.

"Ruth-san, I'm not sure I ever believed the remnant was possessed, but it seemed Satoko grew possessed during the years she underwent the horishi's needles. That is what you want to talk about, isn't it? Her tattoo?"

"I'm sorry, it's really not any of my business. But during my research I met a member of the Tani household who mentioned the tattoo."

"The more people are sworn to secrecy, the more likely they are to blurt out the truth." Miyazaki eyed me curiously, and I could tell he doubted my story.

"That tattoo meant everything to Satoko. It was as if with each new design, each darkening of the ink, more and more of the apprentice's spirit seeped into her skin. She terrified Akira, but there were times she terrified me, too!"

"What do you think about the police reports of her death, then?"

I hadn't intended to talk about Satoko or her reported suicide, but I couldn't help myself.

"I know Satoko began to identify with the young apprentice, his vision of beauty and thwarted ambitions. She believed she had inherited his spirit, a spirit that had been betrayed. Perhaps those feelings took her to the riverbed, like the disconsolate apprentice and his bereft lover. Are you familiar with the Noh theater?"

I nodded uncertainly, not knowing where his question was leading. In fact, I was a great fan of Noh theater.

"Are you familiar with the play *Izutsu*?"

I nodded.

"In the play a woman, missing her husband, pulls on his court robe and hat, and in the glimmering moonlight, stares at her reflection in the water at the bottom of the well. The moon becomes her face, and overlapped upon her own face is her husband, wrapped in his robes of old. In that momentary shimmer on the surface of the water, the lady becomes the beloved, and the beloved steps forward to comfort the woman he has left behind. There is something magical in the association of the cast-off garment. The discarded robe that once enwrapped the husband, combined with the heart of the woman who loved him dearly, are enough to summon him forward. When she puts on his robe, she becomes him. I think it might have been like that for Satoko."

I understood what he was trying to say about Satoko, but I didn't believe it was a spirit that drove her into the Hokigawa River.

CHAPTER TWELVE
BATS

The air was heavy with the scent of white daphne and wild ginger. A moon was rising, breathing mist along the indigo ridge of mountains in the distance and reflecting off the nodding blooms of Queen Anne's lace. I learned as a child never to collect those blooms; they were loaded with chiggers that burrowed deep into your skin. A butterfly floated up from the meadow and drifted towards the woods. I gave chase, laughing, enjoying the way the tall grass felt as it whipped against my legs and arms. The butterfly flattened mid-flight, a paper slip, a tanzaku with a thin line of verse drifting over the smooth white sheet like the trail of bird tracks. When I lifted my hand to catch the sheet, it slipped through my fingers and into a well. I peered over the side into the darkness. The moon sailed across the sky behind me, illuminating a Noh mask at the bottom of the well. Fukai, the grieving woman, her heart as heavy as a deep, deep well. The face that floated to the surface was etched with age, cheeks hollow, eyes pooling with pain. The water wavered and I saw my own face peering up at me. The moon passing behind me joined my reflection.

In Japan, the man in the moon is a rabbit pounding mochi rice cakes. I always had to turn my head sideways and squint to see the rabbit. There he was. My brother. My brother's face beside mine in the well, smiling. I wheeled around to look behind me, but I saw only the waving grass, the nodding Queen Anne's lace, the ridge of the mountain.

The phone rang. I stared into the darkness until it gave way to the grey behind my eyelids, and I knew I was in my room in the house behind the zoo, and my cell was ringing. By the time I managed to figure out where it was, the call had gone to voice mail.

"Moshi-moshi," I answered groggily when the caller called back. It was Maho.

"Oh, I'm sorry, Ruth. Did I wake you?"

"Um, I'm awake now. How are you, Maho?"

"I'm fine, but I saw Mrs. Shibasaki yesterday at the office, and she told me what's been going on. Are you okay?"

"I'm all right. Thanks for asking."

"Look, I know Daté-san's funeral is today. You're going, right?"

"Yes. What time is it now?"

"It's eight. I'm sorry to call so early."

"No, no, I'm glad you called."

"Ruth, do you want me to go with you? I never met Daté-san. I haven't even read any of her books, but if you need a wingman for the funeral, I'm your girl."

"That's really nice of you to offer. I would appreciate the company."

"I doubt I can be much help to you on funeral protocol. I've only been to one. And that was for my grandfather, but I thought you might like company."

"I would. Do you want to meet me there?"

"I don't mind coming by your house."

I thanked Maho again for her kindness. I needed to hurry, plus I'd hardly thought about preparations. I needed a *kōden* envelope for the funerary offering, so I flipped up my cell and called Maho back, asking if she would pick one up on the way.

"Don't worry. I already have an envelope for you, and one for me, too."

Feeling less stressed, I slid open my closet doors. I'd like to wear a kimono, but I did not have one for a funeral. I did have a black suit.

I rushed to the bathroom to work on my hair, trying to convince it to lay smooth. As I brushed my hair away from my forehead, I remembered my dream. Already forty, I was beginning to look like the Fukai mask. The mask was worn by women who had lost a loved one, frequently a child, but also a lover. The woman in the play *Izutsu* that Miyazaki talked about would have been represented with the Fukai mask. Characters wearing that mask were worn thin by grief, but their souls were deepened by the experience, like a bottomless well. I didn't think I was bottomless. There was a limit for me. I just wasn't sure when I would reach it.

Satisfied I had done the best I could with my hair, I carpeted over the stray ends with hair spray, fanned it dry for a few seconds, and returned to my bedroom to dress. Black shell, black skirt, black jacket, black tights. I had a small clutch purse that was black. I pulled it out of the top bureau drawer, holding it open long enough to rummage around for a string of pearls.

I thumped down the stairs, wincing every so often when I

struck a tender spot, and hobbled into the kitchen. My feet were improving. The doctor had said one week, but I couldn't wait that long. I'd give it another day.

I was adding a coat of polish to my shoes when Maho arrived. I almost didn't recognize her. Her hair was black, and she had removed all the wax from her Mohawk, combing it down to one side. She looked nearly normal. She was dressed much like me in a black suit with black tights and plain black shoes. And she had removed all her visible hardware. I could have hugged her!

"My mother told me to bring these," she said, as she held out two Buddhist *juzu*. "We're supposed to hold them when we pay our respects before the altar. Here are the envelopes. I've already filled mine out."

"I can't tell you how much I appreciate this."

I took the envelope upstairs and searched through my wallet for three rumpled bills to insert in the envelope. Maho told me not to use new bills. She said that implies the death was expected. I carefully wrote my name on the front of the envelope, and the amount on the back, then placed ¥30,000 in the envelope. It was the money I had set aside for the dance recital. I wrapped the envelope in the black silk handkerchief Maho gave me, put it inside my clutch, and headed back downstairs.

Apparently, the family was expecting a large turnout and elected to have the service at a funeral hall, rather than in Daté's home. The hall was close to Kiyomizu-dera Temple. We could see the black and white curtains and tall round funerary stands from a block away. People were lining up outside the entrance to the hall and filing in silently, as greeters in dark suits stood outside and bowed.

When we entered the hall, we went to the reception desk where we handed over our kōden envelopes and entered our names in the registry books. The family sat sullenly on either side of the altar. A large portrait of Daté draped in a black ribbon hung at the front surrounded by a sea of white carnations, chrysanthemums, and lilies. A priest was chanting. I watched the people in front of me pick up a pinch of incense powder, hold it up to their foreheads, and sprinkle it over the burning censor on the altar. Maho and I inched our way to the front. When it was my turn, I bowed to the family members, held my hands encircled by the juzu in front of me in a silent prayer, and offered the incense, bowing again before I moved off to the left.

A priest stood before Daté's coffin chanting a sutra. I looked over my shoulder and was surprised to see the room was almost full. I noticed a photographer with an official press armband.

When the ceremony was over, the funeral hall officials came and wheeled the casket out of the room. The family followed, and the other mourners filed in behind them. The casket was loaded onto a hearse for the short drive to the crematorium. I understood Daté's urn would eventually be returned to Mie Prefecture, where she would be interned alongside her father, mother, and siblings.

Maho and I left as soon as we saw the hearse off. The people at the reception handed out white shopping bags full of parting gifts as we left the building. Maho and I sorted through the items once we were in our taxi heading back to my house: an envelope of gift cards, a small packet of tea, and a little bag of salt. Maho told me I was supposed to sprinkle the salt over my shoulder before I entered my house, to ward off the impurity of death. She walked me as far as my doorstep, made sure I'd sprinkled my salt, and then turned to head home.

I sat for a moment at the dining room table, looking out at the garden behind my house. It needed to be tended. Seeing how unkempt it was reminded me of Daté's tidy garden. I wondered what would happen to her house and all her things.

The smell of incense clung to my clothes and my hair. It was not an unpleasant smell, but I couldn't help feeling it was somehow ill-omened. I was getting ready to head upstairs to take a shower when the doorbell rang. Maybe Maho had changed her mind about going home.

"Hello, Ruth-san."

Tokuda stood in the doorway dressed in a funeral kimono.

I could feel the heat rise to my face as I stared at her with stunned, slack-jawed horror before finally recovering enough to demand, "What are you doing here?"

"I stopped by to talk about the translation."

I thought I noted a slight smirk play about the corners of her lips.

"May I come in?"

Come in? I wanted to shout at her. Come in? So, you can arrange for my suicide, too?

"No, you may not come in. And you know as well as I do that there is no translation. It's all been a big game for you."

"Oh? I'm not sure I understand what you mean."

Again, the twinge of a smirk.

"If you don't want to talk here, I understand. Shall we go to a coffee shop then?"

As long as we were in public, I didn't think she could pull

any of her tricks. And maybe I could coax some clues out of her. At any rate, I wanted answers.

I stepped down into my shoes and picked my clutch off the genkan shelf. Tokuda glanced past my shoulder to the print of the woman in the train.

"The Kashō looks very lovely there."

What she said sent a chill up my spine. I wanted to pummel the smirk right off her face. Instead, I slammed the door as we stepped out into the narrow street behind the zoo. There was a coffee shop two blocks down. The sidewalk wasn't wide enough to walk two abreast. Without thinking, I stepped out ahead of Tokuda, intending to lead the way to the coffee house. As I walked, I could feel her behind me, her darkly hooded eyes boring holes into my back. Any minute now she could slip a dagger out of her obi and stab me in the back. I felt the hairs on the back of my neck tingle as I recalled the way Miyazaki described the underside of the obi. Back stab. I pulled to my left and flattened my back against the wall of the zoo, planning to wave Tokuda ahead of me. That's when I noticed she was nearly three feet behind me. I stepped back into the sidewalk and picked up my pace.

The light was red when we reached the end of the first block. We had to wait momentarily for the traffic light to flash green. The silence between us was so thick it formed a veritable wall that repelled other pedestrians. I suppose we did look formidable, standing amidst the frolicking children in our funeral black, like two giant bats. The light changed, and I charged across. The coffee shop was in sight.

A woman in a mustard yellow uniform and crisp white apron

met us at the door. She led us to a table along the back wall. We sat in stony silence until the waitress returned with our order.

"Why did you do it?" I asked as I poured sugar and cream into my coffee.

"What makes you think I did anything?" Tokuda fished the thin lemon slice off the side of her saucer and slipped it into her tea.

"Please, stop playing games. I know you killed Satoko-san and Daté-san, too. I want to know why."

"Have you forgotten Shōtarō-san? I had him killed, too."

I stared at her without answering. Let her think he was dead. "Why?"

"Ruth-san, do you not know who I am?"

"Tokuda, Niida, you tell me."

I saw her eyebrows twitch slightly when I said "Niida," but she quickly recovered. She rolled the spoon round and round her cup, but she did not take a sip.

"Perhaps you don't remember. You would have been just a little girl."

She looked up at me as she spoke, watching for my reaction. "Remember what?" I wanted to ask.

"It'll be thirty years soon. Thirty years is a long time, Ruth-san. It was a long time to wait, but it was worth it. And I've had other moments of revenge along the way. But this will be the best by far."

"Revenge?"

I had no idea what she was talking about. The longer I sat there, the more I began to suspect she was out of her mind.

"You really don't know who I am, do you?"

I shook my head.

"I'm one of your father's patients."

She arched an eyebrow knowingly and looked up at me under her hooded lids.

"My father had a lot of patients. Be more specific."

"Of course. More specific. I am the patient he cheated out of death and then left with no life to live."

I stared at Tokuda bewildered. She pulled the spoon out of her tea and set it in the saucer beside the cup.

"I had one chance. One chance to give birth to a baby, and he took that away from me. He took my baby away from me. He left me to live a life that was as good as death."

"I am very sorry for whatever happened to you, but I am sure my father did the best he could."

It was slowly beginning to dawn on me that this was the woman in the lawsuit my father had faced, midway through his career. It had been a difficult birth, and he had had to choose between saving the mother or saving the baby.

"That's not good enough."

"What did you expect him to do?"

"Deliver my baby. It was all I asked. All I wanted. And he couldn't even do that."

"But you would have died?"

"I died anyway. Do you know what it is like to hear your husband grieve over the death of his son in the same breath that he begrudges the life of the woman who remained behind? Precious, precious death . . . ugly, putrid life."

You saved the wrong one. That's what the husband told my father while they stood in the recovery room. My father was certain the patient had heard, and he worried even then for her mental state. But later, during the lawsuit, she sat silently beside her husband and his lawyer as they accused my father of malpractice. He had erred in his judgment. He had saved the wrong one.

"I was the greedy one, clinging to life. My husband did not want me around. I was sent away. Divorced."

"I am very sorry you suffered so much heartache, but why did you care so much for a man who had so little respect for you or your life?"

"I didn't much care about him, either. He was a beast, violent and unforgiving. The baby was my revenge."

"I don't understand."

"We had been married for five years and still no baby. He tormented me for it. Calling me the vilest kind of names. As the years wore on, I began to suspect the fault lay with him and not with me."

"You mean, for the inability to conceive?"

"Yes. He wasn't quite the man he thought he was. I took a lover on the sly. And in no time, I was pregnant."

"And you assume it was your lover's child?"

"I knew it was. And I wanted to bequeath this bastard child to my husband."

"Did he know?"

"Of course not. And he never would."

"Then what kind of revenge would that be?"

"The best kind. But when the baby died, his tormenting just grew worse. And I had no second chance."

"But none of this had anything to do with Satoko-san. Why kill her?"

Tokuda smiled.

"Ruth-san, this has been so much fun."

"What?"

"Sometimes things really do come together well."

I stared at Tokuda in disbelief.

"*Isseki nichō.* You have this expression in English, too, don't you?"

"Kill two birds with one stone?"

"Exactly. My husband suffered, too, poor dear. The hospital payout from the lawsuit was considerable. Too much for a man like my husband to handle. He took to gambling and fell into a rough life until he finally hit his pay dirt. He married into a very wealthy family, a family that didn't need children because they could acquire heirs when the need arose. Do you see now, Ruth-san?"

"Tani?" The name came out in a near whisper. Was Akira Tani Tokuda's former husband?

"Ding-ding!" She made the sound of game-show bell. "Oh, what a smart girl you are."

The waitress walked over to our table, refilled our water glasses, and left.

"How dare she," Tokuda continued.

"What?"

"How dare she live the life that was meant for me."

"But Satoko-san had nothing to do with your marriage or the loss of your child."

"And not just her but the whole family. Why does it work for some families but not others?"

"And so, with one stone you took out the two Tani birds? Is that it? What kind of vengeance was that?"

Tokuda laughed

"Is that what you think, Ruth-san? Do you think the Tanis were the object of my vengeance? Were they the little birds so easily felled with that single stone? You underestimate me."

"Explain it to me because I'm getting sick of this game of yours."

Tokuda stared at me out of the corner of her eye. She took a sip of tea and then pulled an envelope out of her obi. She set it on the table and put her finger on it, as if to slide it across the table to me. But she paused.

"The Tanis were more like collateral damage. I hated Akira. I hated Satoko more. I hated her father for his role in manipulating the marriage. He was just like my own father, insisting I marry Akira. And your father, too, Ruth-san, thinking he could decide who to have in a family and who to let go. I wanted Old Man Tani to suffer. I wanted him to lose his children. Stupid man didn't know what he had. Let him lose his children, the way I lost mine. He certainly can't expect Akira to stay there with him now. Once the money is gone, Akira will be gone, too. And it won't take long for them to run through it all. They gamble in high stakes. They'll empty their entire storehouse before long, and Akira will be off for greener pastures. Mr. Tani can rot in hell."

"So, you killed Satoko to get to Mr. Tani?"

"No. You haven't been listening. I killed the Tani children to get to you."

"Me?"

"And through you to your father."

She slid the envelope across the table to me.

"I want him to know what it feels like to lose a child. And I want to be the one who makes that decision."

I took the envelope up and glanced across the table at Tokuda as I lifted up the flap. There was a photograph inside. I pulled it out and saw a picture of a little knobby-kneed boy holding a puppy. It was Matthew.

I exhaled a sigh that was close to a low-pitched wail.

"What did you do?" I hissed.

I couldn't take my eyes off the photograph. It was black and white and a little blurry. Several adult men were in the background, but they were out of focus. Two were holding leashed dogs. There was a woman next to the men. I wondered if it was Tokuda. The soil around them was sandy.

"We removed him," Tokuda says.

"What do you mean, you removed him? Did you kill him? He wasn't even seven years old! How could you? He was just a little boy who liked trains and puppies and ice cream! He was looking forward to second grade. How *could* you?"

I thought my head was going to explode. I couldn't see anything except Tokuda's face. She sat across from me with a smug expression and waited until my breaths grew longer. I sat back in my chair and realized the restaurant had grown silent. I hesitated and then glanced over my shoulder. The waitresses had stopped serving and were standing in their tracks staring at me. A few of the other diners pushed their chairs away from their tables and were craning to see what was going on.

"I didn't say we killed him. I said, we *removed* him."

"We removed him. We removed him? I don't even know what the fuck that means! What do you mean?"

I was trying to keep my voice down, but it was hard to fight the urge to fly across the table and strike Tokuda. She sat there haughtily, watching me struggle.

"Your father removed my son. I removed his. How did it feel, Ruth-san? Did your mother cry? Did your father say, 'it should have been you?' Or maybe that was what your mother said."

"You are not human."

"No? But I have a son. A strange, blue-eyed son. Would you like to see him?"

"He's alive?"

"Yes."

"Where?"

"Come with me, Ruth-san. I'll take you to see my son."

Tokuda pushed her chair away from the table. She picked up the photograph, placed it back in the envelope, and stuffed it in the inner fold of her obi. I followed her as she pushed the door open and stepped outside.

Tokuda walked several steps to the corner of Nijō and Jingū-michi. She stopped, and in a few minutes, a sleek black sedan with tinted windows pulled up alongside her. She opened the backdoor and told me to get in. I hesitated. This was the car I saw at my house earlier.

"Don't you want to see your brother?"

I nodded.

"Then you will need to come with me."

I slid into the backseat. It had leather upholstery but was

covered in a white lace seat cloth. I wanted to get out. Tokuda slipped in beside me and closed the door. She leaned forward and said something to the driver. He pulled out into traffic, heading along Jingū-michi. We passed the library and the museums, turning left on Niomon-dōri. The driver took a quick right onto a smaller street and then began wending his way up towards Awata-guchi. I was surprised when he turned at the entrance to the Miyako Hotel. A bellhop dashed out to the circular drive and pulled my door open. I stepped out. The driver's window was down, and when I turned to look back at the car, the driver looked at me over his shoulder and smiled. It was Detective Kimura. Or at least the man who had represented himself as Kimura, when he stopped by my house and confiscated the manuscript. Tokuda alighted from the other side and came around the back of the car before walking through the entrance to the hotel.

"We've been sitting so long, Ruth-san, I'd like to take a walk. Will you join me?"

I didn't think I had much of a choice.

Tokuda went back out the front door and followed the road towards the Keage crosswalk. There were walking paths through the grounds of the power station that led all the way to the aqueducts at Nanzen Temple. Tokuda turned off onto the path and slowed her pace. We were able to walk two abreast now. I was relieved to see there were others out enjoying the break in the rains.

"Where's my brother?" I demanded.

"Ruth-san, it has been such a pleasure to reel you in. You've been so predictable."

"Reel me in?"

"I'd been wondering how to approach you. How to get you to bite. First there was the matter of your marriage, but it didn't take long before your husband grew tired of always coming in second to your many important projects. And then he finally met a pretty sweet little woman, a woman so unlike you! You got just what you deserved, and you managed that mess almost all on your own. But your professorship, now that took a little more work. Lucky for me, the chair of your department didn't like you one bit. Older Japanese woman, unmarried, not many publications to her name. It must have been awkward for her to have a red-headed American with impeccable Japanese on staff. She couldn't wait to get you out of the department, Ruth. All I had to do was share with her the insubordinate emails you sent to students mocking her."

"I never did any such thing!"

"Didn't you?"

Suddenly, I could see Professor Watanabe glaring at me during faculty meetings. I never understood what I had done to irritate her. She was constantly correcting me in public. My annual reviews became more and more negative. The whole tenure debacle began to make sense. Watanabe had sandbagged my case because of the lies Tokuda had spread.

"Oh, such a shame about your career, Ruth-san. What is it that you call the system of life-long employment?"

"Do you mean, tenure?"

"Tenure, that's right. Too bad about yours. I guess it pays to have friends in high places."

"Where's my brother?"

"I'm getting there, Ruth-san. You'll just have to wait for me to finish, and I'm in no hurry."

Tokuda stopped alongside an azalea still in bloom and pinched off a flower. She twirled it in front of her face, smiling.

"I knew you'd come running back to your precious Japan, Ruth-san, once you ruined your career in the United States. When I had you back here, it took me a while to devise a way to approach you. I don't know why I didn't think of using Shōtarō Tani sooner."

We exited the azalea garden and crossed Sanjō towards Anyō-ji Temple. A set of old concrete stairs led us up towards the Keage Incline.

"As I was saying, it has been fun to bait you, Ruth-san. Don't you see? You've been my prize all along. Your losing tenure, your flight back to Kyoto in disgrace. And that's when I saw how to lure you into my trap. You with your insatiable interest in Japanese literature matched only by your unreasonable ego. The translation ploy was almost too easy."

She stopped and turned to me.

"What do you think, Ruth-san? Do I have a career as a writer?"

"You posed as Shōtarō Tani-san to get access to me? But why?"

"Just to watch you simmer away in your misplaced pride, believing yourself to be a great translator."

"But why kill Satoko-san and Daté-san?"

"And Shōtarō, too, you know. I wanted their father to feel what it was like to be bereft."

"But he doesn't know it was you. The police are calling Satoko-san's death a suicide."

"He knows."

Her voice was so ominous, I shivered. The wind whipping along the concrete water trough was growing cold. I was relieved when Tokuda started to walk again.

"But why kill Daté-san? She never hurt you."

"She helped me get to you. I enjoy watching you suffer."

We turned along the path that led to the aqueduct. There were fewer people now. I began to feel nervous. The water in the trough was high and swift after all the rain. Tokuda peered into the current and stepped up on the edge of the concrete trough. It was at least three feet wide and permitted walking. I had walked along it many times in the past, but I felt queasy seeing her up there.

"Where's my brother?"

"Your brother . . . yes. What a sweet little boy he was. And now he's so tall. I suppose he gets his height from his father."

"Stop this. Tell me where he is."

Tokuda turned towards me glaring down at me like some demented guardian statue.

"Did you think it was going to be that easy?"

She pulled the envelope with the photo out of her obi and waved it in front of me.

"You'll never see your brother again."

She tossed the envelope over her shoulder. It floated upwards for a sliver of a second, caught on a gust of wind, and then drifted capriciously over the edge of the trough. Horrified, I reached out to grab it, but the envelope evaded my grasp. Tokuda stepped back instinctively. I turned to watch as she took a second step back, her foot floating momentarily over the rushing water before she plummeted. I leapt to the edge to look over and saw her slide into the water, too far beneath me now for me to reach her. She stared up at me as the current filled her right sleeve and tugged at the hem of her kimono, slowly pulling her in deeper. A sneer played along her lips. I ran along the trough, trying to keep sight of her dark figure gliding just beneath the surface of the water. She then disappeared into the narrow tunnel at the end of the sluice.

I scrambled down the steep embankment as fast as I could, trying not to lose my balance. There were people below, and they looked up at me not certain whether to laugh at the spectacle I cut, or to be alarmed.

"Help!" I finally found words. "Help! A woman has fallen in!"

The people walking near the aqueduct just stared at me. No one moved. I finally had the presence of mind to take out my cell phone and call the emergency number, 119. As we talked, I could hear the sirens.

The water in the sluice eventually spills out into a water treatment plant near the zoo and then feeds into a canal running along Niomon-dōri. Unfortunately, the sluice ends in a floodgate. Once Tokuda's body entered the tunnel, it would not automatically wash out the other side, because it would be trapped by the gate. The police officer on the scene began a process of negotiations with the Kyoto Waterworks Bureau to see if it would be possible to open the gate.

Another police officer had me walk back with him to the site where Tokuda fell. I explained what had happened. He shook his head and drew air in through his teeth. It didn't look good.

"And you say she was under the water?"

"Yes, yes. The current carried her down."

"But she seemed to be conscious?"

"She was looking at me!"

The officer took a flashlight off his belt and shone it into the tunnel. The opening was large, six feet high and just as wide. I couldn't tell if the tunnel narrowed further in or remained the same size. The officer crawled up on the parapet surrounding the sluice and leaned over tentatively to peer inside the tunnel. He shook his head and sucked more air through his teeth.

Another team of rescue workers arrived and roped up a man in a wet suit. He stepped into the sluice. The rope immediately grew taut as he was quickly pulled into the tunnel. I could see his team members slowly releasing more and more of the rope. After a few minutes, they began pulling the rope back, reeling the man in. He shook his head, having not found a body.

"I couldn't get as far as the grate," he said. "I didn't see a body. It's possible the body is snagged on something closer to the tunnel entrance here where it's deeper. If that's the case, we're too late."

He and his crew continued to probe the tunnel. The police officer asked me to accompany him to the police station. We went back to the Kawabata Police Station, the same station Mrs. Shibasaki and I visited after Daté's death. I wondered if I would see Officer Murano again. I hoped not.

We entered the building through the back entrance, and I was led immediately to one of the interrogation rooms. The officer who attended me this time was named Moriyama.

I went through it all over again—Daté's death, the bogus novel, my brother's disappearance. I begged the officer to please find out Tokuda's identity, so I could search for my brother. But the officer very politely informed me that first they would have to confirm the existence of a Tokuda.

"Do you think I could have made this all up?"

"Please calm down and tell me about it again."

"Look, if you don't believe me, go to the Miyako Hotel. The bellhops saw her. They can confirm her existence!"

"Yes of course, we have someone over there now. Don't worry Bennett-san, I believe you."

But something told me he had his doubts.

Once again, I left the police station dispirited. My right knee was throbbing. Even though my house was only a few blocks from the station, I hailed a cab and took it home.

I called my parents as soon as I got in. It was still early in the morning on the East Coast, but I didn't care. It had been months since we last spoke.

"Ruth, is that you?"

Hearing my father's voice brought a lump to my throat. I had a hard time biting back my emotion.

"Oh Daddy, I'm sorry to call you so early, but I have news."

"News? Are you all right? Has something happened?"

"You'd better put Mother on the phone, too."

"Well, sure, just a minute."

I could hear him call softly to my mother. She must have

been next to him in the bed. The phone line was crisp and clear, as if they were just across the street. I could remember phone calls to my grandparents when I was little. Back then the line was often full of static. I always pictured the cable inching its way along the ocean floor, being buffeted by waves. On occasion when we would get cut off unexpectedly, my father would tell me a giant swordfish had cut the line.

"Ruth?" my mother came on the line, her voice thick with sleep.

"I'm sorry to wake you up, Mother, I just wanted you both to hear. I have news about Matthew."

"What?"

I went through the story again, trying to condense it to the most relevant parts.

"Now wait a minute, Ruth, just slow down."

"I'm sorry. I know this sounds crazy. But I think we've found out what happened to Matthew. Daddy, it was one of your patients. The one who tried to sue you. Do you remember?"

"Well, I remember some of it, but Ruth that was a long time ago."

"I know, but I'm sure the hospital still has her records. They'll have information about her family, won't they? She most likely was keeping Matthew with one of her relatives."

"But we can't access her records, Ruth. Those are sealed."

"Daddy, this is important!"

"I know, honey, but it's the law. The hospital will not release that information."

"Well, can't you remember anything? Where was she from?"

"I had a lot of patients. And in the case of the lawsuit, it was the husband who stands out in my memory. I can hardly remember the poor woman."

"Daddy, the poor woman kidnapped your son! Please, try to help me."

"Ruth," my mother chimed in. "You need to get a hold of yourself. Matthew's gone. Remember, honey? The police told us years ago there was no chance of ever finding him. They declared him dead. We've been over this. That woman, whoever she is, is just playing a cruel joke on you. She doesn't have Matthew. He's gone, sweetheart."

"We don't know that, Mother! The police were wrong. They just wanted you to stop bothering them. And you did, didn't you? You gave up way too quickly. But I didn't. I have to try."

"Did she say anything that made you believe he's still alive?" my father tried to defuse the tension.

"She said he was tall."

"Oh, honey," my mother blurted. "Have you looked in the mirror? You're five foot ten. What are the chances of any brother of yours being anything but tall?"

"I know she took him. I know he's still alive. Please, why won't you help me!? He's your son."

I began to cry. It was as if all the anger and fear and pain I'd been storing up these last few weeks just burst forth.

"Sweetheart," my father called out to me several times.

"Ruth," now it was my mother's voice. "It's time for you to come home."

"Home? Where's my *home*, Mother? Is it with you? I seem to recall I was turned out of that home when I was fifteen."

"Oh, honey, don't start that again, you're upsetting your

mother."

"I'm sorry. I guess I just thought you might be a little more supportive."

"I'll see if I can't find any of the documents from the trial. But your mother's right, Ruth. It's time for you to come home."

"Matthew is my home, Daddy. I'm not leaving without him."

CHAPTER THIRTEEN
SPARROWS

As a child, my mother read to my brother and me before bedtime on those evenings when she was not on the night shift at the hospital. We had a collection of Japanese fairytales, and our favorite was the "Tongue-cut Sparrow." She knew it by heart, but we'd insist she hold the book on her lap as we curled up next to her. There were pictures.

"*Mukashi-mukashi*, there was an old man and an old woman."

Mother would begin, her voice taking on the sonorous tone of an old-fashioned storyteller. "They had no children."

"Why?" Matthew would interrupt.

"Sshhh," Mother would say, caressing the top of his head, "listen."

"One day, the old man found an injured sparrow and brought it home to heal. He fed it grains of rice. This made the old woman angry. 'We barely have enough to feed ourselves,' she grumbled. When the old man left to cut wood, the old woman pounded the rice into starch. Then she went to the river to wash the clothes. When she came back, the starch was gone. It had found its way into the little bird's tummy. Enraged, the old woman took up her sharp scissors and snipped out the sparrow's tongue. Then she threw the bloodied bird out to die.

"The old man was heartbroken when he returned and learned what had happened. Then one day, he saw his sparrow friend again. The sparrow took the old man to his house. The sparrow wife set out a feast and the sparrow daughters danced and sang. When the old man had to leave, the sparrow set two parting gifts before him and offered him a choice. Not being greedy, the old man selected the smaller of the two and went on his way. Back at home, the old woman scolded him for being gone so long. But when he opened his parting gift, she saw it was full of gold and silver and other precious treasures. 'Well, I'll just pay a visit on the sparrow myself and get another parting gift!'

"The sparrow received the old woman and served her coarse tea. Neither his wife nor daughters made an appearance. The old woman waited and then decided it was time to go. 'Where is my parting gift?' she demanded. The sparrow graciously brought out two packages and asked the woman to choose between them. She picked each one up and decided on the heavier of the two. Then she left the sparrow's house without so much as a thank you. When she got home, she tore open the gift, only to find it contained the vilest possible monsters. They leapt out at her and tore her limb from limb.

"This must have been a horrible sight for the old man. But before long, he adopted a son and the two of them lived together in peaceful contentment. When the old man finally died, his son inherited all his riches, along with his spirit of compassion."

I have the book my mother read. After all the moves I've made, and all the books I accumulated over the years, this is the only one I've held onto. Matthew had scribbled in the margins of the "Tongue-Cut Sparrow." He had drawn horns on the old woman's head. On the last page of the story, he drew a smiling boy next to the old man.

"What does the story teach us?" my mother had asked.

"Not to be greedy!" I answered.

"Not to hurt birds," Matthew shouted. "Only bad people hurt animals!"

Matthew glared up at Mother with the sharp righteousness of a child. With every breath in his tiny body, he was ready to defend any animal in pain.

Mother laughed and tousled his hair. Then she gave him a quick kiss. She should have told us the story teaches us not to trust mean old women.

In the weeks following Tokuda's disappearance, I continued to haunt the Kawabata Police Station, seeking answers to some of the puzzles I encountered. Officer Moriyama proved to be more accommodating than his predecessor. He told me that when the Kyoto Waterworks Bureau opened the floodgates at the end of the sluice, they found a woman's black zori sandal caught in the metal mesh of the gate, but there was no sign of a body.

Although the bellhop at the Miyako Hotel confirmed seeing me with an older woman in a black funeral kimono, he was unable to provide any other information. At least, he corroborated my story. I was tired of being made to feel I was inventing things or over-reacting. It was the bellhop's corroboration that encouraged Moriyama to investigate. He made inquiries at the Miyako Hotel but was unable to locate a reservation for anyone meeting Tokuda's description. He even tried his best to get information out of the Iwakura Christian Hospital. But as my father warned, they refused to divulge any information on any of their past patients without a warrant.

No one believed me when I told them Tokuda confessed to two murders, three if you count Shōtarō, though, of course, he'd been declared dead long ago. When I tried to press the police to re-open the Daté and Satoko cases, they just waved me aside.

I decided to try a different tack. I asked my parents to try to ferret out information on Tokuda through more "informal" channels. Although initially reluctant to do so, my father agreed to reach out to one of the staff members he and my mother worked with at the Iwakura Christian Hospital. Mrs. Ino assisted my father when he served in the obstetrics unit and was the nurse on call when my brother was born. When he'd gone missing, she spent her vacation days near Yase Hieizan-guchi knocking on doors and asking if anyone had seen the little tow-headed boy. I met her one afternoon at a nearby café.

"Ruth-chan, I'm not even sure where those records are now."

Mrs. Ino had soft grey hair cut in a stylish asymmetrical bob. She wore large red plastic-rimmed glasses and looked more like a fashion-designer or art critic than she did a nurse.

"I know it's a long shot, but if I can just get more information about that patient, I think I can track her family down. My mother thinks the woman is just toying with me. She's probably right. But still, I can't rest until I've exhausted every angle."

"I'm sorry this has happened. Ma-chan was such a good boy."

I hadn't heard my little brother referred to as Ma-chan in a long time. Mrs. Ino gave him the name. When she started working at the hospital, she was a single woman with the last name of Tamura. Matthew was the first baby she helped deliver. She seemed almost more upset with his disappearance than his own mother. It was hard to understand my parents' apparent lack of concern over their missing son. They struggled to keep a calm demeanor in public and never wanted to appear as if they were angry with the Japanese people for what happened. I think the effort to remain passive and positive in the face of intrusive media coverage forced my mother to turn her emotions off completely. She never really turned them back on. She remained competent at her job from a skill level, but she lost the human warmth people usually expect from a nurse, and certainly from a mother.

Mrs. Ino was just the opposite. The press was not particularly interested in her, and she never had to worry about the effect her behavior might have on others. I remember visiting my parents in the hospital shortly after the disappearance and finding her deep in tears. The sight of her blood-shot eyes gave me a huge sense of release. At least someone was grieving for Matthew. At the same time, the sight of her tears only made me resent my mother more. I resented her calm demeanor, and her refusal to break out in a hysterical tirade against the ineptitude of the Japanese investigators. I resented the fact I was expected to persist with my sweet face, like a good little girl, a model Christian girl.

"Ruth-chan, I'll talk to Keiko-san in records and see if she can help me. I wish I remembered more about that patient. But I wasn't there the night she lost her baby. And your parents never talked about the lawsuit with the hospital staff."

I thanked Mrs. Ino and headed back to my house. She hadn't had an easy life either. She married at twenty-eight, late for women of her generation. She hadn't resigned her position after marriage, which raised a number of eyebrows. Instead, she continued working as a nurse. When her husband died two years later, before they could start their own family, many whispered it was what she deserved. Never having had a child of her own, she treated Matthew and me like her surrogate children. I knew she'd do whatever she could to help find him.

A few days later she called to tell me she had taken a look at the file.

"I really owe Keiko-san. She let me into the room while she stepped out to visit the restroom. She just happened to leave the file I wanted on her desk. I opened and read it as quickly as I could. Next time I do something like this, I'm going to have to bring my camera!"

Mrs. Ino jotted down notes as soon as she got back to her station. The patient was named Miyo Yoshida Hamada and her husband was Akira Hamada. Her birthplace was listed as Shirohama City in Shikoku.

I thanked Mrs. Ino for her great detective work, and asked her once again to keep her sleuthing a secret. Then I called Maho. Her boyfriend Hawk promised to sketch my brother based on an old photograph I gave him. More importantly, Hawk believed he could age the sketch by thirty years from the photograph.

I thought the sketch looked surprisingly good. After Maho dropped it by my house, I went to the 7-Eleven and made copies. I had already made copies of an old photograph of Matthew with my phone number at the bottom of the sheet and a request for a phone call from anyone with information on the little boy in the picture, who went missing thirty years ago. The photograph was appealing, with a smiling boy looking mischievously at the camera, his blue eyes the color of the sky.

It wasn't easy to get to Shirohama, but certainly not as hard as it was before the Great Seto Bridge was built. Even with the bridge, though, Shikoku felt remote. It took me little over three hours to reach Kōchi by train, and from there I took a bus for another hour and a half.

The Shikoku landscape was breathtakingly beautiful. Large craggy rocks stacked up along the Pacific—the waves foaming white as they lashed the shore. Here and there as the bus rounded the curves hugging the mountain, I caught sight of steep precipices tumbling sharply to the sea. The townships along the way to Shirohama were rundown and weather-beaten. A lot of the seaside restaurants were boarded over.

Once the bus reached Shirohama, I set off looking for the address Mrs. Ino gave me, the address Tokuda had noted when she registered at the hospital those thirty some year ago. I couldn't imagine anyone would be there who remembered her. But it was worth a try. I felt for the folder in my bag with the photograph of Matthew. I pulled the map out and tried to get my bearings. Ukitsu no. 28. It should be down the road that runs perpendicular to the bus route. I found my first landmark, the local post office, and then turned left down a narrow, dusty road. Ukitsu no. 28 was next to an empty lot, strewn with trash and thick with weeds. No. 28 looked abandoned. I knocked and waited. There was no sound of life. I looked up the street and saw an old woman heading my way. She was pulling a small grocery cart. I stopped her and asked about the occupants of the house.

"No, moved a long time ago."

"Do you know where they went?"

"Old Man Yoshida died a few years back. He had his dog pen right there. It's gone too."

"Dog pen?"

"He raised Tosa dogs."

"The fighting dog?" Her dialect was so thick I wasn't sure I had understood.

"They were so mean. We were all too scared to pass his house. All that barking and yelping. I was glad when he died, I'm sorry to say."

"When was that?"

"It's been awhile. I don't think I really remember."

"Did he have any children? A daughter, perhaps?"

"I believe he did. Some sons and a daughter, it seems. I'm not really sure. Like I said, I was afraid to come too close to this place back in the day. But my husband might know. He had dealings with Old Man Yoshida."

"I'm sorry, but it's rather urgent. May I speak to your husband?"

"Sure, sure, he's not doing anything anymore except sitting. Come on by the house."

I followed her down the street and through a small alley. We came upon a roadside shrine, two oblong rocks wrapped in red bibs under a grey weathered roof. She stopped and brought a bottle of water out from her cart, poured a small amount in the porcelain cups in front of the rocks, and folded her hands together in prayer. She clapped twice, tied up the bag in her cart, and started off again, pulling her cart behind her. I followed. We made a few more turns then came upon a slightly wider street lined by stone walls. She opened the battered gate in front of an old wooden house and led me in.

"Ossan! We have a visitor," she called out to her husband.

The house was dark inside and stuffy with the smell of mothballs, fish, and mosquito smudge. A faded curtain hung between the entrance hall and the inner room. I heard shuffling and then an old man stepped through the curtains wearing rumpled white undergarments of thin cotton, a beige bellyband wrapped tightly around his waist. He was stooped and wrinkled but looked friendly. He pulled a cushion out from the room behind him and had me sit on the entryway step. He knelt beside me on the bare floor as his wife scrambled slowly up into the house, leaving her cart in the entryway.

"I'll get you some tea," she said as she disappeared behind the curtain.

I explained why I was there and asked the man what he might know about the Yoshidas.

"Oh, they were a frightful family."

"In what way?"

"Old Man Yoshida raised fighting dogs. They were as mean as they could be, but he was meaner. His dogs did well, though. He produced some champions even, and breeders came from miles around to breed off his stock. But he couldn't lay off the drink long enough to build up his business. He had two sons who weren't worth a damn. His daughter was rather pretty. He married her off to a fellow from Tokushima who also liked dogs. Seems he got a job in Kyoto and before too long, she came home. I'd see her here now and then."

I pulled my photo of Matthew out of my bag and held it out to the old man.

"Did you ever see this little boy around here?"

The old man looked closely at the photo and shook his head. "Not that I can tell. But I spent most of my time in my shop. I had a fishing supply store down by the harbor. I used to sell Old Man Yoshida the scrap fish the trawlers dragged in."

The old woman came in with a tray of tea and sat beside her husband. She placed a cup in front of me and set another beside her husband. I showed her the photo.

"I can't say I've ever seen a little boy who looked like that around here."

"Would there be anyone else who knew the Yoshidas?"

"Well, let's see. That really was a long time ago, wasn't it? Most everyone who lived around here then is either dead, gone, or senile." The old woman covered her mouth with her gnarled hand as she let loose with a laugh. "I suppose you might ask at the Health and Welfare Center. That's where all the old-timers are anymore."

I gave the old couple one of my posters and asked them to call me if they should ever remember anything about the blond-haired boy—or think of someone who might. I thanked them and left.

The Health and Welfare Center was in a fairly new building, spacious and sprawling. It was cool inside. I found my way to the reception desk and explained my quest. The man staffing the desk looked to be about Tokuda's age. He claimed to have no knowledge of the Yoshidas. When I suggested the father had raised dogs, hoping that would jog his memory, he launched excitedly into a long discussion of the attributes of the Tosa breed.

"Built to fight!" he exclaimed.

The Tosa breed, I was soon to learn, was started in the late nineteenth century. The originator of the breed took the indigenous Shikoku-ken, a smart, compact little hunting dog known for its loyalty, and bred it to mastiffs, Great Danes, bulldogs, and Saint Bernards. The aim was to produce a bigger, meaner dog for fighting. Fortunately, the heyday of the Tosa breed passed, and the dogs were banned in most European countries because of their perceived viciousness. The man at the reception did not seem to find this a problem, though. I thanked him for his time and stepped away from the desk. I couldn't bear the idea of my gentle little brother falling into the clutches of a family who bred fighting dogs.

I tacked some posters on the bulletin boards throughout the Center and stepped out on the gateball courts. It was now too hot in the day to be outside playing. I didn't find any elderly residents, so I spent the rest of the day wandering through the town. I stopped by the city hall and the police station, asking the same questions wherever I went, and getting much the same answer. Some people were eager to talk about the Yoshidas. And it seemed opinion was split on whether they had been an asset to the town or a detriment. However, everyone was unanimous in knowing nothing further about the whereabouts of the Yoshida clan. It seems they all died out. The record keeper at City Hall was very clear about that. All the entries in the family record, save for that of the daughter, who produced no children, were now marked deceased. The clerk had no idea what had become of the daughter. The children listed as the offspring of her two brothers were still shown as living at Ukitsu no. 28. The latest entry to the family registry was dated 1979, when Tokuda returned to her father's household. In a fit of desperation, I let my guard down with the police captain. He had been friendly enough when I first met him, telling me about the declining population in the city and the urgency officials felt there to try to retain their young people. I let him know I was looking for my brother. When I inferred that he might have been kidnapped and brought here, the captain's expression changed.

"Absolutely not! We would have noticed a little *gaijin* boy in our town. And we would not have let him remain without asking questions. Look around. You'll see this is a small town without many secrets. If he'd been here, someone would have known."

I spent the night at a small but tidy inn a few blocks from the harbor. The next morning after a quick breakfast, I checked out and tacked more posters up along the wharf, the local clinic, and the library. With time to spare before the bus to Kōchi, I decided to read up on the Tosa dog in the library. A quick perusal of the card catalog showed the library had an impressive stock of books on the breed. I selected a number and took a seat at the long reading table.

I started first with the photographic books. Most of the dogs were reddish, with big heads and droopy jowls like a mastiff. They didn't seem as beefy as a Rottweiler but were long and lean and almost looked like bloodhounds. Some were pictured next to children, an obvious ploy to demonstrate their gentle dispositions. In other photos, they were festooned like the highest-level sumō champions with the thick white cord knotted around their neck and chest and paper streamers attached to brocade aprons.

The book stacks in the library were not open to browsing. To request a book, I had to fill out a form, drop it in a box, and then sit in front of the counter to wait until my number was called. Given that I was the only person in the library, the librarian couldn't help but note my presence and what must have seemed my peculiar fascination. When I was called to the counter to retrieve the next book I requested, he asked me about my interests.

"Are you looking for a Tosa dog?"

The librarian was late middle-aged with a heavy shock of silvery hair and a very visible gold tooth. He smiled when he asked the question.

I smiled back.

"No. I want to know more about the Yoshida family and their Tosa dogs."

"Oh, well you won't find what you're looking for in any of those books. Just a minute and I'll bring you one of our old pamphlets."

He pushed his chair back, stood, and entered a small office behind a row of loose periodicals. He returned with a clear, cellophane envelope and carefully pulled out what seemed to be a catalog from an old dog competition.

"For years, we hosted the annual Tosa Fighting Dogs Competition and the Yoshida dogs took all the top prizes. Our big year was 1982. We had a lot of dog owners, trainers, and handlers who came here from all across Japan, some even from overseas. The competition went on for a week, so the town was full of life. All the restaurants filled; hotels booked up. You wouldn't believe this was the same town now. Just look at this."

The librarian, whose name tag read "Iizuka," pointed to a photograph showing the street paralleling the wharf. When I saw it yesterday, it was full of boarded up storefronts. But in the photograph, the street was lined with people watching a parade of long-limbed dogs decked out in sumō paraphernalia.

"Yes, and see here. We had visitors from all around the world."

The next photograph he showed me depicted a group of large white men, their hair tousled in the sea breeze, standing proudly alongside their heavily leashed dogs. The dogs were enormous and seemed to be a mixture of different breeds. I could recognize Saint Bernards, but the rest just looked big and beefy.

"Yoshida did really well that year, see. That was after he started collaborating with the Scotsman."

He directed my attention to a photograph of two men standing next to a massive dog. One of the men was Japanese, tan and rugged, with a headband twisted tightly around his bald pate. The other was paunchy. He looked miserably overheated in his tweed blazer and necktie.

"So, this is Yoshida?" I asked, indicating the Japanese man.

"Right. He was the biggest dog breeder in town. His dogs had always been strong, but they got even stronger after he started breeding to foreign dogs."

"Is that one of Yoshida's dogs there?" I asked. The dog in the photograph was huge, with a long, slack, black muzzle, deep-set watery eyes, and massive shoulders. His nose and chest were covered with white splotches.

"Yes. That's one he bred off the foreign dog."

"Is that why he has those white spots?"

"Those? No, that's the ointment they put on the wounds following the fight. This fellow won. I'm not sure what happened to the other dog."

The whole concept of dog fighting made me angry. But I held my tongue, hoping to get a bit more information on Yoshida.

"What happened to Yoshida after this?"

"Can't say for sure. He went the rounds of the championships and did well, but it seems he and the Scotsman had a falling out. After that, things went down for Yoshida. He made some bad investments and word is he gambled away whatever money he made. Or drank it. One evening he got so drunk he fell off the end of the pier and that was the end of Yoshida. His sons came down from Tokyo and sold off the rest of the dogs."

"What was the falling out about?"

"With the Scotsman? He partnered with his son-in-law for a bit, and it seems the stakes got higher than the Scotsman wanted to go. Yoshida bought him out. Traded for his best breeding pair. That's the last we saw of the Scotsman."

"His son-in-law?" I interrupted. "Do you mean Akira Hamada?"

"That's right, but he would have been Akira Tani by then. He changed his registry about the time the Tani family adopted a heir."

"You mean, Mr. Yoshida did business with Akira even after he divorced his daughter?"

"Business is business. As mean as Yoshida was, I don't think he held anything against Akira for leaving the family. The Tani family had connections and money to back them up. Seems Yoshida made better profit off his son-in-law being a Tani than he did with him as a Hamada. Sure, I'd see all three of them down at the wharf some evenings enjoying a beer at the chicken grill."

"All three?"

"Yoshida, his daughter, and Akira."

That was odd. Tokuda made it sound as though Akira abandoned her and then took up with Satoko. Could he have continued to see her on the side? If so, then she would hardly have been motivated to kill Satoko to get back at Akira for dumping her. Something else was at work here.

"Do you have some business with these folks?" Mr. Iizuka asked, noticing my frown. "They aren't a good class of people. Seems like they always had some scam going when they were here. You'd be wise to stay clear of them if you ask me."

I thanked the librarian for his advice and then remembered the photograph of Matthew. I wanted to show it to him, but I had to leave my bags and papers in a locker at the library entrance, so I didn't have it with me. I explained to the librarian I wanted to show him something in the locker and asked permission to bring it into the library. Intrigued, he was more than happy to oblige. He followed me out to the locker room where he peered over my shoulder while I fished out the photograph.

"This boy. Did you ever see this boy here?" I asked, pointing at Matthew.

The librarian pulled a pair of reading glasses out of his shirt pocket and took the photograph from me.

"Well, I'll be. That's the Scotsman's little boy. Cute little fellow. Curious, too. He spoke Japanese like a native. They say kids pick up language fast . . ."

"The Scotsman's boy?" I think I must have shouted the question. Mr. Iizuka looked up at me so abruptly his glasses nearly slipped off his nose.

"Yes, I'm pretty sure that's who that is." He tucked his glasses back in his pocket. "Come back to the desk, and I'll show you."

He started back into the reading room. "Bring that photo with you, too."

I quickly stuffed my belongings back in the locker and hurried after him, my heart beating so loudly I was afraid it was going to explode my eardrums.

Mr. Iizuka thumbed through the catalog, carefully turning the pages back and forth while I danced excitedly from one foot to the other.

"Here, see? Doesn't that look like the same boy?"

He pointed to a photograph of the Scotsman standing next to a thin, towheaded boy. The boy had his arms wrapped around the massive head of the same slack-jowled dog I'd seen in the photograph with Yoshida. The boy was grinning shyly, his knobby knees protruding from his short pants. He looked tan and freckled. It was Matthew.

I could feel my pulse racing, the roar in my head now deafening. I guess my face must have drained of color because the librarian asked with a tinge of worry. "Is there something wrong?"

"No, no. There's nothing wrong. Nothing at all," I managed to utter when I could finally get my tongue to work.

"May I, may I take this catalog with me?"

The librarian almost gasped. "No, you may not," he said, gingerly sliding it off the counter and away from my grasp. "This is not a lending library."

"Then, may I have a copy?" I asked, beginning to feel desperate.

"Oh, it's not the kind of material we're permitted to copy."

"It's just that, I think this little boy is my brother. He disappeared when he was nearly seven, and I have reason to believe Yoshida's daughter brought him here. I really need to show this pamphlet to the authorities in Kyoto. I need them to re-open their investigation, particularly in light of a number of recent murders and Yoshida's daughter's sudden death. I really need a copy. Please."

"We have strict guidelines about what we can copy, I'm afraid I can't help you."

"Isn't there some way? Some exception? May I request an exception? This is the first proof I've found that my brother was taken from Kyoto. Is there another copy of this catalogue somewhere else, a secondhand bookstore? Anywhere? I'll pay whatever it takes, please. He was just a little boy!"

"Wait a minute."

The librarian carefully slid the catalog back into the cellophane envelope, then walked over to a battered filing cabinet, taking the catalog with him. He pulled open one drawer after another until he found what he was searching for. He dragged a well-worn folder out of the open drawer and spread it out on his desk, thumbing through the thin sheaf of papers. I watched, afraid to breathe. He reached in his pocket, pulled his glasses out again, and slowly read up and down one page and then another. Finally, he was satisfied he had what he wanted and returned to the counter where I was standing.

"Fill this out."

I wasn't certain what the form provided, but I filled it out, giving my name, address, and occupation. When I came to a space asking for the title of the material I was requesting, the librarian instructed me to write: Tosa Dog Competition 1982. And then, in the space for "purpose" he recommended I write "research." I did as instructed, handing the form back to the librarian.

"I'll find you a copy, or I'll make you a copy. Give me a few weeks."

A few weeks! I wanted to protest. But I knew Mr. Iizuka was doing the best he could for me. Trying to topple centuries of administrative red tape and bureaucracy was a losing battle. I needed to be patient.

"Thank you," I said and bowed deeply.

I didn't have much time before the bus arrived. I thought about rearranging my schedule, so I could stay in Shirohama another day, but Mrs. Shibasaki was expecting me back in the office tomorrow. Given the stringent library policies and the hostility of the police captain, I felt there was little more I could do here. Probably best to have Mr. Iizuka send the materials and then return when I better understood the way this town worked and what it had to offer.

"Do we know the name of the Scotsman?" I asked the librarian, as I was preparing to leave.

"We always referred to him as the Scotsman. He might be registered with the registry of qualified Tosa Breeders, but that's in Kōchi. I don't think he actually bred the Tosa dog, so he may not be there. The bullmastiff was his dog. That's the breed he brought over and sold to Yoshida."

He went back to his desk and brought the envelope with the catalog. Then he lifted the catalogue out again and thumbed through the pages until he came to a picture of the Scotsman standing next to a large brindle-coated dog.

"That's the bullmastiff," he said.

I really could not distinguish the bullmastiff from the Tosa. I guess the mastiff was squatter with a squarer head, and frankly more intelligent looking. But that was all just based on one dog. And that dog must have been the Scotsman's pride and joy. The Scotsman looked about as puffed up as the dog, standing erect, a cane of sorts in his left hand, his right hand alongside his leg next to the dog. I wondered if the photograph was taken in Scotland. They seemed to be standing in a meadow, behind them a rock wall twisted and wound beyond the horizon. While I studied the photograph, Mr. Iizuka slipped back into the office and made a copy of the request form he asked me to fill out. He handed it to me as I prepared to take my leave. I hadn't thought to ask for a copy. As I took the thin piece of paper, I felt touched by this small but certain kindness on the librarian's part.

It took twenty minutes to walk from the library to the bus station. The buses came and departed infrequently. If I missed the 2:17, I wouldn't be able to make my train connection in Kōchi. But in Japan, even in rural towns like this, transportation systems operate with certain precision. I could trust the bus to be on schedule. I just couldn't guarantee I would be there to meet it. I had to hustle. The sun was high overhead now and the broken blacktop was so hot it seemed almost gooey underfoot. I could feel the sweat soak into the pack I had on my back. By the time I made it to the bus, my hair was plastered to my forehead and cheeks.

The bus was pulling up to the shed just as I arrived. Once the four or five passengers alighted, the bus driver also stepped off and closed the bus door after him, while he sauntered over to the wharf to take a smoke and check in with the scheduler.

The few passengers for the Kōchi trip lined up outside the door, where the engine still blew off heat and fumes. I chose to stand in the sliver of shade cast by the shed. There were only seven people waiting to embark. By the time the driver returned, just five minutes or so later, the crowd had grown to nearly twenty. It surprised me to see so many people. There were more lined up than I had seen practically my entire time in Shirohama.

The driver started the bus and allowed us to board. I took a window seat in the back and enjoyed the cool whoosh of air-conditioned air pouring through the vent overhead. We were on the road in minutes, winding our way back around the narrow curves, veering sickeningly close to the edge. I squeezed my eyes closed until we were almost to Kōchi, my mind in a whirl. Was Matthew alive then? Was he in Scotland? Was I returning with good news or bad? I really wasn't certain what to think.

At Kōchi, I hurried to catch the 4:30 train bound to Kyoto. Once ensconced in my seat, I was finally able to relax a little. I had to change trains once more in Okayama, but that would be an easy transfer. I reclined my seat and peered out the window at the passing rice fields and the occasional mountain shrine.

It was clear to me Tokuda was involved in Matthew's disappearance, but what was her role after that? Had she arranged to hand him over to the Scotsman, or had her father orchestrated that? I couldn't allow myself to think beyond these questions. I wanted to focus on the positive. I wanted to believe Matthew was alive and was living somewhere in Scotland. He had to be.

CHAPTER FOURTEEN
PLOVERS

The train reached Kyoto Station at 9:03 p.m. I bought an *eki-ben* boxed meal at Kōchi just before boarding, thinking I would eat on the train. I hadn't eaten since breakfast. Although the box was stuffed with the scrumptious delicacies famous to Kōchi, I had no appetite. I tucked the unopened box in my pack and filed out of the train. Not interested in standing in a bus line, I splurged on a taxi. The minute I put the key in the front door of my house, I could hear the phone ringing. I struggled out of my shoes and dashed down the hallway to answer.

"*Hai? Moshi-moshi.*" I prepared to launch into my usual greeting, but the man on the other end broke in.

"*Moshi-moshi* . . . Hello? Is this Ruth-san?"

The voice was strangely familiar, but I couldn't place it.

"This is she."

"Oh, so you're home already then. Good! I'm sorry to bother you, but I have information."

"I'm sorry, who is this?"

"Sorry. This is Iizuka from the Shirohama Municipal Library. We met this morning."

"Oh right. Of course I remember, thank you so much for

your help."

"I have information."

"Yes?"

"Well, after you left, I looked through the rest of the catalog … Oh, I was able to process your request and I'll be sending you a copy tomorrow. Shall it go special express?"

"Special express would be perfect."

"Very good. We'll process a COD. Will you be home? It will likely arrive the day after tomorrow. In the afternoon. I'll call you when I have the precise delivery time."

It killed me that the post office would give you a precise delivery time.

"Thank you. You said you had information?"

"Yes. Right. After you left, I looked through the catalog, and I found the Scotsman's name. I used that to search through back entry logs in our Shirohama Dog Championships, and I was able to confirm the name of his kennel. Shall I give the name to you now? Or would you prefer I include it in the mailing?"

"No, no, please. Give it to me now!"

I practically shouted in the phone as I cradled the handset against my ear, rummaging through the drawer of the telephone table for a pad of paper and pen. Succeeding with a pen but failing with the paper, I sat down on the floor, rolled my pants leg up and prepared to write on my calf.

"Ok, thank you. Please go ahead."

"Right. This is English, and I'm not sure how to pronounce it. So, let me spell it out for you."

Mr. Iizuka painstakingly spelled each letter in each name he recited: the Scotsman's, the kennel's, the lane's, the township's, and so on. His pronunciation made some of his letters hard to understand, and I had to ask him to repeat several times. Then, I read the entire list of letters back to him and he had me repeat. When we were satisfied we had successfully communicated, this is what I had, not just on one calf but two:

Mr. Mànus Munro
Glengolly Kennels
11 Durine
Durness

I thanked Mr. Iizuka for his many efforts, grabbed the boxed meal I had carted home from Kōchi, went upstairs and booted up my computer. Maybe Mr. Munro's kennel had a webpage. Maybe Mr. Munro's "adopted" son Matthew would make an appearance. Most businesses these days have an online profile, especially if they do business overseas.

I was hopeful and impatient with my computer. My Internet browser was not loading, so I pulled the paper wrapping off my boxed meal, waiting for the browser to fire up. Then I selected a morsel from the box while reading on my monitor, "Server not found."

Great, the server was down. It happened periodically and for apparently no reason. I popped a few more pieces of whatever I was eating in my mouth and continued to stare at the screen.

I couldn't wait. I couldn't just sit here. I needed to know now.

I tossed my chopsticks on my desk, powered down my computer, and transferred the name and address Mr. Iizuka gave me from calf to paper. There was a twenty-four-hour Internet and gaming center in the Shinkyōgoku shopping arcade called "Net Palace." Before I was living in this house, I had a membership.

I hadn't been to the Net Palace for years, and I wasn't even sure
it was still there. Of course, I couldn't look it up because I didn't
have Internet! I fished through my desk drawer hoping to find
my old membership card. I found an old wallet and thumbed
through the contents. My card was there. I called the number on
the card. They were still in the same spot, with the same hours.

I grabbed my backpack, laced up my running shoes, and
flew out the front door. At this hour, the Number 5 bus was only
running intermittently. I knew I would make better time on foot.
I jogged along Nijō, over to Niomon, and doglegged through the
neighborhoods near Jingū-michi until I made it to Sanjō. Then,
it was a straight shot to Shinkyōgoku.

There wasn't a lot of traffic along the broad Sanjō Avenue.
I was able to keep up a good pace. I made it to Sanjō Bridge
in no time. I stopped for a few seconds to look down along the
riverbank on the off chance Maho might be there with Hawk. I
didn't recognize either of them among the huddled couples, so I
continued along my way, slowing down here and there to avoid
clutches of drunken businessmen staggering uncertainly towards
me. *Chidori-ashi*, they called it, "with footsteps like a plover," one-
foot zagging across the path of the other. It was hard to tell which
way they were going to turn. I stepped down onto the road.

I crossed Kawaramachi without waiting for the light, ran
into the covered arcade, and turned left on Shinkyōgoku. I slowed
to a brisk walk, having forgotten exactly where the club was. I was
slightly out of breath and now damp and clammy in the night air.

The Net Palace was further down than I remembered.
I pulled my handkerchief from my pack and dabbed at the
perspiration on my brow and neck. There it was, next to the First

Kitchen and over the All-Wins Pachinko Parlor. I bolted up the stairs and stepped through the electric sliding doors. The young man at the front desk was sprawled across the counter, his head resting in the crook of his arm. He raised up when he heard the door open and looked at me sleepily, perfunctorily checking my card, explaining I owed back dues. I fished out my wallet, and he handed me my room assignment and a key to a locker.

He went over the list of rules and regulations, no smoking, no alcohol, but I could enjoy refills of free drinks at the machine next to the toilets. I headed back to my assigned cubicle, passing up the free soda as I went.

The single occupancy rooms were miniscule with the rooms for two or three persons slightly larger. I could hear a group of teenagers in the booth across from mine playing a video game. They wore headphones, so I was spared the game noise, but I could hear the manic sounds they made as they banged away at the game controls.

The computer in my booth booted up promptly. I opened up Google and began keying in the search for Mr. Mànus Munro. I tried to imagine how old he might have been in the pamphlet photographs I'd seen earlier today. It was hard to judge. The photos were black and white, grainy. My search for Mànus Munro drew a blank, but I picked up steam with Glengolly Kennels. I came across a newsletter for Bullmastiffs Breeders of Sutherland County. Buried within it, a small notice that a certain Mr. Mànus Munro was fined for endangering the gentle reputation of the breed by engaging in dog baiting and other illegal activities.

The notice concluded that after an exhaustive investigation of Munro, his business partners, family, and other dealers and breeders about the county, he was found guilty of said violations. His sentence was to refrain from any dog training, breeding, or showing for three years with a fine of 750 pounds. If he didn't adhere to the injunction, he would be banned for life from further involvement with the breed.

I wondered if Mr. Munro had managed to behave himself. The newsletters appeared to be annual, with this one dated October 2000. I clicked on the link for the 2001 newsletter, hoping to learn more about Glengolly Kennels. The newsletters were full of photographs and took a long time to load.

In the October 2003 issue of the newsletter, I came across another reference to Glengolly Kennels. I sat up suddenly in my chair and nearly caused it to topple backwards. "Glengolly to Close Effective 15 December." The paragraph that followed was brief and basically reiterated the heading:

> Due to a decline in business, Glengolly Kennels will no longer engage in the breeding and sale of bullmastiffs or any other dog. We have enjoyed a long and happy engagement with this most loyal and dependable of animals. To our former clients, we express our deepest appreciation for your continued patronage over the years. It is now our pleasure to stroll the crofts at leisure with our two remaining dogs, Famlo (aka Famhair Fellow) and Missy (aka Meikle Stane's Missus). Any orders placed and not yet filled shall be reimbursed in full.
>
> In gratitude,
> Glengolly Kennels

No photographs accompanied the notice. No names were introduced to identify the owners of the kennel. I wondered if the decline in profits was a result of Munro's censuring. I scrolled ahead, growing more and more disheartened. I learned much more than I ever cared to know about bullmastiffs and Durness, Scotland, but I gained absolutely squat on Matthew. I jotted down the phone number for the Association of Bullmastiffs Breeders of Sutherland County, along with the other information listed at the end. That's when I noticed the name of one of the association board members looked familiar: Benneit Mathe Munro.

I googled Benneit Mathe Munro. Seven or eight hits came back immediately. Mr. Benneit Mathe Munro was also a dog breeder. It looked as though within months of Glengolly Kennels closing, Benneit Mathe Munro opened Haar Haven Kennels, a kennel specializing in the responsible, humane treatment of all animals great and small. Tired of sifting through page after page on dogs, breeds, and kennel squabbles, I clicked on "images." I was immediately confronted with more images of dogs, kennel signboards, and advertisements. And then, mid-scroll, I saw him. Matthew. Sandy blonde hair, eyes the color of an April sky, a chiseled chin–it had to be him. I pulled a copy of Hawk's sketch out of my backpack and held it to the page. There was clearly a resemblance. Benneit Mathe Munro was somewhat more weathered and heavier. There was a presence about this man that just seemed right. I clicked on another photograph and then another. Benneit Mathe Munro radiated a mischievous warmth, a sweet sincerity I remembered in Matthew. "Only bad people hurt animals!" he had once declared in defense of the tongue-cut sparrow. Benneit Mathe Munro was tall.

I went back to the information pages to look for his contact and found the webpage for Haar Haven Kennel. The contact page listed the kennel at 11 Durine, Durness, the same address Glenngolly used. Several numbers were provided. I clicked through the link for "about us" and read about Benneit Mathe Munro's unique approach to dog breeding. His kennel strongly supported the proper socialization of puppies, allowing them to stay in their litter to establish confidence while simultaneously engaging them with other dogs and pets to encourage acceptance of outsiders. What really struck me about Benneit's kennel was its commitment to contributing a percentage of all proceeds to the Scottish SPCA and to providing a portion of the kennel facilities to rescuing and rehoming.

The "About Haar Haven" led to the page "Introducing Benniet Mathe Munro." It reported Benniet Mathe Munro was the son of famous breeder and champion showman, Mànus Munro of Durness and the late Fione Ogilvie formerly of Inverness. Owing to his father's occasional business in Japan, Munro was born there and spent his first few years in the Land of the Rising Sun. Sadly, his mother, Fione, took ill and passed away while overseas and Benniet returned alone with Mànus to Durness.

It was Matthew! I clapped my hands in excitement and then began pounding the table in front of me. Matthew! You're alive!!! My exuberance caught the attention of the sleepy staff person who clomped over to my compartment and banged on the door.

"You'll have to keep it down."

"Oh, sorry!"

I looked at my watch. It was after 1 a.m. I needed to leave.

I printed off the webpages I had been reading. I would need to pay for the print job when I checked out. I powered down the computer and collected my belongings. By the time I reached the front desk, my printout was ready to go. The sleepy staff person handed me my receipt and printouts and put his head back down on the counter.

I took the stairs two at a time and stepped out into the empty arcade. Most of the stores were now shuttered. My footfalls rang out and the metal shutters rattled from the breeze I made as I passed by. I was relieved when I made it to Sanjō and then out of the arcade. I thought about hailing a taxi for the ride home, but the only ones I saw were already hired. I picked up my pace and without realizing it, began to run.

Matthew was alive! My heart shouted with each step I took. As I ran, I tried to chart out my approach. Did he remember his life in Japan? If I called him out of the blue, would he hear me out? Or would he just think I was some lunatic? Perhaps it would be better to write and include some photographs of the two of us or a shot of him with our parents. But a letter was so one sided. I wanted to hear his voice.

My ideas chased themselves in circles round and round my head as I ran. By the time I reached the house and let myself in the door, I was exhausted. I slipped out of my shoes, and as I headed toward the kitchen for a drink of water, the house phone began ringing. It was half past one. Who would call at this hour?

"Where the hell have you been?"

Maho accosted me before I could even finish my greeting.

"I've been calling you all night! I swear if you didn't answer this time, I was going to go to the police."

That's when I remembered I had promised to check in with her each day. She and Mrs. Shibasaki expressed concern when I told them I was going to Tokuda's hometown. I was supposed to call Maho and let her know my whereabouts.

"I am so sorry, Maho. I guess I just forgot to call."

"Forgot? Dammit, Ruth!"

"I think I found him! I know where Matthew is. He's alive."

"I knew it! I knew you'd find him!"

"He's in Scotland. It's a long story, but I've just been so busy trying to track him down that I forgot to call you."

"Well, I'm just glad you're okay. Anyway, Hawk has something to show you. He found out more about Satoko's tattoo. Do you have time tomorrow?"

"Of course! When would you like to meet?"

I feigned excitement. In fact, I was no longer interested in Satoko, Shōtarō, or any of it. The whole talisman tale felt distant. It didn't have anything to do with Matthew. He was all I cared about now. But if Hawk had gone to the trouble to uncover more information, I needed to at least act like I was interested.

"We can run by your house if you'd like. Or meet at Sanjō somewhere. How about 5:00? When do you get off?"

"I think I can get back home by 5:00. If you want to stop by the house, that'd be great."

"Sure thing."

"Thanks, again. I'm really sorry to keep you up worrying about me."

"I'm just so happy for you!"

After we hung up, I poured myself a glass of water and went

upstairs to get ready for bed. When I pulled my cell phone out of my pack, thinking I might call Matthew, I noticed all the missed calls from Maho. I had turned the ringer off on the train and must have forgotten to turn it back on.

I took my jeans off and lay down on the bed, staring at the phone in my hand. What's the country code for Scotland, I wondered. I recalled that Japan was eight hours ahead. So, if it's two in the morning here, it'd be six in the evening there. How should I start? "Hi, I'm Ruth. I'm your sister. The last time I saw you, you were chasing a puppy."

I closed my eyes just for a minute as the luminescent arc of his slender neck rose up in my memory, gliding white over the silver tracks. The rush of the train blocked my vision, but when it passed, Matthew was there on the other side of the tracks. Only, it was not the knobby-kneed little boy I remembered. It was Benniet, the man. I reached my hand up to wave, starting to call to him. But no words emerged, no matter how hard I tried to force them free. I squeezed my eyes together, willing the words to come. When I opened them again, I was still in bed, clutching my cell phone. It was 6:30 in the morning.

I swung my legs over the mattress and sat on the edge of the bed. I hadn't drawn the drapes last night and the morning light streamed across the floor, chasing dust bunnies and bouncing off the assorted books and papers scattered here and there.

I needed to hear Matthew's voice. I turned on the computer to check the wifi connectivity. It was back up. Next I checked on time differences, 6:30 a.m. in Kyoto was half past ten in Scotland. If he ran a kennel, he probably turned in early. Instead, I settled on calling my parents. It was too early in the evening on the East Coast for them to be in bed. My mother picked up on the second ring.

"Sweetheart, how are you? Are you feeling a bit better than the last time we talked?"

"I have news! Is Daddy home, too? He'll need to hear this."

"Just a minute, honey, and I'll call him to the phone."

I could hear my mother set the phone receiver down as she called out to my father. After some delay and much fumbling about with phone cords and chairs, I had them on the line. My story came out in one long explosion of words. I don't think I even stopped for breath, afraid that if I did my mother would tell me I was delusional and I needed to get myself home.

"Are you sure?" My mother asked when I had finally explained all that had happened.

"I'm positive."

"Are you going to head to Scotland?" my father asked.

"I may. First, I was just going to try to call. Failing that, I suppose I will email him. I guess I just don't want to show up on his doorstep unannounced."

"I feel like we should be there with you," my mother interjected. I could tell she was growing excited. "Would you mind if we stayed with you a bit?"

"Of course not. There's plenty of room."

"Let's not rush into anything yet," my father cautioned. "Let's talk about it. We'll get back to you, Ruth."

"That's fine, Daddy." I was surprised he was so subdued.

"And honey," he added. "Don't get your hopes up. This might turn out to be just another wild goose chase."

The phone call home left me strangely unsettled. Maybe my parents would make the trip, and if I did manage to connect with Matthew, I was sure they would.

I had plenty of time to eat and shower before heading to Logos International. I was wondering how I was going to make it through the day translating brochures without crawling out of my skin. Knowing Maho and Hawk would be stopping by the house later gave me something to look forward to. I jumped in the shower for a quick rinse, tossed on one of my trusty navy suits and squeezed into my pantyhose before heading downstairs to the kitchen. I wondered if I would find any edible food in the house.

CHAPTER FIFTEEN
UBUME, THE CHILD-SNATCHER BIRD

"Do you remember how Hori-ichi nearly went ballistic when we questioned him about Satoko's tattoo?" Maho asked as she settled herself onto the couch. I placed Yatsuhashi cinnamon cookies in a bowl on the table in front of her along with a glass of chilled barley tea.

"That was ballistic?" I remembered the horishi looked fiercely annoyed, but he hadn't yelled at us.

"Well, for Hori-ichi it was. He hardly ever changes expressions, you know. And that morning I thought he was going to blow a gasket!"

Maho reached quickly into the bowl of cookies and pulled one out. She snapped it in two before popping one end in her mouth.

"Anyway, it frightened me."

Maho was back to her Mohawk, as well as her piercings to her ears and eyebrows. I could not imagine her being easily frightened.

"I thought for sure he was going to banish me from the tattoo parlor. So, after that I kept a low profile. But Hawk here," Maho turned to look at her boyfriend who was sprawled in the chair across from her. "Hawk grew bolder. He started going through the print master's sketch drawers to see if he could find any of the earlier tattoo sketches he'd told you about. A few days ago, he came across these."

Hawk placed the black folder on the coffee table and settled on the floor where he could easily spread the contents out for me. He opened the folder and pulled three sketches out. Maho slid down on the floor next to him.

"Are these Hori-ichi's?" I asked, somewhat incredulous.

"No," Maho replied. "They're the drawings Muroya did for him. But they aren't the actual drawings. I mean, Hawk sketched copies of what he found. He wasn't about to take the master's originals out of the studio!"

I studied the first page. It was an intricate design of a wave with a white limbed diving girl in the center. She was naked except for a flimsy cloth wrapped loosely around her hips. She clinched a knife between her teeth, and in her left hand, she gripped an oyster. Entwined along the slender fold of her loincloth were two hiragana syllables "ki" き and "re" れ. Given the proximity to the knife, I assumed it had something to do with cutting.

The second sketch featured a typical noshi motif of knotted strands of fabric swirling on a background of waves that replicated those in the first drawing. The twisting fabric mimicked the tangled tendrils of the diving woman's hair as well as the diaphanous drift of her loincloth. But unlike the monochrome of the woman's bathing attire, the strips of the noshi were heavily patterned in typical kimono motifs. These seemed to all revolve around children's toys—pinwheels, pretty string balls, cricket cages, a tiny puppy, spinning tops, and wheels. At the top of the bundle embedded in the fabric was the graph "ura"裏 the backside, the underside.

The third sketch teemed with arched bridges, pagodas, and temple gates, wrapped in billowing clouds, light beams, and branches of pine. The light beams seemed to illuminate the graph for court—"miyako" 京which stood among the bridges and gates as if it too were an architectural structure.

The sketches were done in ink and very delicately. Here and there, Hawk had marked in pencil the names of colors, apparently to indicate the ink that was to be used. Hawk went to a lot of effort to reproduce the tattoo drawings. I almost regretted he had. My mind was now so far removed from Satoko and her ink. I just didn't feel motivated to worry about her anymore; I wanted to concentrate on Matthew.

"How long did it take you to do these?" I tried to feign interest.

"It didn't take that long. Color would have been more involved, but Muroya sensei's sketches are always just black ink. He suggests the colors. You can see here where the colors are indicated. But the final selection is left to the horishi and his client. And in her case, I understand Satoko was very involved in that selection."

"But look!" Maho interjected. "Don't you think the use of the words here is meaningful?"

She pointed to the first sketch. "I mean, why 'kire'? Why 'miyako'?"

"I tried to find the sketches for the tattoo you asked about, Ruth. If I could find those, we could see what poems she had chosen. But I didn't have time to root through Sensei's sketch cabinets."

"Kire, ura, miyako. What do you think it means?" Maho persisted.

"Well, we already know about the ura, right? I told you about my conversation with Miyazaki, Satoko's lover. He said when he and Satoko opened up the talisman and looked at the underside, the character for ura had been embroidered over the tear in the fabric."

"Hey, wait a minute, Ruth. Doesn't kire mean 'a tear'."

Hawk jumped in before I could reply. "I thought it was the imperative—cut! The diving woman has the knife in her teeth. Looks like she's being told to cut open the oyster shell."

"What does Satoko want to tear into? The truth of the talisman? The nasty reality of the Tani family?" Maho asked.

"I don't know," I replied. "It seems her brother already exposed the nastiness of the family long ago with his earlier fiction. And since we've already established the link between the cut or tear and the embroidered applique of the word ura, what about the addition of miyako? How does that fit?" I thought for a minute. "*The Kimono Killer* was set in Kyoto. Satoko was from Kyoto. But does the combination of these two characters imply 'ura-Kyoto'? You know, like the underside of Kyoto?"

"It does have its underside, that's for sure," Hawk noted. "And half of them come to Hori-ichi's parlor."

"That's not true," Maho fired back. "There are a lot of seedy parlors in town. Hori-ichi's is high class."

"Most of the clients are respectable—like you, Maho. But there are some lowlifes who come by now and then."

"Does Hori-ichi accommodate just anyone?" I asked.

"He can be selective. And for the most part, he tries to avoid clients who are too hooked up. But it's hard, you know."

"I know what you're saying. But it's changing. Hori-ichi is much more interested in clients who are there for the art," Maho shot back.

"Then why do you think Satoko is suggesting an 'underworld Kyoto'?" The tattoo was beginning to feel like a jigsaw puzzle. There were a lot of blanks to fill in and different ways to read the clues. Despite myself, I was growing more interested.

"Do you have a dictionary?" Maho asked.

"You're kidding, right? What translator worth her salt doesn't hoard dictionaries? Red, green, big, little, you name it, I've got it."

Maho rolled her eyes and went off to the kitchen for the pitcher of tea, muttering that maybe it was time I tried to using electronic ones. I headed to my stockpile in the bedroom. When I returned with my arms full of dictionaries, she had refilled our glasses.

We took turns looking for word combinations with ura and miyako. We were well acquainted with the different gradations of meaning for each individual word. Ura referred to the backside, the underside, the inside, the dark side, the hidden, the secret, the clandestine. It could be pronounced "ura," "uchi," or "ri" depending on the graphs with which it was joined. When combined, it offered up words with a whole host of meanings from the lining of a robe to the bottom half of an inning in a baseball game—with lots of nefarious possibilities thrown in, like blackmail, black market, counterfeit, and so on. But, we didn't come across even one instance of the word used in combination with miyako. And that word, in contrast to ura, had basically one meaning. It almost always referred to Kyoto, the old court. There were several ways to pronounce the graph, too: kei or also kyō in addition to miyako.

"So, I guess this combination just makes a reference to the dark underside of Kyoto, home to lowlifes like Akira Tani and Tokuda?"

"They're definitely supposed to be read in some kind of combination," Hawk explained. "See how the motifs are all tied together? The waves become the tangled hair, the swirled loincloth, the fluttering strands of silk, and then the billowy clouds and snaky streaks of light. Pictorially, they are all connected."

"Hey, wait a minute, Ruth," Maho had suddenly grown animated. "What if Satoko is signaling the literal underside of Kyoto, like the freaking tunnel that bitch Tokuda disappeared into?"

Suddenly the image of Tokuda falling into the sluice above Nanzen Temple burst across the screen of my memory.

"And then there was that pipe Shōtaro Tani dragged you into when you were trying to get away from Daté-san's murderers. Maybe Satoko means the world beneath Kyoto."

My recollection of the encounter with Shōtarō was hazy. We were in a pipe of some kind. It was cold and dark, and I could hear the sound of water running.

"We really ought to go over to the Philosopher's Path and see if we can't find where he took you. Who knows? Maybe we'll find the entrance to the underworld."

I don't know why I hadn't thought of it sooner. The night Daté died was so painful, I guess I just wanted to avoid any reminder of it.

"We can't do it now," Maho continued. "I have to go meet my mother in about an hour. Looks like I'm due for my nine-hundred and nineteenth lecture on why I'm such a loser."

"You don't have to go," Hawk said softly.

"I do if I want her to keep paying for my shit. It's a small price, I guess, for her charity. At least it makes her feel virtuous. Mother-of-the-fucking-year. But if you can wait a little, Ruth, why don't we go look for your rabbit hole tomorrow morning?"

"Sure. No hurry. Do you have to leave right now or do you have time to look online and see if we can get anything on 'ura' 'miyako'? I'll be right back."

I ran upstairs to get my laptop. Sometimes, when I get nowhere with a dictionary, I'll use the image search on the Internet. I thought about inviting Hawk and Maho upstairs with me, but then remembered the half-eaten box lunch I'd left on my desk. I unplugged my laptop and carried it back down with me, setting it up on the dining room table where we would have more room.

"Come on in. Let's see what we get when we search for ura and miyako in combination."

I typed in the graphs and clicked on images. Maho peered over my shoulder at the screen.

"Well, that's just weird," she said, pointing to a bicycle. "Why a bicycle?"

"Maybe, it was taking the back roads?" Hawk quipped. But in fact, the images were all pretty random: some manga characters, a baseball team, a salamander. The one that seemed the most relevant was a website for "Ura Kyō Market." I clicked through, but found it was actually in Sasebo, on the island of Kyushu and nowhere near Kyoto. It looked to be a resale shop on Kyōmachi Street. So they named it "Otherside Kyō."

"How clever," Maho snorted.

"See, this is the trouble with searching images online. You get too distracted."

I scrolled a little more. Midway through the screen of images, we came to one of Tosa dogs or what looked like the Tosa breed, tangled up with one another, fighting. I clicked through, hoping I wouldn't come across pictures of dogs in pain. The page that loaded was an article about illegal dog fighting in Kyoto.

"Illegal dog fighting is clearly the gateway to an underworld Kyoto," I said as I strained to read the small print on the screen. "And it circles us back to Tokuda and her nasty family in Shirohama."

The page opened onto a news announcement of sorts, and not particularly recent. Maho reached over and tapped some keys, making the font on the screen larger.

"But, it's not just a concept, Ruth. It's a place. See here. "The bouts were arranged though the infamous gambling club known as the Urakyō, located at 23-55 Inokumachō on West Ninth Avenue," Maho translated from the page as she read. "That's a pretty sketchy area, you know. South of the station. Hori-ichi used to have his studio nearby. I was relieved when he relocated to the Fushimi neighborhood."

I squinted at the article. "Does it say who the owners of the club are? It looks like they were leveraged a fine. What are the chances of this dogfighting ring being connected to Tokuda's lot?" The pulse in my head began to throb.

"Just a minute." Maho began to click away at the keys, moving from page to page too quickly for me to follow. "It looks like the Urakyō has been in business for quite a while. They front for a number of gambling outfits like off-track betting, dogs and horses, but they specialize in the keirin short-track bike races."

Maho continued to scroll through the pages she opened. I couldn't believe she was actually reading what she saw, she scrolled so quickly.

"Ok, here's a 'crimestoppers' report for the neighborhood. Look at all those crimes. It's not just for Urakyō. But, they're at the top of the list. Do you see that?" Maho pointed to the page and the list of infractions was impressive: serving alcohol to minors, indecent sex acts, illegal gambling on the premises, and sponsoring dogfights off premises."

"It doesn't say anything about the owners. Let me try something else." Maho went back to tapping madly at the keys, running one search request after another. Frame after frame of unsavory looking types, clearly gangsters, flooded the computer screen.

"Wait!" I pointed to a photograph of a group of men. They looked familiar. Maho clicked back to the image. The webpage that opened was not from a police roster but looked more to be from an old advertisement of sorts. It showed Tokuda's father, Old Man Yoshida, next to one of his dogs in full champion sumō-regalia. A little off to the side was a younger version of Tokuda wearing a tight, check-patterned dress, and grinning proudly. She was surrounded by two other men. I couldn't be certain, but one of the men looked like the fake police detective, Kimura. The other looked familiar, too, but I couldn't place him.

"Look up Akira Tani," I blurted out, growing excited with the discovery. "I want to see what he looks like."

Maho tapped away at the keys again and an image of Akira loomed into view from a newspaper report on prominent kimono company presidents. He was seated alongside four other men, all dressed in kimonos save Akira who wore a tailored suit. He wasn't particularly large, but he had a round face, small close-set eyes, and wavy hair

"It's the same man. The one with Tokuda, Yoshida, and the dog. So, does this mean they are all somehow connected with the Urakyō?"

"Would it surprise you? But let me do a little more looking." Maho went back to tapping the keys.

"I could ask Hori-ichi," Hawk spoke up. He had been quiet during our web-browsing frenzy.

"Wouldn't that give away the fact you knew about the sketches and the tattoo? I don't want you to get in trouble."

"That's just it, though. I think Hori-ichi and his brother wanted me to see the sketches."

"What do you mean?" I asked.

"Well, Muroya Sensei is always very careful to keep his tattoo sketches in a locked drawer. He feels they're private, not like the sketches he does for his woodblocks. But the other day when I was putting some of his art supplies away, I saw the drawer to his tattoo sketches was unlocked, even opened slightly. These three sketches were there on top. I knew Sensei was out visiting a client, so I had the time I needed to make draft sketches. I put everything back just as it was. And then a few days later, I heard him and Hori-ichi talking over their beers. I could tell they were talking about Satoko."

"Hawk, you never told me that!" Maho sounded slightly aggrieved.

"I hadn't really thought about it at the time. But looking back, it seems like it was a set up, you know?"

"What did they say about Satoko?" I asked.

"They started in on how it was a shame she died. She was almost finished with the tattoo."

"I wonder what else she could have added!" Satoko was not a large person, and it seemed to me her skin was already pretty well covered, at least from the descriptions of her tattoos.

"Oh, come on, Ruth. For most of us, once you get started, you're never through! There's a tradition in Japan where you're not officially done until the horishi signs his work. If Hori-ichi didn't sign yet, then Satoko wasn't done."

"Hori-ichi made one thing clear," Hawk continued, seemingly unfazed by our interruptions. "He kept talking about how Satoko insisted on those particular characters—kire, ura, kyō. And they had to be graphed onto those particular designs. She was very precise about it."

"Then she must have been trying to signal something. Was she trying to draw attention to Urakyō, to this club?"

Hawk got up and went back to the living rooms to retrieve the sketches.

"Look at the design, at the layout. See how all the lines are pointing towards the graph for kyō/miyako? It's like they're directing us there. And here's another thing. See the lines for the beams of light? What color do you think those are?"

Hawk put his thumb over the word he'd written in the middle of the beam. "That word would give the color."

"Yellow, right?" I asked.

"Of course, yellow. What else could it be for the beams of light? Unless she wanted that new invisible ink they have in the States," Maho suggested.

"Invisible ink? What would be the point?"

"Well, it's a special UV ink that only shows up under blacklight," Maho explained.

"No self-respecting horishi would use that, Maho. You know that!" Hawk countered with annoyance. He removed his thumb.

"Akashi?" we both shouted in unison, quickly reading the three syllabes あ か し. Akashi was an old-fashioned term for the color red.

"Could the beams of light really be red?"

"I didn't see the tattoo myself, so I'm not sure. It could be the horishi only added streaks of red. That's what I overheard Hori-ichi discussing with his brother. Satoko was insistent. From what I could hear of their conversation, it seems Satoko meant something more than just color—akashi. Apparently, she said to Hori-ichi something like, it's more than the color, it's the beam of light."

"Oh, I see!" I said excitedly. "Akashi can also mean light, right. It's written with a different graph, in that case.

"Maybe she was playing on the homophonic quality of the word. Akashi. It could refer to the color red or to light, illumination."

"So, she's trying to illuminate this place in Kyoto?"

"Or Akashi. If you're dealing with homophones, right? That could also point to the city Akashi, couldn't it? To the place?" Maho asked.

"I don't think so." Hawk once again pointed to the three sketches. "Like I said before, our eyes are being drawn by the wavy-horizontal lines to the word 'kyō', or 'miyako'. That can only mean Kyoto. And with the pairing of ura, it must mean this particular club."

"So, is there more about the club we should know?"

"I think we need to have a look around," Maho suggested.

"I don't know, Maho. I'm fairly sure they aren't going to let me just go wandering in." Most clubs had tacit rules against allowing foreigners inside. Not that I particularly wanted to push my way into a club like this one.

"Well, no one would notice us," Maho said with a touch of self-criticism, looking over at Hawk. "Lowlifes that we are. I'm sure we'd blend right in."

"Absolutely not. You're not going in there." I was growing nervous with the turn in the conversation. I agreed, we needed to take a look around and find out what was so important about Urakyō, but I wasn't comfortable with Maho's involvement in doing so. And I didn't want Hawk getting caught up in something that could get him in trouble.

"Do you know anyone else who might be familiar with this kind of place and know how to act? I mean, this isn't the kind of place just anyone can waltz into, is it?"

"What about Hiro?"

I stared at Maho in dismay.

"No, seriously. Hiro goes to some pretty seedy places. Didn't you know that?"

"Hiro?" I couldn't quite reconcile the casserole-baking Hiro with a lowlife gambling den. "Are we talking about the same guy?"

"Yeah. Sometimes when I'm in the office with just Hiro we'll trade stories of our escapades. I'll tell him about my earlier cutting days and in turn, he'll regale me with his gambling exploits."

"I know but betting on bikes is legal."

"He wasn't always so savory, Ruth. Our little Hiro has a bad boy streak. He really wants out from under Mommy's thumb and instead of just confronting her, he engages in a total war of passive-aggressiveness."

"Kind of like you, Maho," Hawk's glance was sharp.

I had seen some of what Maho was referring to. At the office, Hiro could be belligerent. That was why it was difficult to reconcile the cordial and considerate Hiro I met at the Shibasaki house. If he hated the job so much, why didn't he just come right out and tell her he wanted his freedom. As much as I wanted to ask Maho more about her behind-the-scenes conversations with Hiro, I didn't want to get sidetracked.

"So, do you think Hiro might know something about Urakyō?"

"Does it hurt to ask?"

"I guess not. I'll see if I can't get hold of him."

It was a little past seven. Maho and Hawk collected their bags, though Hawk kindly left the sketches and a promise to return tomorrow.

After I saw them off, I carried my laptop back upstairs and gave Hiro a call. He was surprised to hear from me, and even more surprised to hear what I had to ask. But he was also intrigued. We decided to meet at a noodle shop on Shijō. I thought about trying to call Matthew but didn't think I had time.

As soon as I left the house, the rain began to come down in buckets. I darted back inside and fished a pair of rubber boots out of the shoe cabinet. I grabbed a hooded slicker and my umbrella as well. By the time the Number Five rounded the corner, I was dry but sweating like a woman in a fat suit. The bus offered little comfort.

It seemed to take forever for the bus to rumble its way to Shijō Avenue. I waited my turn to alight and then darted through the throngs of shoppers the three blocks to the noodle shop. Hiro was waiting for me outside, eager to learn more about my request.

"You want me to go undercover for you?"

"Only if you're comfortable doing so, Hiro. I don't want to put you in danger."

"Ruth, I think you're making this place out to be more volatile than it is. Seedy clubs like this one are a dime a dozen."

It sounded as if he spoke from experience.

"But, the people we're dealing with here aren't your average petty criminals. They're murderers, okay? And kidnappers. I just want you to look around, that's all. Let me know what you see."

"What am I looking for?"

"I'm not really sure. I guess no one will be bragging about their history in kidnapping. Just see what you see."

"I'll wear a camera."

"What?"

"Yeah. I'll head on over to Bic Camera after we eat and see what they have."

"Hiro, I don't think that's a good idea. If you get caught . . ."

"Don't worry so much. The cameras they make these days are pretty good. The video quality probably won't be that great, but I think it's the way to go. I won't know who I'm looking for or looking at, so I'll just walk around recording. We can meet up later and look at the film together. How does that sound?"

"I guess that makes sense."

The waitress brought the noodles we had ordered. Mine was delicious, but I couldn't eat more than a few bites. The broth was a little too hot. But more than that, I was troubled by my request and by Hiro's enthusiasm for it. I didn't want him hurt.

Completely unfazed, Hiro slurped his noodles down in no time. He took the check, despite my protests, and paid our bill. We parted ways on Shijō Avenue and agreed he would stop by my house tomorrow around 11 p.m. to look at photographs before heading off to the club.

It was almost 10 p.m. when I got back to the house. A good time to call Matthew. I found his number, or rather the number for this kennel, and picked up my phone. What was I going to say? "Hello, you don't know me, but I'm your sister. You used to live in Japan."

I jotted down a few opening lines, but nothing I prepared sounded right.

I flipped my phone open again and keyed in the number. The phone rang on the other end, several times. I could feel the pits of my arms begin to sweat. Finally, an automated message machine picked up. I panicked and snapped my phone shut, ending the call. It wasn't even Matthew's voice. I placed my phone beside me on the bed and wiped my hand on my jeans, determined to try again. This time, I would leave a message. Once again, I listened to the phone ringing at the other end, the click of the answering machine, and then the tone. "Ma-chan? Ma-chan? This is your sister. This is Ruth. I know it sounds crazy, but you have another family. You have family in Japan. I'm sorry. This must seem a shock. I wanted to talk with you about your childhood. I just want to talk with you, okay? I'll call you back later."

I hung up, regretting such an incoherent message. Poor Matthew won't know what to make of it, and I forgot to call him by his new name, Benniet. He's not going to remember being Ma-chan.

Or will he? Maybe, he'll know exactly who I am, or maybe, he doesn't want to hear from me. He probably blames me.

I fell back on the bed in tears.

I must have fallen asleep, because when I awoke it was morning. Late in the morning. Maho and Hawk were standing on my doorstep, ringing the bell.

"Oh no, I'm sorry," I exclaimed as I invited them in. Maho looked suspiciously at my rumpled clothing, aware I was wearing exactly what I had on the day before.

"Is everything okay, Ruth? I thought you wanted to go check out the Philosopher's Path."

"Yes, of course. Just a minute, and I'll get my things together."

I raced upstairs to splash water on my face and brush my teeth. I raked a comb through my hair and changed into a clean shirt. Yesterday's jeans would do.

We headed over to the Philosopher's Path. It was still raining but only lightly. We splashed along under umbrellas. It was amusing to walk with Maho and Hawk. Passersby actually stared more at them than at me. I glanced over at Maho and noticed she stared fiercely at anyone who looked her way, seemingly daring them to hold her gaze. Once we made the turn onto the narrow Philospher's Path, there were fewer people to encounter. It was still early, and the rains helped hold them at bay. At the same time, the rains made the path all the prettier. The hydrangea blooms lining the canal were more vibrant than ever, nestling among the lush green bushes. Most were blue, but some were deeply pink, even purple. Because of the rain, the blooms hung heavily over the path. Maho and I kept our eyes trained on the canal, looking for an opening large enough for a man to fit through.

"Ruth, I'm not seeing anything. Where did you say it happened?"

"That's just it. I can't really remember. I ran through the grounds between Daté-san's house and the Hōnen Temple, jumped onto the pavement, and kept running. I turned as soon as I could and was just about to cross over a bridge onto the Philosopher's Path when Shōtarō grabbed me and pulled me down into a hole."

We found any number of small pipes that fed into the canal, but nothing the size of what I remembered.

"Ruth, I don't see your rabbit hole, but even if there was something big enough to climb into, how would you get down there?"

She was right. The walls of the canal were steep and paved on both sides with rough white stones. Nearer the water, they were covered with a slippery-looking algae. I remember Shōtarō pulling me down, but I don't remember being dragged along a stone wall.

We came to the bridge leading off the path to the Hōnen Temple. All three of us leaned over to see if we could find any kind of opening beneath.

"Did you drop something?"

We turned to find a kindly looking old man. In one hand, he was cradling an overweight dachshund. In the other hand, the man held a clear plastic umbrella.

"We were wondering how you get in and out of the canal, assuming you needed to," Hawk said when he saw Maho and me looking like we'd gotten caught in the act.

"Well, with a ladder."

"A ladder?" the three of us asked in unison.

"We keep one stored over by the Otoyo Shrine," he gestured again by tilting his umbrella down the path behind us. "The main shrine's up there, but the one back that way houses the ceremonial cart. We use it to store our path-cleaning tools. The ladders we drag out twice a year to clean the stream bed. More, if someone drops something in the water, like the other day. I found a woman down there." He tilted his umbrella off in the direction we'd come.

We all swiveled to look trying to imagine what he meant.

"You mean, in the water?" I asked.

"That's right. I'd come up to the path from my house, right over there, to hear the cuckoo. It was around dusk, and I thought it strange for the cuckoo to be singing so late in the day. It's a bad omen, you know. And if I'd known what was good for me, I would have stayed inside."

"You say the woman was in the water?" Maho was growing impatient.

"Right down in the middle of it. I thought maybe she'd fallen in. She seemed a bit dazed."

"What did she look like?"

"Maybe mid-sixties. Dressed in black funeral wear."

I could feel the hairs on the back of my neck tingle.

"I called down to her, but she didn't seem to hear me. So, I leashed up Chibi-chan here," he juggled the dachshund in his arm, "and ran down to the shrine to drag out the ladder."

Again, he gestured down the path with a slight tilt of his umbrella.

"How'd you get her out?" Hawk scrutinized the old man, doubtful someone so frail could have helped a woman up the steep incline.

"Well, that's just the thing. By the time I got back, she was gone."

"Gone? How?"

"I have no idea. It was no simple task for me to drag that ladder out of the shed and haul it back up here. I was almost glad she was gone. I'm not sure I could have pulled her up out of there. I was fighting for breath as it was."

"I'm glad you didn't hurt yourself."

"Or didn't get hurt!" Maho said under her breath. "They would have called it a suicide!"

"Suicide?" The man heard better than Maho anticipated.

"She may have been aiming for a suicide, but this stream isn't quite deep enough to do the job, not unless you lie face down in it. But then, maybe she did. She was soaking wet."

I shivered, once again the image of Tokuda sliding into the sluice played across my mind.

"If she'd just fallen in somehow, she'd have been wet here and there. Of course, her feet would be wet, but she looked drenched to the bone."

At the mention of her feet I remembered one of Tokuda's zori sandals had turned up after the search of the water treatment plant. "Was she missing a zori?"

"A zori?"

The old man stared at the dog in his arm, as if Chibi-chan might have the answer.

"I can't recall. To tell you the truth, I didn't want to look too closely at her feet. I was afraid she might not have any. I mean, there she was in the middle of the river dripping wet. Between the nightfall and the cuckoo, I was beginning to believe she was some kind of *ubume*."

Maho and I exchanged uneasy glances. The ubume was a particularly frightening *yūrei* ghost, the kind of creature who haunts old legends. She was believed to be the specter of a woman who died in childbirth, her body soaked from the waist down in blood. In illustrations, she was often depicted wading through the shoals of the river of death, her hair wet and ragged. In her arms was the bloody bundle of her dead fetus. What was even creepier, the graphs that were used to write ubume could be read "child-snatching bird." If that didn't fit Tokuda, I don't know what did.

"No. I didn't stick around," the old man continued. "The last thing I want to tangle with now at my age is a ghost."

"Do you think she might have fallen in upstream and gotten swept into this canal? I mean, assuming she was a person and not a ghost?" I knew my question sounded crazy, but so did finding a ghost in your neighborhood canal.

"Upstream, you say?"

"Yes, like around Nanzen Temple."

"Well, I suppose. Back in the day, there was a whole network of pipes and tunnels connecting the Nanzen Temple aqueducts to this canal. But the Kyoto Municipal Waterworks sealed most of them off and re-directed the flow, so that it ended out there by the zoo. You know where the Biwa Canal Museum is?"

We nodded.

"Well, that's where the runoff goes now, for the most part."

"But the pipes are still in place?" Hawk pursued the point.

"I suppose they are. Years ago, my son and his friends used to play around in there. We worried one of them would get trapped or lost, so we petitioned the city to board over most of the entrances. Maybe they missed one."

Shōtaro Tani had told me something similar about his childhood.

"Where was the opening your son used to enter, back when he used to explore the tunnels?"

"Well, it's right there," he said, nodding towards a clump of tall grass just across the canal from us. We swiveled once more to look behind us.

Maho turned back to look at the man. "Did you call the police after you saw the woman?"

The man looked at his dog for a few minutes and then turned to us a little sheepishly. "No. I didn't think they'd believe me."

He let loose a deep sigh and seemed to shrink a little.

"We believe you, sir." Hawk said to him as we thanked him and took our leave. We skirted the bridge and stepped down along the dirt walkway running parallel to the Philosopher's Path.

It was muddy from all the rain, and the grass on either side was overgrown and wet. Hawk closed his umbrella and used it as a cane, parting the clump of grass to uncover a dark manhole.

"Do you suppose this thing is easy to move?"

"Let's try." Hawk used the tip of his umbrella to pry it up. The manhole didn't budge.

"So, Tokuda turned into a ghost." Maho said with sarcastic venom.

"I still can't believe it. It must be some kind of crazy coincidence. Tokuda's dead. I saw her. I mean, I saw her go under." I spoke with conviction. But in fact, I had begun to have my doubts. If she had fallen in accidentally, wouldn't she have displayed some kind of panic? Far from it, she had smiled up at me, hadn't she? As the current dragged her under, she had locked her eyes on mine and smiled. Not a beatific smile of resignation, but one of spiteful victory. She'd planned the whole thing.

CHAPTER SIXTEEN
MANDARIN DUCKS

"Ruth, don't look so worried," Hiro chided me. "It's going to be fine." He was sprawled comfortably across from me in the living room as we waited for Hawk and Maho. I'd shown him the webpages with the photographs of Urakyō and Akira Tani. He pulled all the video cameras he had just purchased out of his shopping bag and lined them up on the living room table. He had more than he would need, a pen camera, a buttonhole camera, and two pairs of glasses with cameras.

"Won't that pen in your shirt pocket look a little out of place? I know you're trying to look like a salaryman out for a good time, but would someone like that have a pen handy? And what about the light? Won't it emit a light when recording, and the glasses, too?"

"Relax. I already tested them. You can't see the light. Besides, what if you can? What if they find me with a camera? I'll just tell them I'm making dirty pictures to enjoy later. That won't make them happy, but it won't make them kill me either."

"It's just that, I . . . "

"Stop. You're beginning to sound like my mother, and I don't mean that as a compliment, either."

Hawk and Maho were due to arrive any minute, and I was nervous with anticipation. We agreed Hawk would accompany Hiro. Maho would wait with me. When they got back, we'd view the video together to see what, if anything, turned up. When Hiro mentioned his mother, I decided to follow up, as a way to divert myself.

"You were so nice to me right after Daté was murdered. Both you and your mother were amazingly solicitous. I felt as if the Hiro-at-work and the Hiro-at-home were two different people."

I glanced over at him, making sure I wasn't stepping into dangerous territory. He met my gaze.

"Well, maybe that's because I don't really want to be in that office."

"You make it pretty obvious."

"Before my father died, he made sure my mother was well cared for. She doesn't need to work. That translation business is more or less a hobby for her, but one she's passionate about. I just don't share her feeling."

"Then, why are you there?"

"I haven't been there that long, and I don't plan to be there forever."

Hiro looked down at his hands. I could tell he was deciding whether or not to continue. He squeezed the skin on the ring finger of his left hand as if twisting an invisible ring.

"I was married, Ruth, I even had a son. Well, have a son. But, I pretty much screwed things up. I was supposed to become a career diplomat like my father."

Hiro laughed to himself sardonically, still squeezing his finger, and then looked up at me and continued. "When Father died, he left my mother money. He left me a pedigree. He made sure I went to Waseda University, learned French, because studying English would have been too easy, in his eyes. And just when I thought I had failed my foreign service exam, he found a post for me in Marseille, France. I packed off on my twenty-fifth birthday."

"Sounds like an incredible birthday present to me. Marseille!"

"I know. And it was. I was a lower-level attaché in the Japanese consulate. Well, that makes it sound more impressive than it was. I was a pencil pusher. I started having an affair with a Japanese woman who was also employed by the consulate and before long we had a son and got married. And then things just fell apart. I wasn't happy. That sounds so cliché. I was beyond unhappy. I was deeply depressed."

"I'm sorry to hear that. I can't imagine being depressed in France. Was the work just too awful?"

"I wanted to cook."

"Cook?"

"Right. I wanted to cook. There were so many fabulous restaurants wherever I went. The smells! Some days, I'd just wander into whatever restaurant I was passing and push my way back into the kitchen. A few of the chefs I met grew to like me. They let me hang around in the kitchen while they worked."

"No wonder you're such a great cook now!"

"Ruth, I can make a bouillabaisse that is *au-delà extraordinaire!* But my real job suffered as a consequence, and I was constantly being demoted and demoralized. My wife was mortified by my behavior, and she let me know it. I started to drink. And, then I started to gamble. Anyway, I'll spare you the details, but I was sent back to Japan in disgrace. My wife divorced me. My father was dead. And the only one who seemed even slightly pleased to see me was my mother. So, I've been helping her at the translation company ever since."

"But you clearly don't like it. Why don't you do something else?"

"Why do I live with my mother . . . Isn't that what you really want to know?"

I had clearly struck a nerve. "I don't mean to pry."

"I lost everything. Now, I'm just trying to pull myself back together. As long as I live with my mother, I can save a little. Besides, she's got a really nice kitchen."

I had to agree with him there.

"I've got my eye on an old machiya not far from her. It used to be a dry goods shop. If I save enough, I think I can afford the down payment. It's in bad shape, though, so it will take a lot to make it habitable. I want to open a gourmet restaurant, French-Japanese fusion."

Hiro's face brightened as the image of his future restaurant played across his imagination.

"Anyway, I'm a jerk at work because I don't want Mother to start to depend on me. I want her to know I don't belong in her office—or even in her house."

I heard a tentative knock at the door, followed by a louder one. Maho and Hawk let themselves in.

"Let's go gamble!" Hawk called out exuberantly. Clearly, he and Maho were a lot more enthusiastic about this adventure than I was. They were also a lot more animated. I was both exhausted and cagey with apprehension. I pulled some beers out of the refrigerator and handed Maho and Hawk each a can. Hiro planned to drive to the club and was not going to drink.

"I can't afford to get flagged for drunk driving. I'll splash a little beer on my face before I get there, least I'll smell like I'm shitfaced. Clubs like drunk salarymen. We seem like easy targets."

Hawk and Maho thought that was an ingenious ploy. They also found all of Hiro's spy cameras wonderfully exciting. Maho picked up a pair of glasses, pulled Hawk's ball cap down low on her face, and went through a simulated spy routine. Hawk decided to wear the glasses with dark lenses. I worried he wouldn't be able to see well enough. Hiro opted for the clear lenses. With his hair gelled back, he was the image of a geeky salaryman out to blow off steam. They decided they would enter the club separately and act as though they were not acquainted.

After they left, Maho and I settled back on the couch to watch a late-night suspense drama. Maho snorted with laughter at the schmaltzy acting and went in the kitchen for another beer. I checked my watch, it was a little after midnight. Not too early to try Matthew again, I thought. A busy kennel owner, he'd be up and about by 8 a.m. While Maho entertained herself, I went in the dining room to place the call on my cell. I didn't feel quite as nervous this time.

The phone began to ring. The answer machine picked up again.

"Ma-chan?! I mean, Matthew . . . uh, Benniet? It's Ruth again. Your sister. I'm in Japan. I'm sorry to keep bothering you. I'm sorry . . . "

I snapped the phone shut without even finishing my message. What an incoherent idiot I was. I sat in the darkened dining room for a minute fighting back the tears. Maho passed through to the kitchen and pulled out another beer, which she handed to me on her return.

"Do you think Matthew still speaks Japanese?" she asked.

"Probably not, why?"

"Because the message you left was entirely in Japanese."

I stared at Maho in disbelief. I hadn't been aware what language I was speaking. I just spoke. When we were little, Matthew and I only spoke to one another in Japanese. It was our natural language, our home language. We spoke English around our parents and their friends, or when we were in some kind of formal event. With each other, it was always Japanese. I guess on the phone I reverted to our childhood tongue.

"He'll probably think it's a wrong number."

"I wonder." Maho looked over at me sympathetically and then went back to the couch in the living room. I opened the can of beer and joined her. We were nearly through our second suspense drama when Hiro and Hawk returned.

Hawk was drawn, his face ashen. He stumbled into the living room and collapsed on the sofa next to Maho. "What happened?" Maho's eyes widened in fear as Hawk buried his face in her arms. Before she could coax an answer out of him, Hiro walked in. His face and the front of his white oxford shirt were covered in dark, dried blood.

"Hiro!" I shot up out of my chair and ran to him, practically pulling him up into the room. "Are you okay?"

"It's not as bad as it looks. Do you have a towel?"

I ran to the kitchen and grabbed a clean dish towel out of the drawer, rinsing it in warm water. Hiro followed after me. He ran the towel over his face, wiping off most of the blood, but smearing some of it across his cheek in the process. I took the towel from him and dabbed tentatively at his cheek, nose, and neck.

"That much is mine," he said. "The stains on my shirt belong to someone else."

"Someone else?" I raised my voice in alarm. "Did you get in a fight?"

"No. It wasn't me."

He pulled my hand away from his face and looked at me wearily.

"Do you have anything to drink?

Maho and I had finished the beer. I pulled a bottle of red wine out of the cabinet and held it up for his approval. I'm sure it wasn't of the quality he was used to, but it's what I had.

"Don't you have anything stronger?"

"I'm afraid not."

"Ok, then. Set me up." He turned and walked back into the living room.

"What happened?" Maho had wrapped her arms around Hawk and was nuzzling him when we went back in. I had glasses for everyone.

"Let's just say, I'm glad we got out of there alive. Those are some evil people."

"Was the swamp monster there?" Maho asked, meaning Tokuda.

"She may have been. It's hard to tell. There was a woman there about her age, but it was pretty dark. We'll have to watch the videos."

"Do you want to watch now?" Hiro's voice was raspy.

"Of course!" Maho and I practically replied simultaneously.

Hiro pulled the USB cable out of the box his camera came in and hooked it to the TV. We held our breath as we waited to see what he recorded. The field of vision was fairly narrow, and the frame rate was slow, making the images blur whenever Hiro moved his head. While he was relatively still, the clarity of the shot was impressively clear. He made it into the club without any trouble, as there did not seem to be anyone checking the door. Hiro ordered a drink from the bar, a whisky and water, and found a seat at a table near a small stage. Several young women were on the stage scantily clad and gyrating to an awful mashup of a Donna Summer song. A young girl wearing nothing but a short apron came up to Hiro and offered to give him a lap dance. Hiro stared intently at her face, the lens in the camera focusing enough to reveal that behind all the cheap makeup, she was probably not much older than fifteen.

"You're not my type," he said, purposely slurring his words. "I like younger girls."

"I'm second-year of middle-school. Or at least I was. Don't you want me make you happy?" Japanese was clearly not her native language.

"Where are you from?" Hiro asked, as if annoyed.

"Japan!" she said with some hostility. It was clear she wasn't Japanese.

"Get out of my way, I'm trying to watch," his hand shot up in front of the camera, waving her off.

"It goes on like this for a while," Hiro said, fast forwarding the video. "I was shooing off girls all night. None of them looked older than fifteen. Some looked younger. I shouldn't have said I liked them young, because next thing you know I had a tiny little thing come up and proposition me. I wanted to ask her about herself but was afraid to act too interested, afraid she might get in trouble. These are evil people, Ruth. Okay. Here."

He stopped fast forwarding and the video resumed at normal speed as a small girl sidled up to Hiro's table. "He sent me," she said, tossing her head in the direction of a tall man sitting slumped against the bar, staring in her direction, a cigarette stuck in the corner of his fleshy lips. Hawk had entered the club by then and was seated not too far from the man, his dark lenses looking particularly menacing. He seemed to be watching the stage show, a whiskey and water on the bar beside him.

"How old are you?" The way Hiro asked the question made it sound as if he was seeking confirmation she was young enough to interest him.

"How old do you want me to be?" the girl answered with a seductive wink. She'd been well trained to evade possible incrimination. When Hiro waved her off, the man at the bar stood up, stubbed his cigarette out in an ashtray, and ambled over.

"What's the matter? You don't like my girls?" He grabbed the girl who had been standing in front of Hiro, slapped her hard on her bare backside.

"Sorry man, not tonight."

"Our girls can make you come harder than you ever have." The man nodded at a group of men at the table behind him. Hiro slowly turned to look, his camera glasses spanning the room as he did. The men each had a girl squirming atop their laps. Hiro could see the vacant, almost bored look on the girls' faces.

Their bodies were there, but their spirits were somewhere else.

Hiro swung back around to face the man, the video image whirring with him until it focused again on the man's leering face. He was laughing now.

"Your girls are hot," Hiro said. "But that's not why I'm here."

"Oh, one of those?" the man said, holding his right hand up to the side of his face and letting it hang there limply. "No matter. I can get you boys."

"How about an American boy?"

I gasped when I heard Hiro ask this. He reached across the table and took hold of my hand. "I had to ask. The jackass believed I was a player. I thought if I took my chance, I might be able to get some of the information we needed."

"American? That's not going to be easy. I could hook you up with some Russian boys if you give me some time."

"Maybe later. I came here for the tables. I heard you had some hot numbers going on the dog races." The camera whirred to the right and then to the left as Hiro surveyed the room. "But, I don't see anything. Maybe I heard wrong."

"No. We've got what you want. Like I said, we've got anything you want." The man pushed the girl off to the side and waved his hand in the direction of a hallway behind the bar. "Follow me."

The camera shot up over the tables as Hiro stood. Hawk watched him cross the room after the man. Then, the bar disappeared from view as we entered a long hallway, passed a filthy-looking toilet, and came to a closed door. The man knocked and another man opened the door, he was clearly a yakuza *chinpira*, a lower-level thug who wasn't smart enough to do much, except open and close doors.

The room was dark. There were several booths along the walls and a group of chairs lined up in the center, most of them taken. The men seated there had their eyes trained on a television screen. One man kept jumping out of his seat, shouting, waving a sheet of paper around, only to throw his head back in disgust and tear the paper into tiny pieces. The men around him jabbed at him. One stood up and slapped the side of his head angrily until the man sat down. Hiro slowly panned the room, there were people seated in the booths, but it was too dark to make out their features. When Hiro's camera trained on the TV screen, it was clear the men were watching a dog fight. One of the dogs was being dragged off by its hind leg, a trail of blood streaking after it across the dirt floor of the ring.

"If you want to stay here, you got to get in on the action. Place your bets over there," the man pointed to a table on the right of the TV screen where a woman sat. A number of men were lined up in front of her filling out forms. Hiro crossed the room, slowly scanning the darkened booths as he passed them until a man called out, "The fuck you looking at?" Hiro turned in the direction of the voice, and an older man came into the frame. I was pretty sure it was my old friend, Kimura. There was a woman next to him in the booth. It was difficult to make out her features, but instinctively I knew it was Tokuda.

"That's her!"

Hiro stopped the video, but even in freeze frame her face was indistinguishable.

"Are you sure?" Maho asked. "How can you tell?"

"I just know it. So, she returned from the dead!"

"Did you speak with her?" Maho asked. "And where are you, Hawk?"

"I was still at the bar trying to figure out where Hiro went and how to follow him without raising suspicions."

"No, it's good you stayed where you were," Hiro responded. "We don't know what might have happened out where you were. If we were both in one place, we'd have missed it."

"Yeah. I saw them drag that guy in."

"What guy?" Maho asked.

"The guy they beat the shit out of," Hawk said, taking a long swallow of wine.

"Here, I'll fast forward." Hiro pushed the button on the remote, and the video whirred ahead. "Just as I was getting ready to place my bet on the next fight, they dragged some guy in. He was already pretty banged up. His face was bloodied, and it looked like his hand was broken."

As Hiro resumed the video, I could hear a man screaming in terror. "I'll pay! I'll pay! Please."

"You're damn right you'll pay, you piece of shit," the man with his back to the camera shouted. He pulled the man up and hit him so hard in the face he fell into the man behind him, who hit him again, sending him careening into Hiro with a sickening thud. The video images jumped, blurred, and then went black for a second.

"When the man slammed into me, he knocked my glasses off and something sharp scraped my lip."

"Was it the edge of your glasses?" I asked.

"To be honest, I think it was a bone in the man's face. Poor guy. I tried to pull him over into a booth, but the goons yanked him away, threw him on the floor, and started stomping on him. That's when I decided it was time to leave. I wasn't the only one either."

"No shit. I was sitting there at the bar and all of a sudden this stream of men started pouring out of that room." Hawk looked over at Hiro. "I was really glad to see you."

"Anyway, we shot out of there, made a dash for the car, and here we are. We stopped at a pay phone on the other side of the station and left a call with the 119 emergency. We didn't give our names. I'm sorry, Ruth. I just wanted to get out of there. And I'm pretty sure that man wasn't going to need an ambulance by then. Tomorrow, I will make a copy of the video and drop it off at the police station."

Hiro smiled wanly. The crack in his lip opened slightly and a thin seam of blood rose and spread across his mouth. I reached over and pulled a tissue out of the box I'd set on the coffee table and handed it to him.

"Thanks. I'm sorry to ask, but do you have a shirt or something I could change into? I don't think I should go home looking like this."

I dashed upstairs and rifled through my drawers, looking for one of my large sleeping shirts. I found a plain black T-shirt and went back to the living room. Maho and Hawk were wrapped in each other's arms, eyes closed.

"You know, it's really late. Do you want to stay the night? I've got plenty of room."

Everyone looked relieved at the suggestion. I hurried back upstairs to put fresh linens on the beds and pull out some towels. The guest room had two twin beds I had covered with matching coverlets of red silk embossed with *oshidori* ducks. It was one of my recent finds at the Tenjin antique market. They must have been part of a bride's trousseau—meant to top the conjugal covers of a happy couple. The oshidori, or mandarin ducks, are supposed to mate for life.

Maho and Hawk came in behind me.

"Oh, don't go to any fuss, Ruth. We're just going to collapse anyway." Maho said, practically pushing me out of the room.

"It's okay. I'll take it from here." She shut the door.

"Hiro, would you like to sleep upstairs in my room? I'll be glad to take the couch." I stood in the doorway to the living room with an armful of blankets. Hiro stood up, crossed the room, and wrapped his arms around me, burying his face in my hair. "If you don't mind, Ruth, I'd prefer to stay with you. I don't want to be alone right now." His arms wrapped tighter around my back, squeezing my arms and the blankets between his body and mine. I could feel the damp warmth of his arms, the heat of his breath. It felt good.

I tossed the blankets onto the couch, turned, and headed back up the stairs. Hiro followed, carrying the black T-shirt.

"Would you like to shower?"

"Yes."

I showed him to the bathroom and gave him a clean towel. Then I went into my room, slipped out of my clothes, pulled a nightshirt over my head, and dove under the covers. I hadn't had a man in my bed for over a year. I heard the shower turn on, the sound of splashing, and then silence. Hiro walked into the room in boxers and the black shirt. He slid in beside me.

"Thanks, Ruth. I just need to be next to someone good."

Hiro curled up with his back to me, and I folded my arms around him, squeezing him to me. The soapy smell on the back of his neck tickled my nose. I pressed my face between his shoulder blades, sensing the beat of his heart against my arm. We did not sleep right away, but lay there, each aware of the other's presence. Having him so close felt good, but it also made me nervous. This was all so new to me. I was exhausted, but unable to sleep with this man in my arms. I concentrated on his breathing, waiting for it to deepen.

At some point in the night, I slipped off to sleep, and in doing so, I disentangled myself from Hiro. I awoke with my back to his. It took me a few seconds to remember he was there. I could hear him breathing, deep chest-fulls of breaths. A maple syrup morning. The kind of morning when you woke up and all seemed right. I smiled. Squeezed my eyes shut and opened them again. It felt good to be next to Hiro. From the light streaming in between the darkening shades, I could tell it was sunny outside, close to 8 a.m. Hiro turned. He ran his hand lightly along my arm.

"You're a good woman, Ruth," he whispered hoarsely in my ear.

I nodded without turning.

I felt his arms slide around my waist, pulling me tightly to him. His hands were soft and warm, but his body was firm as it pressed against mine. He buried his face in my hair and kissed my neck. An electric current ran through me so sharply it made me gasp. I wasn't expecting to sleep with Hiro. But more than that, I wasn't expecting to feel this jagged bolt of desire. I turned and grabbed Hiro's shoulder just as he rose to meet me, pressing his body down hard on top of mine. Within seconds, we had both wriggled free of our clothes, and I folded my body around his, delighting under his touch. It had been such a long time since I had felt this kind of pleasure with a man. I wanted our lovemaking to last forever, but at the same time, I was impatient, ecstatic, and before too long, sated.

"Thank you," Hiro whispered and softly kissed my forehead. A few minutes later, he rolled out of the other side of the bed, pulled his trousers on and my shirt, balled up his bloodied shirt, and put his hand on the door. "I'll call you later," he said as he walked out. And then, he was gone, leaving me feeling strangely unsettled.

CHAPTER SEVENTEEN
WIZARDS

"Did Hiro leave already?" Maho eyed the folded collection of blankets on the couch, as she and Hawk collected their belongings and readied to go.

"Yes. Uh, he said he wanted to make a copy of the video."

"Well, he left all his equipment here," Maho said, pointing at the eyeglasses and cables strewn on the floor by the TV.

"Maybe I misunderstood," I shrugged.

"I'll call you later," Maho said as she stepped out into the midmorning sun, closing the door behind her.

With Maho and Hawk gone, a quiet fell over the house. I collected the wine glasses, picked up the blankets, and carried them back upstairs. Maho stripped the linens off one of the single beds in the guest room and had smoothed the mandarin duck coverlet back in place. The ducks looked happy.

I walked into my room and stared at my unmade bed. The sheets were wound into a knot. One of the pillows was on the floor. I flung myself across the mattress, clutching the sheets to my face, inhaling deeply, hoping for a lingering trace of Hiro's soapy scent. I couldn't smell anything. The night before, our morning sex, all seemed a distant dream. All that remained was the memory of his body on mine, the press of his hands across my breasts, the heat of his breath on my neck.

"I'll call you later." That's what he had said. It was more a casual utterance than a promise. I wondered if he would call. I wasn't even sure what I thought. I had never looked at Hiro as a potential lover, but last night felt natural. Now, as I lay in the tangle of bed sheets, I wasn't so sure it had been right. I began to feel awkward. He must think I'm some pathetic, over-the-hill, sex-maniac! I stacked both pillows on top of my face to try to stop the visions.

I tore the sheets off the bed, grabbed the soiled towels from the bathroom, the stack of linens Maho had left in the guest room, and traipsed downstairs to run a load of wash. The sun was high in the sky now. Good weather for laundry drying. The Nakatas had a dryer, but it did a lousy job, filling half the house with steam.

Staying busy kept my mind off Hiro. I straightened up the spy cameras and stuffed them in a plastic bag. Even so, I couldn't get those girls out of my mind. They were so young. Had Matthew been tangled up in a sex trafficking ring? Had he been . . . .

No. I couldn't let myself go there.

I concentrated on cleaning the house. Once I finished with the house, I would go to the 7-Eleven to buy some blank CD-ROM discs, so I could copy the video. Then, I'd take the cameras to the police and try to convince them to investigate, hoping I'd have more luck with these girls than I had with Matthew.

I heard my cell phone ringing. I dashed up the stairs in the direction of the ring, not certain where exactly I set my phone. I found it next to my computer and flipped it open just in time to catch the caller. Mr. Iizuka, the librarian. True to his word, he called to give me the precise time my package was scheduled to arrive today. 3:15. And the charge would be ¥1,930. I assured him I'd be on hand to meet the delivery and pay the COD.

I looked at the clock, 11 a.m. Too early to call Matthew. The washing machine buzzed, indicating the end of the cycle. I put the clothes in a basket and stepped outside to hang them. I then turned my attention to the clutter in the dining room. I straightened the papers left on the table, pausing when I picked up the folder of Hawk's tattoo sketches and pulled them out once more to take a look. It fascinated me that Satoko would have been so precise in the designs she wanted. And she'd been so detail oriented, down to the very word she chose to describe the color. Akashi. Why did she use such an old-fashioned word when *aka* would have been more in keeping with the other colors Hawk noted on the sketches: *kiiro* for yellow, *ao* for blue, all very standard. Akashi seemed so deliberate. Like Hawk had said about her color choice, "It's more than the color, it's the beam of light." Akashi. With no kanji graph to fix its meaning, the syllables akashi could indicate both the color red and a ray of light. It could suggest a torch. Evidence, too. Akashi could mean "proof." I looked at the sketches, again. The stylistic beams of light illuminated the character that meant Kyoto. What were we supposed to see? What was the "evidence," Satoko sought?

I spread the three sketches along the dining room table. The diving woman. She was an ama, a woman who traditionally dove for shellfish, seaweed, and pearls. Free divers, they were able to hold their breath for an unusually long time while they probed the seabeds for their catch. The image of the naked beauty, her hair wet and tangled, became the subject of many a woodblock print—to varying degrees of titillation. Satoko's ama was beautiful, but also businesslike. She captured her oyster and would soon pry its shell apart with her knife in hopes of a pearl. Cut! That's what the symbols meant alongside the diver: kire. That's what Hawk presumed. But the ama would not cut the shell, would she? She would force it open. So, what did Satoko mean by kire? I stared at the sketches. The character was written along what appeared to be a seam in the woman's sash-like garment or remnant. Aother meaning for kire was remnant, a piece, a strip. All the words began to add up: cut, remnant, inside, light, proof, Urakyō. And there were the children's toys on the noshi ribbons. I needed to see the Tani talisman. The proof was there; proof that would implicate Akira and Tokuda.

I looked at the clock again. 12:30. I decided to call the kimono designer, Ryohei Miyazaki. If anyone could advise me on a way to see the Tani talisman, he could. I picked up my phone to call and noticed I'd missed a call from Hiro. Should I call him back and let him know about my breakthrough? I decided to wait until I had more concrete information.

Miyazaki was surprised to hear from me, but he was willing to meet if I could be at his shop in twenty minutes. I hung up and rushed into the bathroom to get ready, then hailed a cab at the corner and instructed it to take me to the Ippodo Tea Shop. The clerks greeted me with familiar smiles and were quick to help me select a nice package of tea for Miyazaki. I dashed back to the taxi and off we went to the Nishijin district.

Miyazaki was waiting for me, somewhat impatiently. His wife was out on errands he said, as he invited me back into the

Japanese-style sitting room where he had received me earlier. I handed him the gift of tea, mumbling some perfunctory words, apologizing for taking up his time.

"You have more questions about Satoko?" he asked.

"Yes, if you don't mind," I said, pulling the folder with Hawk's sketches out of my bag. I spread the sketches out on the table and twisted them, so they were facing him.

"I wanted to know more about these tattoos."

Miyazaki picked the sketch of the diving woman up and looked at it closely, set it down alongside the noshi sketch, and then picked it up in turn.

"Yes? How can I help?"

"I've gone over the sketches, the design and the incorporation of the words here, kire, ura, and miyako. I believe Satoko was using her tattoos to point to a hidden treasure." I placed my finger on the diving woman sketch, pointing to the oyster in her hand. "For the diving woman, the treasure is a pearl, but for Satoko it was proof." I pointed to the word akashi Hawk said indicated the color of the light rays. "And the proof is concealed inside the remnant, the kire." I tapped the words kire and ura. "This remnant can only be the talisman. I need to see the talisman, and I thought if anyone could help me do so, it would be you."

I looked beseechingly into Miyazaki's face. He eyed the sketches for a few seconds longer and then returned my gaze.

"Where did you get these?"

I hated to reveal my source, but I felt I had little choice. I told Miyazaki about the way Hawk came across the sketches and hurriedly copied them.

"He's a very good artist," Miyazaki spoke admiringly as he

again picked up the diving woman sketch. "But these designs are not part of Satoko's tattoo."

"Are you sure?"

"I'm sure," Miyazaki smiled. "I was very familiar with Satoko's tattoo."

"Oh, yes, of course." I looked down at the table, flustered.

"I was also familiar with her difficulties with Akira. She was distraught over his actions, and what she felt certain were unspeakable crimes. She struggled to find the evidence she needed to take to the police. She followed him once, and that's how she discovered the Urakyō," he nodded in the direction of the third sketch. "But, she could never quite prove her suspicions."

"What were her suspicions, exactly?" I asked tentatively, wondering if Miyazaki's answer would confirm my own.

"She was certain he was involved in a child kidnapping ring. She confided this to me on a few occasions. I imagine she shared her fears with Hori-ichi, too."

"Hori-ichi knew?"

"I believe so. Tattooists become something of therapists, you know. When you spend that much time lying naked under the needle, you develop a bond. That's what Hori-ichi told me once while I waited for Satoko's tattoo session to finish. That's why I assume he drew these tattoos for you."

"But you just said these weren't part of Satoko's tattoos."

"That's right. I believe Hori-ichi drew these for your friend to find."

"He planted them?"

"From what you have told me, the horishi knew of your interest in Satoko, and he knew your interests exceeded the surface of her tattoo. He wanted to tell you what she had confided in him, but he was bound by his honor to his client not to speak of it directly. So, he devised this method. He must have known your friend was eavesdropping on his conversations; he knew your friend would find the sketches in his brother's drawer. He also knew he would make a copy to show you. He delivered his message without betraying Satoko's trust."

"Then, you agree my interpretation is correct?" I asked.

"Yes. I believe Satoko found the proof she needed, and she hid it in the talisman."

"Then, do you now believe she was murdered?"

"Very likely she was killed because she found the evidence."

"Will you help me uncover the evidence?"

"Yes."

Miyazaki turned around and began rummaging through the stack of bolts and boxes behind him until he uncovered a notebook full of name cards. He turned back around and put the notebook on the table, flipping through the pages until he came to the card he was looking for. He slipped the card out of the plastic holder, reached into his shirt pocket for his phone, flipped it open, and tapped in some numbers. I watched, not certain who he was calling or what he was planning.

"Miyazaki, here," he said to someone on the other end. "I need to talk to you in private. Where? I'll be there." He snapped the phone shut and put it back in his pocket.

"Ruth-san, I have a friend who works with the textiles in the Kyoto Municipal Museum of Art. Akira has called her any number of times trying to spur interest in the talisman. The museum has never been willing to pay what he wants, but I may be able to encourage her to at least offer to analyze the remnant. Part of that analysis would be to open the seam. She might tell him she could only assess the integrity of the piece by looking at the inner threads, or something. Akira doesn't know anything about textiles. He'll go along with it, so long as he believes there's money at the other end. That would allow us our chance to see what if anything Satoko has hidden."

"I want to be there," I blurted out. "I want to be there when she opens the seam."

"Perhaps," Miyazaki nodded. "My friend may not be able to do this. I'd be asking her to compromise her professional reputation by entering a negotiation she has no way to honor. But, let's see."

He stood and waited for me to do the same. I collected my papers and left the room. Miyazaki followed me to the front entrance and waited while I slipped into my sandals.

"I'll call you when I have news. Probably later tonight. I'm going to meet her, now." With that, he bowed slightly and withdrew down the hallway. I barely had time to thank him before he was gone. I stepped out of the house and closed the sliding door behind me.

The rains of yesterday gave way to a vibrant blue sky with fluffy white clouds. Days as fine as this were few and far between. I was tempted to keep on walking the three miles or so to my house but was afraid it would take too long and I'd miss the special delivery letter scheduled to arrive at 3:15. I ducked into the Family Mart convenience store, bought a package of blank CD-ROMs, and headed back out to find a bus stop. I was home just before 3:00. The mailman was already there, twelve minutes early. I accepted the package and paid what was due.

The copy Mr. Iizuka made for me was surprisingly clear. I scanned the pages of the catalog for any additional clues, paying particular attention to the photographs. I couldn't take my eyes off the one of Matthew standing next to the dog and the Scotsman. I decided to give his number another try. It was early in Scotland. I dialed the number, biting my lip in anticipation, only to hear the familiar mechanical message on the answering machine again. I left another message. This time making absolutely certain I was speaking English! And this time, I didn't forget to leave my phone number. I also noted I would follow up with a letter.

I went upstairs, pulled out several sheets of stationery paper, and sat down at my desk. I could write on the computer. I could email. But, there was something about the intimacy of a handwritten letter that just felt right. The letter took longer to write than I had thought, and I had to rewrite a few of the pages to avoid cross outs and corrections. I wanted the letter to reflect the sincerity I had in my heart. I folded the pages and slipped them into an envelope along with copies of the photographs of Matthew I had made for my trip to Shirohama. I carried the letter downstairs to place in the entryway, so I would remember to drop it by the post office tomorrow.

I was just headed outside to retrieve the wash when my cell phone rang again. It was Miyazaki.

"Where are you now, Ruth-san?"

"I'm at home."

"And you live close to the museum, don't you?"

"Yes, just a few blocks."

"Do you know the Marinna Café?"

"Yes."

"Can you meet me there in ten minutes? I'd like to introduce you to my friend."

"I'll be there."

I grabbed my bag, carrying along the sketches, and dashed out the door. Miyazaki was to meet me where not but a week ago, I had had my encounter with Tokuda. I wondered if the wait staff would remember me. I suspected I had left quite an impression. Miyazaki was seated when I arrived. Sharing his table was a woman in her late fifties, stylishly dressed in a light brown peplum suit. As I approached, she looked up at me and smiled.

"Ruth-san, thanks for coming on such short notice. This is Shiori Hayashi. She's the textiles curator at the museum."

Ms. Hayashi handed me her name card. Shiori was the perfect name for a textile curator. The second character in her name, *ori*, meant "weave."

"I've told her about your interest in the talisman. She's willing to help."

"That's wonderful," I turned to Ms. Hayashi and smiled.

"But, she will not be able to contact or interact with the Tani family."

"Please understand, Ruth," Ms. Hayashi broke in, speaking a British-inflected English, "I cannot represent the museum in any negotiations with the Tani family that are, well, for lack of a better word, fraudulent. I can't compromise the integrity of the museum."

I understood her position, but I was disappointed. I didn't know why we needed to have a meeting for her to reveal this to me.

"But, I am willing to help," she added hastily, seeing my disappointment.

"I know what you want to do, and I know why. And, I want you to succeed. What I can do is coach you, or preferably an associate of yours, in what you need to do to gain access to the Tani talisman. Do you understand?"

I nodded.

"Good. And, I don't mean to be rude, Ruth, but I think it would be better if the person contacting the Tani family was a Japanese. They may not be willing to enter into negotiations with someone who isn't."

"I understand. What do I need to do next?"

"Do you have a friend you trust who will pose as a museum curator? She or he should be a little older than you, if possible. It takes years to reach the level in a museum where you can negotiate an expensive purchase."

I thought over my acquaintances. Maho would be more than willing to run a scam on Akira Tani, but she was much too young, and much too "colorful." Mrs. Shibasaki. She would be perfect, and she could definitely convince Akira she was a credible businesswoman.

"I have someone in mind, but I'm not sure she will do it."

"Please follow up with her and get back to me as soon as you can. I have actually heard through the grapevine Mr. Tani has been looking for a buyer."

We talked a bit more about the talisman, and then I excused myself, promising to follow up as soon as I located someone willing to help me. Once home, I called Hiro. I'd been avoiding talking to him, feeling more and more uncomfortable about our tryst, but I wanted to ask his mother to be my accomplice. I needed to run it past Hiro first.

"There you are!" He picked up on the first ring. "I've been trying to reach you."

"I know. I'm sorry. It's just that I've been so busy today."

"I've been thinking of you all day, Ruth. About last night . . ."

"Oh, that's okay. You don't need to explain. It just happened, right? I mean, it's not like we expected it to. I understand. Don't worry about it."

"Ruth, stop!" he cut me off. "Yes, it was unexpected, and it did just happen. But, it was not just one of those things."

"What do you mean?"

"I mean, I'd like it to happen again."

"Oh?"

"Ruth, I like you, and I hope we can see more of each other, but I don't want to force you."

Hiro caught me off guard. I was certain he was going to make excuses for the encounter. Although I could feel my stomach lurch with excitement at the prospect of seeing him again, I was going to have to get used to this new direction. I launched into my conversation with Miyazaki, slowly working my way around to involving his mother. He promised to follow up with her.

CHAPTER EIGHTEEN
SWANS

"Ruth, are you ready?" Hiro called from the front door.

"She'll be there in a minute," Maho shouted down the stairs on my behalf. She stopped by to help me get ready and was putting the finishing touches on the hair she had very carefully dyed and coiffed for me. Her fussing was making me nervous.

"That's good enough, isn't it?"

I brushed her hand aside and stood up, eager to get started.

"Someone's impatient!" she said with a teasing wink.

I was. But, not for the reason Maho implied. I hurried down the stairs. When I saw the look of shock on Hiro's face, I knew Maho had achieved the wanted results. I did not look like Ruth. I looked like Mrs. Shibasaki's colleague. That would be Mrs. Shibasaki in her guise as the associate curator of Japanese textiles for the Kyoto Municipal Museum of Art. Maho had dyed my hair a dark, chestnut brown and had plaited, spun, and folded it into a very well-behaved chignon. With my dark suit and new high heels, I looked convincingly professional.

Hiro released a soft whistle of admiration.

"Okay, don't get used to this look! The color is temporary, and the heels even more so!" With the additional height, I was nearly six feet. I would certainly be a commanding presence next to Mrs. Shibasaki. I pulled the new leather name-card holder out of my sleek attaché and read over my name card one more time, to be sure I had it. Grace Carothers, Textile Research Associate, Boston Museum of Fine Arts. I was to be assisting Mrs. Shibasaki with the textile assessment today, representing the Boston Museum and a potential joint exhibit. It was all subterfuge, of course. But, Akira was too blinded by greed to investigate. Of course, if he uncovered our deception, we'd be in trouble. That is why Hiro, our driver, would be standing guard nearby. We had apprised Officer Moriyama with the Kawabata Police Station of our plan to "interview" Akira about his relationship to the Scotsman. We'd left out a few details, obviously. Moriyama wasn't happy about what we were doing and encouraged us to let his department handle further investigations. Earlier, I had presented him with the spy-cam video Hiro had made. He allowed that there was nothing in the video to implicate Akira or to suggest Tokuda was still alive. Akira was careful. Even though he seemed to be a shadow owner in the business, his name was not associated with the club. We were hoping that this time, in his own house, he would be less circumspect. We believed his ignorance of kimonos would be to our advantage. Both Mrs. Shibasaki and I had undergone an intense, though brief, tutorial with Ryohei Miyazaki and the textiles curator Shiori Hayashi. I thought we knew enough to fool Akira.

Hiro held open the door to his mother's Mercedes, and I slid into the backseat, next to Mrs. Shibasaki. She looked impeccable, as always, in her dove grey Chanel suit. She nodded coolly as I fastened my seatbelt, already working on her serious professional demeanor. Hiro had also dressed for the part in a dark suit, tie, and sunglasses.

"Are those the camera glasses?" I asked, leaning forward and touching him lightly on the shoulder.

"Why, yes they are. Did you bring yours?"

I had. Both Hiro and I planned to film the encounter with Akira. Fortunately, the large, dark-framed camera glasses Hiro used at Urakyō looked good on me, accentuating the bookish demeanor I planned to project when presented with the talisman. Maho tapped on the window and waved to us as we pulled away from the house. She would stay behind.

Mrs. Shibasaki pulled a sheet of paper out of her Gucci attaché case.

"Do you like this little accessory, Ruth?" she asked when she saw me eyeing the case. It looked very expensive. "I borrowed it from a woman who worked in my husband's diplomatic mission. She retired a number of years ago and has little use for it now." She handed the piece of paper to me.

"After our textiles tutorial, I took the time to stop by the city office and managed to wheedle a copy of the Tani family registry. Interesting, don't you think?"

I turned my attention to the document, wishing I'd had the forethought to investigate the registry myself.

"Look who the family head is."

It wasn't Akira. The senior Mr. Tani, Shōtarō's father, was still listed as the head. Normally, the adopted son, once the father had retired, was elevated to the president of the company, when a family business was involved, along with the headship of the family. Akira was the president of Tani Kimonos, but the elder

Tani was still the family head.

"Why do you suppose that is?"

"Hard to say. Perhaps the elder Tani has misgivings? Regrets?"

"But he was the one who invited this wolf into the hen house."

"Don't forget Akira had leverage over the old man in the form of debts." Hiro piped up before slamming on the brakes to avoid a taxi switching lanes.

Traffic was light until we reached the intersection of Imadegawa and Shirakawa. All the tourists around the Ginkakuji Temple backed up the buses, which backed up everything else. I looked anxiously over Hiro's shoulder.

"Relax, Ruth."

"I'm just worried we'll be late."

"And if we are, we'll apologize. A curator has a busy job, you know. I think we should keep Akira waiting, at least a little."

I saw her point. I sat back in my seat. We were only five minutes late when the car glided to a halt in front of the wall surrounding the Tani compound. Hiro parked, then walked over to the intercom alongside the bolted gate, leaned over, and spoke into the box. Within minutes, an old woman in a cardigan and loose-fitting dress opened the small door next to the gate. I felt a rush of fear, worried it might be Tokuda, but it wasn't. She held the door open, while Hiro helped his mother out of the car. I was probably supposed to wait for him to open my door, too, but I alighted on the other side. I brushed past Hiro as I did, and our eyes met. He hurriedly bowed before betraying any kind of familiarity with me.

"This way, please. Mr. Tani is expecting you."

The woman guided us over freshly watered stepping stones dotting an expansive lawn edged with perfectly manicured shrubs and graceful trees. Not a leaf was out of place. She led us into a spacious entry hall, tastefully appointed with a fresh bouquet of flowers and several serene-looking Buddhist statues. I was grateful for the cool air that rushed out to meet us as we entered. Just the walk across the front lawn in my dark suit was enough to start me perspiring.

Mrs. Shibasaki and I removed our shoes and straightened them neatly behind us. We stepped into the slippers that had been prepared for us and made our way down the hallway after the woman. She led us into an overly elegant sitting room, completely western-style, with tufted settees, Rococo-style pedestals, grotesquely ornate figurines, and an enormous tapestry of a wan, golden-haired woman with an arm draped over the slender body of a white swan. Unlike the Renaissance versions of Leda and the Swan, this woman was fully clothed. I could not imagine anyone ever feeling comfortable here. But, perhaps that was the point. Mrs. Shibasaki and I sat gingerly on the claret-colored settee under the alarmed gaze of the swan. The woman left briefly and returned with servings of tea and cake. We heard footsteps in the hallway and then the door opened, admitting Akira Tani.

He was taller than I had imagined, trim and tan, as well. If I hadn't known better, I might have thought him handsome, but there was an arrogance about him. His unrelenting gleam of insincerity when he smiled confirmed this.

"Mrs. Shibasaki?" he said as he walked briskly across the floor. "So nice of you to come." He took the phony business card

Mrs. Shibasaki offered and stuffed it in his shirt pocket without so much as glancing at her credentials. "I've been trying to get you museum people out here for years. What made you finally listen?"

"Well, the museum has come into some money rather unexpectedly, and we are looking to add to our textiles collection. Your talisman has been at the top of our list for as many years, I can assure you."

Mrs. Shibasaki responded with a smooth assurance and then turned to me. "Allow me to introduce you to my assistant, Grace Carothers. She is doing an internship with us from the Boston Museum of Fine Arts."

I presented my card and bowed clumsily. We decided I would speak only rarely and then only in English, not revealing my fluency in Japanese. I mumbled a greeting, and Akira eyed me curiously.

"I hadn't realized you'd bring an assistant. I can't imagine what a foreigner might contribute to the authentication process, but at least she's not hard on the eyes." I had to struggle not to give away the fact I understood every word he said, but the hard, feral glint in his eyes needed no translation.

"Yes, well then." Mrs. Shibasaki snapped her hand up and shot a glance at her TAG Heuer wristwatch. "Shall we begin? Where is the item?"

"I've prepared a room for you."

"This way please." Akira stood and waved us toward the door.

"And you will have it in its carrying case and wrappings, yes?"

"I believe those were the conditions you made, weren't they?"

Mrs. Shibasaki nodded.

"That is what you will get. The lady's wish is my command." He leered back at me.

Akira ushered us down a long corridor and then outside along a covered passageway to a separate wing. This one was Japanese style. Was this part of the house Satoko used for her refuge? There was little evidence of the earlier occupant; however, the wooden floors along the bridgeway were rough and needed polishing. The alcoves placed here and there along the corridor lacked any sort of ornamentation. Akira led us into a tatami-mat room. There were three men in the room, standing silently along the bare wall. I immediately recognized Kimura among them, and my heart began to pound. I did my best to keep my head down, terrified he would recognize me. The second man was the one Hiro had encountered at Urakyō. I had never seen the third. Akira instructed us to sit on the pillows placed alongside a low table. I did my best to position myself, so that my back was to Kimura. How could he not recognize me? I guess Maho's disguise was that good. Once we were seated, Akira pulled his cellphone out of his pocket and made a call, then turned to us. "The talisman is on the way."

Mrs. Shibasaki took that as her cue to begin readying herself. She pulled a small leather folder out of her briefcase, unzipped it slowly, and extracted a white cloth, a velvet pouch with a magnifying glass, a pair of white gloves, and a small set of tools—needles, tweezers, and snips. These she lined up in front of her with the precision of a doctor preparing for surgery.

The door opened and two women entered with a large, flat wooden box which they set before us on the table, and then withdrew to the other side of the room and kneeled on the tatami, apparently ready for instructions from Akira.

"Well, there you are. Do whatever it is you do."

Mrs. Shibasaki looked at the box but made no effort to remove the lid. "Will the elder Mr. Tani not be joining us?" she asked with some surprise. I noticed the two women shift their weight a bit and look stealthily at one another.

"No. He won't be joining us."

"He is in agreement with these negotiations, is he not?" Mrs. Shibasaki looked sharply at Akira. I was beginning to feel squeamish, wishing she'd just get on with it. "I would hate to go to the trouble of authenticating the item only to learn he wasn't ready to part with a family heirloom."

"Trust me. He'll have no objections."

"Certainly, but it's not just a matter of trust. It's my understanding he is still listed as the family head. Is that correct?" Akira glared at Mrs. Shibasaki. She had struck a nerve.

"Not that it is any of your business, but the old man had a stroke and is in a wheelchair. Would you like me to drag him down to witness these proceedings?"

"I suppose that won't be necessary," Mrs. Shibasaki treated Akira to a withering stare. "Will he be able to sign our documents in the event of a sale or is he too incapacitated? I don't mean to be insensitive, but if he can't manage a signature, we'll need to make arrangements."

"Oh, he'll sign," Akira sneered, "even if he has to hold the pen in his teeth."

Mrs. Shibasaki held Akira's gaze and then turned to the implements on the table.

"Very well."

Slowly, as though she were performing an elaborate ritual, she took the white cloth, unfolded it, and spread it over the table, carefully brushing away invisible pieces of lint with a tiny hake brush of pristine white goat hair. Satisfied the surface was clean, she pulled her white gloves out of their special envelope and slipped into them one finger at a time. She pushed her fingers into each other, making sure the gloves were appropriately snug, and then she rose on her knees to peer over the box on the table in front of her. Slowly, she pulled off the lid and examined it inside and out, running a gloved finger down the smooth surface of paulownia wood.

"Clearly, the storage box is not original to the talisman, but it is a fine specimen."

"How do you know that?" Akira asked, sounding slightly offended.

"Well, there are several indicators. The edge on the groove on the rim of the box that creates the seal with the lid is rounded, see here?" Akira leaned in to look. "Box makers in the seventeeth century made them square. Then, there's the choice of wood grain."

"Yeah, yeah. Who cares? It's the talisman we're selling. So, get to it already."

I had to agree with Akira. I was eager for Mrs. Shibasaki to hurry it along, but she had paid careful attention to Shiori Hayashi's instructions about the procedure for analyzing items. Even if her explanations were complete fabrication, her elaborate ministrations were more than convincing.

She carefully set the lid to one side, leaned over the box, and cautiously lifted out the talisman, tucked inside a thick paper wrapping, and placed it on the white cloth. With what seemed a practiced hand, she gently untied the cords to the wrapper. When she pulled away the paper and brought the talisman into view, I gasped. It was breathtakingly beautiful. The lines between frames were crisp and clean, the colors deeply saturated. The remnant was about the width of a formal obi sash, perhaps a bit wider. And it was much, much longer. Mrs. Shibasaki took out a measuring tape and began making detailed measurements, meticulously writing the numbers in a small notebook she pulled out of her bag. She carefully unfolded the fabric, revealing the tanzaku poetry slips I was so familiar with. The artistry in the slips was exquisite. Here and there, the young dyer had inserted mother-of-pearl inflected dyes into the fabric of the slips, giving the cloth a luminescence in addition to a sense of depth. Each slip was inscribed with a poem. I leaned over to study the poem closest to me. The calligraphic hand was so fine and certain, I could easily read:

> The love I have for you
> Now that we have met
> Pales in comparison
> To what
> I felt before.

I recognized it immediately as a poem by Fujiwara no Atsutada, one of the Thirty-Six Immortals of Poetry. It was the kind of poem a lover would give his lady the morning after their tryst. I imagined our young dyer probably had his master's daughter in mind as he labored over this piece. The slip of paper was tied to a blossoming branch of cherry, with soft petals illuminated against the hoary trunk of the tree. Mrs. Shibasaki gently nudged me to sit back. She picked up her magnifying glass and began inspecting the fabric. She then unfolded more of the fabric, bringing the section with the maple leaves into view. I nearly gasped again, the fabric was so vibrant.

"What's this?" Mrs. Shibasaki asked as she neared the end of the remnant. She brought the magnifying glass down close to the seam.

"This is odd."

"What?" Akira wedged his way between Mrs. Shibasaki and myself, leaning in as if to pick up the fabric.

"Please! Don't touch with your bare hands. This fabric is delicate."

Chastened, Akira drew back, but he asked again. "What's wrong? What did you find?"

"Well, these threads do not appear to be original to the fabric. I'll need to lift them out in order to do a proper investigation."

"But, it won't damage the piece, right? I don't want you to do anything that will lower the value."

"No, certainly not. I need to examine the underside of the fabric anyway, so I'll just pick this thread out here. I suspect someone earlier had done the same."

"What do you mean?"

"Well, the only way to authenticate the vintage of a fabric is to examine the nature of the gloss on the inner threads."

Mrs. Shibasaki's deception was so convincing, even I believed her.

"Do you mind?" She turned to look up at Akira.

"No, no. Do what you have to do."

"Very well."

Mrs. Shibasaki tried to pick up the slender needle she set along the edge of the table, but she was having difficulty doing so with her gloves on. She adroitly slipped her right glove off and lifted the needle. Then without touching the fabric with the fingers on her right hand, she slowly began to pick up the thread away from the seam. When she had pulled it out ever so slightly, she set the needle down and picked up the snips. With what could only seem a practiced hand, she snipped the thread and then returned to the needle. It was a laborious process. When she had made a small opening, she slipped her glove back on and gingerly inserted her index finger into the remnant. She then pulled her finger out, lightly touching the items she lined up on the edge of the table. "That's odd. I thought I had a number 911 needle, but I seem to have misplaced it." She rifled hurriedly through her bag.

"Ru—Grace," she caught herself, addressing me in English. "Will you please go to the car and bring my other bag. I'm going to need that smaller needle. I can't seem to make the progress I need with these tools.

It was a ploy we discussed earlier. I was to go to the car and ask Hiro to call Moriyama. Mrs. Shibasaki must have felt something lodged in the remnant, but she did not want to alert Akira to it until we were certain we'd have the backup we needed. I stood up, my knees shaking with excitement, and headed towards the door, careful to keep my face turned away from Kimura. At Akira's signal, one of the women opened the door for me, led me down the corridor, and to the other wing where she showed me to the entrance and waited while I rushed to the car.

Hiro rolled down the window and looked at me expectantly.

"She is asking for needle 911."

We had thought using the American emergency number would be a safe enough signal. In Japan, the emergency number was 119.

"Please pop the trunk, I need to look like I'm searching for something."

I rummaged about while Hiro sat in the front and placed the call. When he was finished, he came to the back of the car. "I reached him. He said he was on his way. Give him fifteen minutes."

"Will he run his siren?"

"I don't know. He didn't say."

Hiro reached down for my hand and gave it a squeeze, then he straightened up and closed the trunk while I returned to the house. The woman saw me back to the room where Mrs. Shibasaki was still busy with her inspection of the talisman.

"I am sorry, Mrs. Shibasaki, but the needle you requested was not in the case. Shall I send the driver back to get it? He thinks he can do it in fifteen minutes."

"No, that won't be necessary," she said, with no change to her expression. "Let's continue. I'll just need to go slowly. This larger needle is causing the fabric to pucker slightly."

Handling the fabric with a respectful delicacy, Mrs. Shibasaki slowly picked at the threads along the seam, gradually making a larger and larger opening.

"How much longer is this going to take?" Akira asked, visibly uncomfortable seated on the floor.

"It's difficult to say. It is of paramount importance to the integrity of the item that I do not pull up the wrong thread, or do anything that might cause the fabric to fray."

Mrs. Shibasaki continued to pick with exquisite precision at the threads. Each tiny piece of thread she snipped, she collected and placed in a slender white envelope she had pulled out of her bag.

My phone began to vibrate in my jacket pocket. Hiro was to send a message when he had more information on Moriyama. I pulled my phone out and flipped it open. "M delayed. Fifteen minutes more." Mrs. Shibasaki leaned over to check the message and when she did the edge of a white envelope peeked through the opening in the seam.

"What's that?" Akira asked.

Mrs. Shibasaki looked down at the talisman and admitted she was unsure. "It must be some kind of lining, you know, to give the talisman more stability."

"Pull it out. I want to see."

"Mr. Tani, please. We must treat this fabric with utmost care."

"Just pull it out."

Mrs. Shibasaki guided the envelope through the opening she had made in the seam. It was thicker than expected. Akira lurched for it across the table. I think by now he had begun to understand what the envelope was and who had put it there. It was clearly of recent vintage, though Satoko had chosen traditional-style washi paper.

"Not so fast, Mr. Tani. We do not know what this is. In the interest of preserving the integrity of the item, I must insist you not touch anything with your hands. If you are determined to interfere with my inspection, I will require that you wear gloves. Grace, please find Mr. Tani a pair of gloves."

Fortunately, we had thought to bring an extra pair. I dove into my attaché to retrieve them.

"Here you are, sir," I said in English.

The gloves were small for Akira, but he managed to get them on. The distraction, though, allowed her time to peer inside the envelope. She used a pair of tweezers to retrieve a folded page of blue stationery paper and slipped the rest of the envelope down onto her lap before Akira noticed. I quietly pulled the envelope from her lap and onto mine, uncertain if Kimura and the other goons behind me had noticed. The fact that they made no move to stop me or to alert their boss made me suspect they had not. The envelope was heavier than I anticipated. I was eager to look inside it but didn't want to draw attention to myself.

While Mrs. Shibasaki unfolded the stationery paper, I tucked the envelope into my jacket pocket.

"It appears to be a letter."

"What?" Akira asked craning his neck to see. Mrs. Shibasaki held it at an angle, making it difficult for him to read it from where he was seated.

"Yes. It is a letter. Please allow me to read it."

If you are reading this letter, then I am dead. These

last few months I have grown increasingly concerned with my husband's illicit deeds. Unable to stop him, I have taken to collecting evidence, which you will find contained herein, that I trust will implicate him in a number of crimes—chief among them kidnapping and trafficking in children. There are photographs. I came upon them quite unexpectedly when cleaning the storehouse. It seems then we will both use this storehouse to hide our secrets. Mine, I have hidden in this remnant, this so-called Tani talisman—beautiful in its own right but layered with so much treachery and pain. How heavy it has become.

"Give me that!" Akira barked, reaching across the table to snatch at the letter, but Mrs. Shibasaki was quicker. She twisted her body away, holding the letter out of reach. This only compelled the men behind her to step closer. They squeezed in around us, standing at our backs, so that we were nearly able to rest our heads on their knees. Akira put his elbows on the table and leaned over, leering into Mrs. Shibasaki's face. "I believe that letter belongs to me." He held out his hand. "Hand it over."

"Better do as he says!" I mumbled to her, terrified he would hurt her.

"You speak Japanese?" Akira wheeled around to look at me. In my panic, I had forgotten to use English.

"Just sukoshi," I answered, holding up my thumb and forefinger to make the sign of the littlest of inches and doing my best to mispronounce suu-KO-shee.

Akira wasn't buying it. He grabbed my hand and nearly

pulled me across the table.

"What the hell is going on here? Who are you really, Grace Carouthers?"

The violent way he jerked my arm caused the envelope to ride up in my pocket, catching Akira's attention. He let go of my hand to grab the envelope, but I beat him to it, spilling the contents on the table. Photograph after photograph cascaded over the polished table. While Akira and the others stared wordlessly at the cache, I spread them around like playing cards, searching until I found one I recognized. Matthew with the puppy. I held it up to Akira.

"Did you kidnap my brother?" I shouted in Japanese, no longer concerned to hide my identity. "Just tell me yes or no!"

"Who the hell are you?"

"Just answer me!" I yelled, hoping these images were being captured on tape. To be extra sure, I secretly pushed the button on the phone in my pocket, ringing Hiro's number. He would be able to hear what was happening. I heard him pick up.

"That depends, doesn't it?"

"On what?" I asked. My pleading turning to desperation.

"On who wants to know."

"I want to know. Matthew was my brother. He IS my brother. And I need to know what happened to him."

Akira looked at the photograph in my hand. I saw a glimmer of recognition flash into his eyes.

"You kidnapped him and took him to Shikoku, didn't you?"

Akira turned his gaze back over to me, his anger softening to a sickening smugness.

"Ah, the little American."

"Then you did take him?"

"I wish I could take the credit; it was quite a heist. But my bitch of a wife was the mastermind of that one."

"Satoko?" Mrs. Shibasaki interjected in shocked disbelief.

"Don't be ridiculous. I mean my first wife, Miyo Yoshida."

"But why?" Again, I could not quell the pleading.

"Money. We had hoped to score big with the lawsuit, and that dragged on and on without the kind of payout we needed. Miyo cooked up the kidnapping. She figured the kid's parents would pay big. I mean, we knew they had the money . . . surgeon in a successful hospital and all."

"You never even gave them the chance. There was never any ransom demand." The pleading had now given way to disbelief, as well as disgust. My parents had been missionaries. They didn't earn much. Besides the hospital treated most patients on a sliding scale, charging them only what they could afford. If they'd gotten a ransom demand, they would have paid.

"We made a better deal."

"What do you mean?"

"We found a buyer."

"The Scotsman?"

That got Akira's attention.

"Wait a minute. How do you know about him? Who are you, exactly?"

"I told you. I'm Matthew's sister. My name is Ruth Bennett."

"Then who are you?" Akira riveted Mrs. Shibasaki with a glare.

"I'm the kimono expert," she replied primly.

"I know you arranged for the Scotsman to take my brother.

I just want to know what happened." I fired back before Akira could question Mrs. Shibasaki further. I didn't want him to evade my questions.

"We were going to send your parents ransom demands, but it took time to get the brat to a safe place where no one would recognize him. That's why we went to Miyo's father's in Shikoku. But, the old man was so wrapped up in his goddamn dogs, he threatened to turn us in if we didn't help him with his competition. That's where we met the Scotsman."

"And he offered to buy the boy?!"

"No, not like that. Not at first. We tried to hide the kid. I mean, how were we going to explain him? But, one day the Scotsman came to Yoshida's house, while Miyo and I were down at the docks drinking. He found Matthew there and started asking questions. Yoshida didn't want anything to do with the kid and told the Scotsman he was an orphan. The Scotsman went on and on about how lonely he was, how he lived in a cold, desolate place and couldn't find a woman to marry him. Real sob story. So, Yoshida agreed to give him the boy."

"And so, he just took him?"

"It wasn't that easy. When Miyo found out what her old man had done, she was furious. I was drunk and beat the old man so badly, I nearly killed him and would have if Miyo hadn't pulled me off. We made him go back to the Scotsman and demand money. We explained he'd have to pay to get the paperwork, because the kid needed to get documents to travel. The Scotsman was willing to give us just about anything we asked for. It didn't take too long to find a counterfeiter who could fake the passport, and it wasn't that expensive either. We gouged the Scotsman to make it worth the effort. And once the documents were done, he took off with the boy. End of story. I don't know what happened to the kid after that and I don't care. Besides, the statute of limitations on that case ran out years ago. You've got nothing on me."

"Except that once your taste for kidnapping expired you graduated to murders," Mrs. Shibasaki said.

"I don't know what you're talking about. I never murdered anyone."

"Satoko-san? Daté-san? Satoko-san's brother?"

"Like I said, that's on my wife, and she's dead. Besides, I heard they committed suicide. You've got nothing on me."

"They weren't suicides," I interjected. "Maybe you didn't have anything to do with their deaths, but why was your wife so intent on killing them?"

"She lost her fucking mind when her kidnapping plan fell through."

"Because she missed her big payout?" I asked.

"Sure, that, and the fact she couldn't get past some crazy idea that life owed her, that she'd been cheated. She was more than a little burned by my arrangement with Satoko."

"You left her because she couldn't give you a child?" I asked.

"Don't be stupid. Do you see any children here? If I wanted a child would I have married Satoko? She was already pretty much dried up by then."

"Then why'd you leave Miyo?" Mrs. Shibasaki asked. "You two seemed perfect for each other."

"For the money," Akira answered, apparently overlooking the sarcasm. "Satoko was the perfect cash cow, but aren't you two just so clever coming here with these questions? You don't think

I'm just going to wish you well and send you on your way, do you?"

"I thought you weren't a murderer?" I quipped under my breath, but not in a low enough tone to escape Akira's notice.

"I'm not a murderer, but that doesn't mean I don't know people who are."

Akira looked above our heads at his henchmen, and I felt a pair of hands grab me under the shoulders and pull me up. I turned towards Mrs. Shibasaki and saw she was receiving the same kind of treatment.

"What do you think you're doing!" she screamed. "Take your hands off me." She struggled to pry herself free of her assailant's grip. I found myself wishing I had thought to study aikido or another martial art. "Don't think we came here without informing others what we were up to. People know where we are!"

"Oh, you mean like these people?" Akira asked, opening the door. Another man came into the room pushing Hiro ahead of him. Hiro's hands were bound behind his back, and his face was bruised, blood oozing from his nose and mouth.

"No, she means people like me."

We turned to see Shōtarō Tani walking through the open door. He was clean shaven, dressed in khakis and a crisp white linen shirt. Except for the grey strands threading through his newly trimmed hair, he looked very much like the playboy of old. "Shōtarō?" Akira mumbled the name but then stood slack jawed, staring stupefied. "I thought you were . . ."

"Dead?" Shōtarō finished the sentence for him. "No, Akira, that was another one of your failed ventures. You and your conniving wife. I'm very much alive."

"Well then, let me correct my mistake."

Akira turned and signaled to Kimura and the others to attack. Shōtarō stepped to his left and we could see a figure through the open door in the hallway behind him. It was the elder Tani hunched precariously in a wheelchair.

Shōtarō held up his right hand, and I noticed it was swathed in a white glove. "Before you cut the fingers off my other hand, do you mind if we invite Father to join the party? Perhaps you should consult the family head before you do anything rash, Akira."

Kimura pulled to a stop when he saw the senior Tani, allowing Shōtarō enough time to step back into the hallway and push his father's chair into the room.

"It's just like Father to hang back comfortably in his boardroom while his minions do his dirty work, barking orders like some malevolent daimyo." Shōtarō turned to look at the crumpled figure in the chair. "I guess you're not barking now, are you, Father?"

The elder Tani struggled to turn his head towards his son. His face was slack, but his eyes glinted.

"I want you to see what's become of your family, not that you really care."

Shōtarō gestured towards the talisman spilling out over the table at the center of the room.

"Your wife is dead, your daughter murdered, and your disowned son disfigured. Your putative son, whom you haven't seen fit to advance to the family headship, is desperate to sell the only thing of value this family has left. But, the sale won't benefit the family, will it? If a museum were to investigate the provenance of the talisman, they'd discover that it is the legal inheritance of the Miyazaki family, wouldn't they? You knew that, didn't you? You knew you'd never make any money off this thing. So, I bet you didn't even know what Akira here was up to, did you? Happy now?"

The elder Tani's body began to tremble as he lifted his right hand with great effort and pointed it at Akira. Spittle slipped from the left side of mouth and his tongue twisted thickly as he managed to say, "Stop."

That's when we heard the sirens.

"The police are on their way," Hiro shouted. "Are you going to tie them up, too?"

"At least two patrol cars from the sound of it. Maybe more," I said.

Akira's face became resolute. "Let's get out of here," he said to Kimura and the other two men. They rushed out of the room only minutes before Moriyama rushed in. He was alone.

CHAPTER NINETEEN
PIGEONS RETURN

The hydrangea blooms along the Philosopher's Path looked parched, their deep blue faded to a powdery grey. The rainy season had ended, only to be met by oppressive mid-summer humidity. Two weeks had passed since my encounter with Akira. He eluded capture for a few days but was caught in Osaka hiding behind a pachinko parlor. Police charged him with seven counts of kidnapping and twenty-three counts of trafficking. He was going to be spending a long time in jail. Urakyō was finally closed, and this time for good. Despite my suspicions that Tokuda was still alive, the police hadn't been able to locate her.

My parents made the trip to Kyoto and had been staying with me for the last week. The police informed us that the statute of limitations had long since expired on Matthew's kidnapping, but they also took time to publicly and formally apologize to my parents for not investigating the case more scrupulously when they had the chance. It was small comfort, and I had to admit, I felt slightly vindicated. Mother said so herself when we were seated in the living room, reminiscing. We were laughing about some of Matthew's antics, the way he tried to rescue cockroaches before my mother would squash them.

"I tell you, that boy could not kill a thing. Not even a cockroach!"

We shared a laugh at that and then Mother reached over and took my hand. "Ruth, honey, we've got work to do."

"Work? Have you found some cockroaches here?"

"No, silly. I mean you and me. We've got some repair work ahead of us."

"I know, Mama. And I think we're going to be fine."

Every evening, we tried to reach Matthew only to be met again by the mechanical voice. On our fifth time, I heard the phone connect before the machine came on and an actual human voice came on the line.

"Haar Haven Kennels."

Suddenly, I found myself speaking with a very pleasant-sounding woman. From her voice, she seemed young. For a second, I was almost too stunned to speak and she nearly hung up.

"Oh wait. I'm sorry. I'm calling for Matthew . . . I mean Benniet . . ."

"Yes. Right. He's out tramping with the lads. May I say who's calling?"

"Did you say he was camping?"

"No, tramping. He takes his dogs out with him into the field for several weeks. It's part of their training, you see."

"Is there any way to get a message to him? This is rather urgent."

"I'm afraid not. Say, are you the woman who's been calling? Almost daily, isn't it?"

"Yes. I'm sorry to be a bother, but I need to reach him. I've sent him a letter, as well."

"There's really not much I can do, is there? The reception out there is not good at all. He does check in once in a bit. I'll let him know you called. May I have your name then?"

It seemed such an impersonal way to reach Matthew, but I gave the woman my name. I told her I was calling from Japan, and I had important information of a personal nature to share with him. She let it go at that and did not try to pry any further information from me.

The next morning, I sent Matthew an article I clipped from the English-language newspaper detailing Akira's arrest and the brief reference to Matthew's kidnapping. The English article focused on the Matthew episode, even including a grainy photograph. Two weeks later, the English papers stopped carrying articles on the topic. The Japanese press continued to milk the story. Of course, they were not focused exclusively on Matthew. There had been other children to consider. While thumbing through the papers, I came across a small article on Shōtarō Tani. It seemed he and his father had mended some of their bridges. Shōtarō was reinstated as the family heir. The article ran a photograph of him with a prosthetic hand standing next to his sister's lover, the kimono designer Ryohei Miyazaki. The two of them were planning to collaborate on reviving Tani Kimono. The article made no mention of the talisman, though. I was curious what had happened to it after we left the Tani estate. I made a note to follow up on it with Miyazaki.

I was finding it harder and harder to run in the morning because of the humidity, no matter how early I started. I was still finding it hard to run by Daté's house. The plantings along the wall in front of her house had become overgrown and nearly lost to weeds. One morning, I noticed a fleet of movers parked along the road, blocking the narrow street. Another day I saw a small for-sale sign posted on the stone wall surrounding the property. I wondered who would buy her place, and if they'd know what had happened inside. People were squeamish about moving into a house where there'd been a celebrated death, especially a violent one.

In general, my life returned to the same monotonous routines it had known before I met Tokuda. I still sat at my desk in my upstairs room, translating pieces for Mrs. Shibasaki and watching the tourists amble happily along the narrow street.

Mrs. Shibasaki kept her promise about finding me more substantial translation projects. I still received the usual fare of computer manuals and product evaluations, but I was also given a number of assignments from the Nishijin Textile Center, as well as a few from the Kyoto Kimono Merchants Association. The challenges these assignments posed were a pleasure for me. They also offered an excuse to visit museums and textile centers for a firsthand look at the products being described in the literature I was translating.

Hiro still did his time at his mother's translation agency, but their bickerings had lessened considerably. My mother loved Hiro. He came to my house one Sunday and cooked us all a pot of bouillabaisse. It was as delicious as he promised it would be.

A white parasol caught my eye. I watched as the tip of it bobbed along the top of the green hedge lining the road outside my house. I wondered about the woman on the other end, waiting for her to turn the corner and come into my line of vision. She was wearing a dark purple kimono. Because it was summer, her kimono was unlined and loosely woven. Not quite transparent, but you could see the white of her under kimono, seemingly pale lavender beneath the purple garment. Where it peeked out at the neckline, at the rim of the sleeves, and flashed occasionally at the hem, the under kimono was pristinely white. Summer kimonos, translucent as they are, gave the impression of crisp coolness.

The woman in the purple summer kimono was late middle age. Early sixties, perhaps. She had belted her kimono with an obi of unbleached flax bearing an eggplant design of even deeper purple. The design was ever so slightly off center. She walked with elegant assurance, her light green zori clipping silently over the pavement. I watched her until she stepped beyond my field of vision. And then I waited, wondering if the doorbell would ring. It did not.

I needed to take a walk. I hurried along the narrow street in front of my house, crossed Shirakawa-dōri, and took the shortcut to Nanzen Temple. The grounds were thronged with tourists and locals. Most were lost in conversation and didn't notice when I walked up to one of the pillars and ran my hands along the smooth wood. I remembered those days so many years ago when Matthew and I wrapped our arms around the pillar, wondering if we would ever be able to touch the others' hand. We must have been so small.

I closed my eyes and breathed in the scent of wood. I imagined the centuries that circled this pillar and pressed into the grain of the wood. Sediment of history. My history, too, seeped into the wood. Tears well up behind my lids, making my cheeks grow hot.

I felt fingers touching mine, lightly at first and then harder, insistent, pulling my hands away from the pillar, encircling my hands with a soft warmth. I opened my eyes and looked up into eyes as blue as an April sky.